The Sweepstakes of Love

TOOMAS VINT

THE SWEEPSTAKES OF LOVE

STORIES

TRANSLATED BY MATTHEW HYDE

DALKEY ARCHIVE PRESS

Translated from the following books (published in Estonian):

Naisepiinaja õnnenatukene, 1996, Varrak
Elamise sulnis õudus, 2000, Kunst
Õnneliku lõpuga lood, 2004, Eesti Keele Sihtasutus
Kunstniku elu: jutte ja mälestusi, 2011, Tulikiri

First edition, 2016

Library of Congress Cataloging-in-Publication Data

Names: Vint, Toomas, author. | Hyde, Matthew Cavender, 1972- , translator.
Title: The sweepstakes of love / by Toomas Vint ; translated by Matthew Hyde.
Description: First edition. | Victoria, TX : Dalkey Archive Press, 2016. |
Translations from Estonian of selected stories never before published in English.
Identifiers: LCCN 2015040723 | ISBN 9781564789471 (pbk. : alk. paper)
Subjects: LCSH: Vint, Toomas. | Vint, Toomas--Translations into English. |
Authors, Estonian--Biography. | Painters--Estonia--Biography. |
Estonia--Fiction.
Classification: LCC PH666.32.I5 A2 2016 | DDC 894/.54532--dc23
LC record available at http://lccn.loc.gov/2015040723

Partially funded by a grant from the Illinois Arts Council, a state agency. Special thanks to the Estonian Literature Center and Traducta for supporting the translation of this book.

www.dalkeyarchive.com
Victoria, TX / McLean, IL / London / Dublin

Dalkey Archive Press publications are, in part, made possible through the support of the University of Houston-Victoria and its programs in creative writing, publishing, and translation.

Cover: Art by Katherine O'Shea

Printed on permanent/durable acid-free paper

I. AN ARTIST'S LIFE

II. A FLOCK OF DELUSIONS

I
An Artist's Life

THAT WONDERFUL HAIRY BEAST CALLED FIB

We lived in our own house, which was bordered by a large and well-kept flower garden. "No one else in the whole neighborhood has such a beautiful garden" was the phrase that was repeated almost every day, sometimes several times a day. "Don't forget that you are well-raised children" was the other phrase that was constantly repeated. And it was true—faces with sincere expressions looked back from every childhood photo, hair combed straight and half-opened mouths that had just said "Thank you" and would soon open again to say "Please."

There aren't many of those photos.

They were probably taken by a professional photographer who had come to the house, or they might have been a present from some family friends. Always in sets of four or five pictures. And to this day, the photos of those two brats are preserved in a thick family photo album, which itself dates back to the time of Estonia's first independence. It shows, year by year, how wonderful the process of growing up is. Although the word "brat" is completely wrong here: those first photos show two little blond-haired angels, smiling, stark naked, surrounded by flowers, and with buttercup crowns on their heads.

The garden was surrounded by a fence, painted reddish-brown and topped with barbed wire to stop the thieving neighborhood boys from climbing over. The gate was always locked, and we could sometimes be seen positioned between the fence posts, staring out into the street for hours on end. About twenty meters away there was a large house that contained several rented apartments and had no fence around it. There was a pack of children living in that house who were always tearing around all over the place—they were scruffy and rowdy, and we found them terribly exciting and sometimes a bit frightening. But we were well-raised children who weren't allowed out into the street, and who were always told that it was "such fun for the two of us to play together in our own garden."

The house was full of heavy furniture, and there were pictures in gold frames hanging on the walls and leather-bound books in the cupboards. The books with cheaper bindings filled the open shelves that lined the walls, and the floors were concealed under carpets that muffled the thud of running feet. Father taught at the university, and the few acquaintances that came to visit were also connected to the university, and therefore knew very well that life consisted solely of the university and that nothing else was of any importance. Sometimes the guests brought their children with them to play with us, and they were well-raised too, they didn't slurp when they ate, and they didn't talk nonsense. And so there would be four or five of us standing behind the fence, gaping at the little rascals who were scampering about in the street and shouting rude words we didn't understand.

Sometimes Father didn't come home in the evenings, and we were told that it was because he had lots of work. When he occasionally went missing for several days, Mother would dress herself up, putting on a silk gown that reached down to the floor and plaiting a fresh flower into her long dark hair, and then sit down at the piano. The melodies she played were sad and they made us feel gloomy. But sometimes it seemed as if the sounds coming from the piano were lashing us like a whip, even though we were of course not to blame for anything. My brother and I would sit on the sofa gently whimpering. Mother would play for an eternity, we would have enough time to fall asleep and wake up again, and she would still be playing, her face motionless, her lips pursed into a thin red line. We would listen in silence, without trying to get away—the sofa held us still, and the sounds emanating from that black box nailed us to where we were.

Mother had dreamed of becoming a concert pianist, and I never found out what made her break off her studies; it was either because she got married, or because one day she simply realized that she would never be up to the required standard. She got married quite suddenly, to a handsome man with a promising future, and bore him two sons, two years apart. After that, she was left to dream about how things could have turned out if she had continued with the piano. All she could do was construct some beautiful fable, cry endlessly over her unfulfilled potential, and then resign herself bitterly to the humble lot of the housewife. Housewife? In her case that would definitely be an exaggeration. Grandma was the real mistress of the house. A stout and overbearing domestic dictator who treated her grown-up daughter just as she did us little rascals.

And so on. Now I've painted a picture of a lovely, caring family with angelic children who would sit and listen to their mother's piano playing in hushed reverence. I could add a bit more gold and glitter, or some more pinkish-blue tones, but the painting might start to get a bit over the top. The reality was somewhat bleaker than that. Our childhood world may have been delimited with barbed wire-topped fencing, but that simply meant that all the stupid things we did were done right there in front of Grandma and Mother. We would constantly dream up these stupid things, and almost always carry them out. We weren't allowed out to the street to fight with the other children, so we fought between ourselves at home. We were headstrong and disobedient, but whenever we did something particularly bad Mother would get it from Grandmother even worse than us. You could always hear shouting and yelling coming from our house. I can't remember what we had been up to that time when Mother suddenly lost her voice. You could see that she was trying to say something, but all that came from her mouth was a ghastly croaking sound. It dawned on our young minds that something was actually very wrong. Huddling close together out of fear, we stuffed our fingers into our ears to block that horrific sound. Then through the window we saw Mother stumble out into the street, barefoot and dressed only in her nightgown. She stood in the middle of the road, shaking her arms as if she were trying to get mud off of them, until Grandma eventually dragged her back indoors. They took her to the hospital that same day. Grandma never tired of repeating to us that it was all our fault. When she went to market the next day, she tied us to the legs of the huge oak dining table with the washing line. We were imprisoned, chained up like dogs. Our tiny little fingers weren't able to undo the tight knots. We hated Grandmother and dreamed of poisoning her.

When Mother came back from the hospital she was like a different person: she slept a lot and was always tired and moody. Father didn't spend any time with us; he was very rarely at home, and when he was sitting there in his office at the writing desk we weren't allowed to approach him. When I think back to my childhood, it seems as if it consisted only of rules telling us what not to do. When we were taken on rare visits to other people's houses, we were like little frightened animals; we didn't know where to put ourselves. There is one photo in the album that was taken when we were visiting someone's house, and it shows me sitting on the edge of the chair peeking shyly or guiltily in the direction of the photographer. I'm not sitting in the middle of the chair, but on one edge of it, so that everyone can see how little room I'm taking up. But I also remember how we were always praised: what well-raised children you have, how polite and well behaved they are.

"Although they do get up to mischief sometimes as well," said Father with a chuckle, stroking our heads with the palm of his hand.

Once when we had been celebrating Mother's birthday, and I was sitting comfortably in my favorite aunt's lap—my head resting between her pillow-like breasts, my nostrils tickled by the smell of flowers wafting from her—I was ordered off to bed. My brother, who had started school two weeks earlier, could stay up for a bit longer. That kind of rank discrimination offended me, because it underlined that I was still little—and I probably bitterly resented having to leave Auntie's lap too. I let the anger well up inside me as I lay there in bed, and then I started to pound my legs against the wall, yelling repeatedly: cock, cock, cock, cunt, cunt, cunt. Those mysterious taboo words that my brother had recently dragged home from school with him achieved the desired aim—Mother ran in to my room, shouting at me to stop. But I didn't stop, and those words continued to ring out throughout the house. Then Father came, and I watched as he undid his belt from his trousers. Mother left the room, and I heard Father order me in a quiet hiss to get down onto my knees in front of the bed. Shaking with fear and crawling humiliatingly, I slid down onto my knees. Very slowly, as if I were trying to gain precious seconds of time, I lifted my nightshirt off my bottom and up onto my back—and then the first blow fell. But I didn't feel any pain. I didn't even feel the belt touch me.

"Yell!" whispered my father.

I yelled, and the blows continued to rain down against the side of the bed. Father put his belt back on, turned out the light, and left the room with a snort. I had no idea what was happening. Mother and Grandmother often beat us, as if it were just part of the daily housework. Grandmother, in particular, would make us kneel for some time with our bottoms bared, so that we would reflect on why we were being punished. I hid my head in the pillow and sobbed and sobbed, until one time when I suddenly realized that there was actually no reason to cry.

I couldn't reveal Father's puzzling behavior to anyone—I knew that was an important rule I had to follow, even though he hadn't actually told me to. I knew that it was wrong to lie. First a fibber then a thief, then you're on your way to hell—Grandmother would say in an ominous tone almost every day, sometimes several times in one day. By striking the side of the bed with his belt and ordering me to cry out as if I were in pain, Father had lied. In those days I believed that my mother and father never lied, otherwise they couldn't demand such honesty from us. I couldn't even imagine them lying. I supposed that there must have been a very important reason for my father's behavior that I was not yet allowed to know, and so everything had to remain covered with a veil of secrecy. I didn't say a word to my brother about what had happened during the beating. I tolerated his mocking grin with indifference—he had told me quite clearly that those words were forbidden and should never be used within earshot of adults.

Childhood suddenly ended for me when I started school. I had studied enough alongside my brother to get the gist of reading and arithmetic, so my parents decided that I was ready for school at the age of six. The rules, instructions, and good upbringing of home life all became irrelevant overnight. I figured out pretty fast that all those things that were considered right or good at home were not necessarily seen the same way by the boys at school. More likely the opposite. I wanted, more than anything in the world, to be like the other boys, but I just wasn't. I was left by the wayside, or more precisely pushed there, since no one had any use for an overfed brat who always had to run straight home after school and wasn't allowed to go over to anyone's house or have anyone over to his place. And I couldn't get my way through force: even though I had practiced fighting with my brother, I was still a softy compared to all the other boys. Since I couldn't win recognition from my peers I had to make do with words of approval from the adult world. I went to my piano lessons diligently and got nothing but the highest marks. Now that I think back to it, I can say with some pride that by the age of six it was already clear to me that if I couldn't be like the others, then I would have to differ from them as much as possible.

I had started school a year earlier than my peers, and this really became apparent at puberty. I can remember once when we had started back after the summer break, seeing my classmates racing for the showers and discovering to my horror that their crotches had started to turn dark with hair and their dicks had suddenly grown to frightening proportions. After that I couldn't undress in front of them to wash when I was sweaty, and they noticed that.

"I can't let my body come into contact with water," I explained. "I got this disease over summer. It's called onparaceticum—it's a horrible illness, if my skin comes into contact with water I get all blotchy. I can only wash with a special solution. Don't worry, it's not infectious, it's an onomatoproblematic illness caused by an excess of white blood cells."

I lied without batting an eyelid, and without changing my expression in the slightest. Those complicated words came to my lips as if of their own accord. I knew that if the boys heard something they didn't understand, they would have to believe it.

Our gym classes began to torment me in my dreams. I was weaker than the others and couldn't do the exercises, and now there was this visible physical defect as well. My brother was growing body hair, the others were growing body hair, but I was different. I stretched my powers of imagination to find credible excuses to get out of gym class. I discovered that a complex fabrication always sounded more credible than some ordinary, mundane lie. I learned that when lying, one should never make the aim obvious. When I arrived to gym class limping with a bandaged knee, I pretended that I desperately wanted to join in. But the teacher ordered me to sit on the bench so that I wouldn't strain my injured leg.

Although we lived in our own house, we didn't have a dog or a cat.

Grandma didn't want to hear of taking an animal into the house. Once we found a kitten on the street and managed to hide it in the shed and feed it for several days. When Grandma discovered the animal, no amount of begging could convince her. Pets just ceased to be a subject of discussion in our house.

One of my classmates had an Alsatian bitch that had just given birth to its first litter of puppies. I went to see them nearly every day after school and decided that I had to get one for myself at all costs. I began to drop animal stories into the conversations at home: how an Alsatian had apparently saved one of the boys at our school from some pervert, how another Alsatian had pinned a burglar into the corner, and he had to sit there trembling for several hours, and had crapped his pants too. One day I told my family that my desk mate was going to Moscow with his whole family for the winter vacation. The next day I brought "their puppy" home, since someone had to feed it while the family was away.

"Take that right back to where you got it!" roared Grandma. "I can't" I said tearfully, "they already left."

"Come on, it's important to try and help other people," said my father, who happened to be at home at the time. My desk mate's father was an officer, so everyone was a bit afraid of him. "Moscow" and "officer" sounded credible, and of course no one had to know that my desk mate had in fact gone to visit his grandmother in Pärnu and that the dog was the Alsatian puppy I had been longing for.

After a few days, the whole family had fallen in love with that wonderful animal. Grandma would hold him close to her chest as she sat in front of the stove, and Mother carried him around bundled up in her bathrobe. Even Father, who didn't care about anything other than work, was constantly kneeling down and letting the dog nibble at his fingers. I was the only one who didn't show any signs of caring for the puppy.

A week later my desk mate came to see us at the house. The family was sitting around, just enjoying spending some time together and playing with the dog. "You'll never believe it," said my desk mate, "but Mother went to see the doctor in Moscow and it turns out that she's allergic to dogs. Could you possibly look after him for few days until we find him a new master?"

I bit my lip so as not to burst out laughing, because I had noticed how all my family members' faces had suddenly livened up. Father cleared his throat, and said: "Well, we might have room for a dog. We've kind of gotten used to it. But what do the rest of you think?"

"I'm for it," mumbled Grandma and blew her nose noisily. I could have sworn that there were tears in her eyes.

Later, when the animal was sitting on me, pawing my chest and licking my chin, I experienced a strangely intoxicating feeling of happiness. My plan had worked out, I had gotten myself a real live hairy beast called fib.

I remember that I lied with reckless abandon back in those days. It was a pretty dangerous pastime, and I always had to be careful not to go overboard. At the same time, it reminded me of one of those games where you have a certain number of lives that you have to try not to lose. Let's say the player has five lives: when he's been caught five times his lives are up, and lying doesn't work anymore since no one will believe him. The lies had to be properly thought through and, if possible, risk free. For example, when I told one of my schoolmates that I was given a bike with gears as a present, but that the very next day it was stolen from our shed, I described everything related to the theft in great detail, and I got great amusement from seeing the genuine anger he felt towards the nonexistent criminal. I guessed that he had already begun to imagine himself tearing around on my bike, and the very impossibility of this image now coming true was what made him angry. Lying sets a mysterious causal chain into motion. You might utter some tiny little lie, but it will immediately grow into another larger lie, and in the end you have to make the whole world somehow fit with some little lie that came into your mind quite by chance, significantly revising the whole of reality in the process.

I read a lot in those days. I found it thrilling to escape from the drab, soul-destroying everydayness of life to a world where something interesting was always happening. Stevenson, Dumas, Defoe, Molnár, Scott, and Verne were magicians who could change reality with a couple of sentences. I knew that they were lying, but they did it so elaborately that I couldn't help but believe them, and I yearned to experience that dazzling bravery, noble-mindedness, self-sacrifice, ingenuity, selflessness, and everything else that was dulled or half-dead in our everyday existence.

In the spring of 1957, by which time I had been suffering for a whole year alongside my visibly maturing classmates due to my apparently stunted development, I started to hatch escape plans. I didn't actually have any kind of credible plan prepared; at first it was all just a hazy dream, assembled piece by piece. As I lay in the dark waiting to fall asleep, I weighed up completely unrealizable possibilities, lived out fantastical adventures, and mentally braved my fears and all possible dangers. At the same time I experienced a pleasant tension in my lower body, a strange tingling sensation. I felt as if I was physically taking part in the adventures, that very soon, at some yet to be disclosed moment, all my senses would be able to partake in a new world of experiences. The images I saw before I fell asleep made way for the reality of my dreams, and it would often happen that even after I had woken up I would continue to search for the solution to some problem from my dreams. And sometimes, although to be honest quite rarely, I even forgot that I had thought something up myself; then, what had been a lie ceased to be one.

One morning, when the rest of the family had departed in their various directions—Father on a work trip at the crack of dawn, Mother and Grandmother to see an aunt who lived in the countryside not far from town, and my brother on a tour with the basketball team—I couldn't be bothered to get out of bed at all. After giving it some thought I decided that it would be best to turn up for just the last lesson that day. I would claim that I had fallen asleep on the bus to town, but that the bus had gone to the depot, and that when I had woken up the bus doors had been shut and the driver had gone home with the keys. So I had to wait until they found the driver, because no one wanted to break the lock just for me. Yes, but why didn't I escape through the window, I thought to myself. I tried to imagine what the bus windows looked like, but instead I saw some writing: Emergency Exit. I decided that I would have to leave that story for some other time—I first needed to carefully research what a bus actually looked like.

I thought about other possibilities, and then suddenly it dawned on me that I could have myself kidnapped. I would ask for ransom money, and that would be that. Then I could run away with the money I got. Maybe to Poland or Germany. Although that plan would need thorough preparation—a month or two—and it would be better to wait until the weather was a bit warmer before going on such a long journey.

It was often the case that one thought would immediately give rise to another one, and in the end the plan would be left hanging, too difficult to implement. I decided to be very cautious this time and just say that a pickpocket had been caught on the bus and that I had been taken to the police station to give evidence. But would it really take several hours to give evidence? Probably not. Instead I could say that some American spy had been captured and had started shooting at people. One of the bullets had grazed my hand—I could even wrap my arm in bandages—and I had fainted and fallen to the ground. At the hospital they took X-rays and did all sorts of tests . . . The spy story was a bit too elaborate. Too elaborate to be believable.

It was something of a special event to be left alone in our house, and I had to make good use of it. During the first half of that morning the ring of prohibitions and orders was breached. I went into Father's study to open the desk drawers. This time they were all locked. I knew that the key that opened the locks was hanging hidden behind a painting of a farm house with a thatched roof. There were dark clouds and a bird flying in the sky. The gold frame was covered in a thick layer of dust, only the right corner was sparkling clean. You had to take the right corner with one hand and pull it towards you, lifting the key from the nail with the other hand. Complete disorder always reigned in Father's office. A brush or a duster had no business here. His office was only cleaned ahead of public holidays, and always under his watchful eye.

Father's collection of rocks and minerals was in the low drawer to the right. I took out one stone after the other. My favorites were the rock crystals, but I really adored the cluster of large mauve crystals. I had just taken a seat at the table when I heard the front door close with a bang. Burglars!—the thought came to me, making my whole body tremble. But then I heard the voices of my father and a woman. In a couple of seconds the stones were back in the drawer and the drawer was locked. Suddenly the woman started to laugh. The sound, unpleasantly shrill and loud, quickly started to get closer. I didn't have time to slip out through the door, the only option was to hide behind Father's leather sofa. My father was supposed to be on a work trip, and I had no idea what he was looking for at home, but it was clear that he was about to come into his office.

For some strange reason they didn't talk when they came into the room. All I could hear were odd sounds like the smacking of lips and the rustle of clothing. Suddenly a heavy weight came down onto the sofa, the leather creaked right by my ear, and when I looked up over my shoulder I saw some small fingers with chewed fingernails gripping the black leather. Suddenly the sofa began to jerk backwards and forwards rhythmically, pressing me ever closer up against the wall. My heart was beating wildly. I thought in alarm that if it weren't for the panting just above me, my heartbeat would be audible, reverberating from all four corners of the room. Suddenly I heard a plaintive, half-groaning sound: "No, no, not inside me." The thrusts got stronger and stronger, I thought I would be crushed to bits against the wall, and after each thrust the plaintive voice repeated: "No, no, no . . ."

I raised my hands and pressed my ears shut with my fists. Suddenly everything was quiet. Then I felt a pleasant twinge in my lower body, quite like nothing I had experienced before, and to my alarm I noticed a warm wetness spreading in my trousers.

When I took my hands away from my ears, there was silence in the room. I thought that they had gone, but then I heard my father's indifferent, somehow bored voice: "What are you doing sprawled there, put your clothes on."

"Listen, if something happens, then come and see me and we'll sort things out. Just make sure you don't do anything silly," said Father in a more conciliatory tone.

"I said not to come inside me," said the girl tearfully.

"Say what you like," said Father impatiently. "Who would bother to listen to a little whore like you. You should be in a brothel, not the university. Oh well, give me your grade book then . . ."

The front door had already slammed shut a long time ago, but I was still squatting behind the sofa, squashed against the wall. This was now my place. A dog's place is under the table, and my place was behind the sofa. Our dog had gone missing that winter. "The dogcatchers probably know to nab them while they're in heat, that's the wages of sin," said Grandma.

Why had it run away? It had a good life with us, I thought as I crawled out on all fours from behind the sofa.

Father's office looked just as if nothing had happened, only the leather sofa, with its dull black sheen, had gotten a bit wet. My trousers were damp and sticky. The chicken-thieving fox was still there running across the painting hanging on the wall. The child with the oddly shaped head was looking out of the darkened gap of the doorway at the chicken thief. I remembered that the key was still in my pocket. I hung it back in its place behind the painting. Now everything was really just as it had been when I had come into the room.

Once I was in the bathroom I took off my damp underpants and hid them at the bottom of the laundry basket. My dick was swollen. I thought that maybe I had been afflicted by some horrible illness. My face was flushed and my forehead was burning hot. I felt a cold shiver run through me.

I only started to feel warm again when I was under my quilt. I tried not to think about what had happened, but it was the only thing on my mind. My father's work trip had been his lie. I knew that when a lie was not watertight, punishment would always follow. My father had been caught, and he deserved to be punished.

By the afternoon, when Mother and Grandmother came home, I felt perfectly fine, but I put on my "sick child face" and complained in a feeble voice that I had been ill that morning, and had felt cold shivers.

I gripped the thermometer tightly in my hand and rubbed it, until the temperature rose to thirty-eight, enabling me to be seriously ill for a while.

In the evening Father came home. From his work trip. He told a colorful story about how some stupid policeman had hassled him on the motorway. I heard Mother tell him that I had been sick that morning. "So he didn't go to school today?" Father exclaimed, as if in disbelief. A moment later he appeared at my door. He came straight up to the edge of the bed and sat down.

"So, how are you feeling?" he said slowly and hesitantly, and he took my wrist between his fingers as if he were feeling my pulse.

I looked straight at him. He turned away and I felt his fingers clasp my wrist like pincers.

"Ah, that hurts!" I cried out.

"I'm sorry," said Father. "Mother said that you had a fever, but you don't look particularly ill."

"That's because I'm not ill," I said quietly.

An odd expression appeared on Father's face, but it was one that was familiar to me. It was exactly the same expression he had used when he looked straight at Grandma and said that it would be all right for us to get a dog. It was a look that was completely resolute and certain, one that makes any kind of resistance crumble into dust. I sensed that Father knew that I knew. His eyes glared at me from under his bushy eyebrows, and his gaze could have bored into a stone wall.

Contrary to any kind of logic, contrary to the sly plan I had hatched as I had lain in bed for half the day, I sighed and begun to tell Father how I had skipped school and gone with another boy to see the gypsies who were parked at the edge of town.

"Why are you telling me this?" asked Father.

"I don't know, I feel awful. I've never skipped school before. I was afraid I couldn't do the math assignment. Then I lied to Mother that I was ill. Father, forgive me, I won't do it again," I lied.

Father was still looking straight at me, but I could see that he couldn't see me, and wasn't listening to what I was saying. I recounted what had happened at the gypsies' and what their camp looked like. I enthusiastically described some scenes from a film I had once seen, and as I did so I had the awful feeling that this time the sentences I devised that were coming out of my mouth were indeed creating a new reality where all the facts would live from that moment on. And then the things that had really happened would no longer exist.

"I really can't bring myself to believe all that, but you could at least promise me that this will be the last time you'll skip school," said my father somehow lightheartedly, almost as if he were joking, as he got up from the edge of the bed.

"I don't know if I can make that promise," I joked in response.

WE ARE CHILDREN OF LENIN, WE ARE CHILDREN OF STALIN

"That boy in your story seems a bit too bright. He is telling us, the readers, that the things he invents actually create reality," said my wife with irony in her voice.

Aili is always my first reader. As soon as a new story is finished, I am too impatient to wait. I sit next to my wife, watching which part she has got to, tensely following her facial expressions, hoping to pick up some important signs. On this occasion she had just finished reading the story "That Wonderful Hairy Beast Called Fib"—the very same story that you, dear reader, have just read.

I immediately began to defend myself: "But a thirteen-year-old is not a little boy anymore. I'm sure that the same kind of thoughts were on my mind back then. It's possible that I've formulated them a little too precisely. But then why should I write imprecisely."

"It sounds too grown-up," said Aili. "Although for me it's even harder to believe that the boy isn't shocked by his father's behavior. It's as if he thinks it's natural for young female students to pass his father's classes that way."

I didn't know what to say in response. When I was writing the story I never considered how shocking it might have been—I didn't have the slightest fragment of a memory of ever being bothered by my father's activities in any way. Naturally I understood that something reprehensible had happened between them, but I was thinking more about the plan I had hatched, the deal I was going to make with my father. I would keep my mouth shut and he would help to convince mother to let me leave the conservatory. In those days it wasn't my father's behavior that made me feel sick, but the piano.

We had a very strict upbringing in our home, but the system of rules and punishments didn't lead us to form high ethical standards. I didn't feel the slightest pang of conscience when I picked the locks of Father's desk drawers or secretly read Mother's diary. Stealing my thrifty brother's hidden sweets seemed more like an adventure than a crime. I believed that lying was an act of cunning, and that any punishment was simply a price you deserved to pay for tripping up. I wasn't capable of knowing, nor did I really want to know, what had really happened between my father and that young girl.

When the boys forced some girl to stay behind in the classroom during the break so they could feel her up a bit, or when some vigorous groping happened in the cloakroom, I didn't understand what it meant. I was a year younger than my classmates and a complete dunce when it came to sexual matters. These days such things might seem impossible, but in the socialist prison we were so good at hiding sexuality that the common anecdote about the young couple, who had been married for three years but couldn't have children because they didn't know how, sadly rang true to life.

But the thing that had taken place that morning in my father's office, to which I had been unwilling witness, began to torment me. It intruded rudely into my dreams. It aroused me as I tried to get to sleep. Those sounds—above all I remembered the sounds—caused my dick to swell uncomfortably, and sometimes I would wake to find that my bed was wet. I didn't dare tell anyone about my illness, and the worst thing was that these bouts were always accompanied by a pleasant feeling that spread throughout my whole body.

I can remember how I tried to translate the sounds that were haunting me into musical language. When I happened to be alone at home I spent most of the time at the piano. Just lifting the lid of the piano got me into a state of arousal and pretty soon I would be overcome by a bout of that awful, sweet sickness which too often ended in me having to hide my wet underpants in the laundry basket.

I was alone with this worrying problem. I didn't trust either

Mother or Grandmother, who always seemed to be looking for a reason to give us a thrashing. Father never punished us, he seemed to live solely for his work. I had no close friends at school or conservatory, I was chubby and younger than the others, an overachiever and a teacher's pet—I had to resign myself to those labels, which were pinned to anyone who was different from the others.

I had a cold, even hostile relationship with my elder brother, who was two years older. In those days he was a good athlete—at the end of the 1950s athletic boys were highly praised and generally seen as superior to the rest—so we lived in very different worlds. It's odd, but both of us experienced a major change of course in the same year, 1957: my brother decided to become an artist and began to mix with an artistic crowd, whereas I ditched music school and started fencing.

I can remember one time at the end of seventh grade when we went on an excursion to South Estonia. In those days it was the custom to organize spy games during our trips out of town. The class was divided into two groups, one of them with white paper ribbons tied to their sleeves, the other red. The ribbons were the lives we had to try not to lose during the game. We ran around playing at being spies. We were the Stalin generation. We had been born during Hitler's time, and our earliest memories date back to the Stalinist period. Our mental world was formed by Stalinist slogans. They tried to cultivate Soviet idealism in us through the romance of the working-class cause and partisan warfare. Spy games were an important part of that.

Once, we managed to capture one of the girls from the enemy side in a clearing in the shrubbery. She was big and strong and kept trying to get away, so we had quite a struggle to keep her lying flat on the ground. I tore her red ribbon to pieces triumphantly. "Lord help me, I'm dead now!" the girl giggled and lay there limply, her arms stretched out wide. Our four-man intelligence patrol looked at her in silence, then my desk mate unbuttoned her blouse. A shiny pink bra covered her pale, full breasts, and to my surprise my ears picked up that familiar heavy breathing—exactly like I had heard a short time earlier when I was hunched up behind the sofa, peeping at those fingers with their chewed nails. I felt my dick getting stiff. I held my hand in front of it so that my classmates couldn't see, but they had no time to watch me: one of the boys had already pulled her breasts out of the bra, and we started fondling the two pink-nippled globes. The girl was still dead. Now they hoisted up her skirt and tugged her flowery cotton panties downwards. The dead girl held her legs tightly together, but a triangle of dark hair was exposed—although only for a moment, because she suddenly jumped up and ran off. Then she stood there at the edge of the clearing and jeered at us: "Idiots, idiots, idiots . . ." The girl's ripped-up red life ribbon was lying on the ground on top of last year's faded grass. Suddenly I noticed the swelling in the other boys' trousers as well.

"Damn slut, could have at least shown us her pussy," one of the boys said.

"But we saw it," I said, as if trying to defend the girl.

"What an idiot," said the boy, and they started teasing me.

When we were on the bus going back I watched the girl from a distance. She didn't differ in any way from the others, she was chatting, giggling, singing like them. A completely ordinary female classmate. But when I looked at her I felt a tension in my nether regions. I imagined that she had already managed to do things that the other girls wouldn't dare to do, but I didn't understand why my classmates used shameful words when they talked about her. I had the odd feeling that this girl had risen above the rest of them, as if she were hovering above our heads somewhere.

I can't remember where or from whom I acquired the necessary wisdom, but by the beginning of summer I had already managed to work out for myself how those "adult things" worked, and I no longer believed I was ailing from some embarrassing illness. School was finished, but that girl from my class appeared almost every evening in my imagination. I would hang around outside her house quite often, and one time we bumped into each other "by chance." She told me she wouldn't be coming back to our class in the fall because her parents were moving to another town and she would be starting technical college instead.

"It's already decided," she said, and smiled at me.

I was soaked in sweat. I blurted out some utter nonsense, and then started laughing idiotically, as if I had said something funny.

"Jeez, Fatty, are you sick or something?" the girl asked in amazement. It was the ultimate humiliation: I just turned around and ran away. That evening I vowed that from then on I would have nothing more to do with anyone of the female sex, they were all stupid, horrible, and full of themselves, and so on. As I look back, it occurs to me that a young man in that kind of state would have been ideal prey for a homosexual. But when I made that vow that evening, I couldn't have guessed that twenty days later something would happen in my life that would forever tie my thoughts and fantasies to the female form, and that there would no longer be anything at all I could do about it.

During the haymaking season we went to the countryside to see our relatives. Those are still the most memorable times from my childhood. Transporting the hay in a horse-drawn carriage. A giant bonfire. Swimming and fishing. Mother stayed in town that year and we went with Grandma. At first we just hung around for several days watching the rain come down. Then the wind dispersed the clouds and the sun began to blaze. Suddenly everyone was extremely busy, it was only little boys like me who just had to wait until it was time for the hay to be transported. I read old crime novels in the loft. It was really trashy literature, what we used to call "yellow press." Literally so, as the pages had turned yellow and tatty from being read so many times. One day, my brother suddenly climbed up into the loft. Without seeing me he ran, stooping forwards in a strange way, to the window at the other end of the room, and then stood there tensely, looking out. He slid his pants down and began to pump away at his stiff dick. I was startled by how big it was. He was breathing heavily, even panting. Then he rushed over to the beds, threw himself down onto Aunt Elina's bed, and began writhing around, moaning and groaning. And then he abruptly fell silent and lay there like a dead man for some time, until finally he sat up and stared at the sheet. "Fuck!" he swore out loud. He pulled up his pants and swapped Auntie's sheet for his own. Then he knelt down for a few more minutes at the window he had been looking out of, before leaving hurriedly down the ladder.

When all was quiet I came out from behind the dusty chest of drawers and stealthily crept up to the window, feeling like some kind of freak. Outside, down between the apple trees, in a nest made in the long grass, Aunt Elina was sunbathing. She was lying on her stomach with no clothes on. Aunt Elina was not our real aunt—as far as I know she was just a distant relative—and was the object of some criticism in our family. They would talk about her disdainfully as some kind of debauched bohemian. She smoked, and she drank vodka with the men. I thought that she was cool; you could always be sure you'd have plenty of fun with her. Now here she was, lying there naked. Then suddenly she sat up. Her tiny breasts were drooping from her body and the dark triangle under her stomach was barely visible. She looked around in alarm, then a grin appeared briefly on her face. She put her smock on, then got up and walked off, and I couldn't see her anymore.

When I pulled up my trousers, I was overcome with a vague, empty feeling. I felt ensnared in a web of depravity. I had spied on a naked woman and jerked off. If someone called you a jerk-off it was an insult, and being a Peeping Tom was humiliating too. For several long minutes I hated myself, but in the end I found consolation in the thought that it was a temporary, chance occurrence, a one-off mistake. I hoped that the guilty feeling had not yet quite taken root, and as it turned out the rest of the day passed by quite free of any worries.

When I went to bed, the adults stayed in the barn to drink beer and belt out some songs. My brother had left that day because his training camp was starting. Uncle's children had gone to town with him. That night Auntie and I were alone together in the barn. I didn't lie down near the window, where I normally slept, but next to Auntie on one of the other beds, which were now free. I made a plan to roll over during the night to get closer to her, and then, as if by accident, touch her breasts. When she woke up I would say that I had had a terrible nightmare and was too scared to sleep alone. Or, even better, I would start making an awful groaning noise, my whole body would start shaking like a leaf, and then Auntie would huddle close to console me.

For most of the night I lay there waiting to fall asleep, tormented by a constant state of arousal, until I eventually nodded off for a bit. But when I heard the ladder creaking I was already wide awake again. I heard the rustle of clothes right beside me and saw a woman's silhouette and bare breasts against the reddish glow of the twilight sky, visible through the window. Then her panties slipped downwards with a rustling sound. Lifting first one leg, then the other, she stepped out of them, and, almost tripping over me, she began to look for something. Now I could smell her, not some sweet scent, but a more bitter, not particularly pleasant smell that aroused me all the more, and then she crawled under the quilt into bed. She had been looking for her nightgown, but hadn't found it, and was now completely naked. The thought that I would soon roll over into the embrace of a naked woman made me start rubbing my over-aroused dick, which then began convulsing violently on its own. I had gone and made myself all wet again. I realized with a strange feeling of relief that I definitely couldn't crawl into my aunt's embrace in that state.

The next day was Summer Solstice, and the loft filled up with revelers, who were also there to celebrate Grandma's hundredth birthday—in any case it was a lively time, which I don't have any particular memories of. A few days later, when we were back home, I pleasured myself again. I imagined that I was putting my hands onto a naked woman's breasts. No, not Aunt Elina's—in my imagination I was touching a woman with big balloon-shaped breasts like that girl in my class who I had touched during spy games.

From then on I was tormented by a remorseless feeling of guilt. Sometimes I managed to resist it during weekdays, but then I would always give in to the guilty pleasure again, and usually several times in a row. My mind was racing with all those invented warnings: masturbating stunts your growth, makes you go blind, hair starts growing on your palms, and you get blue bags under your eyes. And then anyone could see from a distance that you were a masturbator. A long and difficult struggle ensued, in which my appetite for pleasure and the lust for a woman's body always won out in the end.

In July and August of that year we went to Käsmu for our holidays. We rented the top floor of a two-story house, and my brother and I had the cozy attic room. Although we had bickered constantly until then, something like friendship had now started to develop between us. In those days there weren't many vacationers in Käsmu, just one or two families. Everyone looked like they were suffering from boredom. In the evenings we sat on the beach with the waves gently lapping and listened to the sounds of music reaching us from across the bay. There were often concerts on the Võsu bandstand. During the warm August evenings the lights flickered on the far shore. Life there seemed to be in full swing with all those things that made our young hearts race with excitement.

My brother was quite comfortable with sexual matters. All sorts of things would happen during his sports competitions and training camps. He recounted it all to me in great detail, probably exaggerating plenty too. I got the impression that the life of an athlete was somehow special, better, more interesting, more full of adventure. I started running with my brother and doing other exercises, and by the end of summer I had lost several kilos. It might have been my brother's exciting stories that lured me to fencing training that autumn. But it wasn't only sport that brought me and my brother closer together that summer. We would go to peep at naked women sunbathing together, we would get turned on looking at pornographic pictures, and then at night we would both jerk off. I can remember those yellowing pictures to this day. They were photos that had been taken of drawings: doll-like women with elaborate hairdos getting up to all sorts of tricks with muscular men. There was even one vile picture in a comic vein, in which a man had stuffed a goat's hind legs into his boots and was pleasuring himself with the animal.

Towards the end of August Mother came back from one of her trips to town, radiant like the sun. She said that there was a huge surprise waiting for me, but she wouldn't say what it was. She teased me and my brother, who was also bursting with curiosity. In the end she announced that I would be going to "Artek." I was visibly dejected—in my imagination, all sorts of impossible dreams had already come true, but Pioneer camp had certainly not been one of them.

"I don't want to go," I declared sulkily. I imagined that only creeps went to Artek, and I was sure that nothing interesting could possibly happen there. And I couldn't speak Russian either.

Artek was an All-Union Pioneer camp in Crimea. Every Pioneer's dream. It was trumpeted in the newspapers and on the radio, and there probably wasn't a single person alive who could understand why I didn't want to go. In fact, even I didn't understand why. Later, Mother explained that our school had gotten authorization to send one thirteen-year-old boy from seventh grade. It was the first time that had ever happened. But the teachers were at a loss—there was no one in seventh grade they could depend on. Then they came up with me—so what if he was already in middle school, he's an excellent class monitor and always gets top grades, and he can play the piano like a young Liszt. So they had decided to send me—the age fitted, it would be easy for me to say (lie!) that I was in the seventh grade. Since the authorization was for September, and the children also had to attend school while they were there, it was decided that it would be more impressive if I appeared to be cleverer than the others in my year.

In the end I had no choice but to agree. And I guess I did want to see the mountains.

There was a group of around twenty children from Estonia. I was so exhausted after the long train journey and the weight of all those new experiences that very few traces of that period were preserved in my memory. But three very vivid memories do remain. Firstly Moscow, which in the textbooks and children's books seemed to have a golden halo hanging over it. I imagined it would look like a fairy-tale castle, everything there would be gleaming and grand and unlike anything I had ever seen before. But the Moscow that I saw out of the train windows was a grave disappointment: ugly, shabby barracks, grimy factory buildings, and the incomparable dirtiness and squalor of the areas near the railway embankments. Next, the courtyard of Simferopol Pioneer Palace: unbearable heat, scorched ground, daylong boredom waiting for transportation, and the most terrible thing was that there wasn't a single mountain, not even a little hillock within view. It was already nearing evening when they finally put us on the bus. The winding road made me carsick, and I began to throw up uncontrollably. Between the bouts of vomiting I looked out of the window and saw some mountains that looked brownish in the evening light and bore no resemblance to the mountains that had loomed so splendidly in my imagination, with their bluish-gray rock faces and gleaming snowy peaks.

During the train journey I had made friends with Kalev, a strapping boy from Kohtla-Järve. In the 1950s Kalev was a very rare name—at first I thought it was just a nickname he had been given, after the hero from Kreutzwald's poem, because of his strongman appearance. I liked his sincerity and directness, even his slightly rough nature. I don't know what it was he liked about me, and in those days I didn't really ponder over such things. Back then there wasn't much pondering done. Even very odd situations were treated as completely normal.

As I write this story I can't help thinking about how children were selected for the elite camps back then. I'm pretty sure that the regional Party secretaries' kids didn't miss out, to say nothing of the children of the senior government officials working in Moscow. Some of the places were shared out democratically, but then in the schools they would of course take consideration of who the parents were. For example, the Chairman of the Defense Brigade Council at the camp was a boy called Dzhalil—when I checked in the Estonian Soviet Encyclopedia there were two high-ranking Dzhalils: one was a Hero of the Soviet Union, the other a People's Writer from Tajikistan. Certainly, some of the children spending their holidays there were particularly gifted or had caught someone's eye for some other reason, but it still left a bitter taste in the mouth. In any case, my friend Kalev's father was a miner—who just happened to be a Soviet Hero of Labor.

In writing this story it occurred to me that I had already used the trip to Artek in one of my novels. I found the collection, *Just the Two of Us*, on the bookshelf, and read the story. The sequence of events in the story, with the heavily erotic subtext, wasn't very accurate; I had changed several things to make them more palatable. And one should take into account that the story had been written during the Soviet era.

In fact, in those days my position was a little different from other writers—the sexually explicit parts of my stories were left in, whereas I suspected that other writers' erotic passages were mercilessly excised. Erotica and politics were proscribed in much the same way. It seemed like only Heino Kiik could write sharp political commentary and only Vint was allowed to write about sex. Otherwise, however, literature had to be free of any rough edges, smooth like an egg.

When the Sovetsky Pisatel ("Soviet Writer") publishing house was preparing my book *The Return* for print, it became clear from the correction sheets that everything that was the slightest bit erotic had been censored. Some of the stories had even had whole plotlines ripped out, making the contents obscure and difficult to follow. In those days the chief editor of the publisher's Soviet Peoples' department was an Estonian named Tamm. I went with the translator Yelena Pozdnyakov to talk with him. In general, the offices of Sovetsky Pisatel, which was the most prestigious Soviet publisher, created an odd impression: there was a solemn atmosphere there, like in a church or temple. The authors would walk quite literally on tiptoe down the corridor. They wore dark suits, dazzling white shirts, and understated ties. It was clear that they had just been to the hairdresser. I was even a bit embarrassed by my jeans-clad artist appearance. Tamm promised to do what he could, and hung the blame on one of the chief editors who had made the corrections. I pointed out that perestroika was now under way, and stressed how integral the erotic parts were to my books.

"The Russian reader won't understand that," said Tamm with his arms outspread in resignation and an unhappy expression on his face.

I had heard that phrase many times before. For my part I found it impossible to understand what kind of reader doesn't understand screwing.

When the book was published, one or two more things had been left out on top of the earlier edits. Now I was seriously angry. My contract stated that corrections were not allowed without the author's written permission. The statute of the Writers Union contained a provision which promised that the organization would always stand up for its members' rights, and so on.

When I went to the Writers Union to demand my rights, who else should I find as secretary there but Jaan Kross himself.

"Well yes," said Kross in the comfortable and relaxed manner of a man who was loyal to the state. "We can discuss that at the meeting of the management board, then later we will be able to demonstrate that in 1988 we had already dealt with the problem that Russian publishers censor our writers' manuscripts."

I said that I wasn't interested in demonstrating anything; I wanted the Writers Union to help me take the publisher to court.

That evening, after the meeting had taken place, I phoned Teet Kallas to find out what the Writers Union bosses had decided on my question. "Tuulik said that an organization can't make a complaint against another one in court, and that Vint would have to take this matter forward himself. That was that as far as your case was concerned," said Teet.

It was 1988, and I reckon that if I could have been bothered to take the matter forward—Yelena Pozdnyakov bravely agreed to provide a copy of the translation for expert analysis—then the legal process would have caused a stir in Moscow. I knew several people in cultural circles there who had good contacts with foreign journalists. It would have been a glittering advertising opportunity for me as a writer. But I couldn't be bothered. In those days I still believed rather naively that a writer's job was to write good books.

But as I was writing this, one detail stuck out to me. I hollered across the room: "Aili, can you remember what happened to the song '*We are children of Lenin, we are children of Stalin*' after Stalin's death?"

When some time had passed with no answer, I got up from

behind my writing desk and went to see where my wife was. Aili was writing something at the kitchen table. When I repeated the question she looked up and stared at me for a moment: "Do I come and disturb you when you're writing?!" she snapped angrily, and I didn't find out if she could remember the thing that I couldn't.

Without Kalev I might have had a bad time at the Pioneer Camp, with the rush of all those new experiences, and in the company of other kids I didn't know. I wasn't very sociable—a childhood spent within the confines of our garden had probably left a lifelong mark on me. I remember confessing one day to Kalev, on the condition of secrecy, that I was actually in the eighth grade, and that I was thus a participant in a bit of fraud. Unexpectedly, Kalev found that extremely funny: "Hah, you shouldn't take that stuff too seriously," he instructed me. On the first night he had already told me that this would be a great opportunity to go and visit some girls. At first there were only four of them, and the rest of the beds in the large bedroom were still empty awaiting the arrival of the others the next day. After curfew we climbed up the smooth-barked trees (magnolia?) growing in front of the building, reached the second floor and slipped over the edge of the balcony into the room. Just imagine the giggling surprise of those girls! I'm sure that such a brazen act was something unheard of for those goody-goody little Pioneers, and they definitely got a big thrill from it.

Stepping beyond the bounds of what was permitted wasn't actually customary for me either. Although I was a proper ruffian at home, at school I stood out for my good behavior. A model pupil. I used to think: a child who never got caught. In reality there was a fear of punishment lodged deep in my soul that made me weigh up situations from every possible angle before savoring the forbidden act. So that crazy risk I took with Kalev was all the more unexpected. It's possible that I thought I could pin all the responsibility on him. In any case, it was already clear after just a couple of days that Kalev was fundamentally different from the well-behaved flock of sheep sent to Artek. But I still didn't feel any sense of danger.

Before the morning roll call the next day I saw our girls

huddled up in a group whispering amongst themselves, glancing repeatedly over in my direction. I knew what they were talking about, and it made me proud to be alive.

A fairly militaristic system had been established at the camp: squads, platoons, and the defense council. The platoon leadership and the defense council management all consisted of boys and girls who were older than us. They formed a separate group and could do things that we were forbidden to do. They were definitely already Komsomol members, but they wore red neckerchiefs and pretended they were Pioneers, as that made it easier for them to spy on us.

My Russian was pretty bad at first. The Russian campers were quick to take advantage of that, teaching me swear words with innocent looks on their faces and then sending me to repeat the obscenities to the Pioneer leaders. The Estonians were dispersed throughout the camp either alone or in groups of two, and all of them had problems with the language. They were called "Germans" and the jokes made at their expense were the same all over. I was lucky to be in the same room as Kalev. He could speak Russian really well and could swear like the rest of them. There were around ten other boys in the room, and right from the beginning Kalev and a boy called Rutskoy bickered constantly. Although the Russians would normally always call each other by their first names, Rutskoy was always called Rutskoy, and we had no idea what his first name might have been. He loved bossing the others around and teasing them, and the gangly Tolja Lukashenko was like an underling to him. (Although to tell the truth I probably looked like the same kind of loyal underling to Kalev.)

Kalev was assigned as the squad leader and that really got under Rutskoy's skin. He wanted to show who the real chief was, so our room was soon divided into two enemy camps, even if most of the boys swapped sides depending on circumstances. Sometimes they were against us, sometimes with us.

Life in the camp began to take on a regular routine. School lessons, swimming in the salty sea, hiking, excursions, and at least once a day we would assemble in one of the pavilions to sing Pioneer songs. The children were all of different nationalities and it was the custom for us to sing songs from our own parts and in our own languages for a bit of variety. I remember the mixture of fear and hilarity we felt when Kalev and I presented our version of an Estonian national song, "Cock in the Rear and Dagger in the Eye." It made our girls giggle and blush, but they didn't complain, they just waited a bit and then joined in singing it with us. In general it wasn't acceptable to complain in the camp; we were afraid of the leaders, but we were united in solidarity against them.

And what about those camp crushes! Tanja and Ljuda. I still remember their names to this day, and their pictures are still there in my childhood photo album. I remember that I once managed to give Tanja a peck on the cheek, whereupon she burst into tears. I tried for what seemed like hours to get her to tell me why she was crying, until in the end she said, through her tears, that now she would have to have a baby. I didn't understand, and she didn't understand that I didn't understand, and I didn't understand that she didn't understand much about anything at all. And that's how it was for several days. Then I figured it out and tried to explain things. But she said that she knew for sure that children were born from love.

Ljuda's mother was a famous singer. Once when I was a little boy I had overheard my mother evaluate the breasts of a Russian opera diva after a concert. She had argued that they drooped downwards unattractively towards the middle of her stomach. That image stuck in my mind, and later I would observe women at length to see if their tits drooped down onto their stomachs. Ljuda and I met in one of the far nooks of the camp, in a pavilion built on a mound, a lovely spot with a picture-postcard view down to the sea. She listened patiently to my broken Russian, occasionally correcting it, but very tactfully, as if afraid of offending me. She was very mild mannered and gentle. I think that at some point I must have really been in love with her. After the camp we exchanged some bland letters about school life, but then our correspondence fizzled out. Later I saw her in several films, where she normally played the role of a fair-haired fascist, although sometimes she had bigger roles.

Tanja was in love with me, I was in love with Ljuda, but it

was all very innocent and pure, and it had nothing to do with the dirty (?) world of sex. Both of the girls were still children with tiny little breasts. But the young ladies who looked more mature and feminine—who could also be found amongst the campers—often captured my attention and inspired erotic fantasies. Once I managed to have a talk with Kalev about these things. It turned out that Kalev was already "experienced," so I let him describe to me what "it" was really like, dozens of times over.

Towards the end of the camp Kalev informed me, with a conspiratorial look on his face, that something special was in the offing. He was constantly thinking up crazy schemes, but until then we still hadn't gotten in trouble. True, one night when we rowed out to one of the rock islands an ambush had been prepared for us, and it was only by good fortune that we didn't get caught. Someone had told on us, and we guessed that it was the latest example of our enemies' foul play. In order to identify the snitch, Kalev bet Tolja that he could go and take the plaster bust of Pushkin from the Pioneer leader's room that night. When Kalev sneaked off, I clearly heard Tolja and Rutskoy giggling, as if they had played a really good trick on someone. Some time later, Kalev climbed back into the room through the window and gave Tolja a good whack in the teeth. Then in the morning before the wake-up bell, one of the Pioneer leaders came into our room with several henchmen and carried out a search. They found the Pushkin statuette at the foot of Rutskoy's bed. Everyone realized that Kalev had won the bet. Each of us was then questioned one by one, but in those days all good Pioneers had read the books about the Partisans, and not a squeak was heard from any of us.

Kalev had already nabbed that statuette by climbing through the Pioneer leader's open window during the day. At night he had just gone to scout out the situation. Two men had been on guard. They questioned him, hoping to get some information out of him, in the course of which he found out that they knew someone was supposed to come and steal something, although they didn't know who. An anonymous letter had been thrown through the Pioneer leader's open window by a skinny boy from the third squadron, and one of the cleaners had seen him do it. "Damned Lukashenko!" Kalev had cursed.

And so, on this occasion, we were sure to do things very carefully. After curfew we went out to the corridor separately, leaving a decent interval of time between us, and from there we crept out of the window. Kalev had somehow gotten ahold of the key to the witch's house, which stood on chicken legs in the fairy-tale theme park, and a bottle of wine. Soon Nadja and Lenochka, two jolly friends from Leningrad, arrived. Kalev liked Nadja, but she wouldn't come without Lenochka. With two couples in the little house, it wasn't some sort of innocent kids' frolic anymore. When we went our separate ways after a couple of hours together, we promised that we would get together again the following night. We met like that two or three times in a row, until we finally got caught. We were ordered out of our house, and quickly had our arms twisted behind our backs. It all happened in the dark, I recognized Nina Petrovna, a fellow camper, by her voice, but I didn't know who the men with her were. They began to lead us over to the lit-up track around the park, but by some miracle I managed to struggle free after a few steps and disappear into the darkness. I slipped in through our corridor window and waited to catch my breath. Suddenly two other boys climbed in as well: it was Rutskoy and Tolja, splitting their sides with laughter. They had been to watch the spectacle of us getting caught and were very happy with themselves.

But there wasn't any big scandal the following day. At first they had wanted to send Kalev straight home, but they only said that for show, as the camp was due to finish soon anyway, and who would send a child from one end of the country to the other all alone. They cursed us and threatened us, but nothing bad ended up happening. They probably didn't want people to start saying that things like that happened at an elite camp. That evening a big fight broke out. One Estonian boy called Sassi came to help us and some boys from our room joined in. The closing ceremonies for the camp were taking place at the same time; the rostrums were full of people, multi-colored rockets shot up into the sky, and everyone was singing: "Great and wide is the land that is our homeland . . ."

"Damn, my ears are ringing from all those songs!" panted Kalev in the darkness behind the rostrum as he tidied himself up. We were dusty, our clothes were torn, and we were covered in welts. Rutskoy had already taken off with the others, only Tolja was left, crawling along the asphalt begging for mercy. No one was planning to carry on hitting him, and it was strange to see he didn't realize that.

The next day, when we were leaving the canteen, the Chairman of the Defense Brigade Council Dzhalil beckoned me over. He was visibly older than us, a young man who liked to show off his muscular torso. "Let's go!" he commanded. I shrugged my shoulders, assuming that the boys had snitched on me for sneaking out to the witch's house on chicken legs, and now I would get a dressing down for it. When we went around the corner of the canteen building he started punching me, but I only felt the first blows because I lost consciousness. The next thing I remembered I was in the train, where I was being given medical treatment. When I finally managed to stand upright, I saw Kalev. His eyes were swollen shut, his lips were puffed up, and his face was covered in bluish-yellow bruises. When I looked in the bathroom mirror I didn't recognize myself. I looked just as horrible as Kalev.

Several people had come from Estonia to take us home. They (probably?) didn't even blink when two children who had been beaten half to death were handed over to them. They may have been told that we "Germans" were ourselves to blame for picking a quarrel based on ethnic grounds.

"That damn Lukashenko! He went and snitched on us again!" cursed Kalev when he could speak again. Kalev had been beaten up by Dzhalil and one other man, who had spat in his face and said that all Germans should have been killed during the war. "I managed to land at least one good punch on that shithead," said Kalev proudly.

We were still just children, and the guys who beat us up were already muscular young men. I have since wondered in amazement that they went so far as to punch us in our faces. Were they really so sure of their impunity, that they could do whatever they wanted to us "Germans"? Or maybe they hadn't learned yet that it was possible to beat someone up without leaving a trace. I once got worked over by a proper KGB professional in Moscow in the 1970s. Afterwards my body was covered in blue blotches and I couldn't move, but my face was left unscathed.

The day after I arrived home I overheard Mother talking to someone and trying to explain that I was ill, but the person still wanted to speak with me briefly. It was a journalist from the newspaper Õhtuleht. They were alarmed be the state of my face, which was still covered in horrible blue and yellow bruises. I explained what had happened. I believed that it was normal for such things to be written about. I was angry and full of indignation.

There is a yellowed newspaper clipping in-between the pages of my childhood photo album, an Õhtuleht article about a meeting with a suntanned, happy, and eager Pioneer who had just come back from an All-Union camp. *I had been dreaming of going to Artek for ages*—the Pioneer recounted with pride—*the Party looks after all the children with no exceptions, even those who live in the most distant parts of our great homeland. At Artek, under the warm sun and by the blue sea of our beloved homeland, we were united as one fraternal family. Every day at the camp was a full-scale, rousing celebration of the friendship of nations.*

When Aili had finished reading the story, she turned to me with a look of horror on her face. "So what did your mother do about it?" she asked.

I told her that my mother had done nothing. She was probably just grateful that her son had lived to tell the tale.

EARLY SPRING ORANGE

Over the course of time all sorts of odds and ends have accumulated in my cupboards and drawers. Every time I dive into the stacks of folders and piles of papers covered in writing, my fingers come across things, sometimes unexpected and interesting things, that I then have to examine, read, and investigate. I can then be sure of forgetting what I was originally looking for, my initial thoughts having been superseded by new ones, and those by others still, and it's not until some time later, when I again feel the need or desire to rummage in my archives, that the thing I was initially hunting for (the piece of paper) comes to light.

One morning at the beginning of February this year, when I was writing this book, which you dear reader, happen now to be reading—a book that is no ordinary collection of stories assembled from different periods, but more closely resembles a novel in its structure (and maybe it really is a novel!)—I was awoken at half past five by a terrible noise. In my sleepy state I couldn't tell where it had come from, whether it was something right next to my ear or further away. Then I felt a draft, or rather a waft of fresh air from outdoors. I got up and walked towards the kitchen, almost as if I were passing through a corridor or tunnel formed from the cool air. When I got there the balcony door was open. A big black cat with a white mark on its chest was sitting on the stove, and its superior gaze was fixed on me.

I had been worrying that I was missing something important that was needed to finish this collection of stories. I had chosen *Life's Sweet Horror* as the title of the book, which meant that I had to constantly check whether the life I was describing in my stories really was so sweet that it was worth the trouble of living, and whether there were proportionally enough horrible things also included. That autumn I planned to begin writing a completely different type of novel, which I gave the working title "Impressions." I had completed the first chapter several years previously, describing in long Proustian sentences how the main protagonist waited for the local train and then traveled several stops, but then I began writing *The Caretaker's Wife* instead and postponed the other work until the following year. And so every autumn I would sit down with a sigh to start working on "Impressions" again. At first I would go through the whole first chapter (which would always involve changing the protagonist's name and cutting up some of the longer sentences), then I would plan all kinds of (fantastical and unrealizable) structural devices, intended to represent a major advance in the Estonian language and the art of novel writing. But then I was always overcome by an unexplainable black despair, which made me feel like the character in Camus's *The Plague* who can't get further than the first sentence, and so it always happened that eventually I would start writing something else instead.

On this occasion I had thoroughly rewritten that (damned!) first chapter again, given the protagonist a new name (*Enden* = "End") and had once again gone round in circles and got myself tied up in knots. One sleepless night the word combination "Life's sweet horror" came to mind, and I thought it would be a suitable title for a book. In the morning the art critic Ants Juske called and said that he wanted to do a double interview with me and the artist-writer Ervin Õunapuu for the journal *Arkaadia*. My book *On the Weekend. Playing* was just coming out, so any kind of advertising was welcome. What was so wonderfully entertaining about the whole thing was that it was an art critic doing a double interview with two "double" artists. Right at the start Õunapuu said that his novel had come out the previous week, that a short story collection was coming out a couple of weeks later, and that a few days previously he had submitted a new novel to his publisher. My jaw dropped. I eventually managed to close my mouth, but (to my own surprise) I opened it again to say that I also had a new collection of stories called "Life's Sweet Horror" ready, which was to be mostly autobiographical in subject matter.

When I had finished spinning yarns to Juske (being interviewed by him) it occurred to me that there wasn't actually any reason why I shouldn't write an autobiographical book like that. I had just had a story appear in the journal *Looming* in which, among other things, I had recounted how Aili had painted a huge, magnificent seascape on the wall of her studio in Lasnamäe—and how over the previous few days I was unable to do much else other than receive guests who wanted to look in awe at Aili's sea.

What's more, in her review of *An Artist's Novel* Heie Treier (the art critic) had said that Vint should write "using real names and without any surrealism, about himself, his brother, wife, and like-minded fellow artists, about the 1960s and the following decades as he experienced them . . ." The next morning I called the publisher, and they promised to put *Life's Sweet Horror* into the schedule for 2000, which they happened to be compiling at the time. And what could be nicer than an artist fulfilling the critic's wish!

But my text has really started to ramble now. At the start I was supposed to be talking about rummaging in the archives, but then a strange cat sat on my stove, following which I ended up being interviewed by Juske instead. That's how it always goes—you start off looking for one thing and you end up finding something else.

So on this occasion I was standing there glowering at the cat in my kitchen (or maybe it's a burglar who has taken on the form of a cat, I thought), and the cat was glowering back at me (if that man would be so kind as to go back to bed then I could get to work burgling his house!) and the whole time I was tormented by the thought that there was something important missing from my book. I didn't know what it was. I had a vague feeling that it had to be something (very) autobiographical and really horrible. The Soviet period was horrible. My youth was sweet.

There was nothing I could do about the cat. I couldn't figure out how it had gotten up to the eleventh floor balcony. It was plump, with shiny fur. I offered it some milk and mincemeat, but it refused to eat. I started to feel cold so I shut the balcony door. The previous evening my friend Aarne from Canada had been over and had left a smell of smoke behind him. Being a former chain smoker who is now a non-smoker, I had to expel every last whiff of smoke, which was why the balcony door was ajar and the cat—that same black hairy cat—had slipped in through the gap, knocking a saucepan off the bench. That was the source of the noise that had woken me up. Nothing out of the ordinary had happened, I told myself, to try and calm down. One evening I had come back from the bathroom after brushing my teeth to find that my wife was no longer in bed, where I had left her a few minutes earlier. I called out her name. No answer. I ran through all the rooms battling a growing feeling of panic. Nothing! The front door was shut, all the windows were shut, but my wife was nowhere. I don't believe in supernatural forces (although it's possible that I'm so afraid of them that I just say that I don't believe in them!). I sat down, feeling powerless in the face of the hopelessness of the situation, and listened to the silence. My wife had disappeared. Without a trace. Aliens must have nabbed her, that was the only (!) logical explanation. "Aili!" I let out a heartrending yell from somewhere deep inside me and it reverberated through the empty rooms, somehow making their emptiness even bleaker.

"What is it?" asked Aili in surprise, closing the toilet door after herself. I hadn't looked for her there. She hadn't bothered to answer my calls.

"Your jokes are like some kind of brutal barracks humor," I said angrily.

"Looks like you still care about me then," Aili joked.

I didn't know what do with the cat, and I couldn't think why I should have to bother with it anyway. So I just turned off the light in the kitchen and lumbered off to my office, shuffling my slippers as I went. I wouldn't be able to get back to sleep now anyway. I pulled the cupboard door open and examined the shelves, which were full of all sorts of junk. Then I picked out a yellowing folder full of newspaper clippings on the off chance there might be something interesting in it. It belonged to my brother Tõnis (over the course of time, and after various moves, the archives had gotten a bit mixed up). Sixties culture. Or more precisely, the traces that culture had left behind and that an art student had put aside for posterity. I leafed through the clippings: *In recent times it has ceased to be the norm to count how many paintings in an exhibition cover a given subject or another . . . many of our artists feel no obligation to give an annual report to the public when they deal with real life subjects . . . commercial art no longer exists as an isolated form in the public domain, but is instead created for that very purpose, and with its simple and highly visible style it makes up an inseparable component of that domain . . . in order to resolve the major compositional challenges presented by the unlimited possibilities of watercolor painting . . . although Adamson-Eric doesn't directly reflect the most important challenges of our Soviet reality, he does not lack personal meeting points with the contemporary . . . in no circumstances should a person be used as a pretext for resolving some challenge presented in painting* . . . And then a Russian article caught my eye from among the other papers, poorly printed, on yellowing paper, with the photo barely discernible: "The geologist Yevgeny Rukhin's second vocation," describing how the geologist Yevgeny Rukhin used his free time when he was not away on expeditions—he set up his easel on the snowy banks of the icebound Neva River and conjured up unforgettable cityscapes from the tubes of paint.

(I spend some time examining the plant growing in a pot on the windowsill, it has large thorns and small leaves, and red blossoms connected by thread-thin shoots, although some of the blossoms have fallen off and are lying on the white windowsill beside the shiny black ceramic pot. I begin to think that Rukhin might be the missing part of my book. And so I let my memories wander back to the year 1966.)

It is early winter, or already midwinter. The air is ice-cold and when we speak, puffs of steam shoot out from our mouths. We have come to the Hermitage library to look at art books and journals. They are in the private collection; you need a special permit to see them, and my brother organizes a pilgrimage to do so every year. We Soviet art students enjoy a rare opportunity to peek at the culture of the rest of the world for a few days (I'm tempted to write "to peek up the skirt of culture," but I don't).

By then I have already dropped out of university, and I'm not studying or working anywhere. I'm reading. Waiting for something to happen. Father's frown is getting more and more pronounced. He was sure that I would have an academic career, but now he is not sure of anything. I read approximately twenty-four hours a day (an exaggeration of course!). One day I go to put myself forward for a job as a laundry operator (it sounded grand). A pack of women greets me jubilantly. I begin to feel uneasy and decide to leave, promising to think over the matter. One night, in the middle of the night, someone knocks on the window of our apartment. It's the artist Jüri Arrak, who is on skis and has come to visit my brother (in fact he had gone skiing during the day, but then stopped off at a friend's place, where they started boozing, then at three o'clock he decided to ski home but got lost and ended up at our place—or maybe our lit windows were like a lighthouse that he skied towards?). Jüri asserts that existentialism is best illustrated by a situation when a man walks down the road and all the roadside signposts fall on his head. At the time existentialism is like a religion for me. Tõnu Kõiv and I regularly sit in Café Moscow in the late afternoon and talk about nothing but existentialism. Tõnu has also left the university. As has his friend Andres Ots, with whom he studied French. Andres is now training to be an actor. Tõnu reads one or two plays every day. He has started to translate Camus's *Myth of Sisyphus*. For three weeks in a row we talk about *The Brothers Karamazov*, and then for a whole month about *Demons*. Tõnu says that before Camus no one knew how to read *Demons*. I don't argue with him.

One day we go to Leningrad. I don't dare ask for money from my father. My brother asks for me. Everyone respects Tõnis, at home and at school. They are all proud of him. When they see me, they look worried and sigh. There are four of us in the train compartment. Tõnis with his future wife, his brother (me), and one of his fellow students named Aili. When the train departs, none of us know that just one year later the four people traveling together would become two married couples.

In Leningrad we go straight from the station to see Rukhin,

the very same amateur painter and geologist I have already mentioned. Geologists were imbued with an aura of romantic glory in Soviet society. All boys wanted to become either geologists or astronauts. Rukhin hates singing songs around the campfire and loves the city and culture. He lives in a large apartment by one of the canals, where a porcelain collection is resplendent above the grand piano and there are Russian works of art in heavy frames on the walls. He himself paints "churchscapes"—that is, landscapes that must without fail include a church. He has many friends overseas: for example, in America he knows James Rosenquist, Jasper Johns, Roy Lichtenstein, and Robert Rauschenberg. There are spools of reel-to-reel tape, vinyl records, catalogs, and art journals lying in piles in the corners, and paintings given to him by friends propped up against the walls. There is so much to see and listen to that we probably don't even need to go to the library. Zhenya (Yevgeny) is bored of painting churches. Recently he painted his first abstract work, which depicts a blue form growing out of the darkness, culminating in a zinc-white form in the center. Aili likes the painting, so Zhenya gives it to her as a present. He has recently started experimenting with collage, which is later to become his main artistic outlet. Tõnis likes a piece in which a t-shirt has been stuck onto cardboard and painted over with a striking lilac-blue color theme. So Zhenya gives it to Tõnis with generous abandon. We Estonians make an awkward fuss to show our gratitude as we receive the presents. The tall Russian, who has an abundance of hair growing out of him—a shaggy, curly lion's mane and huge beard—shrugs his shoulders indifferently. His whole being is sincere, genuine, and kind. There is something epic about him that makes us Estonians, who grew up on those tiny patches of field between brushwood, cower in awe.

After a day spent in the library and a memorable evening at Rukhin's we collapse in exhaustion, but after fleeting and dreamless sleep we wake up, and then are unable to sleep any more until morning. We are sleeping on the floor and some tiny unidentified creatures are attacking us with merciless bloodthirstiness. I manage to pin one particularly aggressive one against the wall with a safety pin. We think that the little creatures must be bedbugs, and we are probably right. (Holdovers from the Leningrad blockade, and still practicing their bloody vocation to this day.) Later I start to feel remorse for pinning the bug against the wall. By the next evening new accommodations are made for us on camping cots, which have appeared out of nowhere.

In our dream-like state, the Leningrad days pass quickly. I have been devouring art with the same relish as my companions, who had already chosen art as their vocation. During the three years I spent in the army I drew for fun—played with forms, created surrealist structures from them. I had never taken art seriously. Unlike literature. As a four-year-old child, whenever I would read some book or other I apparently used to say that I wanted to write books myself so that I wouldn't have to bother reading them. I don't know if that is true, or whether it was just my mother's fantasy. She loved to invent stories and remake life according to her whims. One time I recorded my mother's recollections of Grandmother's adventure-packed life on a Dictaphone. She had been sent to Siberia together with Grandfather, had seen Lenin with her own eyes, and had traveled in the same carriage as Stalin (during the journey Stalin had apparently swiped Grandfather's gold pocket watch). Grandfather was shot dead on a hunting trip near Tomsk, after which Grandmother, who was by then pregnant, began traveling in the direction of Estonia. In Petrograd she gave birth to my mother, got a sham marriage with a Latvian, then finally arrived home in 1921 with three little girls clinging to one arm and nothing but her two hands and ten fingers as her possessions. Her house on the outskirts of Tallinn had been burned to the ground. A maid who was still living in the servants' house there came to the door and had the nerve to claim that she had never seen Grandma in her life.

Our time in Leningrad (my mother's birthplace!) finished very abruptly. I remember we were in a kitchen somewhere, drinking vodka and waiting for someone or something. Our departure somehow depended on that (on what?). I hoped with my whole heart that we would miss the train so we could spend one more day in Leningrad. I sat there stealing glances at Aili, and started to regret that when we got back to Tallinn art would just be a peripheral pastime for me. Just as it had been before. I had a lot of things to sort out—I had to find a job somewhere and then start seriously writing in the evenings. I had (at whatever price) to live out the story of Martin Eden. I hoped and believed that in the future I would be able to experience the same kinds of powerful artistic sensations I had felt in the Hermitage in many other museums in many other cities. It didn't occur to me for one moment that I could earn a living as an artist.

Rukhin finally surfaced and at the last moment our problems were resolved. On the journey from Leningrad to Tallinn Aili and I talked the whole night through, to the accompaniment of the clunking wheels of the train. We talked about Rudolf Arnheim's life, about the battle of Lilleküla, and about many more of life's important questions. I had never met a girl who was so willing to follow the absurd thread of my fantasies. Aili could fantasize almost as an incidental activity, as if it were an everyday form of communication. When the train arrived in Tallinn we agreed that we would go to the theater together as soon as possible.

My parents were terribly worried about me. My father the academic (who was extremely distant from culture, and who in his whole life would only read one work of fiction through to the end, which would be his son's first collection of short stories), informed me that if I hadn't gotten a job by the first of April, then . . . He didn't say what would happen—probably he didn't know himself. My classmate Peeter Eelsaare worked in television and told me I should apply to be a director's assistant. I imagined that the work might have a creative side to it. At least it would be more interesting than being a laundry operator. My mother took me to the theater to see *Porgy and Bess* so that I wouldn't completely fade away from sitting at home all the time. Aili was sitting behind us with some friends. She introduced me to them and said that they had known each other since they were kids. Then she looked straight at me and said "You see, we did go to the theater after all." I felt uncomfortable as I recalled my earlier promise, and I probably blushed to my ears.

Something awful had happened. Instead of concentrating on writing a short story or a novel, I did nothing but think of Aili. I had previously decided to avoid the company of all females of the species, believing that they only brought sadness, worries, and trouble. I was certain that I had to resist the destructive influence of women in order to realize my grandiose plans. Now I had completely fallen off track. Maybe it would have helped if I could have invited Aili to the cinema or a café. Then I could have made sure that she was just as boring as all the other females of the species, that there was nothing about her that was worth going crazy over. But I had no money to go to a café. I either didn't want or didn't dare to ask for money from my parents, so the whole situation was stupid.

Towards the end of the 1960s everyone knew that the Art Institute parties were major events. People would do anything to get into them and would then talk for several weeks about how Eri Klas, now an internationally renowned conductor, had pounded out a half-hour drum solo, and the floor of the hall had shaken, moving up and down by as much as ten centimeters to the rocking rhythm. My brother Tõnis took me with him to one of these parties, and I went despite having sprained my leg. I was limping heavily and there was no question of dancing. I watched from the doorway of the hall as Aili danced with my friend Tõnu Kivu, and I saw that when they'd finished they walked across the dance floor hand in hand. I couldn't stand seeing that, and I fled as quickly as my injured leg would allow me to. I spent the whole night writing poetry, which I had then ripped into pieces by dawn. I was quite sure that life was no longer worth living.

But soon enough I had to raise my arms above my head in humiliation and surrender myself to a life of imprisonment: Tõnis's wedding was in September, and then Aili and I got married at the beginning of October. We dragged a two-seater couch through town—each holding on to one end—and brought it into our new home in the cellar of a building on Kunder Street. I got the job in television, which was only a couple of minutes away from the cellar studio. Both Tõnis and Aili had graduated from the Art Institute that year. When they started getting ready for the autumn exhibition, which they could take part in as artists for the first time (at that time students were forbidden from appearing in exhibitions) I began to paint pictures as well.

Amazingly, one of my highly decorative paintings got past the jury, but the exhibition curator chose not to display it.

Aili once told a story about how her brother caught a baby fox. They had pampered and spoiled it until it had grown up. Then they took it in a bag to the edge of the forest and let it go. But the fox didn't care much for the forest anymore.

I realized that my fantastical plans and lofty goals for the future would have to gradually fizzle out. It was pretty nice to be able to run back and forth between the television station and our studio, sleeping in my wife's embrace at night, and dragging pictures to the exhibitions at the Art Hall, although to tell the truth they were rejected from two exhibitions in a row. I wrote television scripts about a former prison or a concentration camp (I can't remember exactly which) in Lithuania in order to earn enough money to buy a stroller for our baby. Then I sold my first painting. It was a work that had been on display in the following autumn exhibition in which a butterfly of unidentified species was hovering against an abstract background. Max Laosson was the buyer. When I rang his doorbell with the painting under my arm and my heart racing, all I knew was that Laosson was a writer of some sort. He had an impressive house and a huge number of books. I reckon there must have been even more books than in my childhood home. The writer gave me a signed copy of one of his works: impressions from a trip to Cuba. It was a very Communist book. I hadn't had much contact with writers at that stage in my life. There were Aadu Hint and Minni Nurme, who were the parents of a classmate of mine named Päärn, but at that time we were tiny kids and they were big grown-ups. On this occasion I was able to talk for over an hour with a writer who was the same size as me. When I told him that my painting cost nine hundred rubles (which was the size of our household debt at the time), a strange expression appeared on the writer's face; he fell silent for a while, and then he went into the other room and came back with the money. He had to make up the full sum in kopecks. I didn't know how much my art was worth. Our artist friends weren't able to sell their paintings yet. When I told people how much I had asked Laosson for my picture, they pulled long faces and told me that even half of that sum would have been too much.

I wanted to become a writer, but in my university days (and later as well) I didn't mix much in literary circles. I read a lot, but I was uninformed. I didn't know many of the important things that a budding writer needed to know about the Estonian literary world. It was actually a real shame that for the new generation that was now arriving at maturity—or at least for our group of young artist friends—Laosson was seen as just another writer. As a Communist Party loyalist, he had played a significant role in the destruction of Estonian culture and of Estonian writers' prospects, and over the course of little more than twenty years this had been lost in the farthest recesses of our memory. That was just as terrible as the fact that today, in the year 2000, we have completely forgotten what happened in 1980.

But really, what do today's twenty-year-olds need to know about what took place back then? For them, events that happened ten years ago are echoed in the form in which their mothers and fathers want to remember them. They adopt the positions of their friends and relatives, and these then become the myths which replace reality. For them there can be no actual reality.

I've let myself get really far off track with this story again, and now is probably the final chance to find the right path. Let's say it is 1974, late autumn, and we are going to Leningrad again to a reception for Rukhin's wedding anniversary. And naturally, we are again planning to investigate the journals and books that have arrived from the free world to the Hermitage library.

In the intervening period the "Saku 73" exhibition had taken place, and a brass band had blasted away at the opening, leading Rukhin to point out that if a similar exhibition were to open in Leningrad it would be the lethal shots of the regime's guns you would hear ringing out instead of an orchestra. All four of us Vints had been accepted as members of the Artists Union. We were part of the establishment, but we could create the kind of art we wanted to—so we probably all had happy and contented expressions on our faces back then.

But the reception at Rukhin's stunned us. Butlers (spies?) in white gloves were thronging about with trays. There were a lot of people there—some in old sweaters which had seen better days (Russian underground artists), others in elegant evening wear (diplomats from Western embassies). At least half of them had come from Moscow specially for the reception. It was something completely different from our artist's studio parties. Here there was shape and color, food and drink. It didn't at all fit with our ideas about an artist's life—it was more like watching scenes from a foreign film.

The next morning we woke up in an old-fashioned hotel, with a rather frivolous nineteenth-century painting hanging on the wall. When we were leaving the party Zhenya (Rukhin) had stuffed a bottle of Moskovskaya vodka and some pickled gherkins into my pocket. So I twisted the top off the vodka and was then able to pass the time pleasantly relaxing in an old bed in the old hotel, curing my hangover and exchanging impressions of the previous evening with Aili. We were quite astonished by the conversations we had had with Russian artists, which mostly revolved around selling pictures. They visibly tried to curry favor with foreigners, or sought to strike an anarchistic pose through their behavior and appearance. In this way, what we had seen the previous evening resembled a theater performance. Our young homegrown Estonian artistic community was burning with intellectual curiosity; we were trying to find out as much as we could about everything that was happening in global culture, but we had absolutely no way of knowing what the Western art world really looked like. Only Estonians from the diaspora and Finns visited Tallinn. But foreign diplomats and correspondents of major newspapers had brought their habits and customs to the Moscow and Leningrad art circles, and by the middle of the 1970s the Western art world's value system, with all its emptiness and superficiality, was flourishing there.

If one takes a cynical view, the famous "bulldozer exhibition" was actually a well-planned PR operation, where the KGB simply took the bait. A group of Russian underground artists decided to organize the exhibition on some abandoned land near Moscow. They applied to the city government for permission, which they obviously didn't get. The entire underground elite came to show their works without authorization, and dozens of foreign journalists were invited. Suddenly truckloads of young people started to arrive at the exhibition grounds, all dressed in brand-new work overalls and carrying brand-new spades, looking like they had arrived for one of those regular voluntary work days organized in the Soviet Union at the time. The precise aim of the work was unclear, but the bulldozers drove resolutely in the direction of the artists' displays. They drove right at the people and the artworks; fifteen paintings were smashed to bits, three were burnt in fires, and some artists, including our friend Rukhin, were arrested. The next day all the "authorities" of the art world were talking about it. Art had turned into politics, and the Russian artists reaped the benefits quite cynically.

The day after the grand reception we visited some artists' studios with Rukhin and saw plenty of blood, sweat, and tears being shed. Russian artists are tireless, they can work for days on end, but if they should happen to start talking it's very hard to bring their clever chatter to a halt. They did their hard labor in those studios, although for many of them the work seemed to have little prospect, because they were not wanted at the exhibitions, and only a very few of them made it into the Western orbit. Only one or two of them had emigrated—Zhemyakin was in Paris, and no one else comes to mind right now. But by the 1980s Leningrad's underground artist community had almost been drained dry—some went here, some went there, in some cases depending on whether they had been able to prove their Jewish heritage.

Rukhin visited Tallinn pretty frequently, but for us it was a major undertaking to go to Leningrad. I remember how he would sometimes just turn up, only to depart a couple of days later just as unexpectedly. Tõnis tried to organize an exhibition of his work at the Art Salon, and we almost got the authorization to do it. We stored the pictures intended for the exhibition in our attic for a year, until at last it became clear that the art officials didn't want to take the risk. Zhenya came to take the pictures away; he piled them onto the roof of his massively overloaded Volga, tied them down, and started doing some repairs on the car engine. Never before or since have I seen a car with so much rust under the hood. But after half an hour's tinkering the engine started again.

There were many legends about Rukhin circulating in Tallinn. About how he would arrive in Moscow by train in the morning, leave the paintings he had brought with him standing up against the station wall, and would then come back the next day, or the day after that, and take them where they had to go. And this was in Russia, where anything that wasn't nailed down would be stolen! It was probably true as well. Just like the story about his children playing with bundles of twenty-five-ruble bills, building houses and whole cities with them. They used to say he was operating on a big scale—in the course of one night he could paint four or five pictures that some diplomat had ordered the night before to take across the border with him the next day.

It was April when Rukhin came to take his paintings from our attic, and there had already been several days of warm, sunny weather. At that time all the "authorities" of the art world were trumpeting his forty-work exhibition, which was touring US cities. By then he had become the most famous artist in the Soviet Union. The weather was beautiful, so we decided to drive to Vääna-Jõesuu to look at the sea. Some of the dunes still had snow caps on them, others were already bare. The sea was blue. Zhenya took an orange from his pocket and let it roll down the undulating slope of one of the smaller dunes. The orange rolled a short distance and then stopped. It had left a clear track in the sand. Some men took photos of us. We took photos of them, they took photos of us.

We went to the Kuku Club in the evening. Zhenya bought a jar of orange juice and a bottle of gin, which were rationed goods at the time, to take away. When he was getting ready to leave with his pictures loaded on the roof, he gave them to us as a present. He told us to drink to his health. A few days later we got a postcard from Zhenya. There was a burning car on it—a retro reprint of a 1930s art deco postcard. On the other side there was a brief note telling us he had arrived home without any particular incidents.

"See, that's how considerate people treat each other. We were worried when he left, so he put our minds at rest. But you sometimes go missing for two or three days and don't even call," said Aili.

A week later we received the news that Rukhin had died. He had been drinking vodka with a poet and some girl in a studio somewhere. A fire had suddenly broken out. The poet had managed to jump out of the window. Rukhin and the girl had burned to death in the building. Aili and I had the flu so we couldn't go to the funeral. There were a lot of policemen at the cemetery; they had destroyed peoples' pictures by pulling the film out of their cameras and exposing it to the light.

There was an eerie reoccurrence of oranges in various forms in the run-up to and aftermath of Rukhin's death.

The artist Ohakas's spouse told us that they had gone to see the writer Juhan Smuul at the hospital on the day that he died. Smuul had given them a bottle of vodka and some oranges and instructed them to get drunk. And then he apparently suffocated himself with his pillow. I didn't trouble myself wondering whether this story was true or not, but somehow we became convinced that Rukhin's death had not happened by chance, and that he had sensed or even known it would happen in advance.

About a year later I began painting a picture of an orange rolling down a sandy slope. I put "Early Spring Orange" as the title. The picture appeared in the Estonian national exhibition, and on one occasion I started to paint another version of it. I am sure there is not a single other picture I have put as much effort into. I was striving for perfection. In the end I achieved what I wanted (probably?).

Someone from the Moscow Export Salon chose "Early Spring Orange" to be included in an exhibition in the USA. By the start of the 1980s Soviet "underground" art had become a valuable commodity. The Estonian artists Malle Leis and Jüri Arrak and myself were grouped together with the Russian avant-garde, since we all differed, each in our own way, from the Soviet Union's official art. In America a woman named Natasha negotiated the sale of our paintings, and told us that their retail value was apparently well over ten thousand dollars. This was the high point of the American art market—the crest of the wave before the fall. We only received two to three percent of the sale, part of which was in the form of remittance vouchers for hard currency goods that we had to purchase from the state at an inflated price.

The art world is built on myths, and since in the last quarter of the twentieth-century it was suffering from a dearth of them, the events in the Soviet Union aroused particular interest. The heroes of the "bulldozer exhibition" such as Rukhin and other later victims of the system (who perished in uncertain circumstances) acted as advertisements for the goods (the paintings) and pushed up the prices. Apparently Natasha, who owned a gallery, did particularly well at that time. She liked my "Early Spring Orange" and had it printed on her gallery's posters. One day I got a call from the Moscow Export Salon telling me that a company called "International Images" wanted to order a dozen paintings from me, and that they should depict different kinds of fruit rolling down a sandy slope: apples, pears, lemons, apricots, tangerines . . . I said that I wasn't interested in that kind of work.

"But they pay well"—clearly they hadn't understood my answer.

So I told them again that I didn't want to paint those kinds of pictures.

"What should I tell them, they won't understand," someone complained at the other end of the line.

"Tell them that Rukhin is dead," I said.

"What's Rukhin got to do with it?" they asked.

"A lot," I said. But they didn't understand.

A BUNCH OF FORGET-ME-NOTS

And when at last I do die, if I die altogether, it will not be I who will have died, that is, I will not have let myself die, but will have been killed by man's fate.

—*Miguel de Unamuno*

At the end of a hot and sunny May in 1977, Aili and I went to Poland for the opening of an exhibition of our work. In the rest of the world it went without saying that artists would take part in the openings of their overseas exhibitions, but in the Soviet Union some Party functionary or official would normally go. The trip didn't seem real for us right up until the last moment, and we only believed it was actually happening when we were sitting in the comfortable two-berth compartment on the train to Warsaw.

"We really are going!" said Aili with a sigh. She loves to travel. Like a gypsy, travel is in her blood, it doesn't matter where to or when.

I stretched out my legs and lit a cigarette, and, feeling pleasantly relaxed, I took a small book I had bought in the station out of my pocket. It was a slim collection of short stories by a Polish writer in Russian translation, and it had been printed on very cheap paper and formatted quite atrociously.

In the 1960s and 1970s Poland played a very important role for Estonia. Musicians and artists came into contact with world culture for the first and often last time through the festivals and biennials that took place in Poland. At the end of every year we would stand in incredibly long lines for hours on end to order Polish journals, the quota for which could run out at any moment. Our exhibition was organized by the Polish-Estonian Soviet Socialist Republic Friendship Union, and the "miracle" of our being able to go to the opening came about because the new chairman of the society, the Tallinn mayor Norak, wanted to show himself in a good light—or maybe he just wasn't yet up to speed with the rule about people in the cultural sphere (not) traveling abroad. Both of us had been to Poland before with organized tours—Aili even twice before—but being allowed across the border and then left to our own devices was a truly rare occurrence amongst our circle of acquaintances. Especially to open our own exhibition! In those days it must have seemed to us like the first big, bold step on the path to international recognition.

But disappointment awaited us in Warsaw—it turned out that our paintings hadn't arrived at the gallery, even though we had sent them a month earlier. Something had gone wrong at the station on the Polish border: the boxes with our paintings were gathering cobwebs in some carriage on some siding at the station in Brest—either that or they had simply gone missing. We were very worried, but the Poles were quite relaxed about the whole thing, they seemed confident that the paintings would turn up. Our exhibition was supposed to travel to several towns in succession, and there were only four days left until the first opening in Zielona Gora. Urgent telegrams were dispatched, then we were driven across Poland to a small town near Zielona Gora where an international painting camp happened to be taking place.

In those days artists were still fun-loving bohemians who spent the daylight hours pleasurably painting but enjoyed their parties in the evenings even more. There was a happy holiday atmosphere at the painting camp, and Aili and I decided to take it very easy: we didn't have our painting materials with us, and the weather was lovely.

By the fifth or sixth day it became clear that our pictures would not be arriving any time soon—there was apparently a dire staff shortage at the border station (someone told us that there was a strike on the Polish side of the border). But at that point a storm started raging in the skies above us, and it was pounding the ground below with thunderbolts, so we couldn't go swimming or rambling through the countryside, and I took out the book I had bought in Moscow—the only one I had brought with me—and started reading.

The first story seemed typically Polish in its themes—it was about war and betrayal. But it didn't conform to the black-and-white principles that were customary in socialist realism. From his own perspective, the treacherous protagonist's actions were always fully justified, and it was hard for the reader to condemn him. I was stunned that a story like this could have been published in the Soviet Union. It might have been a slip-up on the part of an ordinarily watchful editor—they had read the work too superficially—or maybe the skilled translator had managed, in the right places, to get the right message across to the right people. But it was also quite possible that good writers—because the story really was well written—occupied an important position in the Polish literary hierarchy, or maybe it was just that this writer had hunted deer with an important Moscow functionary in a Polish forest some time.

The second story in the book took the reader across the ocean, and the author seemed to know his way around the city of Denver, where it was set. It was likely he had been lucky enough to spend some time there—the cityscape was vibrant and the piteous hero (if it is possible to call an émigré loser a hero) acted out his role there fairly convincingly. This story didn't arouse any particular emotions in me, however; it was a rather tedious piece, the plot was too obvious, and in general it came across more as a political commission than a short story. By the time I got to the final pages of the story I couldn't focus my eyes on it anymore, and when I read the title of the third story I was already so overcome with boredom that I had lost all desire to continue reading the Pole's works.

That night a fresh storm gathered above our heads, and we couldn't sleep. For some time I watched as flashes of lightning separated by short intervals lit up the greenery in the darkness outside the window, and the landscape momentarily took on a completely unnatural coloring. We were staying in an old manor house, built in the style of a small castle; the lightning illuminated the wing with its turrets and gothic windows, and I had the terrible feeling that I had ended up in some kind of horror film. A bit later the skies opened, the flashes of lightning started to look hazy through the wet windowpane, and the rain came down in bucket-loads. Suddenly everything went quiet, and it became very dark. I turned around to walk back to my bed, but collided with something soft. For a moment I heard the sound of my own voice, half-muffled and ghastly, then I realized what had happened and started laughing—Aili had come up and stood behind my back, unheard, and I had bumped into her.

I didn't feel sleepy at all now, and so Aili and I chatted for a while until she dozed off. Before leaving for Poland there had been an exhibition of her work at the Art Salon, and she had slogged away for months to get ready and now deserved her holiday.

I opened the Pole's book of stories again. The title of the final story was "Nezabudki," meaning forget-me-nots. I had barely managed to get through a few pages before I started to feel troubled by an odd feeling that I had already read the story, and some of the details of the scene that was described seemed particularly familiar. Suddenly I realized that it wasn't the text of the story, rather it was that the places being described that were familiar. And why shouldn't they be, if we had already spent several days in the very same small town the story was describing. Some writers need individual details from which to construct a fantastical whole, but this Polish writer needed absolute reality into which he could smuggle his creations.

The impression that the writer was describing real life was reinforced on the next page, where I read a description of the very room we were in, with the protagonist sitting in the very same chair where I had been sitting. The view from the window was the same. Even the watercolor of a withered bunch of flowers . . . *from which decay emanated, almost as if they were flower-corpses sending their stench to the nostrils* . . . was hanging in a thin black frame on the wall.

I couldn't keep my incredible discovery to myself, so I had to stir Aili from the depths of sleep again, and read to her what I had just read, my voice trembling from excitement . . . *Wieslaw sunk, fell, collapsed into the depths of the armchair, and for some time he sat there like a ball of rags, like a crumpled piece of paper. His eyes were shut tight, but the picture remained remorselessly there in front of him, he didn't want to see it anymore, but he was powerless against its persistent attack, he was unable to change anything, and when he finally forced his eyes wide open, he saw instead his trembling hand and his fingertips pressed into the reddish-brown cover of the armchair. What fine hands, he thought. These long fingers could belong to a pianist, they would be well suited for playing violin . . . then his eyes strayed to the right, where, resplendent against the gray wallpaper in its narrow black frame, he saw the watercolor depicting a bunch of flowers, from which decay emanated, almost as if they were flower-corpses sending their stench to the nostrils, and he could even smell a putrid stench coming from the vase; then he forced his gaze towards the window, and then from there outwards, to the world outside, where the evening sun was turning the tops of the farthest trees golden but had somehow forgotten the tree growing right by the window, leaving it completely in the shade. In several years the branches of that tree would probably start growing into the room. If no one chops them off before then . . . But that final fragment of a thought—if no one chops them off before then—suddenly took on a terrible significance, and only now, in that brief moment of time, was it clear what he had done. He realized how awful it was in its total irreversibility. In its undeniable reality . . .*

"It's strange, I was thinking exactly the same thought about those tree branches," said Aili. She was wide-awake.

Since my Russian was more fluent than Aili's, I started translating the story to her right there and then. We also started reading the tourism booklet, which had a plan of the town in it, and by morning we had a pretty good idea of where the events in the story had taken place, and we became more certain that the events described in it really had happened at some point.

A certain Wieslaw, a bohemian type portrayed in a sympathetic light, completely loses control and kills his friend. He is tormented by a terrible sense of guilt. No one has any reason to suspect him, and they all believe that his friend drowned. Some time later a half-decomposed corpse is found in the reeds by the lake; at first people think it is the friend's corpse, and they bury it. Wieslaw can't bear the guilt any longer, so he goes to hand himself in as the murderer. He reveals the spot where he buried his friend's corpse. They start digging, and soon a corpse does indeed turn up. But it's the corpse of a dog. A despairing Wieslaw rushes over to the remains of the dog, wailing and lamenting. They tear him away by force. After a couple of months in the hospital he comes back to his hometown. In the intervening period his hair has turned partly gray, and he has filled out. He walks along the edge of the field, whistling to himself in a carefree mood and picking forget-me-nots, which he ties into a bunch. There is a patch of wasteland in the middle of the brushwood where all sorts of rubbish and junk has been dumped. The rusty carcass of a delivery truck is lying there. That's where he solemnly and ceremoniously places his bundle of flowers.

In the morning we slept through breakfast and only got up when the bright sun had already climbed high in the sky.

"They've since repainted the floor in this room," Aili uttered, her first words of the morning.

I jumped up and started examining the floor like a detective—there was a reddish-brown paint under the new gray coat, as revealed in a few worn-out spots. The branch of the tree growing by the window had already been cut back at least once, but it had grown back, and nearly reached inside the room now.

"Looks like several years have passed since that time," I said, without knowing what I would do with that information.

"He's probably not a young man anymore. Those wartime experiences and impressions he writes about in the story happened thirty years ago. Now he would be over fifty," Aili estimated.

I had spoken to her at length during the night about the type of writer he was, fixated with reality, and in our minds he was already equated with his protagonist Wieslaw.

"Look, there are forget-me-nots growing right here!" shouted Aili, almost leaping out of the window. We exchanged a meaningful glance.

This Polish writer describes the murder in his story, but there wasn't a single word about the corpse being buried in the ground. The confession and the revelation of the burial scene seemed genuine, but it came as a real surprise when the dog's corpse emerged from the earth. The bunch of flowers at the end gave the barest of hints that the reader's assessment—that everything was just a figment of the mentally-ill protagonist's imagination—could also be mistaken. But the fleeting hint remained a hint, and the writer also played with a redeeming theme -—the dog as man's best friend

The house was quiet, just as silent as it had been for Wieslaw on that fateful evening. We walked down the same corridor, climbed the same steps, and arrived at the same terrace. The Polish artist Stanislaw had set up an easel in front of the house, there still wasn't a single spot of paint on the canvas, but some of the leaves of the rhododendron growing nearby had turned cobalt blue. "Don't go far, we're going to the Zielona Gora song festival this afternoon, and there's a dinner being organized there in the evening," said Stanislaw.

I asked about the writer whose collection of stories we had been reading. "Oh, he's just some guy who writes nonsense about émigrés. They say that he's never been to America, he just copies the descriptions of the cities from Kerouac," said Stanislaw.

We walked down the overgrown path to the end of the garden, then around a lopsided gatepost out onto the street, at the end of which we could see a small bluish-colored hill, a distant mound covered in bushes. We walked for a while down a road lined with tall hedges, until suddenly two girls in snow-white dresses appeared in front of us. They had garlands of meadow flowers in their hair and were wearing white stockings and shiny black leather shoes. They might have been around six or seven years old, and they were skipping along holding hands right there in front of us. Then another three young girls appeared from a side street, and by the time we had arrived at the main street there were dozens of them.

"If we're to believe what was written in that story, then some sort of Catholic festival is taking place today," said Aili, and I noticed the look of horror on her face.

And it really is an awful feeling when a story that you thought was fictional actually becomes real. The church festival and the girls in white dresses were tangible reality.

"Tangible reality—what a horrible expression," said Aili, a shudder passing through her shoulders.

. . . *He walked ten steps past the door, then abruptly turned around and walked back ten steps to stand facing the door and to stare at the embossed tin coat-of-arms hanging proudly beside it, depicting a tree split by a sword. Probably an oak, he thought. It really is a lot like an oak, he thought as he walked down the steps, descending from the bright light into the darkness. He clumsily groped his way, stumbling downwards, until he could no longer see anything at all. And now he could start walking, with his customary slightly swaying but confident stride, in the direction of the chair where he normally sat . . .*

I told Aili that the tree there on the coat of arms really was an oak.

"I wonder whether he measured the time with a stopwatch before he started writing?" I said in amazement and continued reading . . . *Janina arrived at the post office in five minutes, she wasn't out of breath, which enabled one to conclude that she hadn't hurried, but had walked at a measured pace, certainly not running. She had walked the distance in exactly five minutes, not a second more . . .*

"I really can't understand the reason for that kind of accuracy. Why is he trying to be so precise? I sometimes can't even be bothered to take the book I need off the shelf to describe something more accurately, I just write as my memory or imagination tells me to," I said once we had seated ourselves in a pleasantly cool, dimly-lit bar and ordered beer and sandwiches.

"Maybe the story is some sort of peculiar alibi," said my wife thoughtfully.

"Then the writer must have committed a crime," I pointed out. "It would be pretty horrible if a story that provides the alibi appeared in print before the crime had happened."

"As I understand it, Wieslaw couldn't live with the guilt that was weighing on him, and he thought his only salvation was to hand himself over. But it was by no means certain that he wanted to create a situation where he could be punished for the crime. It was as if finding the dog's corpse in the spot that Wieslaw showed to the investigator no longer had anything to do with the crime. He had admitted his crime: as a Communist, he had confessed his mortal sins to the state authorities, just as a Catholic confesses to his priest. The logical sequence—crime, confession, punishment—has been switched around a bit here. The investigator had no chance of proving the murderer's guilt," Aili deliberated.

"So fate was simply cheated," I concluded, after savoring a mouthful of cold beer.

"Well yes, but then no one really knows what we mean when we talk about fate," I added a little later.

. . . Wieslaw knelt down and moved forwards slightly in a kneeling position, so that to the chance passerby it might seem that he was looking for something, that he had dropped a coin or a button on the ground and was trying to find it. It would not have occurred to a chance observer that the kneeling man was feeling dizzy and that he might keel over at any moment, but then the bell in the church tower started ringing with a hollow chime that echoed all around, and the man jerked upright. His eyes started to take in his surroundings once again, and he saw Janina coming out of the coffee shop door and down the steps. She was around ten meters away, or to be precise, nine—Wieslaw's whole body was tensed, he readied himself to leap forwards at any moment, but then he froze still, supporting himself against a Polish Post letterbox, his hand right against the slot, so that the person behind him who was just about to stuff a letter inside shouted angrily at him. "It was an illusion," mumbled Wieslaw as if to apologize, and that was how the man who wanted to post the letter interpreted his words . . .

"It really is nine meters!" shouted Aili, measuring in paces the distance between the steps and the letterbox again. And so we continued down the street, carrying the book, and becoming ever more convinced that the author had mapped out the town meticulously, as if he had wanted to make some very important thing clear to the reader. For our part, we were becoming more and more certain that the purpose of the sentences printed in the book was more than just literary.

"Although it might simply be that he knew about some crime, and wrote a story that was so realistic that the truth would become clear," Aili suggested.

I replied that if we knew when the story was written, we could go through the local papers and maybe get some idea of what had happened.

Aili laughed at that: "Do you think they write about crimes in the newspapers here? It seems to me that Poland is the same kind of socialist paradise as Estonia, and in these kinds of countries nothing bad happens anymore. It's only the capitalist gutter press that feeds off dirty, blood-stained criminality, ha-ha!"

"But we are talking about a local crime, so local people should know about it and remember. These kinds of things would normally stay fresh in a small town's memories for years."

"Well, go and ask then. But do it in Polish. No one really wants to talk to you in Russian," said Aili.

We arrived at the bus station. There were several people waiting under the awning, taking shelter from the sun. Buses were coming and going.

. . . Softly whistling a fragment of some jolly tune, Wieslaw climbed down the stairs and got off the bus. He was the last one to get up from his seat and the last one off the bus. A content and carefree mood was reflected in his chubby face as he put his bag down onto the ground and placed a cigarette between his lips. The clock on the tower, which made the bus station look inappropriately grand, showed half past twelve. The late May sun was scorching hot. He walked down the steps, stepped on to the gently rocking wharf, walked past the moored boats to the end, bent down and scooped up a handful of water and rubbed it across his face, then with the same measured pace he walked back, turned to enter the bus station, glanced over the bus timetable, joined the line at the ticket counter, and when his turn came he asked for a ticket for the one o'clock service to Poznan, then he strolled back into the sunlight, it was eight minutes before one, but when the Poznan bus arrived a few minutes later, he didn't go to the bus stop, but set out across the square in the direction of the hotel, turned to the right, and started walking along the street in the direction of the light-blue mound, or small hill . . .

"Well, it's certainly not this bus station he describes," I said, putting the book back in my pocket. "There's no lake, no hotel, and no grand bus station building, just a mound in the distance."

"Let's go this way then. I bet that if we do a loop in this direction then we should end up at the lake," Aili decided.

The bus station was pretty close to the edge of town. We turned off the asphalt and continued walking along the dirt road running between the fields, and there was no longer any doubt that if we kept going we would come out near the small lake where we had already gone to sunbathe and swim. Forget-me-nots were blooming abundantly along the edge of the field. We climbed up the slope towards the young pine trees, which were growing on the mound like bristly hairs on someone's head. Down below, between the trees, we could see the glimmering surface of the lake. Normally we would approach the lake from the other end of town. But from this side there was a steep reddish clay trail leading down to it. In some spots it was quite slippery, and the downpour of rain the previous night had washed deep furrows into the ground. Someone had already been down that road before us and left their footprints on the soft surface. Once we arrived at the bottom of the mound we continued to follow the trail of footprints, but in the end we seemed to have veered away from the lake. The track turned marshy and we had to take off our sandals, although it was clear from the footprints ahead of us that whoever it was had not been particularly worried about getting their shoes wet. The brushwood was dense, and in several places we had to clamber over fallen trees. Gradually the ground started getting drier and we eventually arrived at a small clearing where benches made from planks placed on top of stones were positioned in a circle around what had clearly been a campfire. Someone had thrown a fresh bunch of forget-me-nots on top of the sodden pieces of charred wood.

"The fishermen make their fires here," I said to Aili. "The lake is probably close by."

Aili picked up the bunch of light-blue flowers from the velvety black pieces of firewood and started to examine them, but then she suddenly threw them back, as if she had been burnt.

We had followed the footprints, which looked like a bulldozer track, to the clearing, now there were a lot of footprints around the fire, where their owner had clearly clumped up and down, and then the prints turned off to the left. I followed them for about ten meters and then suddenly saw the reflection of the sky glinting through the brushwood. "Look, this track does lead to the lake!" I shouted joyfully.

In the evening we went to Zielona Gora. There was a big Russian song festival taking place there, with fireworks and a grand dinner reception. Singers from several different countries were singing songs in Russian. During one of the breaks we saw our own Estonian writer Lilli Promet, who had come to the concert as a member of the Soviet writers' delegation. They were taking part in some kind of seminar or conference there. I didn't know Promet very well, but on foreign soil we met like old friends.

After a grand fireworks display we went to the dinner reception. There were tables laid in the gigantic hall of the Stalinist-style building, and fat generals and marshals were standing by the walls at either end. We were told that they were Warsaw Pact bigwigs. The upper echelons of the Polish Communist Party had also come. The women were in evening wear, and an orchestra was playing popular ballads on the stage, but on the table there were just a few sorry plates of cocktail snacks and some tiny glasses of vodka. A little later the tiny glasses were refilled so we could drink to friendship between nations.

"Here in Poland we get full on speeches, not food," Stanislaw laughed bitterly. When we climbed into the bus home, he was jubilantly sporting two bottles of vodka, which by some trickery he had managed to procure from the otherwise poorly provisioned dinner. That year Poland was suffering from the first serious economic crisis, and the shops were emptier than ever before; you could only find mushrooms and chicken at the market.

The painting camp started to wind down, and our trip to Poland was nearly over too. The final exhibition of work from the camp and the farewell party still remained. After that we were supposed to travel through Poznan to Warsaw, and from there back home via Moscow. The boxes containing our paintings were still waiting at the border station, and when we saw the scale of public interest and celebration that accompanied art openings in Poland, we regretted even more that it had not been our and our paintings' lot.

The farewell party took place outside on a steep slope on the edge of the lake, where there was a wide, picturesque view onto the landscape below. Towards evening the sky had become cloudy, in the distance there were flashes of lightning, and in the azure haze of the horizon the land and the sky merged into one, as if we were looking out to sea. Then the sun came out again for a bit and everything looked like a Friedrich painting.

Vodka flowed generously, and sausages and other kinds of meat sizzled on skewers over the fire. The writers and singers who had been at the festival came to see us. I told Lilli Promet that I had read a story by a Polish writer, and I asked whether she knew anything more about him, or whether she could introduce me to a Pole who might know him. "But that writer is right here!" exclaimed Promet happily, taking me by the hand and leading me up to a thickset man with a gray hedgehog haircut who was sitting at a distance from the others on a block of wood.

After much hand kissing and all the other familiar Polish gallantries, Lilli Promet went back to join the others by the fire and the writer stood in silence for a couple of minutes before sitting back down on the block of wood. Bolts of lightning came crashing down over the landscape, which seemed to stretch out endlessly before our eyes. There were popular ballads blaring out behind us. The writer took a flat bottle from his breast pocket, poured some liquid into the cap and offered it to me. I told him that I had just read his collection of stories in Russian translation, that I had liked them, and had particularly enjoyed the detailed descriptions that had been carefully intertwined with the portrayal of the protagonist's psyche. I asked if a heightened sense of guilt was a typical national characteristic amongst Poles, and suggested that in my view, Andrzej Wajda's *Everything for Sale* was an attempt to gain salvation from guilt. I offered the opinion that the film probably contains many codes, which a foreigner such as myself, who is not familiar with the background to Cybulski's suicide, would not be capable of cracking.

The writer made a dismissive gesture with his hand, as if he found the subject boring and wanted to change it, and he poured another shot from his bottle. I was disappointed that the conversation hadn't gotten going. He had spoken with Lilli Promet in very good Russian—he had probably studied in Moscow—but he didn't seem to want to say anything to me even in Polish. I took a slug of his cognac and recounted how my wife and I had followed the thread of his story through the town, got lost, and then ended up at the site of the campfire, where someone had left the bunch of forget-me-nots. I offered the view—half joking—that if the events he described had once taken place, then logically there should be a corpse buried right there under the spot where the campfire had been.

No reaction whatsoever. The writer just sat on his block of wood looking at the lightning flashing amid the dark clouds. The storm was gradually getting closer, we could already hear the dull sound of thunder, as if someone was trying to muffle a cough with their hand clenched into a fist. But the hand holding the shot of cognac had come to a halt just before reaching the writer's lips, and I watched as the golden liquid trickled slowly out of the glass. Then he keeled over onto the ground. He was completely drunk.

A couple of men came up to us, and when they saw the writer lying face down on the ground they said something in Polish, hauled him upright and shuffled off. I picked up the half-full bottle from beside the block of wood and brought it to my lips. The cap of the bottle, which the writer had been using as a shot glass, remained in his closed palm. I couldn't understand how he had managed to get drunk so quickly; just a little while earlier he had been speaking with Lilli Promet completely normally. Toasting Polish literature to myself, I took a healthy swig of cognac and went to look for Aili among the crowd of people so that I could tell her about the meeting I had just had.

"Just imagine, when I saw you kneeling down by some man, I thought for some reason that he must be that very same writer.

I don't know why I thought that, but as it turned out, that's who it was," said Aili.

When I next opened my eyes I was lying fully dressed on the bed, and the sun was shining directly onto my face. Aili was packing our things.

"What a pain," said Aili. "I asked that boy who helped me drag you to bed to hold on to your jacket, and now he's disappeared along with the jacket. You didn't have anything important in your pockets, did you?"

I replied that there would have been nothing more than a packet of cigarettes. My tongue was sticking to the roof of my mouth and I generally felt vile.

"After the storm it suddenly got quite cold, and that boy only had a wet shirt on," Aili explained.

I looked at the time. In a quarter of an hour we had to leave, and I felt a horrible hangover coming on. "Screw the jacket," I mumbled to myself, glancing guiltily in Aili's direction. She didn't seem particularly angry.

"But it really was a nice jacket," I said in a louder voice.

When we got downstairs the bus was already waiting in front of the building. Around twenty people were coming across the clearing from the direction of the slope, like a large colored blotch. Someone was being carried on a stretcher. A woman was crying hysterically.

"Jozef fell off the cliff. He's dead . . ." explained Ewa.

The first thing I saw was my fancy light-yellow jacket, which had been stained red on one side. How despicable—I thought numbly—someone has died and I am lamenting my jacket. Aili was shaking next to me. An ambulance drove up to the building, its siren blaring. Men in white smocks came rushing out.

"We can't help anyone here," I said to Aili, taking her by the hand and pulling her towards the bus.

Everyone was talking about the accident the rest of the day. It was sad, depressing, and stupid. They had wanted to build a fence at that spot for years, but had never got around to it. Someone fell every summer, but no one had been seriously injured before then. This time the sudden downpour had caused a landslide, a few large rocks had shifted from their previous positions, and the poor boy split his head open against one of them. Aili just remained silent, I couldn't tell whether it was the effect of the accident, or whether she was angry with me for getting drunk again. But when we were alone in the train to Warsaw she started talking.

"I think that writer, whose story we were reading, pushed him," said Aili.

"What are you talking about?!" I said, and explained quite agitatedly that from what I saw the writer had been so drunk he couldn't even stand upright.

"He wasn't drunk at all, he was spying on us."

"Who? Us?" I said.

"After we brought you to bed Jozef stayed with me, but that writer started to follow us everywhere. After the rainfall the ground was damp, and at that same spot where he had been standing for some time there were the same kind of marks on the ground that we saw near the lake, like bulldozer tracks."

I broke out in goose bumps. Through the carriage window the Polish landscape raced by like a patchwork quilt—tiny patches of field, of many different colors, woven tightly together. The sky was partly covered in dark clouds again. There were peals of thunder and flashes of lightning somewhere nearby.

"I think he thought that Jozef was you," said Aili, almost whispering.

"Did you look like a married couple when you were with him?" I couldn't resist asking.

"I also think that someone's corpse really is buried there besides the lake, under the campfire . . ." Aili said after some time, still in a whisper. Then we didn't speak about it anymore, we didn't say anything at all until we arrived in Warsaw, and all I could think of was why fate had apparently decreed that I should remain alive yesterday.

The next day, before catching the train to Moscow, we went to eat at the hotel restaurant. Our host, *Pani* Hanna-Danuta, placed a red flag with a hammer and sickle on our table. They brought us big pieces of meat for the main course, while at the other tables that hadn't been adorned with flags people were eating mushrooms and other vegetables. Hanna-Danuta spread her arms in resignation—the country was living through a crisis. In Warsaw your only indulgence was going to the cinema to see *Man of Marble*.

We had gone to the cinema in the morning. Although the film had been showing for two months already, it was sold out, and we only got in thanks to Hanna-Danuta's contacts.

"Our traditional saying is: the worse it is, the better it is," our host explained in a hushed voice, but I just felt ashamed to have that eye-catching red flag on our table.

Suddenly a woman came up to our table and said something agitatedly in Polish. *Pani* Hanna-Danuta interrupted her twice to exclaim something emotionally, and then got up, apologizing that she had to leave us on our own for a bit—a writer, some member of the friendship union, had apparently died, and she had to take several telephone calls straight away.

"He killed himself," she said in a conspiratorial tone, and gave us a loaded look.

"I've got this strange premonition that it was our writer who killed himself," I said a little later. "Perhaps this story has finally found a fitting ending."

I could still picture clearly the writer's somehow crumpled, prematurely aged features. The glazed look in his eyes, as if he couldn't see anything. Suddenly I realized—those eyes that had looked straight at me, they were fish eyes. And then I started to explain: "That writer was a murderer who wrote a story to try and get salvation from the feeling of guilt that was tormenting him; he admits his guilt in the story and describes the actor's murder down to the tiniest of details. But there are nevertheless limits to how much of the truth he is prepared to reveal. From the description of the bus station onwards the story becomes fantasy, and the tracks are blurred. Now, some time later, because of this literary song festival, he ends up back where those events took place, and he decides to make the fantasy described in the story a reality—he takes a bunch of forget-me-nots to his victim's grave. But the murderer is taken by surprise when a stranger begins speaking to him about the campfire site and the bunch of flowers. In his drunken state he begins to panic—he starts to believe that his interlocutor might expose him and the secret hidden in the farthest recesses of his soul. But it is the man's striking jacket, rather than his face, that embeds itself in his memory. Under cover of darkness he follows the wearer of the jacket, waiting for the right moment, then sets upon him and shoves him down the steep slope. He might have even smashed his victim's head in with a rock. In the morning when he sobers up, the writer is weighed down by an even greater burden of guilt, and he simply can't bear it any longer. He decides to take his own life . . ."

We are finding the food hard to stomach. The people sitting at the neighboring tables are eying our big juicy pieces of meat with obvious envy, but we can't manage a single mouthful. When Hanna-Danuta comes back, she asks us in dismay what's wrong. "Nothing," I say and ask her if the name of the writer had been the same as the one we had met.

"No, it wasn't!" exclaimed Hanna-Danuta in amazement. "I know that man very well and he would never take his own wonderful life."

After a long and awkward silence Aili cleared her throat and said: "Hanna-Danuta, when you see that writer, please give him a bunch of forget-me-nots as a present from us."

Noticing Hanna-Danuta's growing confusion, I try to explain: "Tell him that we discovered his work quite by chance and that it made a very deep impression on us."

THE THEATER MINISTER AWAKES

I remember that the weather was terrible in early spring of 1981. There was constantly a misty rain coming down, the streets were full of slush, and there were heaps of gray snow, black in places, that seemed to start melting and collapsing in on themselves almost overnight. Trying to pick out the drier spots to place our feet, we skipped along the sodden (that's a good word for it) suburban streets towards my house. We had no money left for a taxi, but we managed to buy some sparkling wine with the last coins we found in the bottom of our pockets, and I held the bottle tightly against my chest in the unfounded fear that it might just suddenly break—it could fall onto the hard ground, or fly into the sky and collide with a meteorite, smashing into fragments. That fear characterized our mood and feelings at the time very accurately: we had been traveling for two or three days, had visited Riga or Leningrad (who remembers all the details now?) and now wanted to make a soft landing and a gradual transition back to everyday life.

"The snow looks just like a cake baking in the oven. It rises quite nicely, but then a puff of cold air and *pop*, it collapses." I tried to sum up in a couple of words some hazy childhood memory of my grandma sitting in front of the oven, but Aarne didn't latch on to my talk about snow, he hadn't really latched on to anything over the last hour, he was somewhere else altogether. He had gotten bogged down in his worries, fallen into an abyss of doubt and uncertainty, looked into the dark unknown of the future. He was troubled by practical everyday thoughts and was fretting about all the work that was still to be done. But a free-lance artist and master of his own time like myself was able to reflect on other things, and so I happened to be thinking about why the sky was spooking me out so much that morning . . .

"Hey, why is the sky spooking me out so much this morning?" I asked, more as a rhetorical question, since I knew Aarne wouldn't answer. But this time he opened his mouth and said: "Damn."

A couple (or more?) days later we met by chance (or perhaps it wasn't chance) in town. I had just been paid a large fee and the money was itching to jump out of my pocket and run down the street to spend itself. "Hey," said Aarne, "do you want to go to Paris?" I said that that was a very difficult question and it would need to be meticulously dissected and talked through at length. "Well, let's talk then," said Aarne, and we went to the restaurant Gloria to talk the matter over.

Aarne was known as the "Theater Minister," which meant that he was the head of the Theater Administration in the Culture Ministry, which was almost a ministerial position. His career began when he took charge of a student building brigade, after which he had worked in the Komsomol City Committee, then in television, then managing one theater, and then all the theaters in the country. Having become a Nomenklatura post holder he began to mix in Party circles. All the former brigade members had become big operators. Aarne's friend Indrek Toome had risen to become Communist Party boss in Tartu.

I came to know Aarne through working in television, and over time it became clear to me that this was not a man who was meant to have a Party career. The position just pulled him along like a whirlwind, when in fact he would have much rather been teaching arts and crafts to kids somewhere out in the sticks, like he had done when he first finished school. His career was for him what alcohol is for an alcoholic—he would have liked to quit, but he liked everything that went along with it. This contradiction, which had been growing inside him for years, had evidently become more acute in recent times. He had begun spending his evenings painting and drawing caricatures—a highly unusual activity for a senior Party member, particularly since his pictures mocking Party leaders were the funniest of all.

"I don't know what this damn thing is that plagues me," he confessed as he downed a shot of something. "I wake up in the morning and I don't dare open my eyes because I know that I am in some foreign city. The scariest thing is that I have to sort out some important business, but I don't know the language that everyone is speaking."

"I reckon you've got a pretty decent command of Russian," I say with a smirk. It was a jab, referring indirectly to his friend Toome's career, which had gotten going after he had spent several years in Moscow playing the role of some southerly republic's Komsomol secretary.

"The thing is that the city in my dreams is not Moscow; I guess it's somewhere else, farther away, in some overseas country," mused Aarne, sounding genuinely unhappy. I could guess what he was thinking—he was longing to be me. He was dreaming about an impossible world where he could just get up in the mornings and sit down at his easel.

"You could get a different job," I suggest casually.

"I can't," he says, also casually. Once, many years earlier, he had disappeared one morning. Everyone was panicked, the telephones were ringing non-stop. Around ten days later he came back home, like a dog after it has been in heat, his tail between his legs, a subservient look in his eyes. After that he was transferred from television to theater. This time to a directorial position.

Wc had arrivcd at my gate. I go through and traipse up to the front door. I can already see the next few days very clearly: hangover, my wife not talking to me, pangs of guilt over what was done and what was left undone. Someone is unlocking the door from the inside, but I don't know who.

"Aili, do you want to go to Paris?!" I call out in a cheery voice. It's an intriguing question, and it has clearly intrigued my wife, who appears with a questioning look on her face.

"It's not a joke," I say, "Aarne is putting together a tourist group, and he offered a spot to me, but I thought that maybe you'd want to go, since you haven't been to the capitalist world yet."

And so they go. To Portugal and France.

It was still September and I remember the warm, pleasant

weather. The sky was blue and the trees were bathed in golden rays of sunshine. I bought a bouquet of tiny yellow roses and began to wait. The train from Moscow was delayed. Among the people waiting for the train I noticed Leena Kimm, the wife of Kimm the painter, who worked in the Culture Ministry.

"Toomas, don't be too alarmed now," said Leena in her soft accent, "but someone from our group has run off."

My legs suddenly went so soft that I could barely hold myself upright. It occurred to me at that moment that when we refer to legs going soft it is not just a metaphorical expression, it is what actually happens. And then another thought came to mind, that in a group that mostly consisted of actors there was no sense in anyone defecting, since an actor can't get work in a country where they don't speak the language, and the only person who wouldn't be affected by the language problem would be the painter Aili Vint.

Aili was my wife, and in the space of a few seconds a vision of everything that would happen to me after her defection crystallized in front of my eyes, and it seemed so awful that I was ready to burst out crying right there on the spot.

"It was Aarne," said Leena hurriedly, probably alarmed by the look on my face.

"I really must not understand anything at all about how the world works," I said to Leena. "That Communist, Aarne Vahtra . . . ran off?! You must be joking."

"I'm not," said Leena.

Finally the train arrived. We watched as it crept slowly towards the station. Familiar actors descended the carriage steps and I felt an unbearable sense of anguish—maybe Leena hadn't said everything she knew—but then I saw Aili, and I sighed in relief. I rushed forwards, but a fair-haired man blocked my path. "Aili Vint?" he asked, and hearing an affirmative answer, asked her to come with him.

"Hello Aili," I said, as if we just happened to be passing in the street.

"Hello," said Aili, and I could tell she was very stressed. For some reason she had three or four bags with her, so I took one of them, which was unexpectedly heavy. The other man obligingly took two of the bags. We walked along in silence. The actors and the relatives who had come to meet them stood to one side, and we walked past them. I noticed their alarmed looks, and it was clear that they all guessed what was happening and could well imagine everything that was going to follow.

We got into a black Volga. Nothing was said, no explanations given. For some reason the car didn't turn on to Pagari Street, where the KGB headquarters were situated, and our journey continued instead in the direction of the city center. I didn't know what was happening, but my heart was heavy with foreboding.

When we got to the Ministry of Culture they asked us to get out. We went up the stairs, straight to the Minister's office. I saw a row of chairs in the corridor and said that I would sit there and wait. But they ordered me to come with them. A ministry official with a familiar looking face took a seat behind the Minister's table. We sat down on the sofa behind a small table. The fair-haired man opened his notebook and started asking questions. The ministry official seemed to be very familiar with the case, and he took part enthusiastically in the questioning. So this is what an interrogation looks like then, I thought numbly. Maybe these ministry people are also on the KGB payroll, and that's why this official is so worked up. They probably had a mole in the tourist group, or even several of them. Although I still didn't understand why Aili should be singled out.

I tried to force myself to relax and listen. Eventually I found out exactly what had happened on the trip, almost minute by minute. I listened to Aili's recollections; the truth about those ten or so days, if it really was the truth—Aili probably knew what she was supposed to say. The fair-haired man didn't seem to make many notes, but I guessed that this meant that the conversation was being recorded. So that's why they brought us to the Minister's office, I thought, because there are microphones here. I wondered if the Minister himself knew about the microphones.

Two or three hours passed. Suddenly Aili turned towards me and looked as if she had seen me for the first time: "Hello Tom, so you're here as well!" she exclaimed. The bunch of flowers was still blooming in my hand, although I had frayed the bottoms of the stems with my fingernails. I reached out and gave her the flowers.

"Oh, how beautiful!" Aili said. The flowers weren't particularly beautiful anymore, they were already starting to wilt.

"We will call for you very soon," said the fair-haired man as he stood up. I wondered if this was the new Raus. Raus was a KGB officer who was responsible for culture and was always hanging around boozing in the Kuku Club. There had been rumors circulating recently that he was about to retire.

"Your work must really be a bore," said Aili. "It's such fine weather outside, but you have to sit here in the dark."

The fair-haired man glared straight at Aili, trying to work out if he was being mocked, but then he seemed to accept Aili's sincere tone, and, with a sad expression, he spread his arms in resignation. The light really was dim in the Minister's office. I had not been asked a single question. I didn't understand what point there had been in including me as a witness to the questioning. But they probably knew what they were doing, I thought uneasily.

They drove us home. The driver lifted the heavy bags from the luggage compartment and placed them on the footpath. He was probably amazed that a poor Soviet tourist had acquired so much. I was amazed as well. I was willing to wager that this would be the first thing they would discuss in the KGB offices. When the car drove off, Aili told me that they were presents for Makarenko's relatives. Makarenko was a friend of ours. He was an artist who had already lived in Paris for several years and was very successful there. Before that, he had earned a living as a stoker in Tallinn and lived in a cellar apartment on Kunder Street, in the same place where we lived for six years.

We started to drag the bags in the direction of the house. "What really happened with Aarne?" I asked. Aili didn't answer.

"Have you swallowed your tongue or something?" I asked in irritation. She gave me a poke with her elbow, but didn't say a word. I sensed that there were things we couldn't talk about right then. That there might be reason to fear that a black Volga was parked ten meters or so away, with a highly sensitive microphone pointed in our direction and KGB men who were itching to find out what had really happened to the loyal Party boy abroad. But I was also dying to know the real story.

After we were inside I tried, in a whisper, to get the conversation started, but Aili kept her lips firmly sealed. She went up to the telephone and covered it with a thick layer of old newspapers. I didn't laugh, as I also felt uneasy at seeing my wife, who normally isn't scared of any damned thing, suddenly so afraid. We sat in silence for a while. Then we started talking about all sorts of trivial stuff, and then after that—roughly half an hour later—we went out for a walk.

When we clumped down the steps and started walking through the pine trees in the wooded park nearby, I had the horrible feeling that some invisible person was watching us. "It's likely that they're already rummaging through your bags," I said quietly. Aili cast fleeting, furtive glances at the surroundings, although she tried to not to make it too obvious that she was looking around.

At the beginning of the 1970s a very frank article appeared in an Italian newspaper about my brother Tõnis's work, his other activities, and his private life. Afterwards, the KGB started breathing down his back. I remember once, we had been staying at my mother's vacation house in Vääna-Jõesuu for a few days. When we returned to town we went straight to Tõnis's place. There was a foul stench in the toilet, as if someone with a heavy hangover had just used it. It was a clear sign that the KGB guys had rifled through his apartment while we were in the countryside, and one of them had just recently used the toilet. I suspected that someone was watching us now as well, so that their colleagues could rummage through our house, and especially Aili's bags, while we were out. I imagined in horror how shocked our daughter would be if she came home from school to find some strangers making themselves at home in our apartment, and I hoped that she would get home at the normal time, not earlier.

I didn't have any particular hang-ups about the KGB. I

actually used to laugh at them for seeing foreign agents lurking behind every corner and suspecting their acquaintances of spying, but that was before the time that someone smelling of a hangover had used my brother's toilet. The KGB was a grim reality, and its all-powerful fist was raised menacingly over the heads of anyone who didn't take it seriously enough. In the 1970s Tõnis was a unique selling point for Estonian culture. All the foreign journalists, art fans, critics, and other cultural people who came to Estonia never failed to visit Tõnis. When the US Chief Consul came to Tallinn, he didn't even pay a courtesy visit to the Party boss Käbin, but spent a couple of days with Tõnis instead. Tõnis was particularly well known in Moscow cultural circles. The compositional forms of his paintings were imitated, and his opinions were quoted. Legends circulated about the group sex and depraved orgies that were apparently organized at his place. For Russia, Estonia was like a foreign country, but even better, since you could come to Tallinn without a foreign passport, which for most honest members of the Russian intelligentsia was beyond impossible to get hold of. The Italian article had depressing consequences for Tõnis. The journalist had earned his money by writing a sensational story (exaggerating plenty) about someone living in the Soviet Union who was able to do all the things that were forbidden for everyone else. Once he got his fee he didn't give a damn about what happened to the people he had written about. But the Soviet Union was not indifferent to what was written about it. The organs of power took action. To prevent something even worse from happening. To frighten people. To tighten its iron grip. And they achieved what they wanted. Tõnis recoiled in fear. He retreated back into his shell like a snail, and from that moment on he would only move his feelers infrequently and cautiously. And so the malign influence was rooted out of public life.

By now Aili and I had reached a clearing in the woods, and there wasn't a soul nearby.

"So?" I asked impatiently.

"He ran off," Aili said laconically.

I started to get irritated: "It was already clear that he ran off, but what was the reason?"

"I don't know," replied Aili.

We sat down on two nearby tree stumps. We could feel the warmth of the early autumn sun. There were some Mourning Cloak butterflies flying around next to us.

"We were in the Louvre and were looking at the Cézanne painting—you know, that one with two men playing cards. I couldn't work out which angle the light was shining from in the picture. It looked like it hadn't been that important for Cézanne. He wanted to create the impression that each layer and each spot of paint was radiating its own light, coming almost from inside the picture. At that point I felt someone nudge me. It was Aarne. He was green in the face. I thought he had fallen ill, and so I asked what the matter was. He didn't answer. He just stepped painfully on the toe of my shoe. Suddenly he turned around and hurriedly left the hall. I didn't understand why he was behaving so oddly, but I started to get an uneasy feeling. Then I noticed that the man with the hat in Cézanne's painting couldn't actually be wearing a hat, because the brim had cut away part of the back of his head. This was a major slip-up by the artist, but it had benefitted the picture in an odd way."

A jogger appeared, running in our direction and then passing right in front of us. A strong young man, glowing with health.

Once the fitness fan had disappeared through the bushes, Aili continued telling her story: "On the previous evening Aarne had come to my room to show me the presents he had bought for his wife and children. When he left he forgot the things on the table. Now I realize that he did that deliberately."

"But wait, he'd been abroad several times recently. Why did he suddenly get the idea this time? And why the hell were you taken in for questioning as soon as you got back?"

"I think the spy in our group thought that I was Aarne's lover. Why else would an artist be taken on a tour with a group of theater people? And Aarne and I often went wandering around Lisbon and Paris together."

Now I realized—or at least I thought I realized—why I had been allowed to be present at Aili's questioning. They had probably hoped to take advantage of the situation (or at least have some fun with it) by letting the cheated husband hear how his wife had been having fun with her lover in Paris.

A few days later Vahtra was on the radio. It must have been on Radio Free Europe. The theater producer Kalju Komissarov taped his performance and it made him very angry. Vahtra said that he had decided to cross over to the other side, but that he had left behind many loyal intellectual allies in his homeland. After that, all of Aarne's friends and acquaintances were summoned down to Pagari Street, one after the other, for questioning. The KGB worked diligently to identify all those intellectual allies. At that time I had just had a novel published by the Finnish publisher Gummerus. A couple of days before the planned trip to Finland the Writers Union director, Paul Kuusberg, invited me over to tell me that the trip had been canceled, as there had apparently been too much traveling in our family recently. Later on, Mart Mäger, who was then working at Tampere University, told me that someone had told him that Vint didn't want to come to Finland anymore.

Whenever someone went to be questioned, a group of interested persons would wait for him or her at the Kuku Club to hear the news. Rude jokes were cracked at the expense of the "brave men" of the security services, and no one seemed to care much that the tables most probably had ears.

I remember one morning when Aili had to go in for another round of interrogation. We happened to have been partying for two days on end—in those days we knew how to party properly, and we did so often—when Aili suddenly remembered that she had to go to Pagari Street. She phoned the investigator and told him she had diarrhea. The investigator wasn't happy about that, and he objected that his day would now be wasted. "But I can't come and see you with diarrhea, now, can I?" objected Aili in turn.

The whole situation started to feel like a game. The people who weren't invited down to Pagari Street felt that they had been unfairly deprived of something. Of course the whole of Vahtra's circle got the clear message that none of them was going to get a whiff of foreign travel for some time to come.

One fine autumn day my turn came. I'm the kind of person who enjoys the home life, and I avoid having too much contact with official establishments, which I don't particularly trust. It was particularly disagreeable to have anything to do with the police or the KGB. I had a nasty feeling of unease when I arrived at the notorious building on Pagari Street. The entrances there were marked with the letters A, B, and C. Before opening the door I cast a glance around, and saw someone I half knew turn the corner. I slipped in quickly, hoping that he hadn't noticed me, for if he had, then later that day there would be a rumor going around town that Vint was letting himself in and out of the KGB headquarters like it was his second home.

Although it also occurred to me that I could just as well ask that person what they had been looking for on that particular street.

Inside, the building was like a barracks, painted in cold shades of green, ochre, and brown. They called someone from the guard desk. A little later a short man with a boyish face wearing a plain suit came to meet me. He inquired in decent Estonian whether I was me, and then asked me to come with him. We arrived in a fairly spacious office and he sat down behind the desk, as if to underline that here he was boss. He told me he was Lieutenant Colonel Ilyashevitch, and that he was conducting the investigation into the circumstances of Vahtra's defection. My jaw dropped—the person I had thought was some errand boy turned out to be a high-ranking officer. Knowing the hierarchy of the Soviet military, it was hard for me to believe that I was being questioned by a senior officer of one of the larger organizational structures, but I couldn't see any particular reason why he should lie to me.

"There's no getting around it, we have to investigate your friend's case. If he had simply stayed abroad, then the situation wouldn't be so serious, but he spoke on the radio as well—and that is already a serious crime against the Soviet Union," said

Ilyashevitch, handing me the Criminal Codex, where the relevant paragraphs were heavily underlined in red.

"He didn't just betray his homeland. He betrayed his friends," said the investigator, once I had spent a while trying to tame the lines of words dancing in front of my eyes. "Take a moment to think about that."

I counted the hours passing by. The investigator and I tried to work out what could have led Aarne to such treachery. I didn't really know why I was willing to be so cooperative with him, but I really just wanted to wipe my hands clean of any guilt stemming from my association with Vahtra. I couldn't work out what it was that forced me to speak at such length, but at some point I had the feeling that I was standing with two feet firmly in the real world again, in the investigator's office, with some KGB officer sitting behind the desk who was despised by everyone. "Friends, and friendship in general, were very important to Aarne, I'm afraid that he won't survive a lonely life abroad for long, and eventually he'll have enough of it. He'll buy a cheap gun, rent a room in some shabby hotel, and blow his brains out. And the following day the headlines in the Western newspapers will declaim in big letters that Soviet agents had shot the dissident Vahtra dead."

Ilyashevitch (later Olev Mill, Vladimir Ivlev, Ants Arukas, Vello Pärnaste, Mauno Saari) paused his one-fingered typing. A strange silence came over the room. Ilyashevitch stared straight at me for a while. I remember seeing two dull brown buttons in the middle of his face (although were they actually brown?), and then seeing the buttons suddenly fall down onto the table. The pause became long and awkward, and suddenly, for some reason I couldn't discern, I started feeling sorry for this man. I almost wanted to cheer him up, so I said, "People are saying that Vahtra was Stirlitz, and that the state organs sent him abroad to spy."

"If only that were the case," sighed Ilyashevitch, and he carried on prodding away at the typewriter with one finger, dragging out the completion of the interview protocol. Tapping away like a chicken pecking at gravel.

When he finally instructed me to read the protocol through

and sign it, I discovered that many details from my and Aarne's lives had been changed, had become more comfortable, easier for the state organs to understand. I was tired, bored, and I could imagine him starting to prod away at the typewriter again, so I signed off on those thoughts that I hadn't uttered, that hadn't even occurred to me. I knew it wouldn't make any difference anyway. It was unlikely that anyone would ever read those texts. And if Vahtra had enough sense to register himself as a permanent resident in some foreign country, then there was no risk of him ever having to answer in court for what he had done.

Gradually life started getting back to normal. I wrote the short story "Message," which described a writer who writes a story to pass on a message to someone whose whereabouts he does not know. In the story I described scenes and situations that Aarne and I had experienced together, our shared memories. I imagined him somewhere at the other end of the world, eagerly reading the story—it appeared in *Looming*, and the Estonian diaspora obviously subscribes to journals from the home country—and realizing that there was a message hidden somewhere within the memories. He would look and look for it, and he would carry on looking, because the story "Message," with its double meaning, was itself the message. That was the first story in which I consciously addressed the problem of literature's nonliterary functions, which is something that still fascinates me to this day. However, the effect of my "Message" was somewhat unexpected and unwelcome for me at the time.

One night—at precisely the moment when I was finally dozing off after battling for some time with insomnia—the telephone rang. I picked up the receiver reluctantly—the telephone was by the head of the bed, and if I didn't bother to pick up it would have carried on ringing noisily for some time—and heard that I had a call from Munich. What the hell, I thought, and then I heard Aarne's voice asking how things were going. It was a simple and polite question, which I answered very briefly: "So-so."

"How are things there, are they slamming your fingers in the desk drawers then?" asked my old friend, slurring his words.

"Yeah, yeah," I answered briefly, the rage boiling up in me and starting to bubble over the edge. The idiot, I silently curse, he gets plastered in Munich and decides to call me up. Has he completely forgotten, in the course of one month, what kind of country this is that we're living in, or has he gone so soft in the head, that he no longer realizes that telephone calls are recorded, and that tomorrow a whole team of spooks will be drooling over our conversation? Perhaps he could ask when we're going to start overthrowing the Soviet authorities as well!

"I didn't understand the message," he babbled.

"Yeah, yeah," I continue saying in response to whatever he says, but I don't want to give the spooks the pleasure of hanging up and refusing to talk to a traitor, so I just repeat: "Yeah, yeah . . ."

The year was starting to draw to a close, and vague information would occasionally turn up about Vahtra having been spotted in one country or another. A couple of postcards with no name, but written in familiar handwriting. Aarne had departed from our lives in just the same way as some of our friends who had died young. Then one day at the end of summer, a woman walks in through our garden gate. She speaks to us in Russian, with an accent. She brings greetings from Vahtra. We invite her indoors, but she prefers to walk around the garden. There are ripe apples hanging from the branches. As we chomp away at the sweet fruit the woman tells us that she's a tour guide for a group of American tourists. She visits Tallinn nearly every month. She says that Aarne wants to help us. He wants to organize sham marriages for us. We would have to get divorced quickly, and then Aili would be sent a groom, and Toomas a bride. It would apparently be as easy as that.

We are quite taken aback. Nothing of the sort had ever occurred to us.

"You have a month to think it over," she tells us reassuringly. She consults her notebook for a moment, and then says: "I'll be in Tallinn on the 21st and 22nd of October. You should be clear about what you want to do by then."

The apples taste sweet. The garden lawn is glistening in the sunshine. Some Red Admirals are flying around the gooseberry bushes. Kati the cat stretches from tip to toe, and then comes to rub herself against our legs. In the distance a train whistles, and we can hear the faint rattling of wheels. I've been listening to that sound since I was a child. Especially at night, at around four, the rumble of some cargo train can be clearly heard.

"We'll think about it," we promise our guest. "Say hello to Aarne," we say as we see her out through the gate to the taxi. "These are really sweet apples you have," said the woman in place of a farewell.

In the evening some guests drop by unexpectedly. Some really good friends. We get the party started. I have the silly habit of saying things I shouldn't when I'm drunk. That's probably why no one has ever tried to recruit me as a spy. It really is a stupid habit. That evening I vividly recount how Vahtra is going to send us brides and grooms very soon, and how we will fly away on silver birds to New York, Paris, London, Vienna, Venice, and Barcelona.

"Hey, careful with your chatter," Aili reproaches me.

"Ha, what are you fretting about, they're all close friends here," I say blithely, and shrug my shoulders.

As far as I recall we didn't discuss Aarne's proposal much more over the following days. When it was almost mid-September, I said to Aili that I had no desire whatsoever to be waking up in strange beds for the next several years.

"I still remember from my military days how awful it is when you see your home in your dreams, and you hope to see it when you open your eyes, but instead you just see all those things you don't want to see every day."

"That's what we'll say to that woman when she comes, then," said Aili.

But the woman never came.

THE TIME WE WENT TO SALVADOR DALÍ'S FUNERAL

When Estonia regained its independence and life started getting more and more complicated by the day, the writer Mihkel Mutt frequently liked to point out that back in the early 1980s our lives had been one long worry-free party, like they had never been before, nor ever would be again. Actually, the party continued into the late 1980s, but with more worries, as it was hard to get hold of vodka during Gorbachev's perestroika. A scant monthly quota of it was allotted per person, and you could only buy it if you had the requisite tokens in your pocket. In the Kuku Club, where the artists drank, there would be only five bottles a night, and sometimes even less, for everyone that was there. But of course that wasn't enough to stop people drinking. All my good friends drank, to greater or lesser degrees. The process of getting hold of vodka had a special kind of thrill associated with it, although unfortunately it often turned into a dangerous adventure.

I remember one party in the garden of our house in Nõmme. Aili's brother and wife had come to visit us from America, and they had bought so much vodka from the hard currency shop that we couldn't finish it all in one night. So we sat under the large chestnut tree in the freshness of the following morning and got started on the remains of the previous night's party. Each time we emptied a bottle of vodka, all we had to do was go inside, open the fridge door, and take out another green-labeled bottle of Moskovskaya, covered in sparkling beads of condensation and exuding coolness. I was about to go and get the next bottle, but the poet Ott Arder stood up and angrily exclaimed that this was no way of drinking vodka. Instead of having to pool our money together and then work out where we might be able to get hold of it, all we had to do was go back and forth between the garden and the kitchen. Having said his piece, he left with a snort.

We could manage the evening drinking sessions, but when it came to having some hair of the dog the next day, the situation back then was particularly dismal. They only started selling wine and vodka late in the day, and that was for tokens. There was very rarely any bottled beer, because the loyal Party trooper Indrek Toome had declared that people shouldn't drink beer as if it were fruit juice, and had restricted its production to almost nothing. Draft beer that looked like (and tasted like?) horse piss was sold in one or two places, but there was always a huge crowd of people there, standing in impossibly long lines, clutching their three-liter jars.

In 1988 they finally started to reshuffle the ranks of the Soviet Arts Academy, and when someone in Moscow put me forward as a candidate and I rejected the dubious honor the very next day, Ott got very angry with me. "I can't be a member of a reactionary organization like the Art Academy," I said, trying to justify myself. "You're a fool!" Ott cursed. "Just imagine—we're hungover again, the line is at least three hours long, and no one knows if there's going to be enough beer left for the people waiting. You might pass out right there waiting. But if you were an Academician, then I could say: Citizens, let the honorable Academician Vint through to the beer stall! And our fellow citizens would have to stand aside respectfully."

It would have been interesting to find out if they actually would have elected me, given that I was just a normal guy without any higher education in art. There were some people in Moscow who liked my paintings, and some of them were even crazy about them. But then there were others who simply loathed them. Once there was an exhibition in Leningrad called "Academicians and their Students." For some reason the exhibition organizers displayed one of my works as well. The next day it had disappeared. Towards evening they discovered the picture behind a cupboard in the corridor. At first they suspected that someone wanted to steal the painting, but when the story repeated itself the next day, they realized (or verified) that a certain respected Academician found my work so irritating that he thought it necessary to remove it from the exhibition.

In those days I often drank, but it was usually large amounts "in one go" (that was how the actor Volkonski put it). Periods of work would be interspersed with drinking binges. The general view had already taken hold that I was a tedious and unpleasant alcoholic, and no one wanted to be in my company when I was drunk. We hadn't been invited to gatherings, or as guests in peoples' houses, for some time. I consoled Aili by saying that in every period in history the royal court had always tried to avoid the artists, who reeked of vodka and garlic. Essentially the situation suited me—when I was sober I couldn't tolerate social settings, I felt shy around other people, and I found it boring spinning out idle chatter for hours on end. I would only clamber out of my studio or my study at home when the thirst for vodka came over me. Drinking seemed to be an honestly earned reward for all the efforts I had made, and getting drunk was a vital means of relaxing the nervous system. I once heard that it had been compulsory for knights to get blazing drunk twice a month to ensure that their nervous systems would be in good order. That information, which I first heard a quarter of a century earlier, had become the golden rule of my life. At least twice a month, for several days in a row, local club-goers could witness Vint staggering from table to table, disgustingly drunk. That's how many people still remember me. But I'm not bothered by that.

"Sure, they see me when I am relaxing, but they don't see me when I am slogging away at work," I used to bluster self-importantly. "And if I didn't drink vodka and relax, I wouldn't be able to do my creative work."

As I write this now, at the beginning of the new millennium, I chuckle gently at my idée fixe from back then. I have now been sober for over five years—during that time I haven't even had a mouthful of beer—and I feel like I have been born again. I heartily relish every day I live. My nervous system is in very good order. I am in excellent creative form and I believe I am getting better and better. I understand why my former drinking buddy

Mihkel Mutt says, wrinkling his nose, that what's good for Vint's health is bad for his art. And I forgive him. Just as I forgive Vint the alcoholic all his former delusions.

Late one evening in the early spring of 1989 I was gazing from my studio window at the town roofs and the church towers, which were swathed in a faded ultramarine haze. I was swigging whisky and mulling over some thoughts. It had been a good day. A very good day. I had found out that in June there would be an exhibition of ten Soviet artists in Italy, and that I was to be included in the group, and that contrary to the "finest Sovict traditions," all the artists would be present for the exhibition opening. Also that day, a Finn had bought a painting and given me a bottle of whisky as part of the deal. So there I was swigging at it. Life was fine, and getting finer by the moment.

At the end of the previous year Aili had finally got her own studio and could now enjoy being alone. This resolved the stupid situation where we had to take all our things off the easel if one of us wanted to look at a picture. But that situation had endured for years—first in the fourteen-square-meter cellar studio, then in the ten-square-meter studio room in our house in Nõmme, then in front of the three-meter window in the studio at the Art Hall gallery.

We were strong candidates to get a room when a new studio building was built on Raja Street, but when the decision was made they must have reasoned that we were used to painting together in a ten-square-meter space by now. Someone had even suggested that if we had managed to build ourselves a U-shaped swimming pool at our house, then we must also have the means to build our own studios. In those days we told everyone that we had a U-shaped pool at home, describing how wonderful it was to jump straight out of bed into the water every morning, and then surface in the dining room. Aili and I used to concoct all sorts of stories like that. Towards the end of the 1980s we started telling the critic S, as a joke, that the artist A was awfully taken with him, and the next day we would whisper in the artist A's ear that the critic S couldn't live without her a day longer.

Before that they hadn't even noticed each other, but they soon got together and are (probably?) living happily together to this day.

So I was sitting there sipping whisky late that evening and I started to get in the mood for going out. A boozing urge had already been building itself a nest inside me for several days by then. It's a tormenting, soul-destroying state of disquiet, when life seems more and more pointless by the hour, and doing any work is just like trying to carry water in a sieve. I'm gripped by an unbearable feeling that something important is missing, or that it has been lost somewhere, and that mood literally radiates from me. Aili always spots this unfailingly, and then she retreats into her shell like a snail and doesn't poke a feeler out until her husband has calmed down. I don't even really want to drink; it's like a heavy burden that has befallen me, and I have to summon all my strength, all my will, to bear it. The first shots are vomit-inducing and make me feel awful, but I always hope that after a few more I'll get over that feeling and become jolly and worry-free again. And happy, probably. I'm allowed to shed my somber character for a while, as if I were hanging up a winter coat. At long last I can love strangers—particularly women. A bubbling cascade of words flows from my otherwise taciturn lips.

When I finished high school and went to university, I had big problems with drinking. There were very strict rules on alcohol in our house. Father had been an active member of the temperance movement during the time of the first Estonian republic, and its shadow hung over our upbringing. But tough times had done away with Father's temperance. Drinking became the thing to do during the Soviet period, and he had to join in. He soon started lifting glasses in public quite enthusiastically, although he never got drunk. During the German occupation he started smoking just to get his quota of tobacco that he could then sell on, but smoking got into him and he became a chain smoker—four packets of strong Priima cigarettes was his standard daily dose.

I think that the real reason my father abandoned the temperance movement were actually the endless interrogations, during which he would often have matches pushed under his fingernails.

He would usually have to go to Pagari Street after work. They wouldn't come to his office or home to get him. It was some kind of strange ethical rule they had. Sometimes he would sit at work for hours on end, and would hardly ever be seen at home. He probably didn't have the strength to leave his office His brother had been an Estonian officer. When the Russians took power, he hid in the forest and only came out when the Germans pushed out the Russians. After that they put him in a German uniform. After the war the NKVD showed some interest in him, but the German DV security organs were even more interested (or so I later read). I remember we always had suitcases packed and ready in the corridor in those days. The whole family lived in constant fear that the authorities could come after us at any moment and throw us out. It's a mystery to me why my father was not put in prison or sent to Siberia. Maybe it was thanks to former Party Secretary Karotamm. Father was a very well-trained cooperative labor specialist. Karotamm hoped (as one can read from several sources) that the agricultural sector would avoid collectivization in Estonia. He saw the cooperative model as a possible option for the country, and so my father's brains needed to be looked after. When Karotamm died, my father, who was not a Party member, was the only person from Estonia who went to his funeral in Moscow.

Father never talked about his life in much detail. He was a very private person. One could often see him sitting with a distant look in his eyes, as if he were thinking something over. No one had a clue where those thoughts were taking him. I remember one occasion when I helped him build our holiday cottage in the countryside. At the end of the day's work we had a drink with the workman, and when he left and Father and I were alone, I tried to coax him to open up. I was over twenty by then and thought I could talk to my father about anything. So I tried to start up a conversation about women. "I haven't touched a single woman other than your mother," he said in a resolute tone.

In my university days I discovered that alcohol is a wonderful aid to self-deception—after half a bottle a bad mood turns good, cowardice turns to courage, and more often than not a ghastly looking woman becomes a beauty. But I wasn't used to alcohol, I didn't have a high tolerance for it, and I got very drunk after two or three hundred grams. My head would start spinning and I would vomit like crazy. I practiced, I trained myself to drink with an athlete's determination, and by the second year of university I could already outdrink my classmates—twenty-seven half-liter bottles of beer and I still wasn't under the table! I still remember that day very clearly. The autumn sun was shining low in the sky. At the Tartu train station restaurant bright patches of sunlight played across the walls and the faces of the beer drinkers. There were four of us: me, one guy who later became a respected professor, and two other guys who eventually drank themselves to death. In our school the biologists were the real tough guys. They drank the ether used to kill butterflies, and had supplies of surgical spirits in every laboratory. The geneticists even liked frying pigs' embryos as snacks to go with the drinks.

But the evening in question I was drinking whisky. I was relaxed, and it felt good to be alive. Thoughts raced around my head as fast as the wind, new ideas were born and then died away, memories spooled before my eyes like reels of masterfully produced color films. There's a wonderful view of Tallinn's red rooftops from my studio window, you can see five different church spires. I remember waking up one morning in my studio after a party and looking out to see that the Niguliste church spire had started to melt and drip like a scoop of ice cream in a cone. I couldn't believe my eyes, and I really feared for the worst. I staggered back to bed and vowed that I would never drink again, or at least that I would never drink myself drunk again. Then someone knocked at the door. When I opened it, the situation became clear. I hadn't been hallucinating, there had really been a fire at Niguliste and the tower really had melted. My friend Ants wanted to photograph it from my window. Niguliste was sealed off by police and spooks, and they were checking to make sure no one took pictures. Ants started snapping away with his camera, I found half a bottle of something, and we drank to Niguliste's health.

Now Niguliste has been rebuilt and with its rustproof tin roof it stands there like the odd one out among the other churches. The windows of the Music School are shining brightly over there. A choir is singing in the hall, and the faint sound of the song slips in through the half-open window of my studio. In the school corridor someone is waving their arms around. They practice from morning to evening in the corridor. I try to envisage the choir leader in an exam, how he waves his arms about and performs the music in front of the teacher. I'm not completely sure that it happens as I imagine it. Then the artist Valerian Loik arrives from around the corner and makes for the trash cans. Four or five cats are running behind him. When the old chap tips the garbage out of the bucket, the cats try to rub up against his legs. Several stray cats live in the Art Academy building. Valerian normally feeds them sausage and milk in the mornings. He himself seems a bit embarrassed about it, and normally blurts out, "Well these pieces of sausage were left lying about, no sense in just throwing them away."

But on this occasion, when Valerian Loik appeared in my field of vision crossing the Art Academy yard with his herd of cats he had in fact already been dead for three years. I quickly poured another two-finger measure and gulped it down. When I looked out of the window again there was no one to be seen. I don't believe in supernatural phenomena, but I couldn't imagine who else could look and behave so much like Loik. A month or so before his death, Valerian brought a picture to an exhibition in which a sentimentally depicted stray dog was drinking water from the gutter. Instead of a cat, he had painted a dog.

I think that artists are very lucky people. Their real life is spent sitting in front of an easel. Everything else is an illusion. Unreal. The older an artist gets, the smaller that unreal part becomes. An older artist is pure—in the course of time everything apart from art is expunged from him. My studio neighbor back then, Alo Hoidre, will die a while later, in 1993. In the final years of his life he paints every day from morning to evening. He is finally completely free. One fine sunny October evening he rinses his brushes and goes out onto the street. The light of the setting sun makes the mottled leaves on the trees look even more colorful. He arrives at the Art Academy gallery, falls to the ground, and dies.

At the age of forty-five a person is not capable of imagining themselves at sixty or seventy. They think that the unreal is real and that the purpose of painting is to become rich and famous. They think that life should be like a sparkler that goes up in a short blaze of glory.

I twisted the top back on to the bottle of whisky and decided to go to the club. It is depressingly easy to get from my studio to the club—you get in the lift, you travel four floors, you open the door, you go down the steps, and there you are. But this time, quite unexpectedly to me, I stepped out onto the street instead. It's possible that the blast of fresh spring air that reached me from outside was to blame. When you're sitting in your studio you can't properly comprehend spring. The sun doesn't shine directly into the window, and the rays of light turning the rooftops golden are too unreal to make you succumb to their temptation.

Near St. John's Church, in the shadows away from the street lanterns, I saw two people melting into one, probably hugging and kissing. A man in a tweed cap was walking and dragging a bag with him. When he reached the shadows of the church he stood still. He took a breather, then suddenly started to walk hurriedly away, leaving the bag beside the church wall. Cars, buses, and trams were driving along the road. I tried to think what someone else would do in my place at this moment. Would they go and see what was in the bag? I decide not to go, since I am not that someone else. But then who am I?

The bus arrives at the stop, wheezing slightly from old age, the doors slide open, and I get into the dimly lit, half-empty space. A bus is simply a moving space. It's nice to sit there and let oneself be transported forwards, observing the passing scenes through the window. But there isn't a single spare seat by the window, so I have to resign myself to not seeing the city scenes on the other side of the glass. Instead I have to observe the knees of the person sitting next to me. They are visible between the flaps of the coat and are very pale. Too pale, given the dim lighting of the bus.

I cast a sideways glance at the person sitting by the window, but all I see is the back of their head wrapped in a shawl, because they are looking at something outside the bus that is about to be lost from sight forever. I let my gaze travel downwards. Small hands in black leather gloves, resting in a woman's lap, positioned in exactly the spot where the coat opens, leaving the shiny, smooth, excessively flesh-colored legs visible. I shift in my seat and feel the woman's hip against my own. It's a good feeling. The woman's elbow is lightly touching my appendix region, and when the bus sways I can feel the pressure more firmly. I don't know if the woman is beautiful or ugly, young or old. My male hip is touching the female hip. There are just a few layers of clothing between our naked bodies. I can see the slit in the coat and the legs covered with thin stockings, and I could be forgiven for thinking that other than those stockings there is nothing else under that dark-blue coat. The coat material is probably dark blue, although it looks completely black in this light. The eye of an experienced artist always hopes to see color where others cannot. It always makes me chuckle when people talk about "the artist's eye," as if artists somehow have a "special" way of seeing. They don't see differently, it's just that they know how to look.

My shirt cuffs are protruding from my coat sleeves, and it makes for an eye-catchingly colorful sight. A spot of sky-colored paint has ended up there. A sliver of blue sky on the shirt sleeve and a white spot of cloud in the middle of the sky. Due to my slovenliness I can't always be bothered to put on a painting smock. My studio is normally so covered in paint that something inevitably always ends up on me. I usually warn my guests about this and then watch from the corner of my eye as they stand awkwardly in the middle of the studio trying not to get too close to any of the paintings.

I pull my coat sleeves downwards—I am actually a little embarrassed that I'm covered in paint. And that I smell of wine and garlic. But some women find the artist type attractive. A bad guy streak is all too often attractive to them. A life of sin has a kind of mysterious appeal about it. Maybe this woman—sitting by my hip and baring her knees temptingly—has at one time lain lonely in bed dreaming of a passionate romantic encounter with an artist somewhere in a loft apartment in the Old Town? I stretch out my gloveless hand a little, the spot of paint is once again visible, and other blotches of paint can be made out on my (hastily cleaned) hands. I have given a hint about what my profession is, and brought some color to this gray world. Unexpectedly (although maybe even in response to my provocation) I feel a gentle pressure against my shoulder and a waft of perfume in my nostrils. It's a delicate, spring smell and I experience an odd feeling, as if my heart has stood still for a moment. The woman's hand has dropped onto my hand, covering the blue spot of paint.

When the bus starts moving again after the next stop, I try to inch my hand gradually away from under the woman's hand in its black leather glove, but it moves together with mine, gradually sliding upwards, and when the bus takes a bend and I finally manage to pull my hand free, the woman's limp hand falls (or is gently placed?) straight into my lap. I shut my eyes tight, then I open them, and cast a quick glance around. The other bus passengers are minding their own business. No one is peering inquisitively in our direction. We drive on. I'm finding this quite arousing. The woman is evidently sleeping (or pretending to sleep?!), and when I turn my head in her direction I can see her shawl, with an art nouveau pattern against a dark-red background, right in front of my face. The dazzlingly white knees have parted a bit wider and the right thigh is slightly more visible. It looks temptingly firm. I want to lift the woman's hand from between my legs, but I can't bring myself to, its weight (or just its presence?) has already had its effect, although the hand doesn't feel (or pretends that it doesn't feel?) that something inside my pants has started to push it gradually upwards.

I've broken out in a sweat. The woman leaning on my shoulder is breathing so quietly that I can't hear her. If she were also aroused then her chest would be rising and falling more rapidly. That's how it normally goes, sometimes they even fake it. The woman is evidently drunk and asleep, although she would probably sober up from the shock if she were to wake up right now.

My neighborhood, Nõmme, is now approaching frighteningly fast. I breathe in deeply. I am now so incredibly turned on that I want nothing else but to go to bed with this woman as soon as possible. It doesn't matter where.

"Hey, we've arrived in Nõmme, I'm getting off here," I say quietly, and I hear my own voice, stammering and uncertain (as if it were someone else's). The woman sleeps on and for a moment I'm glad that she didn't hear my stammering. I shift carefully to try and release my shoulder, but the woman's head comes with it. So then I lift my shoulder decisively, but the head lolls limply downwards, and I have to support it with my right hand to stop it from falling. Now I have no choice but to push the slumped body towards the back of the seat, and at that moment I see that the woman is staring right at me with her eyes wide open. But her gaze is fixed on one spot. And there is a thin trickle of blood coming from the corner of her mouth and down her chin, dripping onto her blindingly white scarf.

My mind goes blank. I shove the woman back towards the window, for a moment she sits there just like any other person on a bus, then her head falls against the window with a light knocking sound. My mind is still blank. I get up and head towards the exit. The bus is waiting at a traffic light. It starts to move. It takes a bend. I look in the woman's direction again—no, she hasn't fallen to the floor, the sharp turn has just pushed her face flat against the glass.

I don't want to think about what has just happened; I get off the bus, walk a few steps in the direction of the market gates, and then come to a standstill. My knees are shaking. It is late. Some passengers get off, and a few people get on. As the bus starts moving I can see a woman pressing her nose flat against the bus window, staring out.

There weren't many people in the Hiiu pub that evening. It was a weeknight after all. It was an old building that had been rebuilt several times, although nothing good had come of it. In the old days my favorite spot was at the table with the single chair, behind the piano. They used to dance on the stone floor there. Now no one danced anymore, and money wasn't wasted on a band. A ruble was just a worthless bit of paper by now, but I had some Finnish marks in my pocket.

I woke up in my studio. The telephone in the corridor was jangling away. It's not a real telephone, it's a device to open the door downstairs.

It was Aili who had rung. In my view she is a very well-trained wife—if her husband doesn't come home to bed, she politely informs him in advance that she is coming to see him. "Listen, Masha is here, we're going to go and eat now, and we'll come back in half an hour. Make sure that things aren't in too bad a state there. By the way, Salvador Dalí has died."

That device that people call a head just didn't want to start working. The studio was a complete mess, and some of the pictures had holes in them. As far as I could tell, the painting "In the Suburbs," which had been particularly successful and was reproduced in several journals, had been ripped to pieces. I tried to think positively: at least there was a reproduction of it somewhere. The floor was covered in fragments of glass, cigarette butts, and tubes of paint. A large number of the empty bottles had been shoved into the fireplace and someone had tried to set fire to them, without success. There was a human form under a sheet on the sofa.

I do mean just a form. I didn't believe that it was a real live person. I approached it cautiously, and came across a cup on the floor containing some cloudy liquid. Miraculously the cup was still half-full. I sniffed it. I concluded that it smelled of alcohol. I drank it up. But I still couldn't work out what the disgusting liquid could be. It tasted vile, but at least it brought some moisture to my mouth. I walked a few steps forwards. I lifted the sheet and could see what appeared to be toes with nails painted dark purple and someone's body covered in loose pieces of leather like scales. I tugged the sheet upwards and the scales started getting bigger.

Sovetsky Khudozhnik ("Soviet Artist") was supposed to be publishing my monograph. They were doing some fancy series like the "Rizzoli" publishers. Masha, a Moscow art historian, had to write some text for the book. Fragments of thoughts gradually started to fill my head: Masha and Aili were supposed to come up to see me very soon! I carefully shook the form under the sheet, which was probably human. "Hey, get up, my wife is about to get here!"

The answer came back in slow, sleepy Russian that the person lying there hadn't understand what I had said.

I said something in an angry voice, and went into the bathroom so as not to see what would happen next.

Water was coming from the tap. It happened to be cold water. And it kept coming, flowing into my mouth, and then out again. It poured down my face.

In the evening we went to the Salvador Dalí funeral at the Kuku Club. Masha was supposed to go on to Leningrad, but she delayed the journey until morning. She was dressed in black from head to toe for the funeral. There was a naked woman lying in the open coffin in place of Salvador, and she was covered in pieces of fruit.

When the men carried the coffin out of the Kuku club basement the morning after the funeral, a stranger with a straggly moustache and a familiar looking face asked me, "Who died? Was it the doorman? Well, that guy had looked like the living dead for some time anyway."

CAR STORY

I held the hand that was offered to me between my fingers, gave it a gentle squeeze, and received a similar superficial squeeze in return.

"So give me a call tomorrow" said the slim, elegantly dressed young man. He might have been a well-paid member of staff at the bank, or a branch director, but it wasn't particularly important—I had been treated well here, and now it was important to get back home as quickly as possible. Precisely that possibility was being offered by the middle-aged gentleman who was roughly my age or a little younger, whose hand I had just touched, and who had just said to his boss that he would probably be in touch on Tuesday. The man who was supposed to drive me home seemed familiar at first, but not so familiar that I could recall any details about him—it is entirely natural, when you have lived for half a century in one small country, that many people look familiar. Sometimes it's impossible to tell if the person walking towards you on the street has entered into your memory from some social context or from the TV screen.

The car we came to was handsome and shiny. When I opened the door I immediately felt a rush of warm air and that indescribable sensation of comfort one only experiences with new cars, which always made me feel ill at ease. For someone like me, a comfortable chair was the chair with the worn out cover in my studio, where I was in the habit of sitting to examine a half-finished or finished painting, to "gawp" at it, as I used to say.

I had just hung a modest exhibition of paintings in some rooms in a small-town bank. The suggestion had come from the bank, which had some empty white walls after doing some renovation work, and I didn't have anything against displaying my pictures free of charge. Probably the small hope of selling something played its part as well, although considering the situation in the country at the time that did seem very unlikely. The bank took responsibility for transporting the pictures, and when I had them hung up and started to head to the bus station, the member of the bank staff with whom I had organized things suggested going to have lunch.

"No thanks," I swiftly excused myself, "I have to get back as quickly as possible, I've got another important meeting today," at which he asked how I was traveling. On hearing that I was planning to go by bus he made some efforts to find another option, which he succeeded in doing after a couple of phone calls. I was surprised by such obliging behavior, but for those kinds of people bus travel clearly wastes too much time, and public transportation is generally some kind of unspeakable punishment, so it wasn't actually so considerate of him. I was a little worried as I got into the car. I had managed to avoid the tedious conversation that would have accompanied lunch, but I now had to survive two hours of wearisome chatter with the driver. To be honest, I would have preferred to hang around for a bit at the bus station and then take a long bus journey, which would have left me independent and alone with my own familiar company. But I couldn't find a single convincing reason to turn the offer down.

To tell the truth, I had a real aversion to being left alone with other people and tried to avoid it as much as possible. I found those kinds of situations artificial and boring, but my innate politeness didn't allow me to simply stay silent, even if it was also against my nature to want to exchange empty words with a stranger. In the company of friends I was always talkative, I felt open and relaxed, I knew what to talk about, and there was always plenty of talking done. But my verbal cramp became especially evident when I was sitting in the passenger seat of a car. I always felt that I had to earn the lift, to justify the free transport with conversation. And my vanity also forced me to make an effort to leave the impression that I wasn't some sort of weirdo.

"So, how are the artists doing these days?" I was asked as soon as we had driven off from the bank and set out on the road home.

"It's difficult, especially for our generation," I answered in the usual terms, glancing sideways at the driver. He was elegantly dressed, and a pleasant, slightly bitter smell wafted over from his direction.

"The thing is that at the beginning of the eighties we managed to gain a certain amount of recognition—on the international scene as well. In other countries, that would have meant international exhibitions, fame, and of course financial security, but thanks to the closed nature of the Soviet system we didn't get any of that. In the nineties we were like hapless travelers who had been forced off the train between stations who would never reach their destination. The tragicomic side of it all is that Estonian culture suddenly changed from being the elite culture of the Soviet Union into a provincial culture, and it is the inevitable fate of small countries to go unnoticed." I read out the prepared text, which I had thought over ad nauseam as I tried to find a satisfactory explanation for the situation as it was back then, at least for myself.

It looked like the driver didn't want to show any sympathy for someone like me, nor did he seem willing to pick up the thread of a conversation that did not fit with his own views. We had left the town by then, the straight road ahead seemed to demand a bit of chatting, and it would have been polite for me to offer up a new subject of conversation; but nothing came to mind, and I was itching to say a bit more about the artist's life.

"Sometimes I feel like an elite athlete who's been left out of the team because he's too old, but who carries on training out of pure habit, even if every exertion has now lost its original purpose." I could have added that painting had always been the main thing in my life, and that come what may I would carry on with that work as long as I could still get hold of paint and canvas, but it seemed as if I had already complained too much. And my pride probably held my moaning in check, because in the end it felt better just to thrust out my chest and say: "But I'm convinced that painting is never going away."

A typical early spring landscape flashed past the window, uniform and gray, with patches of snow still visible in some shaded spots, but in the fields the green tones still had not sprouted up from the earth. The man next to me could have been a businessman—a job title that a few years earlier would have left a bad taste in the mouth, but which was now amazingly widespread and had acquired more and more prestige. In any case, it looked like the man was doing well for himself. I kept glancing sideways—there was definitely something familiar about the man at the wheel, maybe if I could have observed his face for longer I would have remembered, but it would have been pretty weird to start ogling him like that.

"What model of car is this?" I asked after a while, trying to move on to safer ground.

"Last year's," came the answer, in a tone of voice that let me know I had asked something very obvious.

"I'm quite ignorant when it comes to cars," I hurried to make good my blunder. "I'd like to live my life in such a way that I never have to touch the wheel of a car. It would be a kind of green motto to live by, although a pretty stupid one, just like a meat eater who abhors the slaughter of animals and condemns all hunters. The Soviet Union was the only state in Europe where one could happily live according to such a motto, and now it seems as if owning a car and driving one are becoming unavoidable—that is, if you don't want to spend your whole life squatting in the corner of a room. But at my age learning to drive would be a pretty impressive stunt to pull off."

"That's what they all say," chuckled the man at the wheel as we passed another car. And suddenly I felt jealous of that man—it was a strange kind of jealousy, the kind you feel when you admire someone's beautiful home or attractive partner. The man's self-confidence, his outward appearance, and the car formed one harmonious whole. I thought that if I were someone like him then I would look a little happier.

"But having said that, I normally stay clear of motor vehicles. Once I almost got arrested for car theft," I said, trying to keep the conversation going. A story that had been gathering dust somewhere in the recesses of my mind suddenly came back to me with unexpected freshness, and it now seemed oddly interesting.

It had lost its earlier horror, and for some reason I thought it wouldn't be a bad idea to recount the story in an attempt to amuse my traveling companion.

"It happened in the mid-seventies, at the end of summer, most probably in September—yes, it was September. Most of our friends had come back to town from their summer houses, and the club was full of drunkards who had finally managed to escape their wives and reunite with their friends . . ." I sensed I had to go quite far back in my memory to tell this story, and why not, since most of the journey still lay ahead, and there was no sense in rushing—on the contrary, the more sentences I could feed my companion, the more pleasant the drive would be.

"By then I had managed to attract a good deal of attention for my young age, and I had grown pompous from my success, so when someone I half knew started buying me drinks I thought it only normal that I should be treated like that, and I didn't lose much thought over his motivations. I still don't know to this day what that guy did for a living, but in those days he would often be in the club with different groups of people, and he seemed to know everyone, although no one else had a clear idea who he was. When he invited me to his place to continue the party, it seemed like the natural progression of the evening. But at his place an argument broke out—I can't remember what over, and it's not important anyway. In any case I left with a slam of the door, and then my last memory was of sitting on the tram. That was followed by a long blank space, after which I unexpectedly found myself sitting in a holding cell—a dimly lit hole with several open doors and a dodgy-looking man with a dog. Some detainees were asleep, others were pacing up and down. I looked for my cigarettes and discovered my pockets were empty. Then came the gradual realization that I had been arrested, although at first that didn't cause me any grief, since I was still extremely drunk.

"There was a window with bars in the door of the cell, and opposite was the police guard desk. I brashly asked for a cigarette. There was one uniformed policeman behind the desk and two characters in plain clothes. Seeing my face, one of them, a young man with a hedgehog haircut wearing a building brigade strap, sneered, 'Look, our customer has found his feet pretty fast.'

"They gave me back my own pack of cigarettes and offered me a light, and now I had a chance to think things over. This wasn't the drunk tank, but as far as I knew I hadn't caused any other problems that could have given reason to arrest me. Then while I was lying sprawled on a bench, a girl appeared in the cell and asked for a drag of my cigarette. It was very strange. It didn't fit with my idea of prisons and detention cells at all. The girl had a lot of makeup and bulging breasts that were only loosely covered by her clothes. She casually put her hand in my lap and felt around for what was there. And then something definitely appeared down there. A strange euphoria came over me, and I told the girl that I had some money and that when we got out in the morning we could carry on partying. But then suddenly I felt very tired and dozed off. When I woke up everyone else was asleep. I went to ask for a cigarette again, and to my surprise that same girl was sitting at the guard desk talking to the policeman.

"This time the waking up was far from fun because a hangover had set in. I was nauseous and could feel a dull pain at the back of my head. When I put my hand there I found a large bump. In those days I had long hair and the obligatory bell-bottoms. I often got hassled by the police due to my appearance, and I assumed that this time I had been a little careless with my language, and that was probably why they arrested me. The bump on the back of my head must have come from a whack with a billy club. The future did not look bright.

"In the morning I was the first to be called out. The police captain sitting behind the table started to put together the report. After questioning me he looked through the drawer containing my things, found my notebook in there, and started to leaf through it carefully.

"'Hey, what right do you have to pry into my things?' I shouted angrily, trying to identify the only obvious right I had in a situation where I otherwise had no rights at all.

"'I suggest you calm down a bit,' said the sergeant who had been on night duty. 'You're looking at one and a half to two years for car theft.'

"I'm afraid I'll never be able to properly describe the emotional impact those words had on me. When a person who considers himself to be a law-abiding citizen is told one morning that he has to go to prison, his whole world suddenly collapses. I wrote something at the bottom of the report without looking at it, then I was returned my things, released, and told that I had to be at the investigator's at nine. And as strange as it now seems, at the time there seemed to be nothing odd about the fact that I, a criminal who didn't have a single document confirming his identity, was let go just like that. The only thing that made me stop and think was that the young man with the hedgehog haircut in plain clothes had been present for the whole questioning, and I couldn't work out why he had been hanging around the whole night instead of peacefully sleeping in his bed. I didn't like that man, and I particularly didn't like the expression on his face, which looked like he was constantly suppressing a smirk.

"I took a taxi home, shaved, put on some more formal clothes, and then was back at the police station at the right time. The girl from the night before waved at me from behind the barred window. "Wait for me, I'm getting out soon," she hollered. But this time I was like a different person, I no longer wanted to have anything whatsoever to do with those sorts, and my only thought was how to save my own skin.

"The investigator, who was a relatively young man, explained that I had broken into a car and the police had arrested me just at the point when I had gotten the engine started and looked like I was about to drive off. I explained to him that that couldn't be true, as I lacked the most elementary driving skills and it was impossible that I could have started a car without a key.

"'The facts tell a different story,' he answered icily. Then he got up and left the room for a while. When he came back there had been a remarkable change in his previously harsh demeanor. Now it seemed as if he wanted to understand my side of the story and help me. He gave me the car owner's address, and advised me to go and pay for the broken lock.

"The owner lived a few blocks away from the police station, and when I timidly entered his house and informed him that I was the car thief, he looked at me like he had seen a ghost. There were a couple of Wiiralt prints and some beautiful icons hanging on the wall.

"'Wine or brandy?' asked the host with unexpected kindness. I guessed that it was to help with the hangover I was obviously suffering from, but I couldn't understand why he would want to treat a criminal to a drink. It turned out that we had both been at the wedding of a mutual acquaintance recently, and that he was a big fan of my paintings. In the evening he had been out driving, he was sure he had locked his car, but then he had been woken up by the police during the night and asked to come to the station to make a statement. The car door was open and the ignition was on. The lock was completely untouched.

"'Someone is trying to set you up,' he said to me. 'Someone clearly planned all this.'

"A week later the investigator called and said that he wanted to speak with me, and that he would be quite happy to come and see what my studio looked like. He came and we chatted for an hour or so. He said that the case was closed because the car owner had taken back his statement. At first he wanted to give me the report as a memento, but then he changed his mind and claimed that they needed it for their archives. He invited me fishing and promised to call me when he next had some free time, but I wriggled out of it—I didn't particularly want to socialize or make friends with policemen."

When I looked over at my driver he seemed to be trying to suppress a smirk, and when I asked if he found my story boring, he started laughing and said that no, quite the reverse, he found stories like that about the old days very interesting. I didn't see what was so funny about the story, but I carried on telling it, because I got a thrill out of traveling back in time and experiencing everything again without any of the fear I had felt at the time.

"Actually, that strange car theft business had already started to become clearer to me even before the investigator visited me. Back then we produced what we thought was world-class art, and we tried to live in step with the values of the wider world. The global wave of sexual revolution had flung some foam onto our shores, and group sex sessions were even organized in our circle of friends sometimes. Exactly at the time that this story took place, an interview appeared with my brother in an Italian newspaper with a headline that read roughly: 'Artist T.'s Orgy in the Face of Soviet Hypocrisy.' He had said one or two things to some Italian in passing, and this had then been used to knock together a long article, without any thought to the possible consequences, which, of course, were grim. My brother said that he didn't even dare masturbate anymore, since every sound he made was eavesdropped on and every movement was photographed. That was probably a bit of an exaggeration, but there was a black Volga that was parked permanently by the entrance to his building, and another just under his apartment windows.

"In those days we were all suffering from spy mania—those were just the times we lived in. But I was fairly sure that the whole car theft ordeal was connected to that Italian article. Some government agency had organized an operation that involved getting me completely drunk and staging a car theft. Maybe even that girl in the holding cell had a role to play in it. But for some reason it hadn't gone according to plan; some oversights or miscalculations were made, and in the end they weren't able to force me to become an informer. That was possibly the explanation, although it could have all just been a coincidence as well."

We were starting to approach the edge of town—the journey had indeed gone by quickly—and the driver asked where he should take me. So I even get taken right up to my doorstep, I thought happily, and added: "But this story had a really odd conclusion. Two weeks later I was asked to come down to the Central District police station. I couldn't sleep the whole night, fearing the very worst—the story must have been warmed up again for some reason, handed over to another police station, and now they were going full steam ahead with it. I stumbled over to the police station with my knees trembling, but it turned out that all that had happened was that the street outside my house hadn't been swept and I had to pay a fine. The Olympic Games were approaching and someone had started, for the first and last time, to take responsibility for keeping the city clean. But it still remains a riddle to me why they left me in peace, even that investigator who wanted to make friends didn't call anymore."

We had arrived at the gate of my house. "Maybe they found someone else to be an informer, someone easier to work with," said the driver by way of farewell, and he seemed to be suppressing a smirk. I thanked him, and the car door made a hollow thud as I shut it. The street was muddy and covered in winter sludge. Only when I had opened the door of our house did it occur to me to mentally compare the driver's face with that of the young man with the hedgehog haircut who had been hanging around the police station that time, and then it no longer seemed strange that the man had seemed so familiar to me. I couldn't help bursting out laughing as I realized what a bizarre trick my brain had played on me, finding that particular story from among all the others to tell in return for the lift.

A LANDSCAPE DEMARCATED BY A SIGN

One August afternoon in 1993 a well-known Tallinn antiquarian named S. phoned me and told me he had been offered a painting of mine, but that the way it had been painted, and particularly the low price, had aroused his suspicion. I was amused by the thought that someone had gone to the bother of copying one of my paintings and was asking money for it. But I couldn't see any particular problem with the fact that this alleged forgery existed, and I took the whole thing fairly light-heartedly. I told S. that it wasn't of course a good idea to buy suspect goods, even if they were being offered cheaply.

The antiquarian seemed disappointed by my attitude. He was quiet for a while, and then he started to try and persuade me that I should come and look at the painting anyway. I tried to avoid taking up his offer. I pleaded a lack of time, and told him that it would help if he could describe on the phone which work it was. The antiquarian told me what format the painting was, describing the backing board in great detail, and then the frame, and then eventually he told me that it was a green landscape in summer, with a yellow and red pillar or post at the left edge. I couldn't visualize it at first; I had painted quite a few green landscapes, and those red and yellow roadside posts could be found in many of my paintings dating from the 1970s, so I didn't know what to think.

"I'm convinced that the right thing to do would be to look at the painting yourself," the antiquarian informed me. "I've got some business in Nõmme tomorrow anyway, so I'll bring the painting for you to see."

As I hung up the phone I was thinking that, given the situation in the country at the time, there was something tragicomic about art forgery. A functioning art market was a phenomenon that did not exist in Estonia, and never had. By the end of the 1930s there were indeed the precursors for the development of a market—artists began to form a hierarchical structure, and the middle classes had enough spare money to spend on less practical things—but within five years the proletarian dictatorship ensured that all of that ceased to exist. Now, especially since adopting our own currency, every single kroon represented a tangible, practical value. No one wanted to think about buying art. It would be ten years or so before one could even dream about the existence of an art market in this kind of country. Estonia's artists were in despair; it was probably the first time that they realized what a useless activity they were engaged in. All of a sudden no one needed their work—or them.

"It's hilarious to think that someone decided to try and sell some fake Toomas Vint paintings when the artist himself can't sell a single painting," I said to a self-portrait hanging on the wall. I had the habit of sharing my thoughts with it when I was alone at home.

The writer in the self-portrait was sitting at a typewriter puffing a cigarette and had his fish-like gaze fixed on some invisible point in the distance, but because of the cigarette in his mouth he couldn't say anything to me in reply.

When I came home the next day my daughter, who happened to be mowing the lawn at the time, told me with a grin that someone had brought a painting for me to look at, as if she wanted to warn me not to be too surprised when I saw it. I was overcome with a strange feeling of apprehension, so I stayed sitting in the sunshine for a while longer. Eva-Maria silenced the lawnmower motor and sat down by my side. "It's a pretty ugly sight," she said. "You probably don't really want to see it, but the man who brought it said that he needs your answer by six o'clock."

I asked what sort of answer he could want.

"Well, whether or not you painted it."

"Listen, if that picture is so ugly then you could have told the man that it must be a forgery, since as far as I know I don't paint ugly pictures," I said, a bit offended.

"But I couldn't have said that for sure, because the painting seems really familiar. I've got a feeling that you really did paint it."

Her last sentence made me jump up like a shot. I started walking quickly in the direction of the house, but I came to a standstill by the door, sensing that my daughter was following me. I didn't like the idea of her looking at the picture with me—or to be more precise, of her looking at me looking at the picture. When I glanced back my eyes probably conveyed enough of what I felt to make her turn round and go start up the lawnmower again. A monotonous drone intruded into the suburban silence, followed me into the room, and only died away when I pulled the door shut behind me.

The painting had made itself comfortable and was leaning against the back of the sofa. I recognized the picture, I had painted it for a personal exhibition in 1977, where nearly all my works had contained red and yellow objects, in some of the paintings the objects had even started to live their own lives and communicate on a human plane. This was my second personal exhibition, and I got to hang it not in the Art Salon, but in the small hall of the Artists Union, where the meetings were normally held. I had a lot of new works, and in order to fit them all in I had to cover the windowless walls literally from floor to ceiling with pictures. The result was strikingly conceptual, although at that time no one in Estonia really knew what that word could mean. The writer Hannes Varblane later praised that exhibition in one of his articles. For some reason he remembered the event as having been kept secret, hidden from the authorities.

And now, sitting there in front of me was a painting with a motif that was definitely my own creation; however, the work was so poorly painted that I somehow couldn't accept it as my own. When I examined the surface of the painting a bit closer I noticed that a red base layer had been used. This shocked me—at the end of the 1970s I often painted base layers with complementary colors in my paintings so as to especially increase the intensity of the greens, and it's unlikely that some one-time amateur forger would have paid attention to those kinds of technical nuances.

I put the painting down, perplexed. I tried to fight the depression growing inside me by looking out at the green grass in the yard, which was joyfully illuminated by the sunlight. Did I really paint so poorly back then—a muddy blue sky, and a faded green landscape that was an affront to the very concept of perspective? I felt uncomfortable looking at it, and uncomfortable even knowing about it. I didn't otherwise have a single painting left from that period, as over the years they had been either sold or given away.

Eva-Maria went past with the lawnmower and cast a glance in my direction, but she didn't say anything.

Could it really be? I reluctantly picked up the painting again and looked at the reverse side, and I noticed right away that the backing board had been sloppily knocked together: it was made from a thin piece of wood and didn't have the movable clips that were normally used on painting frames. So!—I breathed a sigh of relief. But then again!—in those days the canvas could have been fixed onto any kind of frame that happened to be lying around. The reverse side of the canvas was dirty, as if it had been lying around in a pile of soot. The artist's name had only recently been written on the frame with a ballpoint pen, and underneath it one could make out some text, but it was too faded to be legible. In those days my favorite format was a fifty by fifty-two centimeter square. This picture also seemed to be square shaped, but it was clearly larger.

I forced myself to examine the surface of the picture again, and I saw that although the red paint of the base layer was visible, it didn't particularly make the chromium oxide tone more intense. Chromium oxide! The picture was dominated by that grayish-green tone, which definitely wasn't the paint I used. Nor did I use the light ochre that had been used to try and paint the sunlight shining on the tops of the trees. Now I was almost certain that this was a forgery. But I still wasn't completely sure, since it was possible I had departed from my usual approach in this picture to try and achieve a softer color scheme.

I didn't know what to think. I couldn't call anyone to act as judge. My wife would have probably been able to help, but at that time she happened to be traveling on the American West Coast.

Eva-Maria knocked on the window. I opened it wide and tried to smell the fresh air, but there was only an unpleasant stench. Mowing the lawn with a gas mower is a disgusting habit, I thought. "Well?" asked my daughter.

I shrugged my shoulders and wrinkled my nose.

"Isn't there a black-and-white print of that picture in a book somewhere?"

"Which book?" I asked, starting to regain the will to live.

"One that was published in Russia, I think."

I rejoiced at the strength of young peoples' memories. After lengthy and vigorous rummaging through the shelves I found my copy of *Master Soviet Landscape Painters*, and the same picture that was leaning against my sofa was looking back at me from its pages. In the black and white reproduction one could see that the two pictures had the same shades of light and dark, and the composition matched one for one. "Damn!" I swore loudly.

Then the telephone rang. "If that's the antiquarian, tell him I'm still not back!" I hollered to my daughter.

I was drowning and I didn't have a single straw to grab at.

I could imagine the antiquarian selling the painting on, and how it would then hang on someone's wall like a disaster scene, and there would be absolutely nothing I could do about it. I once happened to see one of my better-known paintings, "Building," hanging in the Foreign Ministry. Over the years the picture had traveled across Russia from exhibition to exhibition, then had arrived back at the Art Foundation and was immediately deposited at the Foreign Ministry. I was dumbstruck when I saw it. The surface of the painting was covered in cracks, in places someone had tried to restore it with watercolors, the sky had been retouched with God knows what kind of varnish, and many years' worth of dirt had permeated the surface. They just stared at me in amazement when I requested that it be sent straight back to the Art Foundation—but it's such a beautiful painting, they said. I guessed that other people couldn't see what I could. At the Art Foundation they just shrugged their shoulders indifferently when I asked them to fix the painting, and they told me they had no money for restoration. My painting no longer belonged to me and I couldn't do anything about it. I'm afraid that it's still hanging on the same wall in the Foreign Ministry to this day. In just the same terrible condition.

I listened to my daughter lying into the phone. The painting was in front of me with the initials painted into the lower right hand corner: TV 77. In the reproduction in the book, the horizontal part of the letter T had been written with a slanted stroke, but on the painting it was straight, which was a very significant difference.

"It's a forgery!" I bellowed joyfully.

"So what should we do with the picture, then?" I asked the antiquarian when I had presented him with my expert findings.

"I don't know," said S. "The man claimed he bought the picture for five hundred dollars. It's his private property. Sacred and inviolable."

"But what if we hand it over to the police. Then we're talking about intellectual property theft, right?"

"I don't think anyone could be bothered to investigate that kind of thing here in Estonia. They would just grin at you if you asked. Or laugh out loud."

"So are you just going to give the picture back then?"

"Well, we could smash it into pieces, the two of us . . . but I bet that, to the owner, this would sound about as good as suggesting we throw five hundred dollars in the fire."

We agreed that he would get the forgery from me the next day and then try to look mean when he saw the owner. And that was all we could do.

I examined the picture a bit closer—I had been rescued from that horrible feeling that had constrained me earlier—and it became quite clear how ineptly the painter had selected the colors as he attempted to achieve the same effect as my landscape. When I finally put the picture down, facing the wall, I wondered how I could have ever suspected it was anything other than a forgery.

At one time all my pictures were accounted for. With an accountant's orderliness, the details of every work were written down, and what happened with the work was added later. One hundred and fifteen works were noted down in this way, and the accounts came to an end in 1977. Later, only the more important pictures were added, and with a delay of about a year or so.

As I write this story I sift through my accounts from that period, and read:

16) "Child playing with stones" 1972. Oil on canvas. 100x100. Roughly 90 hours' work. Child (Uta) squatting and looking upwards, next to a toy cart containing pieces of stone, the child looks like she is submerged in the grass. Blades of grass painted onto a slightly wet surface, second layer onto a slightly drier surface, the third onto a sticky layer—which gave it depth; light and shade corresponding with the figure. Glazing from top down (from dark to light). Autumn exhibition (1972). The work went unnoticed by critics. Sold in Japan. Reproduction in the catalog. Payment 250 (!) rubles . . . I am reminded of one very sunny afternoon, the day before Summer Solstice in 1974. The gates burst open and the yard is flooded with three carloads of people. Our ten-square-meter studio is suddenly so crowded that you can't even see the pictures. The Japanese push anyone who isn't necessary out through the door. Paintings are lifted from one wall on to the other. Then a camera starts flashing, and at every press of the button someone—probably the Art Foundation director Andrus Kompus—says in a joking tone: "There, that's another new car for the Vints."

In advance of the Japanese coming to Estonia, legends circulate about the fantastical prices they pay. They were beyond our comprehension at the time. We are shocked, lost for words. After half an hour there is a pile of used disposable flash lights on the studio floor, and the group whizzes off. As they are leaving Aili picks a large poppy flower and gives it to Mrs. Nakamura, who is an art dealer and art advisor to the Japanese Emperor. Suddenly they are no longer in such a hurry. Nakamura takes the flower and examines it closely for around three minutes. The accompanying group is fixed to the spot. The gentle breeze is not strong enough to move a single leaf. Then Mrs. Nakamura takes the first step onwards and everyone else hurries after her with comical haste.

Later we find out that Nakamura had bought two of Aili's seascapes for her personal collection. They were put into three hundred dollar frames and kept in a hermetically-sealed environment. We got 250 rubles for each picture. Moscow organized it all—set the price, did the deal, and decided how much to pay the artists. And it didn't occur to anyone to object.

Returning to the day we saw the forgery, after I calmed down I found my archive folders in the drawer and checked what there was to read about that picture.

105) "A Landscape Demarcated by a Sign" 1977. Oil on canvas. 68 X 70. 47 hours' work. The torpor of a summer day. A view of Stroomi beach. The red base layer just gets in the way. Used as a symbol, the roadside post has a clear significance as part of the picture's inner universe, the meaning of this sign is given in my earlier pictures. The sign's real meaning is a sign. The significance depends on how one reads the sign, which can be different for every reader, but is more likely to be accurate for those who are familiar with my work. Different interpretations have no bearing on me. They are not my problem. Personal exhibition in the Art Hall gallery, 1977. Moscow Export Salon. Exhibition in London 1980, probably in several other places as well. Received back in very good condition. Given as a present to Valdur Ohakas in 1982. Black-and-white reproduction in the book Master Soviet Landscape Painters.

So, then . . . At the beginning of the 1980s the artist Valdur Ohakas let it be known that he would like to have one of my works. He had given me a large, beautiful painting for my thirty-fifth birthday. Once when we were at Kütiorg I had painted a small picture of him, more an etude, and promised a more serious work for his birthday. In fact, he got it some time earlier than that. To tell the whole story, it was to cover damages incurred.

In the early autumn of 1982 the customary gang of friends gathered at Ohakas's summer house in Kütiorg. In those years a large part of Estonia's intelligentsia would frequently enjoy the host's hospitality. On that occasion we partied for several days in a row, savoring the autumn tones of the countryside. One dark and windy evening we went to visit Milde, a local farm woman who sang beautifully. We had the fine idea of organizing a singing competition between her and the singer Elsa. To get to Milde's we had to walk a kilometer through the forest. My physical condition wasn't anything to be proud of at that time, and I was afraid of getting lost in the dark forest. I was sure that as soon as I took a step beyond the confines of the yard something terrible would happen, and so I stayed behind under the cover of the barn roof, by the fire, in the company of half a bottle of vodka. When the others came back they found me sitting by the fire, looking at—not listening to—the radio. I had placed it onto the glowing embers and was watching in raptures as the multicolored flames devoured the plastic. When morning came it was all terribly embarrassing. I wanted to pay for the radio, which in those days was an expensive import. Valdur just brushed it off: "Can't be helped, accidents happen."

"It wasn't an accident," I said.

"Well alright then, if you can't pay with money, then you could give me a painting," said Valdur.

And so the painting "A Landscape Demarcated by a Sign," which happened to have just arrived back from Moscow, ended up being given to Valdur. I gave him another picture for his birthday. But later all the pictures I gave him were destroyed by a fire at their house in Merivälja.

Some time after the forgery came to light, a young man whom I half knew came up to me in town and told me that there were apparently copies of my works doing the rounds in Võru. He said that he hadn't seen them himself, but that his friend had apparently held a smaller version of the picture "Game" in his own hands. The larger version was hanging on the wall in the Tartu Art Museum. I asked if the copy had my initials on it. The acquaintance promised to investigate. A couple of days later he called and gave me the address of the man who was allegedly making the copies.

"He is known by the name of Tom, I didn't find out the surname," said the caller. I wrote down the address, although at the time I had no desire to investigate the matter further. At the end of September, I embarked on a road trip around Southern Estonia with Aili and her brother who lived in America. We were drinking coffee by Tamula Lake when the story came to mind and so we decided that when we got to Võru we would go and pay the man a visit.

It was a large and shabby 1970s house on the edge of town. We could see flashes of bright yellow and red between gaps in the hedgerow. They were painted water pipes, many of them twisted into strange forms, one of them thrusting through the hedges. "It's your 'Troubled Landscape'!" Aili shouted.

We sat in the car and peered through the garden fence at what was a familiar scene. In May of 1977 Aili had an exhibition at the Art Salon. My own exhibition had already been up for a couple of months, and the paintings I exhibited there were all of yellow and red objects. After the opening of Aili's exhibition, a group headed over to Nõmme, where I opened my exhibition of objects called "Troubled Landscape." The signs that up to that paint had featured only in my paintings were placed in a natural environment, and so the paintings became "land art." At that time Estonia's art critics weren't ready to properly appraise this kind of art event, and it was treated as a pretentious joke. But I can imagine that if someone—someone else of course, not me—put on that kind of exhibition twenty years later, then the "ecosemiotics" of the piece would provoke raptures amongst our critics.

"Listen, why don't you let me go," said Aili's brother Vamps. "I'll pretend that I want to buy a painting, and I'll see what's really going on here."

"But don't buy anything right away if they try and sell you a Vint painting at a reduced price," said Aili.

"He's used cheap strontium yellow—he hasn't even bothered to buy the right paint," I muttered staring at the painted pipes.

In the 1980s there was a trend for painting all kinds of roadside marking posts yellow and red. In particular, children's playgrounds started to be painted in brighter colors. I don't know if my paintings had anything to do with it, but all too often one could see yellow and red used, very effectively, against a green background. I even heard that at Nõmme Gymnasium they changed the color of the posts in front of the gates. "I assume they did that in honor of you, as a former pupil of the school!" joked a woman who had been a classmate of mine.

Vamps was gone for quite some time. Eventually he came back and got into the car. He didn't say anything, but from the look in his eyes it was clear that he found something very amusing. "So what's so funny then?" I finally asked, annoyed.

"Well, the artist wasn't home, he's coming back at seven, but an old woman there showed me the paintings. I selected a couple of them, and if you give me a couple of bottles of brandy to trade I can go and get them this evening. The old woman couldn't give me a precise price, but she assured me several times that they wouldn't be expensive."

"Did the paintings have red and yellow signs in them?"

"No, no nothing like that. I'm pretty sure that I've seen one of them before, it's of a boy standing in a meadow full of buttercups. But the other picture I liked was of a giraffe nibbling the top of a tree, and I don't think I'd ever seen that before. When did you paint that one?"

"As far as I remember I have never painted any giraffes," I said angrily.

"You definitely have," said Vamps.

I repeated that I never had nor did I plan to.

"Listen," said Vamps with a chuckle. "When I told the old granny that someone told me I could buy a painting here to put on my wall at home, she told me that her tenant was a famous artist, and that he would definitely sell me a painting. I asked what the tenant's name was. She said it was Toomas Vint. Of course that got me interested, so I asked whether I could see the paintings. The old lady didn't have anything against that, so she invited me in to a room with an easel and a load of paintings. I started looking at them, and the granny stayed standing in the doorway the whole time, probably afraid that I would nab something. I chose a couple of pieces and said that I would come back in the evening. So if that man really is the artist Toomas Vint, then I would like to know who you are, and if my sister is married to Toomas Vint, then she should be living in this house too . . ."

At that point I remembered one time when I was in Vilnius, at the opening of the painting triennial. Tõnu Kõiv, who at that time was working with the Panevėžys Theatre, had started to upbraid me for behaving so loutishly in Lithuania. I was stunned speechless when I heard all the things I had apparently gotten up to. When I told him that I had only arrived yesterday, he wouldn't believe me. A little while later Juri Palm, who had spent his holidays with friends in Lithuania, came to see me with the same story. When we discussed the matter further it turned out that someone had spent two weeks in Lithuania living it up under my name. He had even borrowed money from several of Kõiv's friends. In spring that year two good acquaintances Ando Kesküla and Peep Lepik had seen me stumbling around Nõmme market. They had felt sorry for the wretched drunk Vint, so they picked him up and dragged him back home. Since there was no one at home, they had placed the man—who they thought was me—under a bush to sleep. A couple of hours later Ando bumped into me in town and couldn't contain his amazement at seeing that I was already stone-cold sober.

"It's a doppelgänger," I said, sitting in the car in Võru. "I've had trouble with doppelgängers before."

We sat in silence for a while. "You have to do something about it," said Aili at last.

"But what?!" I started to get irritable. "Maybe I should start painting giraffes as well!" I added, trying to make a lame joke out of the situation.

"I don't think this is funny at all," sighed Aili, and she started to tell Vamps the story of how we had been at Pitsunda Artists' House, and a young miner had been sitting at our table. He had boasted, not knowing who we were, that he had appeared at a dance as the writer Toomas Vint, and had made quite a splash there. Since we kept to ourselves and didn't socialize much with other writers, he was able to happily carry on performing the Vint role.

"We couldn't do anything to stop him! To crown it all, he was, by his own account, a real ladies' man, and so from then on Toomas lived in constant fear that letters would start to arrive at the Writers Union trying to locate the father of all those babies that were about to come into this world," said Aili.

"There might be some law to protect people against identity theft. We can go to the police and make a statement that such and such person, at such and such address, has stolen my identity," I said.

"And that he did so with the intent of making some personal gain," Vamps added.

"Sure, then the police would go straight off with their sirens wailing to such and such address and confiscate the stolen identity," Aili continued. "But then it turns out that the man's real name is the same as he is claiming. His passport proves it, and that's that."

We drove a few kilometers out of Võru to spend the evening with one of Vamps's former classmates. As it approached seven o'clock, I started to get an uncomfortable restless feeling. People were roasting meat on the barbecue and drinking beer. Vamps was talking about life in America. In 1993 the majority of Estonians still thought that anywhere abroad was paradise, with flowing rivers of milk and towering mountains of porridge, and that one in ten people there were millionaires. Vamps's critical account was supposed to have a sobering effect, but the looks on the listeners' faces showed that nothing at all could spoil their rose-tinted dreams about America. I had heard those stories before, so I asked if I could try out the host's bike. He didn't object. I rode along the small village roads until I reached the main road. It was only six kilometers to Võru.

The closer I got the more I started to doubt whether my undertaking was sensible. I could feel my curiosity and my misgivings battling inside me. But my feet pushed the pedals steadily, the distance between me and my destination became less and less, and by the time I jumped off the saddle by the garden gate, curiosity had won a resounding victory. I am certain that

I can't be recognized by my face. I'm not some TV personality who the whole of Estonia says hello to, and what's more, I had recently shaved my head bald on a sudden whim, so even good friends had a hard time identifying me.

A man was sprawled on a wicker chair in front of the house. He was drinking beer and reading a newspaper. "Hello," I said. "I'd like to buy a picture for my friend's birthday."

"Ahaa!" said the man like he was glad to see me, but his voice suddenly changed in mid-exclamation, as if he had somehow swallowed the happier sounding part of it. He peered at my bike. "Actually I'm waiting for an American," he said.

"So don't I look like an American then?" I asked.

"The bike doesn't look right," he said. "My name is Toomas Vint, maybe you have heard of me."

I apologized that I didn't know much about art. "I was told that I could buy paintings here, and I'd like to give one to my friend as a birthday present," I said, arms outstretched in a kind of forlorn gesture.

The man—Toomas Vint?—was lean and of smallish stature, and his nose was unnaturally large for his face, which was strikingly ugly. He could have been ten years younger than me, or at least that's what it looked like to me. He had no gray in his hair, but on his right cheek he had a small scar just like me. But why shouldn't his name be Toomas Vint, I suddenly thought, recalling the time at the polyclinic when I had been given the medical records belonging to someone with the same name as me.

"I'm thinking of something like a landscape . . . with a blue sky, peaceful . . . green," I said, using words that were terribly familiar. I had heard words like that repeatedly over the course of the last thirty years. But this time the roles were reversed—I was the customer who would soon be critically examining the works of Toomas Vint.

"I've got several," the artist drawled. "But I'm afraid to say that two of them were already reserved this morning. A foreigner came. From America."

"You've already mentioned that," I interrupted him quite abruptly. The man flinched, like he had woken up from a dream.

"Come in, let's go and have a look," he said and started

moving vigorously in the direction of the door. But his burst of energy didn't last long. When we had passed through the kitchen and living room and he opened the door to a room which was about ten meters square, he said in a faint, feeble voice, "Be my guest, have a look and see if there's anything you like."

He pushed himself rudely past me through the door, and sat down on the only chair in the room.

The pictures were spread out along the walls. There were around twenty of them in a circle. Mostly small format. Some of them were familiar. "Game," "House," "View of the Garden II," "Let's Return Here." On the corner of the bookshelf there happened to be an open copy of a book published by the Art Museum, where alongside a reproduction of a Lembit Sarapuu painting there was a very darkly printed, upside-down reproduction of "View of the Garden II." Leaning against the wall was the picture itself, similarly dark, upside-down, and much smaller than the original. But due to the darkness, the motif now had an unexpectedly mystical effect. The nasturtium blossoms and individual cold green leaves were glowing against an almost chaotic background. I squatted down in front of the picture and examined it more closely. The dark paint had soaked into the canvas and had made the various shades almost indistinguishable. The surface of the picture needed to be retouched with varnish before carrying on painting.

I stood in the middle of the room and let my eyes move across the circle of pictures. A good number of them had been thought up by the man himself. In those paintings the green was greener and the sky bluer than in mine. Some strange creatures, like the egg character from the Klaabu cartoon, made the pictures look childlike or kitsch. The pictures were not signed. Apart from the one the antiquarian had brought for me to look at. Compared to the others that one was a very poor work.

I squatted down in front of one of the pictures and I could see how much love and attention he had put into painting the stalks and flowers. I started to feel quite sad, and I couldn't keep my eyes from welling up. I shrugged my shoulders like I was trying to shake off an irritating insect. Or scare off some mosquitoes.

Or wake up from a dream. Or quite the reverse—I pinched myself and hoped that I wouldn't feel pain, because I wanted to replace this reality with a dream. I took the open book from the shelf and browsed through it. Kristjan Raud, Wiiralt, Köler, Mägi, Laikmaa, Roode, and then this same picture that was here in the room. "Hey, wow, your works are on display in the Art Museum?!" I exclaimed in quite genuine sounding amazement.

"The critics think that by representing individual elements of nature, Vint achieves an illusory correspondence with nature. But I think that it's quite the opposite—in these individual elements, nature achieves an artistic maturity, wherein the sensory impression of nature is on the border between reality and dream, and this produces in the viewer a poetic image of a pure, light, and happy world," he said in a monotonous tone, as if he were reading out a prepared text from somewhere.

My jaw dropped. "Wait, wait . . ." I mumbled trying to bring order to my confused thoughts.

"I mean to say that without a clearly defined artistic experience people are not able to properly perceive nature. To put it simply, a person has to have the artistic experience first, and only then can they have the corresponding experience from nature."

"So first art, then reality?" I exclaimed, in disbelief that this art forger had come up with such a bizarre, but thought-provoking statement of his position.

"Well yes, people don't see, because they don't know how to look; the artist guides them. It's the same with critics—one artist directs them towards another artist, who they otherwise wouldn't be able to understand properly. I would even say, for example, that if an art critic has acquired enough artistic experience, then he is able to perceive even the nature surrounding him as a form that provides an aesthetic experience."

I asked hesitantly where the exit was. I apologized, explaining that I had drunk rather a lot of beer that afternoon. As we walked out of the house I thought that he hadn't understood me, but he led me up to a lilac bush, behind which was a wooden toilet. I rushed in, ready to burst. Once I had relieved myself I started to feel vaguely apprehensive about going back outside. I guessed that the man was waiting for me right there, a couple of steps away. He needed money. He wanted to sell me a picture. It was all deeply familiar to me, I had experienced it many times myself.

I put down the cover over the toilet hole and sat down. I weighed up the option of sitting here for a while. The man would probably get edgy and start walking around the toilet like a cat around a bowl of hot porridge. I tried to imagine what the cat and the porridge and the man would look like. He wasn't at all like me. But then why should he be?

I didn't know what to do. But I had to decide right away. There was no signature on the paintings. Anyone could have made the copies. There was nothing illegal in that. In my agitation I remembered that I had a book coming out very soon that contained dozens of reproductions. The Moscow publisher Sovetsky Khudozhnik was supposed to publish the book in 1991, but the editors decided that there was no longer any sense in promoting artists from other countries, as Estonia's impending separation from the Soviet Union was quickly becoming fact. They had said (lied?) that all the materials that were ready to print had been lost. When an Estonian publisher decided to put out the book and approached the Moscow publisher about buying the materials, they continued to state with stubborn determination that they didn't have anything to sell . . . The book would probably keep this man busy with work for a pretty long time, I thought, becoming increasingly vexed, and finally opening the door.

The man was in a visibly happier mood than earlier, and he was rubbing his hands together. "Everything OK then?" he asked in a tone of voice that answered his own question.

"No," I said defiantly. He stiffened and looked straight at me, surprised. I started walking in the direction of the house without stopping to explain anything.

"Wait, wait!" he cried out a moment later. "I want to show you something," he shouted.

We walked over to the sheds at the other end of the garden. There was a field behind them. In the distance there were one or two tall trees, and further still a bluish belt of forest was visible.

The man opened the shed door. There was a wide window in the back wall, framed with a gilded picture frame, creating the effect of a beautiful painting hanging there.

"That's a landscape painting," said the man. "A landscape that changes with time. In the morning it's a morning landscape, in the winter it's a winter one. This painting has no measurements of dimension. It stretches out infinitely in every direction. It is in fact a little piece of nature, and at the same time of the universe. Universality is exactly what it is—everyone can understand that as they want, or are able to . . .

"But now come closer," he said, and he took me by the hand. I don't like to be touched by strangers, so I quickly pulled my hand away.

"Come, come, don't be afraid," he said.

I walked forwards. In the window, at the lower edge of the framed landscape, a post which had been painted red and yellow started to come into view. Soon it was in the foreground, already a definite part of the picture's organic whole, and the light of the setting sun gave it a distinctly darker shade.

"Now it's a landscape demarcated by a sign," said the man who claimed to be Toomas Vint.

I could restrain myself no longer. I told him that I was Toomas Vint and that I had painted that picture.

"So what," said Toomas Vint perfectly calmly, as if he hadn't understood what I had just said. "Do you want to buy it?"

BALCONY

Towards the end of the winter of 1999, when I had just delivered my recently finished novel *On the Weekend. Playing* to my publisher, I felt an unexpected desire to write a play. I hadn't been a particular active theatergoer over the previous decades, but some of my good friends are actors and I'm sometimes forced to sit in the auditorium at their invitation. I fully understand—they want me to experience their creative output, but I'm afraid that they just can't comprehend what a bore going to the theater is for me. I write "bore" although it really isn't the most appropriate word—it's too mild, too blasé—"horror" would probably better express the feeling that gradually comes over me as I sit in those remorselessly dark theater auditoriums.

Every time that very specific smell of the theater auditorium greets me—have you noticed how every theater has its own specific smell?—I want to believe that maybe this time I'll be able to watch the show peacefully through to the end. At the beginning everything is as it usually is, and for almost the whole of the first act I can follow what is happening on the stage like any other good theatergoer; but then—maybe as a result of some actor's comment that demands a reply, or maybe only because of their provocative tone of voice—I suddenly feel an irresistible urge to rush onto the stage. My desire to take part in the performance in a speaking role is so strong that I hold on to the armrests of my chair with all my strength, biting my lip so hard that sometimes it starts bleeding. This internal struggle has no sober, rational explanation, but when it subsides I start to notice the people sitting near me, and the situation becomes particularly difficult if my neighbor happens to be taking a lively and attentive interest in the performance. It's bizarre how someone who has briefly caught my attention in the darkness of the auditorium can fascinate me so much—instead of watching the performance I follow all their facial expressions and slightest movements with greedy curiosity. And so a stranger suddenly becomes familiar, and when they start clapping and showing their sincere appreciation for the actor's performance, I really want to embrace them, hold them tight, kiss them right on the lips.

Once many years ago, when I was studying biology at university, I was a serious theater fan—a real theater buff, as they say. I prowled around the theaters like a wolf around a sheep pen. But now it is hard to explain even to myself what exactly I hoped to get out of theater. It had never even entered my mind to become an actor, even though my mother, who had run the school theater group, had me perform several different roles and take part in recitation competitions. I was probably in the ninth grade when I had to sing Gustav Suits's "Crazy Song." After the first couple of verses I forgot the rest of the text—completely, beyond all hope. I was unable to retrieve a single fragment of an idea or find a fleeting reference point from which to proceed. I stood in the middle of the stage like a fool—and the longer I stood there, the more foolish I became. It took some time before I finally realized that I should make my exit. Those experiences during my school years haunt me to this day: I have relived that situation again and again with horrible vividness.

During the period when I loved going to the theater I never made an attempt to write a play. Later in Tallinn, when the theater had fallen by the wayside, I discovered two short plays written under the pseudonym Juku Muuli in the semi-underground journal *Heesi*. I remember that in one of them they burned rags behind the stage, causing the audience to panic, thinking the theater was on fire. When the desire to write a play came over me I wanted to reread those plays, but those copies of *Heesi* were nowhere to be found. I couldn't even remember whom I had given them to. I wanted to phone Jaak Jõerüüt, with whom I had once produced *Heesi*, but then I remembered that he was now the ambassador to Italy. I remembered nothing about the other play.

My desire to write a play might have come about as a result

of the extensive use of dialogue in the novel I had just finished—something that I had tried to avoid in my works up until then. I had been of the opinion that dialogue simply wastes the writer's and the reader's time, and that direct speech sometimes cannot convey all the ideas the writer may want to include in a work of fiction. Natural speech contains a lot of verbal garbage, and in the course of sifting the unimportant from the important the dialogue becomes false and overblown. But in my story "Weekend" I managed to achieve a relationship between what was spoken and what was said that had not existed in my work before, or that I had not previously discovered.

"You know, when we talk we can say all sorts of stuff," I said one morning to my wife. She happened to be in a hurry. She didn't understand, or didn't have time to try and understand what I wanted to say.

After I had finished the novel my days became mind-numbingly empty and boring. Although a monstrous pile of books was waiting to be read, I couldn't get into a single one, and my thoughts constantly wandered from the books back to my own text. It was like the waves after a storm, bringing all sorts of dregs to shore. I stared blankly at the television for several days in a row, getting preemptively angry—no one would get why I had created that particular kind of text, and they were bound to treat the elements that I saw as the strong points of my book as failings. One morning I realized that I wasn't going to be able to get the text out of my mind anytime soon, and that if I were going to start writing a play, then it would just be a continuation of the text I had already written.

I informed my wife in a decisive tone that I was going to the studio to start painting. Aili didn't say anything in response, just looked briefly in my direction and smiled. She happened to be speaking on the phone at the time and was saying: "And I don't believe that either . . ."

I chuckled when I saw my wife's happy smile. In quite a few interviews she has pointed out that living with me is like living with two different people—a writer and a painter—and that she prefers the painter, because the writer is tortured and moody, and can often be a cranky domestic tyrant into the bargain.

I had already pulled on my coat and was about to go, but my wife was still talking on the phone: "And then I saw some guy staggering around on the balcony, holding a cat by the scruff of its neck in one hand and a vodka bottle in the other, and all of a sudden he threw the cat from that ninth floor balcony, but it stretched out its paws and glided down like a tablecloth. At first I didn't dare to watch what would happen next, but in the end I forced myself to look, thinking I might be able to help the injured cat. But the cat was already speeding off behind the house, its tail standing proud. A funny thought occurred to me, that maybe that's the cat's usual way of getting from the house to the garden. A couple weeks later the police and an ambulance were outside the building—this time a woman had been thrown off the same balcony . . ."

As I walked past the Drama Theatre on the way to my studio I met a limping Mati Unt, who told me he had sprained his ankle at a rehearsal. I suggested he send someone by our place to get some comfrey tincture, and assured him that it would help, providing him with several amazing examples of how it had done so in the past. Unt was evasive, like reserved people tend to be, but I realized that he actually seemed to want to do his rehearsals with a limp. He had recently distanced himself from writing and now mainly produced plays. When his Brecht book had come out two or three years earlier, some critic who had become influential gave an assessment of it pretty much after a single glance at the book, and had decided it was very poor. I was taken aback by how fast and categorical he had been in his judgment. I got the impression that he had wanted to prevent positive reviews at all cost—reviews which a good writer naturally receives—because he personally didn't like the book for some reason or other. When I read the book a few months later I realized that there was nothing in the whole of Estonian literature of such high quality as this book about Brecht. The documents, letters, footnotes, and additions seemed like superfluous and tedious repetition of the main themes, but they didn't reduce the pleasure of reading the original text or its relevance in the contemporary Estonian context.

Once Unt had limped off to the theater I recalled an episode that had taken place long ago, at the university café. Some man sitting at the neighboring table gave Unt a gigantic—as it seemed to me at the time—manuscript, and from fragments of their conversation I understood that it was Unt's novel *Goodbye, Yellow Cat.* Mati was visibly happy, but I had had a particularly bad day. I looked out of the window of the balcony room and assessed that if I jumped from there I would probably only break a few bones. In those days I was not yet afraid of heights, I was quite happy climbing up towers, and when the pedestrian bridge was built across the river in Tartu I was one of the first to take the dare of climbing across the high arch. As I looked out of the window of the balcony room on that occasion the weather was particularly dreary, and the asphalt was wet from the relentless rain.

I hadn't been to my studio for some time, so when I opened the door I felt a blast of warm, muggy air. I pushed the window open and felt strangely excited at the thought that the smell of turpentine and oil would soon greet me every time I opened the door. This tingling sense of excitement that came over me as I arrived at the studio could be compared with the fisherman's excitement on arriving at the fishing waters. Before one throws the line into the water anything is possible, it's only a little while later that the real situation becomes clear: the fish doesn't bite, or if the float does bob then it's just a stickleback nibbling at the worm. After several months spent at the computer, coming to the studio to paint felt like a release. Although as I walked up to the window I had the thought that if I fell from the fourth floor then I might break my neck on the asphalt of the Art Institute yard. But in the best—or worst—eventuality I would still be alive.

I only had to look down from the studio window to feel a light spinning sensation; over time my fear of heights had gotten worse and worse. I hate going out onto the eleventh floor balcony at my wife's studio, and if I have to I try not to look down. Looking down from a closed window doesn't bother me at all, but an open balcony drives me crazy. "Balcony," I thought out loud. "The title of the play could be 'Balcony.'"

The first scene took shape before my eyes with incredible

clarity. A man and a woman arrive in their new luxurious penthouse apartment, which has a balcony that looks like a beautiful little ornamental garden. After some trivial conversation, the door bursts open and an anonymous person runs across the room and jumps off the balcony, committing suicide.

I recall that Genet once wrote a play called *The Balcony*, which I haven't read or seen. Édouard Manet painted a "Balcony." René Magritte painted the same picture, but represented the people as coffins and called it "Perspective II: Manet's Balcony." I have also painted a similar composition with coffin-shaped ornamental trees, and put "Group of Ornamental Trees" as the title, which doesn't refer to anything at all.

The title Magritte used for his painting was not very subtle. Normally he chose titles that were unrelated to the picture, sometimes completely absurd, but with this picture the title "Perspective" is somehow too direct, as if he were pointing with his finger—it gives the impression that he didn't trust the viewer, he was afraid that he would not be understood, that no one other than him was capable of reading the picture properly. But the title of a piece is usually a fairly accurate reflection of the artist's relationship to his work. It occurred to me that some good research could be done about the titles of works of art. It would provide an interesting picture of the mental world of artists through different periods in history, and the titles would be like codes that could be used to break the locks into those mental worlds.

I picked up a book of Magritte paintings and leafed through it, and my eyes came to a halt on a picture of a man sitting on a rock, resting his legs. In his left hand he was holding a stick, and by his right leg there was a small case. The man was obviously a traveler, he had a straw hat to protect him from the sun, a red cape to protect from the winds and storms, but he had no face—in place of a face and chest there was a white sheet of paper, on which the viewer could see the silhouettes of a key, a wineglass, a bird, and a pipe. Clutched tightly in his right hand was an absurd object, with two eyes and red lips encased in an ornamental grille of pearls in the form of a face. The background of the picture was a green landscape with a broad river, with light blue triumphal arches rising through the clouds into the black sky. The name of the picture was "The Liberator." It occurred to me that I should have given my recently finished novel an appropriate title, which would have led the reader by the hand down the right track, or an epigraph, which would at least have provided critics with the rules of the game. But the phrase from Poe's "The Purloined Letter" that I used in *An Unending Landscape*—". . . I fashion the expression of my face, as accurately as possible, in accordance with the expression of his, and then wait to see what thoughts or sentiments arise in my mind or heart . . ."—was supposed to give the reader the code to reading it pretty much on a plate, brought to their bedside with their morning coffee. But to my astonishment people read the text literally, and every sentence was taken to represent the author's deeply-felt position.

When John Dexter called me a couple of weeks earlier and heard that I had just finished writing a novel with the title *On the Weekend. Playing*, he burst into raucous laughter. He managed to laugh away several dollars' worth of phone bill before regaining the gift of speech.

"What a rogue you are! Writing a novel called *On the Weekend* to mark the turn of the century and the turn of the millennium!" he guffawed down the phone.

I tried to explain to him that the book actually dealt with one weekend, and that it covered various themes that had nothing to do with the turn of the century.

"Don't give me that!" he scoffed. John is a writer. In my view he is as good as Auster, but he isn't Auster, so he has to come up with scenes for C-list films just to get by.

I had avoided personally intruding into my recently finished novel—no epigraphs, recognizable references, or quotations. I believed that the text should remain open and that the protagonist's thoughts should be italicized only to separate them from the rest of the text and to bring out their dynamics better. I wanted to leave the text to its own devices and wait calmly to see what happened. Just like a fisherman waiting for a fish to bite—that was how I imagined the situation figuratively. The fisherman is sure he has put some really good bait on his hook, and now all he has to do is sit and wait for the big fish to come.

Outside the window, the weather was typical for late winter, still and sunny. A few degrees below zero, with the snow melting in the sun. Icicle season—you're warned to walk in the middle of the road. For some reason I recalled an excursion with some theater folk to North Korea in 1980. My friend Aarne was at that time head of the Theater Administration, and he was the one who fixed me up with a place on the trip. It was a memorable trip, to a tragicomic country. The young actors Oja and Vaarik got a certain well-known critic completely drunk, and he started eating his main course with a knife and spoon, loudly commenting on the antics of the Korean policeman-clowns in the circus show, believing them to be real policemen. "This will be your last trip abroad!" promised the angry group leader Jaak Allik. That year, balconies were being added to all of the buildings in North Korea, both old ones and new ones. The Great Leader and Teacher had said that if people had the chance to have a balcony, then they could be truly happy.

I found the painting "Group of Ornamental Trees." I had to sort through several piles of paintings before I set hands on it. I could have called it "Balcony" or "Perspective"—the latter would have resulted in a particularly satisfying riddle, since the picture depicted some green coffin-shaped objects, like trimmed bushes or trees, and one of them seemed to be sitting on a stool. In order to make the vision truer to nature, I hadn't painted a balcony rail. Now, examining the picture some time later, it seemed that a green balcony wall was needed. The longer I looked at the painting, the stronger I felt that some detail suggesting a balcony would have completed it.

When the telephone rang I went to answer it very reluctantly. At first I didn't understand who could be speaking to me so familiarly, so I said something off the top of my head, but in the end everything got really confused and I had to admit that I didn't actually know who I was speaking to. "It's Peeter K., you remember don't you, that time with Aarne . . ." I still couldn't work out who it was. I assume he must have been a former building brigade or Komsomol character. I had heard nothing from them over the last few years. I don't know why, but I had the impression that most of them had died.

"I'll come to see you then," he said, as if it were solely for him to decide.

If someone is interested in an artist's paintings and wants to come to his studio, the artist can't say no. That person may want to buy something, and whether you like it or not art is a commodity. You have to get by somehow. I tried to create an illusion of order in my studio by moving a few things around, and I put a new cassette into the Dictaphone. I was in the habit of recording the conversations that took place in my studio—guests sometimes bring out new ideas or opinions, and I can't stand letting them go to waste.

When I opened the door his face was familiar, but probably from the newspaper or television, we definitely were never close acquaintances. I thought he might tell me his full name or give me a business card, but at the same time I guessed that he didn't realize I didn't know who he was. Once Käbin had come to my studio—by then he had already retired to the position of Supreme Soviet Presidium Chairman. Someone called to say that the boss apparently wanted to see me and would come at three. Nothing more. And then when a bloke wearing an Astrakhan hat came to the door, I couldn't place him. I knew that I should know who he was, and he was sure that I knew. This unclear situation lasted for quite a while, but at last the man who was accompanying him realized that things weren't quite as they should be, and so he put things right with one deft sentence. Of course Käbin had prepared himself for coming to visit an artist. He took a piece of paper from his wallet and read out what Repin had said about painting—colors like a person's veins . . . and so on. Then he requested that I paint a picture of a grouse for the wall of his hunting lodge, and when I politely explained that I don't do work to order, he agreed to buy one of my landscapes instead. They apparently had a certain amount of (state) money left over at the end of the year. I said that it would not be enough, since the painting was especially expensive. When

I started to leave for home, I met my studio neighbor Kangilaski, who asked what Käbin had been looking for in my studio. I said that he had wanted a painting. "Well, did he get one?" asked Jaak in a sarcastic tone. I said that he hadn't because he didn't have enough money.

Be that as it may, on this occasion there was someone standing in front of me who seemed familiar, but at the same time was a complete stranger. "I'm thinking of one particular painting. It's got the walls of Toompea on it, partly covered in moss," he came straight out with what he wanted.

"That picture is already on display," I said.

"So maybe we could do a deal," he said with a cunning wink.

I explained that the gallery wasn't allowed to sell the pictures in its collection, and that at any rate I was very happy that the painting was there.

"Listen, why don't you paint me a similar picture then," he said. "Tell me the price and I'll pay. I live on Toompea, you see, and so it would be great if Toompea was on my wall as well."

I told him that I wasn't interested in that kind of deal, that I didn't want to waste my time painting some picture over again, and that a landscape with some other motif would suit a Toompea apartment much better.

"I believe you, but you see it would be more something for my wife," he said meekly. "I know nothing about art, our apartment was recently renovated, and there are several empty walls where we thought we could hang some paintings. Maybe you could come and have a look. You could decide yourself what would suit."

I wanted to wriggle out of the situation straight away, to get rid of the annoying guest, and get out of going to visit him, but it suddenly occurred to me to ask if there was a balcony at his place.

"Well, you couldn't really call it a balcony," he said, suddenly getting enthusiastic. "The door from the guest room leads to a terrace, from which there's a magnificent panoramic view over the lower town and out to the sea. That's the apartment's trump card. No one has anything like it in all of Estonia!"

"Alright, we'd better get going then," I said putting my coat on.

The narrow cul-de-sac was jam-packed full of cars. Peeter swore freely and profusely as he nudged his car towards a dilapidated building with faded paintwork and a window with open ventilation slots. I noticed a fancy old vase with a blue pattern sitting on the windowsill, and I also saw that the curtains were brown from cigarette smoke, and ripped in places. A pinkish white wall gleamed at the end of the *cul-de-sac.* It had recently been painted and was in stark contrast with the sorry state of the neighboring buildings. The oak door was adorned with copper handles and a knocker. Peeter opened the door and let me in first.

"Well what do you know, my wife is home as well!" he exclaimed in surprise and hollered out loudly: "Hello, hello, we've got guests. Come and say hello to Mr. Vint. Darling, can you hear me?!"

We took off our coats. "She's probably busy," said Peeter, standing there and rubbing his hands together. He stood in the middle of the hallway and coughed emphatically. "When we got this house it was really just a ruin," he eventually said.

He started to recount how one thing and the other had worked out, stepping from one foot to the other the whole time. I felt awkward, so I took a step back, leaned against the wall, and tried to pretend that I was politely listening to him. He was half a head taller than me, with a powerful build, short graying hair, and a nose that jutted out proudly from his face. He may have been older than me, but he could just as well have been younger: somewhere between fifty and sixty. He goes to the gym and the swimming pool I decided, feeling vaguely envious of what good shape he was in.

"I was away for a while in the United States, and I came here straight from the airport. The hall had just been finished. It was empty, white, the doors onto the terrace were open, the curtains were flapping in a gentle wind, and the warm afternoon sun was flooding into the room. I was smitten. Well, anyway, what am I blathering on for, see for yourself . . ." and he walked forwards a few steps and pulled the sliding door open.

It certainly made a powerful impact. The large and bright room had a glass wall, and behind it white clouds were floating past in a blue sky. "We'll be finished in a second," said a young woman with a blond bob, smiling as she rolled up some papers on a low, glass-topped oval table.

"We've already finished," said a youngish man, getting up from his chair.

"I'd like to introduce you: my wife Eva. And this is my friend Mel."

"Meelis," said the young man, offering me a soft, limp hand to shake. His whole being was somehow soft. I thought to myself that this was probably a man with no character at all. The woman didn't offer me her hand, but just carried the rolled-up papers from the table into the other room. I noticed that there were three doors leading out of the room. I imagined how the characters would walk in and out through those doors, just as if it were a stage set.

"Of course you won't remember me," said the wife coming back into the room. "You came to our school to meet the art class. We made you suffer for a couple of hours. I wrote a very long final paper about your work. Mainly about the triptych 'Views.' It was being exhibited that year."

I mumbled "Oh really?" in response, and started calculating—if she had been a schoolgirl of no more than eighteen in 1991, then now she was a wife of only twenty-six. A little too young for a man who was approaching sixty. I suddenly saw myself in my youth, sitting with Jõerüüt in some café, talking endlessly about literature. The writers Smuul and Remmelgas would also come to this café with young, pretty girls, to drink wine. We thought it was totally wrong, as if these old men had unfairly taken something that belonged to us, but at the same time it looked like the girls were having fun with those famous men. That was probably the end of the 1960s. Smuul and Remmelgas weren't even fifty then.

"I'll be going then," said the younger man. "I'd be happy to chat with you, but I've got a consultation in a quarter of an hour. I'm always rushing around. That's life."

"I'll see him out," said the wife to her husband. "Of course, of course," said Peeter, hurriedly sputtering out the words.

The young man turned around in the doorway, gave me a perplexed look and asked, "Is the writer Toomas Vint your relative? When I heard your name just now I suddenly remembered that Mother was given *An Artist's Novel* as a present, and I just wanted to check."

I answered with a grin that the writer was indeed my relative; he was actually my wife's husband.

"Your wife's husband isn't your relative though," said Meelis swiftly and with a didactic tone of voice, but then he quickly fell silent.

"Why not, if Mr. Vint is thinking of his daughter's father," said Peeter, starting to laugh.

"Well of course," said the young man, now laughing too. He laughed wholeheartedly, clearly feeling no embarrassment over his mistake. For my part I was amazed that Peeter knew that we had a daughter. I told him that we may have met at some children's birthday parties, recalling those times when all the families in our circle of friends had young children of roughly the same age. It was a long time ago, over a quarter of a century now.

"So this is where we live now," said Peeter, spreading his arms out wide as if to suggest he was resigning himself to some kind of misfortune. I looked around, and my eyes came to rest on a white grand piano, and it occurred to me that someone could play the piano in my play. Chopin preludes and mazurkas. The piano would be like a tangible character in the play. Then I had a look at where they wanted to put my painting and it seemed to me that the room's sparse, modernist, light-blue, black, and white design needed some sort of abstract modernist work hanging on the wall.

"I think a pair of paintings by Sirje Runge would suit here, or a Lill in pastel tones," I said.

"You'll have to discuss that with Eve, I don't know anything about art, but we had actually planned to put your picture in my office," said Peeter, and he opened one of the doors, revealing a grand staircase that led upstairs.

On the upper floor there was a corridor with a window at the end of it. Through the window I could see a dense clump of white cloud moving across the blue sky. There were also three doors leading off somewhere. Peeter opened one of them and showed me into the room. It was decorated with dark-brown wallpaper with a gold pattern on it and bookshelves that stretched from floor to the ceiling. I noticed a number of reference books, but also a shelf with some works of Lenin in brown binding. There was a meter-high locked wardrobe against one of the walls, and above it an empty space that was just right for one of my paintings. There was a high window in the side wall, which in fact turned out to be a balcony door. It occurred to me that this and the glass wall on the lower floor were elements that shouldn't be allowed in these old buildings on Toompea.

"It's cozy here," said Peeter as he sat down at a large writing table. The table was covered in books, papers, notebooks and files, and the computer was switched on. I sat down next to the window. The roofs of the old town were visible below. I imagined how awful it would be for someone like me with a fear of heights to have to stand on that narrow balcony. I wouldn't put one foot through that door. The floor of the balcony was covered in frozen ice. No one had walked on it for a long time.

"So here you are," said Eve from the doorway with a happy voice. "Has Peeter already shown you the balcony? It took forever to get the authorization to build it. Well, open the door and show the artist what a head-spinning view there is from there. You can't imagine how much Peeter loves his balcony! But not without reason, standing there feels exactly as if you are hanging suspended above the street."

"I don't know, if . . ." said Peeter getting up from behind the table.

"I'm not sure . . ." I said in a very skeptical tone.

"See, that's the wall where I want to put that painting," said Eve, as if she had suddenly forgotten all about the balcony. I told her that the picture in question belonged to the museum and that there was no way she could have it.

"If I can't, then so be it," said Eve unfazed. "I wanted to

become an art critic, but it didn't work out. One of my relatives was a woman who unfailingly looked fabulous and beautiful all the time. Oh, how jealous I was of her."

I didn't ask why she hadn't become an art critic, I didn't have time to ask anything at all, because someone started cursing loudly downstairs, the hosts froze in surprise, and then Eve ran out of the room, followed by Peeter. A little while later the bawling subsided, and then completely died away. I realized that the intervening doors had been pulled shut and although I edged the door of the room open, I couldn't hear anything discernible.

There may have been people other than them living in the house. The woman's father or brother, the man's son or daughter from a first—or second?—marriage. I didn't have a good sense of how large the house was; only a small part of it adjoined the street, and the rest of it was positioned on the outer cliff side of Toompea, held in the embrace of the neighboring buildings.

I was curious to see what was on the bookshelves. It was predominantly technical literature in Russian, the majority of which had been published quite a while ago, and it didn't tell me anything in particular about my host. I thought they might be books that had belonged to someone else, and had been stacked here just as shelf filling, to make the office look more impressive. I didn't dare to start rummaging through the papers scattered across the table. There are at least some limits to my writer's curiosity.

I liked this office. I had probably once dreamt of having a room just like this, when I could still be bothered to dream of things like that.

For me the only really important thing is where to look when I'm writing. It's become particularly important over the last few years, when I have had to spend countless hours sitting at the computer and I need somewhere to rest my eyes while I am thinking. In the old days I kept postcards in my writing table—pictures of landscapes or reproductions of paintings—but those images aroused too many emotions, sometimes so strong that I even ripped up some peaceful evening lakeside scene, or some beautiful pre-Raphaelite. I was particularly bothered by how static the pictures were as I looked at them; I was always waiting (!) in suspense for what would happen next, but nothing happened.

In March 1994 Erica Jong sent me an hourglass as a sort of birthday present—God knows what possessed her. It was a fancy timepiece, housed inside an ivory casing with erotic motifs carved onto it. It turned out Erica had been the classmate of my wife's brother's wife—what a small world—although I first met her some years ago through the Moscow artist Vadi Mirsky. When the birthday festivities were over I put the hourglass on the table and watched the time flow through it. Over the previous seven years I had drunk a great deal of vodka, and managed to write just one or two mediocre stories, and I had this anguished feeling growing inside me that I was finished as a writer. By that time all those prose writers who had started writing at roughly the same time as me—Vahing, Saluri, Saat, Jõerüüt—had for some strange reason all "thrown in their pens," and I had probably resigned myself to joining their ranks. But now Time flowed past right there on my table in front of me. Every moment brought some change, right before my eyes. I had somewhere to focus my gaze and my attention. At first it seemed there was a lot of time, but then that time started to run out. It is most likely thanks to Erica's present that I have managed to write a book every year since then.

I now have 104 hourglasses. I can accurately measure a wide range of different units of time, so I can chose the kind of time which passes at my writing table. I reckon my novel *Hourglass* will come out in 2004. I haven't written a line of it yet, but in my thoughts I've turned the hourglass over and the sand has started to flow.

"Have you thought up anything for our wall?" asked Eve, who had entered the room while I was thinking. I said that I could offer my advice, but she would have to make the final decision. A work of art hanging on the wall is a bit like a spouse. You have to be ready to spend a lot of time living together.

"Peeter's not really one to choose pictures. It's rare for him to even glance in the direction of a painting. But who knows. I actually had a mental image of some de Chirico painting with a green sky hanging on this wall. Of course we don't have enough money to buy a de Chirico, but then I thought that a Vint would be just as good," she said coquettishly. "Have you painted any landscapes with green skies?"

I was unsettled by this woman's disarming, seductive tone, like a siren's song or even worse. They should be tied up—my friend Vanapa used to say about the kind of men who let themselves be taken in by such voices. I told her that I should be able to find a few paintings that would suit that spot, and we agreed that she would come to my studio soon.

When we went back downstairs, the man of the house wasn't in the hall; he had made himself scarce and left me in his wife's hands. "What do you drink?" asked Eve. Mineral water, I answered, amazed that Eve didn't find it necessary to apologize or explain with a polite lie why they had stormed off as if the house was on fire, and why Peeter had now disappeared somewhere.

"Before you go you should definitely step out onto our balcony," said Eve, pushing the glass door open. Air streamed in, carrying early spring with it, and there were giant icicles melting above the glass wall.

"I'd prefer not to go clambering out there," I said with a sigh. "I'm afraid of heights," I added a little while later by way of explanation, and I thought to myself that there had been a clear hint in the woman's last sentence that I should now think about leaving.

"You too!" Eve started laughing softly. "Peeter can't even watch someone in a film climbing up somewhere high. He shuts his eyes tight and has me tell him when the scene is over. But just imagine what happens in summer when we have guests over. They all go out on the balcony, but he doesn't dare take more than a couple of steps from the door. It's really funny."

I didn't think that there was anything funny about it, and I told her that now was definitely time for me to think about going. "What a shame," she said. "We still haven't had time to talk about art."

I responded that these days there was nothing one could say about art anymore.

"Do you seriously think so? I have the feeling that something really interesting is happening again, but that only a few people have picked up on what it is."

I couldn't be bothered to explain how things looked to me. I rarely let myself be dragged into discussions about art, as I have found that culturally aware people tend to misunderstand me in one way, and those that are not culturally aware misunderstand me in some other way. All of them want to hear some definitive truth, but I am neither willing nor able to find that truth for them. I figure no one wants to know what the real state of affairs is, because it is not in anyone's interests to know.

"Things are what they are," I said in a lighthearted tone, and it was all the same to me how she took that.

Over the course of the day the weather had become uncharacteristically fine for the season. I wasn't in a hurry to get anywhere so I walked around Toompea enjoying the weather. The snow had melted from the benches and so I found myself a spot to sit in the sun. I had decided that Peeter's fear of heights was a wonderful detail to use in the play "Balcony." I could make really good use of it. I had a vivid image of a young wife tormenting her older husband. She dances literally on the edge of the balcony, where her husband doesn't dare follow. I recall how she tried to persuade Peeter to show me the balcony. Some of the things they said that had sounded quite ordinary to me definitely had some kind of mocking subtext for the two of them.

It's odd to watch the relationship between two strangers as a bystander, to form one's own impressions, to interpret the individual known facts and create for oneself some picture that seeks to be a watertight, realistic whole. It occurred to me that I could use these observations to write a play with the title "Balcony," where the final outcome would be that the fantasy that the protagonists had constructed, which had been wearing the mask of truth, would be visibly and audibly revealed to the public.

A few years ago, when I began to properly research a whole range of questions surrounding contemporary art, I became very interested in the issue of how ideological, arbitrary, and highly questionable mental constructions could take on the appearance of truth. The kind of truth appearance that convinced venerable institutions to fork out a lot of money to support it, to help consolidate it, and to make clear to the upcoming generation—our children—that harmony and beauty are something ugly, and that cynically spitting in peoples' faces has some deep intellectual meaning. I naively believed that if I could use my writing to make contemporary art transparent—to show that things are as they are only because it is in the interests of people who occupy the key positions in the art world, then people would open their eyes and realize that the truth that is propagated is not in fact the truth. But I didn't take account of how heavy the contemporary art machine had become as it careened downhill. Living in a country as small as Estonia, it had already become impossible to bring it to a halt. All that was now possible was to gloomily watch on as the machine dragged along more and more people who happened to get in its path.

In my view, the contemporary art world operates by putting on a performance for the public, and the public have now started to believe that this performance is real life, and to fully go along with it.

The thought of writing a play, which had already been bothering me for several days, now started to torment me with renewed vigor, and when I went back to the studio I didn't start browsing through my folders of sketches or leafing through slide materials, but sat gazing out of the window for some time, deep in thought. From time to time I saw people I knew walking across the yard of the Art Institute. I suddenly recalled that when Peeter came I had switched on the Dictaphone and shoved it into my coat pocket. It should have recorded a good forty-five minutes of what was going on when my coat was hanging in Peeter's apartment hallway.

My hands were shaking with excitement as I rewound the tape roughly half the way back. Then, as the tape spooled forwards I heard Peeter's swearing, silence, our conversation in the hallway, silence again, then a sudden sputter of voices. I went back a bit further and listened:

EVE: Listen, you, I can't stand waiting any longer. How long am I supposed to go on like this?

MEL: Dearest, you're not the only one, I'm suffering as well . . . look it's getting hard again.

EVE: Idiot! Cut it out . . . someone might come.

MEL: That's why it's such a turn-on. Imagine if Peeter and that artist walked through the door right now.

EVE: Stop it! I'm not joking. You should remember that you won't get it until the thing is done.

MEL: Well, I wonder which of us loses out the most from that. You can torture yourself if you want. Or start sleeping with your husband. Ha-ha.

EVE: I can't go on like this. My nerves won't stand it . . . I might just end up doing something stupid one day and spoiling everything.

MEL: My dear little Evie . . .

EVE: Oh, you little fool . . .

MEL: You're the fool . . . Everything will work out. It will all work out. Don't worry.

EVE: Well, ciao ciao then! Just think of all the accidents that happen to all sorts of different people every day.

MEL: But keep your chin up. Don't get in a flap.

A door closes with a thud.

A period of silence.

PEETER: Wait, I'll come with you.

A MAN'S VOICE: I don't want to even look at a piece of shit like you, even lying in the gutter.

PEETER: But you do want to see the money.

MAN: I'll see that anyway.

PEETER: Probably a bit more is better than a bit less.

MAN: Fuck off!

PEETER: A little accident needs to happen.

MAN: You can sort out your own accidents. I'm not going to move a finger for you anymore.

PEETER: Wait!

A door thuds.

Silence.

I gawped at the Dictaphone as the last bit of tape wound on in silence before coming to an end. There was a faint click.

"So much for that play," I said out loud, and started at the sound of my own voice.

My writer's imagination had set to work, and I had some pretty terrible ideas about how the story could proceed: Eve wants to get rid of her husband and Mel has to organize it. An accident would be a good solution. Peeter wants to get rid of Mel and someone—judging by their voice not someone you could imagine wearing a white shirt and straight tie—might organize another tragic accident. A bizarre race begins—who gets there first. It could even be possible for both of the accidents to happen, which would probably (?) be the best outcome for Eve. If something were to happen to Mel then a new Mel would turn up before too long.

A misfortune would be fortunate for Eve. Fortune plus misfortune would equal zero, just like plus and minus. Zero would mean that nothing—neither good nor bad—had happened.

I listened to those dialogues three times over. There wasn't anything particularly dramatic in their voices; it was as if they were talking about some ordinary, everyday thing. Nothing indicated tragedy. There were different kinds of accidents that could happen. If a vase falls to the floor, that's a small accident; if the vase is expensive, then the accident is quite a bit bigger. I thought I might be able to change the course of events. I could play the tape to one party and then to the other. I could demand a hefty sum of money for that tape . . . but I could also end up causing an accident to happen to me instead.

I could almost feel the Dictaphone burning my fingers, so I threw it onto the couch. I sat and stared at it. In the end I slid the cassette behind the bookshelf. The right thing to do would have been to delete the dangerous recording, but I couldn't bring myself to do that yet.

I phoned my wife and asked what she happened to be doing. "I was actually just about to call you and ask what you were doing," she said. "If you're not doing anything important you could come over here. I've just finished a painting," she said in a voice that sounded almost timid.

"A seascape?"

"A seascape."

I knew that my wife had been working on something for some time, but she had been doing it in such secrecy that she hadn't let anyone take so much as a peek into her studio. She hadn't produced a single oil painting since 1988, and had announced that she didn't plan to paint the sea anymore. Although she doesn't want to admit it, I think our wonderful critics can take the credit for that.

And so I was extremely happy now that she had managed to put her negative experiences with the art world behind her.

When I arrived at the Lasnamäe building where my wife's studio was, who should I see coming out the door but that very same Mel who had been at Peeter's place. He got into a car parked in front of the building and whizzed off. I wondered what someone like him was doing in Lasnamäe, as he seemed like someone who wouldn't have much to do with that particular district.

As I was traveling upwards in the lift I deliberated whether I should try to summon up the courage to go out onto the studio balcony and peek over the edge. This would enable me to describe with the immediacy of recent experience the fear that Peeter, the character in the play, confesses to his young wife. In so frankly revealing his feelings he never suspected what his wife was about to do with the knowledge. He still believed—and was likely to believe until the very end—that his wife loved him. He had gotten used to seeing the world as he wanted to see it.

"Well?!" I asked my wife as she opened the door. She shrugged her shoulders, but I could sense how tense she was, since I was going to be the first person to assess her work. It's just like an actor's stage fright before an opening performance. Aivazovski would organize opening performances for paintings, after all. In the hall of his Feodossia house there was a stage with curtains that could be opened and closed. The public waited, watched, and applauded.

I took my coat off slowly, as if I wasn't feeling the slightest bit impatient or curious, and meanwhile my wife prepared me for the worse: as if this were the first thing she had ever painted, as if nothing she painted ever came out right, as if she didn't even know how to paint or understand why she was trying to do something that was so beyond her abilities, since it isn't actually possible to paint the sea anyway. I know. I had heard it all before, time and time again over many years, and I had also seen the wonderful seascapes that were produced to the accompaniment of all this sighing.

I entered the studio and just stood there, stunned. Looking back at me from the opposite wall was a huge painting—roughly three by four meters. For a moment I tried to work out, in astonishment, how one would take something like that out of the studio, and then I realized that one wouldn't. The picture had been painted on to the wall.

The wall of the studio was silvery-gray iridescent water. Through the cloudy skies sunlight fell in sparse patches onto the surface of the sea. The glow on the horizon culminated in the sunlight reflected on the crest of a wave, rolling peacefully towards the sandy shore. The calmness of the picture created a tension like I'd never felt before. One felt in one's heart the terrifying desire to be engulfed in this sea forever. So as to reach a state of bliss.

I realized that this was the best painting that my wife had ever painted. I don't believe that there is anyone else who is capable of painting anything like it.

The painting was situated in a shabby residential district of Tallinn on the wall of a shabby building which was soon to be pulled down. I couldn't come to terms with the fact that the painting would imminently and inevitably be destroyed, and that there was absolutely nothing that anyone could do to save it.

"Hey . . ." I said in a tone that was both sad and angry, despondent and accusatory.

"I didn't have a big enough canvas to fit the sea onto . . . but tell me what you think of it."

"What do I think . . . what do I think . . . I think that

standing in front of a picture that is so good there is nothing at all that I can say."

"Do you think it's a good picture?" my wife asked again, although I could tell from the tone of her voice that she was happy.

In fact I was also incredibly happy. So what if the picture was painted on the wall of an apartment block in Lasnamäe.

Maybe that was for the best . . .

When we had looked at the sea for long enough, and assessed many various aspects of it, my wife told me that someone had recently been hassling her to paint a picture, and that he wouldn't accept that he couldn't get what he wanted.

"Someone has told him that only Aili Vint is capable of painting a sunset," my wife complained. "Today he brought me a load of materials for the painting. He's apparently got a grand house on Toompea that's just been restored, with a view of the sun setting over the sea from the balcony. He wants me to paint him a sunset, or more precisely the final moment of the sunset, just before the sun disappears completely, and he wants to put it up on the wall in the same room where the balcony with the view is."

There were around twenty photos. They had been taken at different times of the year, with the sky looking different in each one. There were also a large number of slides. A familiar-looking balcony railing was visible near the bottom of several of the photos, and then I realized—of course it was familiar, I had seen that same balcony railing that same day, a couple of hours earlier.

"Had that customer been to see you just before I arrived?"

"He had indeed," said my wife in amazement.

"Did he say that he had a house on Toompea?"

"That's what he said. Do you know him?"

I replied that I could hardly claim to know him, and that in general it was impossible to truly know other people. I opened the door onto the balcony and felt a blast of wind. It is always windy in Lasnamäe, even in calm weather. I thought how well Magritte's family of coffins would suit the poster for my play "Balcony." I imagined Eve and Mel coming to see the performance. Eve would still be wearing a black dress, with a neckline that was a little too low for someone in mourning, demonstrating that despite everything that had happened she wanted to get on with living her life. Suddenly Mel hears someone on the stage repeating his own words, and Eve hears someone uttering hers. They realize that they have been found out. With faces as white as limestone, the criminals admit their guilt.

Although they wouldn't actually realize or admit to a single thing!—I thought. They would firmly believe that the people on the stage plotting a murder are the real bad people, and they are the good ones.

"What are you doing there in the balcony doorway getting cold," my wife chided. "Tell me what you decided in the end, are you going to start writing a play now or are you going to paint?"

"I probably won't write that play after all," I said, shutting the balcony door. "If I did I would have to go to the theater several times, and you know what a pain that is for me."

AN ARTIST'S LIFE

It happened on a fine sunny day, some time just before the turn of the millennium. I suddenly felt a strong urge to get seriously involved in contemporary art. I want to stress the word "serious" from the start, since my debut piece of contemporary art, shown at the exhibition "Biotopia" in 1996, had a double meaning at its core. I temporarily adopted the guise of a contemporary artist, constantly deep in thought, creating art that is open to many possible interpretations. On that occasion I exhibited an installation that consisted of a computer screen with a freakish-looking garden gnome standing in front of it flashing his dick. My most vivid recollections from that memorable opening are of several apologists for contemporary art warmly and appreciatively shaking my hand, congratulating me on creating such a wonderful work. One of them even mentioned that if my gnome had been positioned right in front of the computer screen then the installation would have had even greater significance—it would have been recognized as a reconceptualization of Nam June Paik's landmark work "TV Buddha."

The mystical word "reconceptualization" seems to condone all manner of things, and whenever I hear it the corners of my mouth start to twitch uncontrollably and strong expletives come to mind. But this time I didn't swear. Instead I just feigned sincere surprise and said: "But Nam June Paik only made 'Techno Buddha' last year, and it was basically a reconceptualization of his 1974 Buddha—strange that you didn't know that." The person who had congratulated me was dumbstruck, and this time it was the corners of his mouth that started twitching as his expression turned sour.

"My garden gnome is prodding the computer mouse with his dick, which represents his desire to find a virtual means of flashing," I explained in a lecturing tone. As I look back on those events today, I can't help feeling some pride—what seers we artists are! In 1995 no one could have dreamed that in only ten years the internet and web cameras would become so widely used, and that any exhibitionist pervert could satisfy his desires in real time, at a distance of thousands of miles. Looking back, it's strange to think that in the year in question it took serious effort just to print out a half-decent color picture.

"Don't joke around, I'm sure you are well aware that there is a much deeper meaning in your work," the apologist for contemporary art declared as if offended, and he went off to see the international jury to sort out the prizes. There was nothing I could reply to that, but it suddenly occurred to me that they might even give me a prize. There would certainly be black humor in that. None of them could have guessed that I had a surprise in store, which was intended to mock contemporary art—the following day a two-page article of mine was supposed to appear in *Sirp* (which was then called the *Culture Page*), with the title "The Birth of the Work (of Art) and its (Short) Life (Story)," in which I wrote a highly ironic exposé revealing that an artwork of mine that was being exhibited in an exhibition of contemporary art was in fact the most idiotic abomination I was able to dream up.

I mumbled a few obscenities to myself and tried to ignore the growing feeling that something absurd was about to happen. On the one hand it would be good if my article in the *Culture Page* was accompanied by a whiff of scandal, but at the same time I felt extremely uncomfortable putting a certain person who was associated with the exhibition, and whom I respected, in such a foolish position.

By the time they started announcing the prizes I was already feeling an irresistible urge to make an early exit, although I had cobbled together a fairly emotional speech in my head, the culmination of which was to be an ironic promise to use the money I received solely for purchasing paintbrushes, canvas, and paints, in order to immerse myself even deeper in painting. I am definitely no public speaker, and I was completely overcome by stage fright. I was sure that as soon as I opened my mouth I would start talking about deeply theoretical things that would be incomprehensible to the majority of people there. It was simply not possible to explain all the things that were weighing on my heart in simple phrases. When they announced that the prize winner was a different piece—one that was directly linked to the theme of the exhibition, and whose central message was that the pedigree dog should be allowed to mate with every dog he wants to, mongrels included—I felt a welcome sense of relief, and a mocking smile appeared on my lips. At that, the ceremonial part was over and the public flowed into the exhibition halls to experience the star attractions of contemporary art.

I noticed a couple of painters standing near my installation, assessing the abomination with contemptuous looks, whispering between themselves and sniggering. I was afraid one of them would come up and say: "Et tu, Brute . . ." But they didn't. Instead, people kept their distance from me, as if I was carrying some particularly dangerous infection. It went without saying that in my colleagues' eyes I had betrayed all of my previous convictions. I had rudely turned my back on all the art I had created up until then.

By the middle of the 1990s the situation that had developed in Estonia meant that if you wanted to be an artist you had to be a contemporary artist, which basically meant writing project applications, making installations, and subordinating oneself to the dictates of the exhibition curators. The curators behaved just like former Communist Party instructors, making categorical assessments about the ideological appropriateness of works of art. The curators seized hold of the reins of the art world and announced that the former hierarchies no longer existed. One female curator who occupied an important position even boasted that it was for her alone to decide who could be an artist in the Republic of Estonia. I recall that Peek and Einmann, who had assigned artists to their positions during the Stalinist 1950s, expressed themselves in a very similar way. The 1950s were quite an ugly time in the artistic life of our country; literally overnight, people started painting in line with the stipulations of socialist realism. Probably the most vivid demonstration of this were the pictures in Estonian children's books, which suddenly started to look exactly the same as the ones that were painted in the wider Soviet world.

I could see all too clearly that history was starting to cynically repeat itself. Without much thought being given, practices were adopted that had originally come into being in completely different circumstances. Artists had bravely struggled for artistic freedom during the Soviet period, but once freedom was achieved they were mercilessly abandoned to the whims of the curator. Indeed, artistic life in the country started to bear a horrible resemblance to the situation half a century earlier. But the worst thing was that the God-given gift of artistic talent was rendered of secondary importance at a single stroke, and even came to be seen as superfluous or a hindrance. Ambitious "wannabes" set the tone. Although they possessed no artistic skills, they had decided to call themselves artists, and their output was prized as elite art.

On the computer screen of my installation, or abomination, as I called it, there was a message that could be read in two different ways: "*The manipulative artist Toomas Vint presents his cutting-edge work 'Still Life,' rejects his former ethical and aesthetic principles, and is therefore able to take his place in high culture.*" The text could either be read as the self-exposure of the artist, or interpreted as critical irony. The double meaning of the installation was only supposed to turn into a single meaning the next day, when I would say everything I really thought about the state of national artistic life in that *Culture Page* article.

I couldn't have suspected how many enemies I would gain on the day the *Culture Page* article was published. And I couldn't have guessed that that wouldn't be the end of the story, but rather the start of a long one-man battle against the "dragon of contemporary art," during which I would try to reveal the ideological pressure on art policy and expose its hidden principle that "if you're not with us, you're against us." In fact, the 1994 congress of the AICA chaired by Julia Kristeva declared that the word "ideology" had become taboo, which was entirely understandable, since the real roots of contemporary art lay in an unacknowledged adoration of the Marxism and Maoism of the 1960s.

I had a mental image of the art world resembling a finely-tuned machine. There were no signs of it being sent for repair, and it just continued to produce the same standard product. But it seemed to be a really well-made machine: an Ideal Machine. If one investigated more closely, it became clear that for the past twenty years the machine was being supplied with power from a single source of radical leftist ideas. It should be noted that this Ideal Machine sometimes malfunctioned—by letting a really high-quality piece of work appear in an exhibition. But then an endless number of imitators all around the world would immediately start to reconceptualize it, and the defective item became just another one of the machine's standard products.

Rumors were spreading that Vint and his article were only the tip of the iceberg, and that there were several famous artists acting under my name. But at the time I hadn't heard about this speculation, so I couldn't understand why some of my colleagues started looking over their shoulders as if they were scared or sometimes even downright terrified whenever they talked to me. I only learned much later that people were afraid of appearing to be in cahoots with Vint.

I can remember the friendly reproaches that I was wasting my time and effort, that I should realize that contemporary art was just a passing phenomenon—they would have their fun and kick up some noise and then everything would get back to more rational lines. I chose not to listen to them, but I couldn't explain even to myself what it was that made me swim against the current and collect enemies. I hadn't been particularly active during the Soviet period or at the start of independence, I had focused solely on my creative work and lived a pretty bohemian life. It's possible that the sudden change in lifestyle and the retreat from social life that took place in 1994 created an empty hole that I needed to fill somehow. I was definitely seduced by the game—since all those hostile encounters could be treated like a form of entertainment—and it was possible that everything I did was spurred on solely by my desire to play it.

In 1997, when a joint exhibition of works by Uuno Roosvaldi, Peeter Ulas, Peeter Linnapi, and myself called "Unending Landscape" was showing at the Art Hall, I was already closely involved in contemporary art's postmodern games. But none of the theorists understood, or rather they didn't want to understand. I didn't add A4-sized texts to my paintings to direct the viewer's attention to what I wanted to say with that given work. All I had was a label hung on the wall next to the work, with text so small it could have been used by an optician to test someone's eyesight.

In addition to my paintings, which were open to different interpretations, I exhibited some photographic art, which was fashionable at the time, in the form of black-and-white reproductions of works that were hanging in gilded frames in the Tretyakov Gallery, the Russian Museum, and public buildings in the US. To my astonishment one famous critic decided that the black-and-white pictures displayed the metaphysical content of my paintings in stronger relief. The day after the opening of the exhibition, the "FUCK YOU" graffiti on my "Do It" painting had been crossed out and replaced with new graffiti reading "Freedom for Tiit Madisson!"—the same message voiced by the picketers who stood outside the Drama Theatre in support of the nationalist politician who was in prison at the time. The defacement of the picture was very eye-catching, and was basically criminal vandalism, but amazingly, no one noticed it.

Following that long diversion into events of the distant past it's time to return to the present day, to the start of this millennium, and the next occasion when I felt a strong urge to produce contemporary art. The sun was shining, a few lone white clouds floated by in the wide expanse of blue sky. Aili and I were sitting in the backyard at our white table eating spaghetti. I can't remember what we were talking about anymore, but something had gotten me so worked up that I couldn't contain my anger, and I grabbed the plate of spaghetti and sent it flying off the table. I've got a strange character trait of taking almost everything that happens in the world seriously, and I take some things really to heart, which means that an internal or external conflict of some kind can provoke me to act quite unpredictably. On this occasion the plate I'd just let fly hit the ground side-first, unloaded the spaghetti, and rolled happily onwards. The mound of spaghetti lay there, pale against the green background, with the melted butter on it glistening in the sunlight. I stepped a bit closer and then kneeled down to investigate. The mesmerizing spectacle penetrated deep into my consciousness, and the visual harmony of the spaghetti and the summer greenness conjured up strange abstract images. I stood there frozen for a few moments. When I came to my senses I rushed straight indoors to get the camera and proceeded to photograph the glowing mound in the grass from every possible angle.

All kinds of landscape paintings loomed before my eyes, each one more fantastic than the next. I could already imagine them covering the walls of exhibition halls with spectacular variations of green and white. An endless succession of thrilling reflexes, mysterious shades, exquisite undertones. Rivers of spaghetti flowing between trees and bushes, forming clouds above the treetops, flowing freely in the open expanses of sky . . . Clusters of raw spaghetti looming behind the trees, lurking there as if to warn of some hidden danger.

I felt that an exhibition like that would provide a unique, vivid representation of the real world, positioning itself somewhere on the boundary between reality and the imaginary.

Over the next few days I felt a buzz of enthusiasm for work, and I was full of inspiration from the spaghetti experience. I was planning a series of fourteen paintings. Most of them would be one square meter in size, although three of them were two-meter-wide panoramas. I had spent some time searching for a pale form I could use to convey a certain meaning, and could paint onto a Toomas Vint landscape. The spaghetti was that form. The fact that it was depicted as a gigantic monstrosity intruding onto a sunny landscape could provoke astonishment, shrugs of disbelief, and all manner of strange reactions from the viewer, but that didn't bother me. I have always responded with stoic composure to all the strange situations that life presents to me. I like to think that if I can describe or paint the unreal as if it were real, then that becomes reality. So what if it has been created by me and did not previously exist. It's true that the critics responded cautiously to the strange situations represented in my exhibition "Clouds and Sofas," occasionally referring to the artist's fantastical games as a pre-meditated form of madness. I got the impression that if an artist were genuinely crazy, then his crazy works of art would be exalted, but the crazy imaginings of a sane artist were approached with more trepidation.

I was planning to play with the idea of madness in my forthcoming series of paintings, and this time they would go well beyond the bounds of reason. But even though I was plotting all of this, I wasn't actually in any hurry to make it happen. It was still summer and I never allow myself to work during summer. Summer is a precious time for forgetting the creative travails of winter, and instead I took pleasure from gardening or fishing by the lakeside during the silent summer nights, delaying the realization of the series of paintings until autumn.

But that year summer was already finished for me by the start of September, as the editor had finished with *The Sober Moon and Drunken Sun*, and I had to make the corrections to the manuscript and hand the novel over to the publisher. In addition to the writing work, I had to choose a set of suitable paintings for an exhibition of my work at the Latvian Embassy in Estonia.

On the 11th of September New York's twin towers collapsed and the next day my exhibition opened in an atmosphere of mourning. Many of the guests stopped in silence in front of the painting "The Third Possibility," which portrayed New York with the Hudson River overgrown with grass. The twin towers were looming over Manhattan just as before, but they were covered in moss, dark green like the rest of the town.

When I finally managed to sit down in front of a blank canvas in my studio, the moment was ripe for my spaghetti paintings. I had seen these new paintings in my dreams many times, but on waking I had only remembered an amorphous, undefined, white monstrosity crawling across the happy summer landscape. Nothing concrete. And I couldn't understand why I felt so good when I woke up, as if I had achieved something really significant.

It's one thing for an artist to paint pictures, but it's much harder to find a place to exhibit them. In three years I would have an important birthday and I wanted to organize a decent retrospective exhibition for the occasion. The last one like it had taken place at the Kadriorg Art Museum a quarter of a century earlier. I wasn't sure if the Art Hall still offered space for painting exhibitions, so a fallback option would have been the Freedom Gallery. But in order to keep this option open, I couldn't use up my turn in the gallery space with my "spaghetti exhibition." I had to find some other option that would also be acceptable in the context of contemporary art politics.

And then it struck me. A vision of a grand spaghetti party took shape in front of my eyes. Long tables groaning with pasta dishes of different forms and colors, with lots of different sauces. More and more pasta would be served from a steaming pot, until the gallery rooms were awash in a sea of spaghetti. The hungry visitors would enthusiastically munch pasta and would thus become an important component of the spaghetti space. People would literally become spaghetti portraits. A few video installations of starving African children would send a meaningful message, creating a visible contrast with the spectacle of sickening gluttony. An assortment of boxes of pasta and cookbooks with recipes for pasta dishes would be arranged on the windowsills to lure guests. Why did I just use the word "pasta"?! "Macaroni" is probably the correct word in the local vernacular . . . but maybe we can now replace a macaroni paradigm with a pasta paradigm . . . and we can refer to "makarony po flotski"* as a landmark from the Soviet past.

A yellowy-white jumble of pasta and macaroni spun around in my head. I had actually been a fan of pasta and macaroni dishes all my life. I remember that in the early years of our marriage, when we lived in the cellar studio, macaroni was the main food we ate—at least Aili's sister's husband thought so, since we always offered him macaroni when he stopped by to see us. It's easy to make excellent dishes from pasta without much effort. Especially if you happen to have some mushrooms. When I served in the Soviet military "macaroni po flotski" was a normal

* Russian: "Macaroni navy style," a pasta dish made with minced meat.

Sunday dinner. Then towards the end of the 1980s, when we started going to Finland more frequently, we would always buy a bag full of spaghetti from the harbor shop to take home with us.

I knew it was a silly idea to put on an exhibition where the hall would be bursting with pasta dishes and the gallery walls would be covered in paintings where weird spaghetti shapes lived their strange lives against the background of Toomas Vint's nature scenes. But I also knew that it had turned into a hopelessly irrational obsession.

I briefly entertained the thought of presenting it to some recognized curator, but I realized straight away what a stupid idea that was—no curator wanted to spoil their CV by putting on some painting exhibition.

Although at the same time, I knew that in the contemporary art world it was possible to present any sort of nonsense as a high-flown project. One just had to play with the words and sentences so that even if they had no intrinsic meaning, they would at least appear to mean something on the surface. I remember how someone once wrote a particularly effective project proposal, got a generous grant, and then spent three months sitting in Hiroshima library, writing out every single name of the victims of the atom bomb . . . With each name it was as if this person personally experienced the tragic circumstances in which the victim had perished, and the person might have even sighed deeply for each name as well . . .

I mulled over the idea of writing an application to turn my silly idée fixe into a large-scale project and making some sort of a breakthrough. But I couldn't force myself to write that particular type of text that is used to describe contemporary works of art and always faithfully accompanies them on display. The phrases you find in them are often just linguistic absurdities that you need to read several times over to escape from the verbal swamp out onto dry land. Strain as one might, the verbal slime will often pull the reader in and leave him to drown—although he somehow manages to summon up a false look of enlightenment as he drowns. More often than not one gets the impression that whoever wrote the text simply had nothing to say, and just hides behind a wall of empty words hoping that no one can be bothered to climb over it.

I hated those convoluted texts with a passion, but I knew that the only way I could earn approval in the eyes of the people who were responsible for allocating exhibition space was by using those kinds of words. I considered the idea of lifting whole phrases from some experienced project-writing wordsmith, and then simply copying and pasting them together as new texts. That would have been a pretty cynical ruse. I remember how Vaal gallery called me the day before my exhibition "Clouds and Sofas" was due to open and complained that Eha Komissarov, who usually puts together their press releases, had refused to do so for my exhibition. The reason was simple—the two of us didn't get along. I had recently offended her by writing that she was just a high-ranking employee of a public museum who had somehow gained control over the operation of a private gallery, pointing out that this situation was unheard of in the modern world . . . and I'd probably written some other stuff about her before that she couldn't forgive . . . No problem, I told the Vaal girls, and produced a shamelessly copied-and-pasted press release, using text previously written by Eha.

"*. . . By changing the context of the forms used in the picture—the sofa and the clouds—the artist achieves a surrealist atmosphere, opening up intriguing possibilities for interpretation. It is particularly striking that the author does not seek to exhaust the chosen discourse, which gives grounds to assume that we are dealing with a postmodern game in which the trump card is the viewer's thirst for reality, which allows eternity to be perceived as the present . . .*"

I was very happy with that text, which managed to say everything and nothing at the same time. One paper even published the press release with the usual sign-off "E.K." On the opening evening of the exhibition I savored the opportunity of speaking on the "Echo of Culture" radio program about what a great joke I had played. After that Eha wouldn't even say hello to me or to my wife. When the exhibition was over, Piia from the gallery told me that people there had complained about what a jerk Vint was for plotting secret deals with clients so that he could sell his paintings himself, bypassing the gallery. Naturally it hadn't occurred to me to do anything of the sort. The fact that no one had bought the paintings from the exhibition could be explained by the sorry state of the art market following the financial crisis. But this was a vicious stab in the back for me, intended to destroy the trust between myself and Vaal, and one didn't need to be particularly clever to work out who had made the complaint.

Copy and paste is a wonderful invention, I thought rubbing my hands together, and set to work looking for more texts written by apologists for contemporary art that could serve as suitable raw material for my postmodernist plans.

In order to investigate the values associated with eating habits the author uses collective, social, and synergetic methods. In the exterritorial part of the exhibition, the artist immerses himself in society's archives, and positioning himself on a sub-orientation, he exposes his interpretations to the light of day.

The project's concept can be seen as the subconscious fear of hunger mapped out through pious sentiment. The author analyses unreal situations and objects, the way in which everyday reality mixes with paranoia, and even phenomena linked to the keyword "terrorism." The exhibition does not so much create a link with third-world problematics or the mental and physical manifestations of terrorism, rather it involves itself with earlier meanings of the aforementioned concepts—fear, terror, and the feeling of being in danger. It provides a visual narrative dealing with the little-discussed subjects of "everyday horror," addictive greed, unthinking actions, and uncontrolled behavior. The question running through Toomas Vint's exhibition is, according to the author himself: at what moment does a game become reality? When is an imaginary threat replaced with a situation that exists in real life (here and now)? . . .

I'm not going to reproduce the whole of the text I composed back then—probably no one could be bothered to read it to the end, but I have to admit that after I had added relevant quotes from Jacques Lacan and Michel Foucault I had the strange feeling that I had just stealthily slipped my hand into my trousers and pleasured myself.

Work could now start on the paintings. I had to get at least three pictures done to use as indicative examples to apply for getting exhibition space. Time was moving steadily on. The trees became more colorful, and then they were bare. During one cold night the grass was painted white by dawn, and in the morning the chestnut tree had shed almost all of its leaves. The following week a sparse covering of snow fell and it became very cold. I went to the studio every day like a normal salaried worker. From dawn to dusk. There was less and less daylight to be seen. In my lunch breaks I drank coffee in the Wiiralt café and chatted with colleagues, but when I tried to tell them something amusing about my project, serious expressions immediately appeared on their faces, and they quickly changed the subject of conversation.

I had the sad feeling that I might already be too old for contemporary art, that it was the inheritance of the young, and that if I tried to get a leg in the door, then the door would eventually be cruelly slammed and I'd be left with a bloody leg. But my friend Leo Lapin read the project and said, grinning diabolically: "Andres Vanapa would say that this man needs to be tied up . . . I advise you to wait a bit and offer your macaroni project to the 2003 Venice Biennale . . . At the very least you should offer it to them!" he added in what was now a serious tone of voice. Then he took another swig of tea and hurried off.

But autumn was already coming to an end, the exhibition space for next year had already been allocated, and I wasn't in any hurry to reveal my project to the public. And I couldn't stop a certain thought from forcing itself into my mind. What if I really were to follow the rules of contemporary art and make a serious attempt to get into the Venice Biennale?

At the beginning of December the Italian artist Vittorio Mazzoli came to visit. We had become friends a dozen or so years earlier in Vares, where an exhibition of ten Soviet artists had taken place. He had been our guide, and thanks to his Russian skills our interpreter as well. We were very well received in Italy, and Vittorio had the opportunity to show us all around the treasure troves of art. Milan, Florence, Venice—what more could one want. We got to enjoy Italy for a few days before the opening of the exhibition, and sometimes it just happens that when you get along with someone, you stay in touch. Over the following years we sent each other postcards and called each other now and again. He had recently had some things to take care of in Moscow, and it looked like he had permanently swapped art for business. When I showed Vittorio my most recent works he was very enthused by the mounds of spaghetti. He praised them generously in Italian, Russian, and English, photographed them all together and separately, and even positioned them side by side in such a way that they told quite an odd story. I don't know why, but I didn't want to say a single word to Vittorio to explain my spaghetti project. I wanted him to see my pictures as art, with no confusing labels attached to them. Vittorio's enthusiasm did not wane. For supper he made spaghetti with a tomato, butter, and garlic sauce—like they only make in Italy.

By December there was so little daylight left that I could only paint for a couple of hours a day at most. Most of the time in my studio was spent sitting and staring at the picture on the easel, often until it had become very dark outside. For artists who live in northern countries, the end of the year is the most depressing time. I normally try to transform myself into a writer then, but that year I had finished writing a novel a month or so earlier, and my batteries were seriously depleted. So I sat like that for days on end doing almost nothing, until one day it all became too much for me and I did something very silly. After that I stopped going to the studio altogether.

Before Christmas Vittorio called and told me that he had some good news. One of his acquaintances was opening a new restaurant in Moscow and wanted to buy my spaghetti paintings as soon as possible to use as part of the interior design.

"I can't sell them," I said curtly.

"He's willing to pay a really good price for them. Don't worry, his vision for the interior design of the restaurant is based on those paintings, and you would definitely have a say in creating the interior. In some ways it would be a fantastic kind of art project," added Vittorio with a sigh.

"I can't sell them," I repeated, this time more despondently.

It was indeed true that I couldn't sell them, because one

horrible dark afternoon I had turned against everything having to do with art. I couldn't understand what it was that had made me want to do some stupid contemporary art project. I had stared at my reflection in the mirror and hadn't been able to recognize who I saw. So to rid myself, quickly and permanently, of this thing that had started to obsess me, and which had now grown to idiotic proportions. I cut my spaghetti pictures into shreds and burned them in the fireplace right there and then. Later, I would bitterly regret my actions, but creativity by its very nature consists of a mysterious oscillation between reason and madness, and a fleeting emotion can sometimes cause disruptive chaos in the protagonist's internal world, with consequences that are impossible to foresee.

It can't be helped, that's just the artist's life.

AN EXHIBITION IN PARIS, AT MONTPARNASSE

In the Soviet period there was a joke doing the rounds among the artists. A bearded bohemian is enjoying the company of close friends, there are plenty of pretty women there, and the vodka is flowing freely. And then he says, with his voice full of yearning: "I want to be in Paris again." An awkward silence comes over the company, then someone asks: "When did you last go there?" "I've never been there, I just got that feeling again, that I wanted to be there," comes the reply.

I suspect that young people these days wouldn't get that anecdote, as the first thing they would ask is why the artist doesn't just go to Paris if he really wants to. Drink less, save your money, and get on the plane. But there is a lot about the Soviet period that people don't understand these days. I could tell them, for example, about the time when the Export Salon in Moscow sold my paintings overseas and I was paid a mere five to seven percent of the retail price, of which I would receive only a small part in hard currency, and I had to buy that off the state at the official ruble exchange rate. Buy is probably the wrong word to use, because in fact the state just gave me checks to the value of the hard currency, which I could then use in the hard currency shops to procure foreign goods that were not available on the shelves of the Soviet shops. But at this the reader probably just shrugs his shoulders and asks: "But why did you sign such a humiliating contract?" I didn't sign any contract, because in those days there were no contracts—everything functioned according to the dictate of the state, and the author had no legal ownership of his work.

The story about a yearning for Paris came to mind when I was putting together this book, and I realized that along with the story "An Artist's Life" that gave the book its title, the collection should contain one or two stories about the paradoxical nature of our lives back then, something that tends to get lost from view these days. It was particularly striking to me that the last two "true life" stories were literary in style, and even similar in places, because in both stories a mystery was constructed that was eventually resolved. I deliberately use the term "true life stories," meaning that the stories were very much based on events that actually happened, although for some reason this term isn't particularly common.

And so I had to write a story about my life for this book, but at first nothing interesting came to mind—by then it seemed I had been keeping my distance from every kind of public event for an eternity. I asked Aili if she could recall any of my thrilling escapades. The kind of thing one could construct a longish short story from.

"Write about how it took you just a couple of quick movements to get the pants off that girl you had painted on the canvas," said Aili with a grin.

The story had indeed caused a grin. In the winter of 1989 I was working on a particularly large painting intended for the Sotheby's auction taking place in Moscow, although for several reasons it eventually ended up in the private collection of the Greek collector Kostakis instead. The painting had an end-of-summer metaphysical mood to it. It portrayed large pyramid-shaped juniper bushes that cast heavy, dark shadows on the ground, and in the foreground I had painted a woman wearing a white hat and red blouse, standing with her back to the viewer. I had planned to paint her half-dressed with a bare backside, but then I suddenly felt like giving her some blue jeans. I don't know why, but I decided that the picture needed some dark blue in the foreground. I worked through the morning and by lunchtime the figure looking at the juniper landscape was wearing pants. But I was sitting quite worried in front of the painting, staring at the backside covered in blue-jean material with growing unease. Contrary to my expectations, the blue color didn't merge into the structure of the painting at all. Instead it was the pale flesh color that created a powerful culmination point against the late-summer grass that covered the ground and was already starting to dry.

In the end, I finally decided to get rid of the irksome trousers, to wipe them off to reveal the flesh color underneath. At that point, the doorbell rang, and a whole detachment of French people descended on the studio, led by Heinz Valgu, the secretary of the Artists Union. It was part of the official entertainment program provided for foreign guests—intended to show real-life Soviet artists hard at work. Our studio was situated in the Art Hall, so we were easy prey for such a program. The French people were very interested in discovering what Soviet artists actually looked like, and investigating what it was we did, and they started to examine the painting I was doing from every possible angle. Then Aili said unexpectedly: "Listen, those jeans really don't suit that figure, maybe you should take them off?"

"You've got a very good point," I noted, scratching the back of my head. So I poured some turpentine onto a rag and wiped off the jeans I had painted that morning. That took ten seconds or so, and it was followed by a chorus of "ahhs" in the studio. The woman in the foreground was now standing there with her naked, rounded backside visible to all.

"Hey, you could do that at an exhibition . . . every single day, at some prearranged time . . ." Heinz suggested, finding the frivolous joke particularly good fun.

I remember that we asked those French visitors whether they had been to my exhibition at the Gorky Gallery in Paris. They hadn't, but one of them knew Basmadjian, the Armenian émigré who ran the gallery, very well, and was full of appreciation for him as a poet.

So that was how that trouser-removing story went. But memory works in such a way that one event reminds you of another, and that of yet another, and a little while later I suddenly remembered everything else connected with that ill-fated Paris exhibition.

At the beginning of the winter of 1985 a letter arrived from the Moscow Export Salon informing me that the Gorky Gallery in Paris would like to put on an exhibition of my paintings. For the first few moments I imagined something big and important, and such unexpected good fortune made a Soviet artist like me quite giddy. An exhibition in Paris! The city that for my generation was still associated with all the good things art had to offer. The fact that art's main artery now ran through New York couldn't erase the symbol fixed in our subconscious. Paris . . . Paris! I could already imagine myself at the center of attention of all those cultured Parisians, at the *vernissage*, with cameras clicking and flash bulbs flashing.

"Hey, where is the gallery located?" I asked Aili when the first glow of irrational happiness had started to fade.

"I seem to remember that it was somewhere near the Luxembourg gardens, on the Boulevard Raspail, which means in Montparnasse," my wife explained, since she had been to visit the gallery when she was in France with a tour group in 1981.

Back then, they had gone to the Gorky Gallery with our friend, the artist Vladimir Makarenko—the same Makar who we left our cellar studio to when we moved to Nõmme, and who had managed to emigrate in 1981. Makar had evidently made himself very at home in Paris, and had probably been helped by the artist Chemyakin, who had already left ten years earlier and made himself an international name; we also figured that Makar's previous move from the Ukraine to Estonia had been a kind of emigration training for him. And so, one afternoon Aili and Makar stepped into the Gorky Gallery, which was known for promoting Soviet underground art, and was owned by Basmadjian. When the latter heard that Aili came from Estonia, he started boasting that he had recently bought some paintings by an Estonian artist and when he showed a reproduction to the guests, Aili was happy to confess that it was her in the picture.

"Are you a model?" the gallery owner inquired. "No, I'm the wife of the artist," Aili explained, at which the gallery owner was moved to tears—he simply couldn't believe that, after getting ahold of a painting from within the closed Soviet system, the woman portrayed in the painting had walked through his door the very next day.

"Damn! So the gallery is even in a nice area. In Montparnasse itself . . ." I said quite loudly, as if I wanted to see how that sentence sounded to my own ears.

For an artist, the location of an exhibition is very important. An exhibition displayed in some foyer somewhere or some out-of-the way gallery has no impact. It's like the exhibition had never taken place, because it's inconceivable that anyone important from the art world will set foot there. If someone starts boasting that he had an exhibition in London or New York or some other large city, it's always a good idea to inquire where exactly the exhibition was displayed. But the Gorky Gallery's location in Montparnasse was noteworthy, because the name of the area alone was enough to make you think of Picasso, Modigliani, Apollinaire, Hemingway, Cocteau, Fitzgerald, Henry Miller, or Miró, to mention just a few of the major figures who come to mind. Montparnasse was basically the artistic and intellectual heart of Paris during the first half of the twentieth century. Ideas that at first seemed crazy by the standards of the time were conceived in cafés there, quickly became mainstream, and went on to change world culture.

When my first wave of enthusiasm had passed, and I had sent off my agreement, I began to get nervous. Twenty or so pictures would be needed for the exhibition, but sadly my studio was just a gaping hole at the time. And there was a gaping hole inside me as well. I couldn't just send any old paintings to Paris, the pictures had to be ones that I rated highly myself and that best showed what sort of artist I was. There were barely five months left until I had to send off the works, but the most frightening thing was that the days were getting shorter and shorter, with only enough daylight left for a few hours of painting each day.

There is no sense in giving a detailed description of the days of work that followed. There is nothing romantic or interesting about an artist getting ready for an exhibition. The beginning is always the hardest—you need to have a pretty clear idea of how every individual picture and the exhibition as a whole will look. Once you start to paint the first planned picture the work becomes pretty routine—one motif helps you find the next one and then pretty soon you get a feel for it. Having the right feel for a painting in progress means having the certainty that the paints you put on the canvas are the ones that the painting on the easel is expecting and recognizes as its own, otherwise you take a risk with the harmony of the colors, which at first you can only see with your mind's eye. There is no greater pleasure than painting the picture you can see in your imagination! For me a good final result is when the painting contains some of Toomas Vint's metaphysics, with the addition of something new or unexpected in just the right proportion.

It was probably January when I started to lose my grip on things. The short daylight hours frayed my nerves and tried my patience, and more and more often I ended up crawling out of my studio and going to the artists' club, where I tried to achieve some sort of deceptive internal balance through strong alcohol. One morning—one of those terrible hangover mornings—I woke up in my studio to find myself surrounded by a scene of devastation. Some half-finished paintings and even some earlier-completed and valuable ones had been kicked to pieces and were lying around on the floor with piles of smashed glasses and cups. I stared at the chaos and couldn't believe my eyes. Finally the tears I had been trying to hold back made my vision hazy and I thought that I must be having a bad dream. But it wasn't a dream . . . After a long search I finally found a glass of vodka behind the sofa. Stale vodka. It was Mati Unt's favorite cure, and was supposed to relieve even the most awful symptoms. There was even a saying doing the rounds that stale vodka was disgusting but good for you. During that period I always tried—if at all possible—to hide a glass of vodka somewhere before I started getting drunk. So as to hopefully find it the next morning.

When the Mati Unt first aid had been administered, I looked around me with clearer eyes. One of my most prized paintings—the kind I couldn't bring myself to sell—had been battered to bits with a hammer, and two nearly finished paintings and another I had just started had been damaged beyond all repair. I can remember feeling vaguely happy that I hadn't destroyed all the paintings, but then it dawned on me that all that destruction was clearly a sign . . . and so I thought, almost as if trying to justify myself, that enough was enough! To hell with that exhibition. There was no point in working so hard that I ended up going crazy. I had to take better care of my health.

And what damned use was that Paris exhibition to me anyway.

Now I understand that it really wouldn't have been any use to me. It couldn't have brought me fame or glory. But this was 1986, and people like me didn't have a clue how things worked in the art world. I lived in the backwaters of a closed system, where the only ray of hope for an artist was to struggle his way out via the Moscow Export Salon. So I had no qualms at all when the Export Salon ordered my pictures again and again for foreign exhibitions. I could take the positive view that some part of me was traveling to Japan, Belgium, the USA, and some dozen other countries. My paintings went wandering abroad and often ended up staying there, so in the end there were around fifty "emigrated" paintings, and some of them were undoubtedly my best works. Of course I felt proud when a guest from Pennsylvania, an art historian who worked at the International Images Fine Art Gallery, told me about the important public buildings where my paintings were hanging.

But all those grand exhibitions all around the world were just sales exhibitions, I thought to myself as I recalled those past events.

After I laid waste to my studio back then in 1986 I didn't pick up a paintbrush for a whole week, but then my friends started pointing out that there weren't many Estonian artists who had managed to have an exhibition in Paris . . . Wiiralt, and who else? What choice did I have? My internal rebellion subsided, and telling myself that an artist's life consists of painting and that painting is all that is important to him, I gave in. An artist has to paint, paint, and paint, regardless of whether there is any sense to the whole thing. I gave my studio a thorough clean and ordered some new picture backings. Ten new paintings were ready, and my task was to paint another ten.

At the beginning of spring I dispatched twenty-three pictures to Paris. Lauri Lees had helped me think up French names for the pictures, and once that was done this Soviet artist could sit back and wait for his invitation to the exhibition opening. But the invitation never came, and I didn't even find out exactly when the exhibition took place. The Gorky Gallery had a tradition of producing fancy exhibition catalogs, with colored reproductions stuck in as inserts, but I never saw my exhibition catalog. It was rare for anyone to personally bring back a catalog from some overseas exhibition. Normally they ended up getting lost in Moscow, and the story was always that they had them somewhere, but they didn't know where they had gotten to . . . A woman at the Export Salon once pretended that she would personally look for my catalog. That was how things were back then. It's possible that if I were to rummage around enough in some Moscow antique shop, I might actually get to see my exhibition catalog with my own eyes.

It was already 1988 when I was informed from Moscow one day that my exhibition had taken place in 1987. Eleven works had been bought and I would get the rest back. Looking at those dates, it now seems unbelievable how long the whole business took back then. There was almost no feedback whatsoever. No one in Moscow could give a sensible answer to my inquiries. Vagueness was the norm, and I didn't get the unsold works back until the start of 1989. The money side of things was the same as ever.

In December of 1988 there was a terrible earthquake in Armenia. The gallery owner Basmadjian had apparently traveled to Moscow to hand over a valuable gift as a donation to the Armenian people. After that he had wanted to travel to Yerevan, but the Russian authorities hadn't given him permission. It was said that he then made the trip in secret. And then he went missing. I found out about all this when a guy from the KGB questioned me, and then a bit later someone from the Estonian Procuracy also interviewed me. For them I was a visible track to follow—a Soviet artist whose exhibition Basmadjian had recently organized. But they somehow couldn't believe that it had taken place without any personal contact between us.

"But you must have at least been to the sauna with him?" the KGB man asked with typical perspicacity.

I once happened to hear from the news on Finnish TV that

Basmadjian had been involved in some diamond smuggling business with the ballet dancer Nureyev and some woman. Later still I heard on Finnish radio that Basmadjian had apparently turned up in Israel. Our friends in Moscow said that customs had seized the works from an exhibition of Basmadjian's collection that had taken place at the Tretyakov Gallery and the Hermitage. It was also said that someone had seen him in the Butyrka prison in Moscow.

Back then, Basmadjian's disappearance in Russia caused a major international scandal. When the next group of French artists visited our studios, we asked what new information had surfaced about that story. They didn't have any fresh news, and all they could do was express their sympathy when I pointed out that the gallery owner owed me money. They said that if a Frenchman disappears with no trace then his accounts are frozen and his financial affairs remain in limbo for years.

A very confusing period followed that, and then suddenly Estonia was independent. It was bizarre to watch how all links with Moscow were so suddenly and decisively broken, as if they had never existed. When I finally started to track down the payment for my paintings from Moscow, I came up against the problem that I didn't have a single document to present to them that could prove that the paintings had been sent from Estonia to the Moscow Export Salon. Interesting, a modern-day reader would probably muse, this was a valuable shipment, how can it be possible that the artworks crossed a state border without any sort of contract?

Those kinds of things certainly wouldn't be possible today, but back then my pictures were dispatched to Moscow with just a postal slip. But I couldn't find that postal slip in either the Art Combine or anywhere else. Pretty soon the Moscow Export Salon ceased to exist anyway.

When the Paris exhibition story came to mind, I started tracking down Basmadjian and the Gorky Gallery on the internet. I tried different ways, changed the spelling of the names, added additional search terms, but got no answers. I started to feel that what I had taken to be real for so many years was just the bizarre imagination of a Soviet artist who lived a bohemian lifestyle.

I complained to my daughter one day that I couldn't find a single trace of those earlier events in the whole vast expanse of the internet. "Yes, sometimes it's like that. We had the period before Christ's birth, and then the period after. Now we can say that there was the time before Google, and the present day."

"Is that so," I grumbled.

Everything that happened before Google is lost in the mists of time, and no one can really be bothered to go the library to research old newspapers or journals for their writing. They just type the name into a search engine and the story is written using Google search results. It was sad to think that my most productive and important years had just disappeared. But despite everything I can still be optimistic. I take a strange satisfaction from the thought that there are dozens of my paintings hanging all over the world, in many homes, offices, and public buildings, and through them the viewer can witness Toomas Vint's unreal reality, and hopefully experience something in the process.

II
A Flock of Delusions

PEDIGREE MALE, FREE TO A GOOD HOME

Meralda was a woman of fine character and fine looks, but she hadn't been lucky in life. First her husband, and then three subsequent partners, had packed their bags and left after a short period of cohabitation, quickly becoming little more than strangers to her. When Meralda bumped into them later, she literally took them to be strangers, and it was then awful to remember that she had in fact shared her table and even her bed with them. Our lovely Meralda had now lived alone for over a year, and single life had already started to get to her. The weekends were particularly wearying—a succession of dull, pointless days, in which only the ticking of the clock gave her the fleeting, false feeling that she had some company.

When the weekends approached and her colleagues with children started discussing all the things they had to do at home, Meralda would have been happy to help. But there was no point—she noticed that when she became single her colleagues stopped inviting over, as though they were trying to keep their men away from her, or as if they were afraid that Meralda would try to grab one of them for herself if she got the chance. She would listen to the women's chattering with tears welling up, and when everyone went their separate ways at the end of the day she felt useless, like an expensive bottle of perfume that was all used up.

After work Meralda would normally go to some shop and then walk slowly home through town, hoping that someone would wave to her or call out her name; but no one needed her. When she arrived home she would cry a bit, then make herself a cozy nest on the sofa and start checking through the personal ads in the newspaper. It was a silly habit she had gotten into recently, and she knew that if she got her hopes up too much she could end up pushing herself into a dead end, but it was thrilling to read the ads placed by all those men who were looking for companions for one reason or another. She would return to the ads that had caught her interest and try to imagine what the men looked like and what it would feel like to find herself in their arms. Up until now, however, she had not thought seriously about responding to any of them—the ads may have all been written with different words, but the exact same thoughts and desires emanated from every one of them.

On this occasion, as usual, there were some younger men calling themselves reliable and looking for a relationship on the side or a lover, and some older gentlemen who hoped to find a serving maid they didn't have to pay. The Finns, for their part, wanted to save money on hotels and bordellos and hoped to find free board, together with someone to warm their bed, when they came to Tallinn. But then suddenly, like a lone ray of sunlight appearing over a rainy gray sea, one of the ads caught her eye: "Available free of charge, pedigree male in his prime. Strong, domesticated, excellent capacity for work. With a character like his, he is sure to become your best friend."

Meralda read the ad again and again. It wasn't a message for dog owners that had ended up in the wrong section. Instead it was a nice joke, intended to convey a promising truth. Unlike the majority of the ads there was no anonymous email address under this one, just a name and a home address—something very rare in the personal columns.

It looks like this man has nothing to be afraid or ashamed of, thought Meralda, feeling full of respect for him. And the best thing of all was that he seemed to be the kind of person who always had a hatful of jokes ready for all of life's eventualities.

Nothing ventured, nothing gained, Meralda thought as she decided to heed her racing heart. So she wrote in her reply that she would be happy to take in a domesticated male and take him for walks on fine spring evenings. Then she weighed up at length whether she should go along so wholeheartedly with the game the man had started, but in the end she decided that playing along was exactly what would raise her above the competition.

So she added that although she had no experience keeping dogs, she had longed for a four-legged friend her whole life. Once she had finished the letter she wavered for a bit longer before adding her phone number, and then took it to the mail box that very same evening.

A difficult, nerve-racking week followed. The newspaper with the ads became frayed from constant reading, and she mulled over every word of her letter hundreds of times, until in the end she was no longer sure whether she had actually sent it off or not.

Then on Monday morning the telephone rang. "Hello!" said a pleasantly gruff male voice. "I'm the one who put that ad in the paper."

Meralda quickly composed herself, and she was surprised to find how easy it was to talk to the man. When she later reflected on that call she decided that it must have been so easy because for the whole duration it had felt exactly as if they were really talking about taking in a dog.

They met the next day. It was a warm evening in early spring. The trees were covered with a gentle green mantle and the air was ripe with all kinds of scents. They walked around a pond several times and Meralda noticed how the onlookers, in particular the women, were following them with jealous looks. Arvi Tuuksam or Tuks, as he let her call him as soon as they met, really was very good-looking: a powerful muscular chest, hairy forearms, closely cropped black hair, and on top of all that such alluring brown eyes. It was his eyes that enchanted Meralda. He was the kind of man who might be silent for a while, but the look of sincerity in those eyes would always be speaking for him.

In the evening they went to eat at a restaurant on the seafront. The red sun was slowly sinking into the mirror-smooth water, and they spoke about life. Meralda told Arvi with almost total honesty about her failed marriages, and Arvi confessed his own sad story. His marriage had started to go awry a year ago, when his wife had decided to take in a dog. Arvi had been against it, but nevertheless one evening a giant growling Great Dane arrived there in their home. Naturally Arvi was livid and told his wife that she would have to choose between him and the dog. The next day the dog had disappeared. But after that incident their married life started to come apart. Arvi's wife was almost never home. When Arvi came back from work the hearty supper was no longer waiting for him, and he had no one to go out with in the evenings. And then, almost a month ago, it had become clear that Arvi's wife had been spending nearly all her time with the Great Dane. She had apparently rented a filthy little room where she whiled away her time fawning over the dog.

"I couldn't get my head around the fact that she swapped me for a Great Dane!" Arvi exclaimed and his eyes expressed the bottomless pain he had been forced to endure for months on end.

Meralda wanted Arvi to lay his head in her lap so she could gently stroke his hair and affectionately scratch behind his ears, but there were people all around who wouldn't have understood such displays of affection, so Meralda just smiled sympathetically. When she looked at Arvi again it seemed like he was reading her thoughts, and she blushed.

Night had fallen when they finally arrived at Meralda's house, and she didn't have the heart to leave Arvi on the other side of the door.

"Why should I put on an act just to make a good impression. Take me as I am," she said, and Arvi put his chin on her knees and looked straight at her with a gaze which promised eternal loyalty.

The next day Meralda awoke at the crack of dawn. Never in her life had she felt so indescribably happy. Some joyful classical music was playing on the radio. Arvi had already gotten up and the smell of coffee was wafting from the kitchen. Rays of morning sunlight peeked in through the curtains, shining onto her pillow. Next to the pillow she saw the pair of red oven mitts Arvi had put on during their love making. "I'm worried that I might hurt you with my nails in the heat of passion," he had said jokingly.

Oh that Tuksi! Meralda said with a knowing sigh, and closed her eyes so that she could luxuriate in the incomparable feeling of happiness for a few more moments. Then suddenly she heard an odd hissing sound, like running water. She got out of bed, pulled on her bathrobe, and looked down the corridor. She was astonished to see Tuks standing there, spraying piss against the kitchen doorframe.

A DOG'S LIFE

I really am a dog, but I can't show them that I am, thought Arvi as he tried to find the tram ticket in his pocket, and he began to feel a bit panicked. He remembered that he had stamped the ticket on an earlier journey and shoved it somewhere. He found all sorts of rubbish in his pockets, but the ticket itself seemed to have disappeared into thin air.

"It must be here somewhere," he said in a louder voice.

The ticket inspector—a vigorous, strapping young man, better suited to pitchforking dung than hassling passengers—eyed him with a superior gaze that said: we've seen hundreds of your sort, they beat their chests and swear they had a ticket, but for some inexplicable reason it got lost somewhere.

"There is no such thing as an inexplicable reason," said the young muscleman, rubbing his eye with an index finger.

Arvi wanted to bare his teeth at him, but he took great efforts to restrain himself, and then his fingers finally located the right ticket. The ticket inspector examined it with visible disappointment before reluctantly handing it back to him. "You were lucky this time," he snapped for no particular reason.

You're the lucky one, thought Arvi with relief and then chuckled to himself as he imagined how flustered that lump of muscle would be if he found out that Arvi was actually a dog. He wouldn't know how to react. He would simply lose his mind—with such a tiny brain he would be totally incapable of comprehending anything of the sort.

That's life, thought Arvi, and his mood turned gloomy again. He had to do something to sort out all his problems. At the moment his life consisted mainly of finding food, water, and a place to sleep, and no one wanted to give him these things simply out of the goodness of their hearts, or because of his handsome eyes. No, he had to earn his sausage, thought Arvi, and his mouth started watering uncontrollably. He hadn't found anything fit to eat for a while now. He had to try to make ends meet until he got himself a new master or mistress. Or, in the most extreme case—and his situation was now pretty extreme—he would have to find a job and earn himself a living.

Just a living, just enough to keep body and soul together. He didn't need any luxuries—mountains of porridge and rivers of milk—he wasn't dreaming of trips to warmer countries, he didn't need a fancy car or a castle to make people jealous. Instead he longed for an affectionate stroke and a kindly word spoken from the heart. It really wasn't much to ask for, even if it sometimes seemed completely unattainable.

The tram rattled to a stop by the edge of a park lined with ancient trees, and Arvi got off. The grass had recently been trimmed and the smooth green expanse tempted him to come and romp. Arvi would have rushed straight onto the lawn, yelping with joy, but he knew that onlookers wouldn't understand, and that running around for no particular reason would arouse suspicion. And some sort of unpleasantness would be quick to follow . . .

Arvi had twenty minutes to spare, so he sat down on a bench in the shade. Two young dogs, both of them with black coats, frolicked in the middle of the lawn among patches of bright sunlight. They were taking turns chasing each other. It might look like a ferocious fight but Arvi knew that it was only a game. Even when they really went at each other they were still only playing.

A dog with a spotted coat, clearly a stray mongrel, was rummaging about in a trash can with abandon. Its head was buried up to the neck in garbage and it was rooting about with such vigor that pieces of paper and plastic were flying in all directions. I definitely won't let things come to that, thought Arvi. When you lose your self-respect and end up exposed to the elements like that, there's no longer any sense in living.

It would soon be a full year since Arvi made the life-changing discovery that he was a dog. But it hadn't happened overnight. In retrospect he realized that back when he was a child he had probably already felt that people didn't treat him right, but he had been unable to see things clearly, and had thought that they were right to treat him like that, and that the problem was instead his own peculiar character and unusual behavior.

He had lived a false life, but over time he got used to it, and in the end he became quite sure that no other type of life was possible.

He remembered one autumn day in particular, when the wind had been howling outside and the rain beating against the windowpane—it was the kind of awful weather you wouldn't even put a dog out in. He had been watching television, and he had seen a young man lying stark naked with a leash around his neck in front of an ordinary dog kennel that had been placed inside some hall somewhere. He was resting his head on his paws and glaring distrustfully at the people jostling around the kennel. Suddenly a woman bent down, probably wanting to stroke him, but the dog misinterpreted the movement, suspecting that she wanted to grab his bone, and he jumped up with a snarl and sank his teeth into her ankle. The presenter's voiceover explained dispassionately that this was an exhibition of contemporary art in Stockholm, where the young Russian artist Oleg Kulik had apparently bitten one of the critics.

"Say what you like!" Arvi vociferated. He knew the shocking truth that the young man on the TV screen really was a dog, but for some inexplicable reason the bystanders had gotten the idea that he was a Russian artist. But then one encounters tragic misunderstandings at every step and turn of life, thought Arvi, trying to draw his tongue across his wife's face. She just thrust him cruelly aside.

"I was trying to be affectionate," Arvi whimpered dejectedly. "I've had enough of your idiotic behavior!" his wife screamed in response.

Their married life had started to stink, like the dregs of some soup left in the bottom of a saucepan for a few days. You would have to be really hungry to lap it up, but it was still food of some sort. And that was how they went on, day in, day out, dragging the heavy burden of their married life with them. To be sure, Arvi sometimes felt that things were gradually getting back on track, but then in a moment everything would become completely unbearable again. Those were the times when it was most distressing to hear other peoples' jealousy-tinged praise: what's wrong with you, everything seems to be going so well . . .

"From a distance, things might seem to be going well," he snarled back at the latest honey-tongued eulogizer, and they were left just guessing what he had meant, with a look of incomprehension on their faces.

The end came quickly. He was dismissed from work in the middle of winter, and when it came out that instead of going to work in the mornings he had just been walking around town, his wife stated harshly that she couldn't bring up children and support a scrounger on her salary alone. Arvi realized that she was being serious, and so there was nothing left to do but slope off with his tail between his legs.

A week had not passed before some Dane had made himself at home with his wife. It turned out that she had being having a relationship with him for a while already, and she had probably just been waiting for a reason to put Arvi unceremoniously out onto the street.

But strangely enough, this injustice didn't drive Arvi to despair. In truth he didn't even miss the children, since they had done nothing but tease him. As the days passed he started to feel an indescribable sense of freedom, which grew stronger and stronger. His entire former life, which had been forced upon him, receded further into the distance until it became unreal.

But as time passed, he started to feel that he may have started his new life on the wrong footing.

After all, a dog is not a wolf, which can roam through the forests on its own when it gets separated from the pack. A dog needs a master, a dog needs someone to care for it, otherwise it grows unaccustomed to people, turns feral, and in the end has to be put to sleep. One morning a muddy gray truck pulled up on the sidewalk near Arvi, and he watched as two men built like wardrobes jumped out and used giant nets and wire nooses to catch some dogs who had been consummating their love in an abandoned house. He looked on in horror as the men mercilessly dragged the poor beasts into the truck, and he guessed what fate awaited them.

Later, as he sat in his tiny rented room mulling sadly over what he had seen, he felt incredibly lucky, for the first time in his life, that no one knew who he really was. He realized that in the future he would have to be cunning and careful, so as not to suffer the same fate at the hands of the dogcatchers.

But the loneliness oppressed him, and became more and more unbearable every day. Once, Arvi walked out to the wasteland outside of town and began wailing with great sorrow. This unburdened his soul, but it was only temporary. He couldn't share his troubles with any of the friends from his former life, and at any rate it seemed as if they were always avoiding him for some reason. If they saw him on the street they would turn their heads or cross over to the other side. He was pretty sure that some of them were also dogs just like him, but they had been forced to hide it throughout their whole lives, even from themselves.

In early spring he had the bold idea of starting to look for a master himself. After much wavering he finally placed the ad in the paper, announcing that a pedigree male in his prime, with a character that would make him a good friend, was available. He didn't entertain any particular hopes, but when a woman with a strange name, one Meralda, eventually wrote to him, he couldn't have been happier.

The woman told him that she had dreamed for ages of having a dog, and had finally decided to get one. Arvi figured that even if the woman had been dreaming about a dog, she probably didn't have one like Arvi in mind. Only after long deliberation did he finally decide to phone the woman and tell her his whole story, just like it was. His amazement knew no bounds when it turned out that the woman didn't make a big deal of it at all, and was fine with everything he told her.

Looking back later, he could only grimace bitterly as he recalled the crazy dance of joy he had done after the call.

For the first ten days or so he had no reason to doubt that he really had found himself a good mistress. Meralda looked after

Arvi well, and his coat already started to shine. But one day she adopted a serious, downright angry tone of voice and asked if he ever planned to go to work and start earning some money.

"What work?" asked Arvi, not understanding what she meant. "My work is protecting you, and when you're away from home I guard your property."

"Listen man, come to your senses," said Meralda resolutely. "I would understand if we were talking about some dog, but . . ."

Everything fell apart right there and then. It turned out that the woman had never had any desire to try and understand his predicament. She had taken him in as a man, and now she wanted him to be man enough to go out and work. But how could a faithful dog start earning money out there with strangers? The woman's foolishness knew no bounds. It seemed as endless as the desert sands.

He recalled how he had planned to kill himself back then. He could no longer bear to live in such a hypocritical world, where someone could pretend for days on end that they had taken in a dog, without actually believing for a single moment that the dog really was a dog.

"What do people truly believe in this world?!" he asked despairingly.

But dogs don't kill themselves. Stray dogs are caught and put to sleep. That's life.

He somehow had to cope with life's problems. He had to eat, drink, and find some shelter when the weather was bad. Life pushed all animals cruelly into a corner, forcing them to struggle for their survival. Now Arvi was looking impatiently at his watch, watching the minutes pass until it would finally be time for him to go to his job interview. As far as he was concerned he had enough experience for this job. In his former life he had taken part in dozens of interviews, but back then it had been him who decided whether to take the jobseeker on or leave them to their fate.

Full of optimism, he rose from the park bench. But the sun disappeared behind the clouds, and Arvi remembered how two days previously he had gone to offer his services as a night watchman. "Do you know your way around a computer, and can you drive?" he was asked at the start. "Why is that required? You advertised for a guard," he said, confused.

"We're not so rich that we can pay a separate person to perform every single movement," they snapped in response. "Where did you work previously?"

He certainly couldn't tell them that, so he just muttered something vague about having some previous experience as a security guard. In fact he had only had one unfortunate experience. On his first—and last—day guarding a store he had sunk his teeth into one brazenly light-fingered customer.

"But he was trying to steal something," he had said, trying to justify his actions, which were entirely proper but seemed odd to the shopkeeper.

"We will be in touch shortly," he was informed after a short interview, and he realized as he sloped off home just how empty the words were, since no one had asked where he lived or what his telephone number was.

He hoped with his whole heart that it would go better today.

The firm that had placed the job ad in the paper, Dogsnout, was situated in a small, handsome building by the edge of a park. When Arvi opened the door he heard the bell hanging by the doorway ring gently. One of the walls in the room was covered from floor to ceiling with shelves holding piles of pet products. On the other wall pictures of pedigree dogs were proudly displayed. A white curtain was flapping in the gentle summer wind and pleasant music was coming from the radio. Behind the table there was a man wearing light-colored summer clothes with strikingly hairy forearms and a dog mask on his face.

"I've come about the ad," Arvi mumbled.

"Aha," the man's voice echoed dully inside the mask. He rose briskly, took the mask off and walked towards Arvi with his hand outstretched.

"The thing is, I need someone to do some good advertising for our company. He would have to wear a dog mask and costume and look just like a happy dog who has eaten his fill of our wonderful, tasty dog food. But I have to warn you that it's pretty tough work. Especially when it's hot—it's murder running around the parks and streets in a mask all day long . . . Although of course you know yourself what you are capable of . . ."

"I think I can manage it," said Arvi, trying to conceal his excitement.

Just recently a huge bird had given him a fright outside the optician's, and he had thought sadly to himself that people had started to go mad in the hot weather—why would a human dress as a bird? But a little later, when he saw a wolf in a policeman's helmet standing by a blue-and-white car, he couldn't help wondering whether the wolf really was a wolf or not . . . In any case, Arvi reckoned that if he put on a dog costume, then there was a good chance that everyone would say, look there goes a dog. He could run, bark, growl, and lift his hind leg and no one would hold it against him. That dog is behaving just like a dog, they would say as they watched him.

But he himself would still know that people only thought that because of the dog costume he had on.

"If you're interested in the job, you could do a trial right away," said the man with hairy forearms, offering him the dog mask.

"By the way, did you know that at first we wanted to call our company Laughing Dog. Like dogs would be given our products in return for laughing, or something like that. What do you think, do dogs actually laugh?"

"Why shouldn't they," said Arvi as he took off his coat. And then he surprised even himself by bursting out into a laugh of pure happiness.

SWEEPSTAKES OF LOVE

It was raining on the day of the sweepstakes. Flurries of big raindrops fell from the heavy clouds as gusts of wind pushed them on their way. It had already started the previous evening, raining hard, then dying down for a bit, before starting up again with renewed vigor. When Fallon awoke and opened his eyes to look towards the window, he couldn't see anything outside. There was just a wall of rain.

Fallon felt a sudden pang in his heart—so, the rain would have washed away the blades of grass. He closed his eyes and tried to delay the arrival of the harsh truth. Two years ago he had put a bit of soil into a hollow in the concrete ledge outside the window, and started to wait. Now he had gotten used to rushing to the window as soon as he got up to see if there were any signs of life in the soil—and two days ago he had seen two pale green blades of grass. That meant the start of new life, that some seeds had been carried there from somewhere far away by a chance gust of wind. But after such a heavy and prolonged downpour there was a real danger that the stream of water had washed away the earth, and with it the blades of grass, from the fissure in the concrete. If the plant had been bigger, then its root filaments would have penetrated into the tiny cracks in the concrete to hold the plant firm, like ropes, in the event of any danger.

I should have made a protective dome over the grass, Fallon thought, but he sensed right away that such behavior would mean cheating nature, and was almost as unsophisticated as getting hold of a seed from somewhere and sticking it into the earth himself. Fallon wanted to observe the true wonder of nature at work, to witness how it brings order to everything all by itself. He had once read a book that had argued vehemently against extinguishing forest fires. He had been inspired by the idea that man should never interfere in the course of nature. From time immemorial, lightning had set forests ablaze. Beginnings and endings are completely natural phenomena. Death and destruction are inseparably linked to birth and growth. Be well aware that the slightest change to the natural order of things just brings the end of the world closer!—the book had fulminated.

Fallon liked to think about the natural world sometimes. That blade of grass outside the window was something real. He imagined how it would grow a bit bigger every day, and how he would eventually be able to spend many a happy hour conversing with the fully grown plant. Fallon sighed unhappily, and then the thought came to him that if the blade of grass outside the window was still untouched by the rain, intact and full of life, then he would be sure to win the sweepstakes that day . . . It was a kind of game he played with himself, where one good bit of fortune would lead to another. And one bit of bad fortune would, in turn, bring more bad fortune with it. In this case the saying that every cloud has a silver lining didn't apply. Quite the reverse: bad things were in alliance with other bad things and any last glimmer of hope would be extinguished for good. Fallon actually believed that the whole world consisted of interconnected events. He believed that life was made up of chains, that life progressed onwards from link to link, so that every man had to travel along his own chain from beginning to end, and there wasn't the slightest hope of jumping from one chain over to another.

Now that he had made that contract with causality, Fallon couldn't carry on pretending that he didn't know what had happened to the blade of grass. He stood up decisively, went over to the window, and saw that it was still there. What a day! he thought in jubilation, and his heart was brimming with joy.

Fallon was a copywriter by trade—he thought up advertisements: the situations, phrases, and words. He injected them into people's brains, and if the ideas were viable, they would take root there and start growing, just like the green blade of grass in the concrete crack. His life consisted mostly—in fact almost entirely—of work. From morning to evening he rummaged through garbage heaps of words, where earlier generations had already gathered up anything that was of any real value, and tried to find some usable word combinations which, with enough time and effort, he could clean up and improve. Adding some fresh color to try and give them more value.

As well as his daily work, Fallon's life was given meaning by the handful of earth in the concrete crack, and the blade of grass growing there. He lived in a part of town inhabited by professional people; there were professionals just like him living in the apartments above, below, and on either side of him, and they had nothing in their lives to worry about or care about other than their work. But sometimes in life, even when you already have more than everyone else, you still want more—and so Fallon had been playing the sweepstakes for eight years now. The sweepstakes of love. It was an expensive pleasure that swallowed up nearly all of his income. The prospects of winning were faint, almost nonexistent. It was entirely possible to play until old age, to scrimp and save your whole life, turn your back on everything else, and still end up with nothing. And yet the faint chance of winning was always there, haunting him. Four times a year—on every equinox and solstice—the excitement reached a climax point. For the thousands of participants in the district sweepstakes there were just five prizes to be won. This time the prizes were Aneri, Geir, Etti, Keddy, and Urlis. They smiled back from the pictures on the sides of buildings, websites, and TV screens. It was big business.

But it was still worth taking part.

By 2021 science had done away with aging for good. And so people were left between a rock and a hard place. A choice had to be made between birth and death. Humans of course chose the moment they happened to be in. A death sentence was passed on death, which of course meant the same sentence was passed on birth. The feminist movement raised its voice, which led to a bloody conflict between men and women. In 2027 men won a final victory. The slightest expression of feminist sympathies would be met with the most horrible punishment. The world's affairs were arranged to support this new order of things for eternity. Mandatory sterilization of the few remaining women began. Humanity's numbers diminished. Some people—quite a few, in fact—became bored of living and preferred death. In order to preserve the ideal number of humans, special laws on reproduction were passed, and farms of childbearing women were set up. In 2038 the "Sweepstakes of Love" system was established in order to give every man a democratic chance.

It had been raining endlessly. Fallon could picture the eternal water cycle vividly in his mind's eye. The process involved drops of water rising towards the sky, sparkling in the sunlight, only to be repelled back downwards. A huge number of people had lived on this earth in much the same way, bouncing back and forth between life and death. This drudgery definitely had its charm—people took empty activities like looking for food or building their dwellings very seriously. Fallon had consulted old texts and got the impression that for many people life's entire meaning and content had come from those activities, and this had made him smirk. But he longed to experience the mystery of the birth and death cycle for himself. To beget, and to behold his own children. In his circle of acquaintances, and even amongst his acquaintance's acquaintances, there wasn't a single person who had won the sweepstakes. Some said that the wins were fabricated, and that the whole thing was a con. There were all sorts of rumors circulating. Any materials that depicted birth and all films about children were banned, so as not to arouse people's parental instincts. Children were brought up in special establishments, and were only allowed to mix with other people when they became young men and women. The concepts of past and future became more vague with every year. People lived in the constant safety of the present.

The waiting was dragging on, so to try and pass the time more quickly Fallon clicked on the websites for the previous sweepstakes, using the screen on the wall. Motley crowds of sweepstake partygoers, filling the city square, slid past his eyes. Until a certain moment had passed, any one of them could potentially be a winner. On the last occasion it had been raining too. A rain cover had been inflated above the square, and it had depicted a clear sky, with a golden sun blazing between white clouds. Despite the fact that the temperature was only a couple of degrees, the heat of summer had persisted under the rain cover. People were dancing. They sang songs, and their voices merged into one. They watched the programs about the legendary suffering of their forefathers. Fallon saw himself among the others—happily jumping up and down locked arm-in-arm with his friends and swaying in time with the songs. As the party reached a climax, the winners of the lottery were revealed. They announced the first winner, who was shown in close-up on the screen. His face reflected genuine happiness and surprise. Fallon was sure there wasn't a single actor who could play surprise so true to life. The winner rushed up onto the stage. Then he froze awkwardly. As the first prize winner he had to make his choice. He was obviously confused. He couldn't decide which to choose.

Fallon paused the film. He tried to imagine himself in the place of the winner. He tried to make the choice in his place. To perform the task that so rarely presented itself in real life. Naturally everyone who took part in the sweepstakes had already picked out their favorite ages ago. True, their choice may have changed several times in the course of the preceding months, but by the day of the sweepstakes it had already been finalized. But in the harsh light of reality the winner was confused—suddenly he realized that the choice he would make was final, and that he couldn't start this game over again from the beginning. He knew that everything that would happen in his future life depended on this one moment, right here and right now.

Now then, muttered Fallon, and he opened the website that showed the girls who were being offered as prizes today. First there was Geir, a chubby girl with a sweet smile, then Aneri, a blonde with a haughty expression, then a perky little brunette called Keddy, then Urlis with her thick legs but kind heart, and finally Etti.

Etti . . . etti . . . et-tett-ti, Fallon sang, watching a slow-motion video of her. There she was. The right choice. The dream woman. He liked Etti's sincerity, simplicity, modesty—everything about her. He savored her every movement, he ran his eyes repeatedly over her wide hips, well suited for bearing the embryo that would grow in her womb, then at her slender waist, then upwards towards her large, round breasts, from which their baby could suck rich milk. Fallon fell into a dreamlike state as he replayed the video of Etti, and he lost all sense of time. He came back down to reality at the very moment that the official festivities were about to start.

He had to be there in person. He couldn't watch such an important event from the screen. He had to capture every sound, smell, and movement in his memory. He hurriedly spruced himself up and ordered a car. Before leaving he had a farewell look at the green blades of grass outside the window, which already seemed to have grown a bit taller, and he felt very sure that fate had chosen him this time.

Fallon punched the destination into the map on the dashboard and saved it to the car's memory. He tried to suppress a strange feeling of excitement as he considered that tomorrow he would have to order a two-passenger car, and his vision of the future started to fill out with various changes, large and small. By the time the car had stopped in front of the town square and he had woken from his daydream, he had already painted himself a vivid picture of a completely new and wholesome life. He was reeling slightly as he passed through the gates of the square, but when he joined his friends Alpo and Keithnal, a strange thought crossed his mind: if he didn't win today, he would never be able to get over the disappointment.

He danced and stamped his feet with the other men, some of them younger, some of them older, and they all chanted slogans and sang in one voice. An absurd thought pounded away ever more insistently in his head: if he didn't win, then he simply couldn't carry on living. He was powerless in the face of the brutal persistence of that thought. In his mind's eye an awful, catastrophic image of the future kept appearing, where some other man would triumphantly take Etti from that stage in the town square.

Although the weeks had been dragging on before, and the day of the sweepstakes had simply not wanted to arrive, the time now started to race fecklessly past. It seemed like he had only just arrived at the square when the girls stepped onto the stage: Aneri, Geir, Keddy, Urlis, and Etti. Fallon tore himself away from his friends and started rudely elbowing his way towards the stage. What he now saw before him was not a moving three-dimensional website on his apartment wall, but something completely different—real and true, just like the blade of grass alive in the concrete crack, just like the pain of pushing one's fingernails into the skin on one's arm. Fallon had now arrived directly in front of the stage, face flushed and breathing heavily.

The sweepstakes machine was already working. Fallon closed his eyes, and then opened them again right away to see the name that appeared on the screen. It was Severi Viirpuu. When the winner climbed up to the stage, Fallon felt like there was an enraged monster inside him that he had previously known nothing about. If he even touches Etti I'll run onto the stage and smash his face in, thought Fallon. He had never had thoughts like that before, but it only took a moment for them to seem normal. Now they seemed familiar, almost instinctual.

Severi Viirpuu rolled his eyes and looked visibly disoriented. "I'll take that one," he mumbled indistinctly.

"Which one?" yelled the head administrator. "Once the choice is made, take the girl in your arms!"

Severi took a couple of shy steps forward at first, but then he started to walk like a proper man, and he went right up to Aneri and put his arms around her. The ear-splitting cries of jubilation reverberated around the whole town square. The orchestra blasted out a fanfare, and the unified choirs began to sing songs of praise, but Fallon realized that he was already soaking with sweat, and he started shivering to the core.

Then silence fell on the square again. It was such a deep silence that one could hear the gentle hum of the sweepstakes machine as it worked away. Then a name lit up on the giant display: Fallon Alanit.

What happened next was like a beautiful, vivid dream.

Late that night, after much celebrating, the two-passenger car finally stopped in front of Fallon's house, he helped Etti out, and he felt that his feet were finally back on firm ground. There he was, alone with his beloved for the first time. It was a wonderful feeling.

"I love you!" he exclaimed, putting the full force of his feelings into those three words. Etti didn't answer. Fallon's lip drooped. He had never seen a film where a declaration of love went unanswered. Those films just didn't exist!

His stupid expression made Fallon's moon-shaped, pig-eyed face look even uglier. "I love you!" he repeated.

Etti looked him over from head to toe. The young woman's face didn't express love, just undisguised contempt.

A VIEW OF A LATE TRAIN

Panting, his heart pounding, the palm of his hand pressing against his chest with fingers splayed, Enden crashes down onto the bench with the whole weight of his body. The warped plywood takes his frame and supports it, as if he were sitting in someone's lap. For a moment it occurs to him that the bench is unexpectedly comfortable, and then he looks over at the electric clock jutting out from the wall above the ticket office. The big hand is just in the process of moving, shifting one minute forwards with an audible click, and then it comes to a standstill, waiting for the next sixty seconds to pass. Waiting, calmly counting the time, without realizing that its own forward motion is unimportant, that in fact it is its smaller colleague that gives its movements meaning.

As soon as he notices the clock, the person sitting on the bench could compare two numbers—the time in the timetable and the time on the station clock—and he would be surprised to note that the convergence of the two numbers does not mean that the train has already departed, for he would be able to see it through the window to his left. The panting traveler would realize that there is still some time left, and despite the agitated clanging of the bell and the cars waiting behind the railway crossing gate, now visible through the windows on the right of the station building, he wouldn't have to hurry. He would be able to walk up to the ticket office with a measured pace.

"Into town, please," Enden would say, catching his breath and pushing the money through the half-moon-shaped hatch. He would say "to town" without mentioning the name of the station, and he would be listening carefully in case the rumble of the approaching train is already audible.

In fact Enden could say that he is already in town, or more

precisely in the suburbs of the town, on the edge of town, which to anyone coming from further afield would mean already in town. But not for him, and not for the elderly ticket vendor with graying blond hair, who would type on the ticket machine keyboard using just the tips of her fingers, and then observe with a slight air of ceremony as the machine ejects a ticket, accompanied by a whirring sound. One could imagine that this is the high point of her job, her moment of glory, since it is only thanks to her handiwork that a correctly printed ticket would now be ready to be torn from the machine. She would appear to take a modest pride in the whole process—her work has not turned into a daily routine yet, and as she sits at the cash till on what would be her second or third day there would still seem to be some sense in it all. She still curls her hair or styles it in the morning and puts on one of her best dresses, giving careful consideration as to whether it looks too fancy . . .

Of course it would be possible that this is just be the panting customer's fleeting impression, to be forgotten the next second, lost from his thoughts, but that wouldn't mean that the ticket vendor's slightly ceremonial expression couldn't come back some time later (a week, or a couple of years later), completely unexpectedly, this time for no certain reason, just for the sake of it, like a star falling in the August sky or the ripple caused by a fish on a smooth lake surface.

If Enden were to turn around in front of the ticket office and walk in the direction of the station exit, he would see for the first time that he is not alone in the waiting room. It's understandable that he has not had the time nor any reason to look around earlier, as he would not be used to running, so his legs would have felt soft, like they were made from cotton wool, all his energy had been expended, and all he could see was the seat with its plywood back. But now, satisfied at the thought that he had arrived in time and even managed to buy a ticket, Enden would let himself have a better look around, casting his gaze around the station building until it alights on two people: a young man with a bottle of beer sitting on the bench in front of the window and a youngish woman sitting opposite him. One look would be enough for Enden to establish that these people weren't about to get onto a train, or at least that they didn't plan to travel on the train that, according to the timetable, was about to arrive. As he lets the door with its over-tightened spring close with a noisy thud behind him, Enden would suddenly get the mistaken impression that there was something uniting the people sitting in the room, that the bonds between the two of them might be greater than any differences. He would think the strange thought that had just popped into his head while simultaneously looking appraisingly over the dozen or so helpless people waiting for the train, standing in a row on the platform, their heads all turned expectantly to the left.

The jarring warning sound of the bell would grow in volume and then die out, but it would still be felt during the moments of silence, making everyone tense. The sense that the moment is fast approaching would penetrate every single brick of the station building, although it is not there yet.

Enden would walk from the doorway straight along the track to a bordering plot of grass, and from there he would see a two-hundred-meter stretch of track. All of the people standing on the platform would be looking in the same direction, but there would be no train on the tracks. Only now would the sudden decrease in air pressure cause Enden to feel slightly dizzy. His legs would grow heavy and he would still be short of breath, and he would not be particularly surprised if, to top it all, an image of a curtain catching fire were to appear in his mind's eye, completely dominating his senses.

Enden would have expected and feared that something like that would happen. He would have been subconsciously preparing for it for some time.

(Just as one could have assumed: *the yellowy-orange-red heating element sooner or later sets fire to the bleached, faded cotton curtain with blue spots, and most probably a flame of the same color blazes upwards through the curtain material.*)

Now Enden would step onto the first concrete step of the platform, but he would turn his whole body to the left and would stay standing level with the window of the station building. Through the window the round clock would still be visible, and the large hand would have already reached three markers beyond the time in the timetable, making the timetable irrelevant, creating a new version of the timetable.

Then he would watch as a running man appears from behind the white-plastered building and arrives at the railway crossing—with no hat, his coat flapping wide open. Suddenly he would stop running and start walking at a deliberately slow pace towards the platform, he would come to a halt in the middle of the tracks and would begin buttoning up his coat.

To the left of the man buttoning his coat, next to the roof of a two-story wooden house, from somewhere behind the leafless birch trees, a dark plume of smoke would shoot upwards.

Enden would shift his eyes quickly away, he would look through the gleaming, recently-cleaned windows into the station building, where a shapely young woman would be sitting in the light of the sun which would have come out from behind the clouds, and right in front of her he would see a young man's spiky-haired head, jerking rhythmically backwards and forwards.

Suddenly an even more jarring sound would be heard above the nightmarish ringing of the bell—a siren, like the sound of a voice crying out, distorted by fear.

Enden would fleetingly perceive a red blur of something moving quickly past and a blue flashing light, but nothing recognizable, just an interplay of colors impinging on his senses.

He would choose not to turn and look in the direction of the main road, because he already knew what he would see there.

Enden would instead look through the windowpane at the woman bathed in sunlight, with her ample breasts rising and falling under her gray coat. It would seem as if she were looking him straight in the eyes, but she would in fact be watching the young man, who was closer to her, sitting in the same room. The woman's plump lips, coated with red lipstick, would part slightly, a black hole or abyss would start to appear, and a surprised expression would come over her face. The woman's pale knees, illuminated provocatively by the sunlight, would suddenly close firmly against each other, then the woman would stand up, rush quickly out through the door, walk past Enden, and come to a standstill a few steps away. (Her breasts still rising and falling. Her face flushed. Shifting her weight from foot to foot.)

A little later the woman would lazily lift a bag that had seen better days up to her stomach and grope around for something in it. She would take out an apple which she would quickly sink her teeth into with an audible crunching sound.

As far as I'm aware the bell should only start ringing when the train has departed the previous station, Enden would think, recalling something he had once heard, or maybe thought up himself.

He would assume that something had happened to the train.

At that moment a fire engine would come racing down the main road with its siren wailing and would turn onto the side street (its brakes grinding or its tires screeching). Behind the bare trees the smoke would already be rising into the sky.

Suddenly Enden would feel unable to stand in one spot any longer, and he would hurry over to the platform. The rails would be shining bluish white, and ocher-colored stones, black in places, would be piled up around the sleepers. Enden would recall that during his childhood the other boys had pressed their ears against the metal of the tracks to hear the distant rumble of the train. He just pretended to do it, keeping his ear away from the track and shouting out to the others that he could hear it as well.

"This train is usually on time," Enden would hear the voice of a woman standing nearby say, and immediately a cap-style hat would enter his field of vision—or more precisely a beret-style cap—together with a brown coat with white flecks, and they would both lean over the edge of the platform to have a look. The platform would be long and would make a bleak impression, and there would only be around ten people waiting by the stopping point for the first and second carriages, all visibly tense. More precisely: five women, four men, and three children. They would be little children, four or five years old, one boy and two girls, and the whole time they would be holding on to the hands of a very beautiful woman with dark hair

The clock's big hand would have passed the time in the timetable by a good five minutes now.

The queue of cars behind the railway crossing gate would be growing longer and longer. He would count eleven of them, and the rest of them that he imagines are there would be hidden behind the white-plastered building. There would only be eight cars visible on the other side of the railway crossing gate, because the station building would obscure the others from view. The station building itself would be built in the style of the early 1900s, but later daubed over with an inappropriate strontium yellow color. Enden would locate another color in his memories—a dark greenish-blue—and as one would expect he would then have a different mental image of his surroundings.

I shouldn't have come here, he would think.

The thought "I shouldn't have" would enter Enden's consciousness for the first time, initially by chance, triggered by something else, but it would immediately make itself comfortable and would stretch out next to the thought "I must." It would be an unfair competition, and like it or not it would redirect and alter many other thoughts, and Enden would sense with alarm that the new thoughts are much more familiar to him than the old ones. The old thoughts would have been borrowed like a masquerade costume, intended to be used just once, and if his heart continued racing, he would know that it wasn't from hurrying for the train, but because of all those unfamiliar thoughts that had installed themselves in his head.

Maybe he would notice that the black smoke coming from behind the bare trees had now turned a whitish blue.

Thinking about why the train was late, Enden might conclude that an accident had happened: it could have been some drunk, some elderly person, some child—it wouldn't matter which. It would be someone who wasn't fully responsible for their actions, and who out of carelessness, a lapse in attention, or drunkenness might have taken a fateful step and ended up under the wheels of the train. Enden could deliberate that the accident—the tragic event—would unavoidably lead to a situation where the plans, schedules, and meeting times of many decent, honest, considerate people would be thrown into disarray, and they would then have to make efforts to retie the threads that had unraveled due to someone else's actions.

Enden could conclude that the accident was caused by a careless motorist.

Or the railway switchman's carelessness, or that of the railway company in general.

Enden would love more than anything for everything to be in good order. To have an orderly and predictable life. He would like to think that every movement had some sense and purpose through which life would create a harmonious composition, which even some glaring dissonance could not spoil. He was haunted by a specter, a strange memory of being taken as a young man to an old master painter's studio, where the air was blue with cigarette smoke, and where there had been cigarette butts and bottles lying all around. The half-drunk painter sat slumped in his chair, which creaked and squeaked as he rocked backwards and forwards, and in front of him on the easel was a fairly large landscape painting that was already finished (95 x 130 cm—for some reason those numbers, carelessly scrawled onto the back of the canvas, had fixed themselves in his memory). It depicted a forest grove painted with a Corot-style color scheme, where the weather was gloomy but some gay yellow flowers were radiant in the grass. The visitors gave the painting reserved but sincere praise. They knew that it was a picture intended to be displayed in a gallery, and that it would take its place in the history of art.

"Too harmonious, disgustingly harmonious," the master grumbled, and he daubed a tiny orangey-yellow dog into the right hand corner of the painting, in between the blades of grass. But it was out of proportion and ugly. "There should always be at least one dog in the picture somewhere," the master mumbled contentedly. At the time Enden had giggled as he thought to himself: The master has put a dog in the right hand corner of the picture, just above the signature, but it hasn't spoiled the harmony.

If Enden were to turn his head to the left again, there would be something different in the railway scene, although he wouldn't initially realize that it is the nose of the approaching train. It would be blackish blue, having lost its original color over the course of time and taken on an indeterminate dark tone. It would get bigger and bigger, bringing the thunderous noise with it, looming above the straight line of the railway track. It would devour the line as it approached, sucking it into its long stomach.

For no particular reason Enden would take a step closer to the edge of the platform, much closer to the meter-and-a-half-deep gulf, where he would be able to see the metal rubbed smooth by the train wheels, the joints in the rails, and the dark nails that fastened them to the sleepers. He would see a large blackish-brown patch of oil on the gravel with a few cigarette butts with golden and ocher-yellow tips lying in it, and he would feel a strong desire to smoke. His hand would slide into his jacket pocket, where his fingers would grope around feeling for the edges of the packet of cigarettes. He would see the outlines of the box, the red upper half and white lower half with the black writing on it.

Enden would squeeze the pack between his fingers to try and ease the intolerable, overpowering urge to smoke. He would knock the box of matches against the back of his hand, making a rustling sound, but the front of the approaching train—like a giant wall—would by then be little more than a meter away, and now—in the course of this split second—he would be able to jump down from the platform edge.

Enden would step forwards, but then quickly recoil, pulling himself back from the edge, and his body would even bend backwards, trying to get as far away as possible from the arriving wall. He would feel a weak but perceptible rush of air against his face. The train would now barely be moving, but it would still easily be able to pulverize Enden under its wheels.

The arriving train would bring nothing more to the passenger, who had pulled away to a safe distance, than a gust of wind that would blow across his face and then expend itself in the bare bushes behind the platform.

The carriage doors would open right in front of Enden; in one of them the glass would be missing from the window, while the other would be cracked. An old woman carrying a bag full of empty bottles would appear in the doorway and then step off the train. One by one she would carefully place her feet, clad in woolen socks, onto the safe concrete.

At that moment the round clock on the platform would show that the train was six minutes late.

Enden would step a little to one side to let the old woman past, but right away someone would shove in front of him into the carriage—a youngish man in a blue jacket, who would look like he was troubled by a constant fear of missing out on something. But this time the young man's shoving might be justified, the carriage would be full of passengers, a mixture of different people all similarly dressed, who would have occupied nearly all the seats.

Having got into the carriage Enden would stop for a moment between the sliding doors, then without much further thought he would make straight for an empty seat that catches his eye. As he sits down, Enden would look at the old man sitting across from him, who would have put his hat—a worn-out fur hat he had had for years—on his knees and would be fiddling with the strap with his bony fingers. A moment later Enden would happen to turn and look out of the window in the direction of the smoke, which was still coming from behind the bare trees.

The train would start moving with a jerk, the landscape outside would start sliding past, at first slowly, then faster and faster. The smoke rising towards the yellowy-white clouds would recede to the left until it disappeared completely from view. Now the smoke would only be visible if one turned one's head, which Enden would have done from time to time if the body next to him had not been pressing him towards the edge of the seat.

Enden would feel more and more oppressed by the unpleasant thought that his leg would have to be pressed tightly against another person's for the rest of the journey.

He would decide to change carriages at the next stop to look for a better place to sit, but very soon his eyes would alight on the knees of the woman sitting next to him, which would be exposed under her open coat, and he would notice that they are naked and whitish pink, and would surmise that she had pulled her boots directly on to naked legs, which would seem peculiar, considering the chilly late autumn weather. Enden would lift his gaze in surprise and he would see that the woman was the same one who had been sitting on the bench in the station building.

They say that things turn red from the cold, he would think, but the woman's knees were a whitish pink instead. And he would start to feel increasingly aroused, as if he had seen something really explicit.

Suddenly the leg situated next to him would cease to be a chance encounter, something irritating, it would become a woman's leg, the flesh of the opposite sex, positioned provocatively close to his own body. To Enden it would seem that the woman's proximity was not accidental (maybe she really did push the toe of her boot against his shoe?), but premeditated and purposeful, and he would shift his trembling foot gradually to one side, further away from the other foot.

He should get a grip on himself, he would think. But then, doubtlessly thinking nothing of it, the woman sitting next to him would scratch her nose or eyebrow, so that when she lowered her hand Enden would be able to feel her ample breast weighing against his arm. He might momentarily smell wine on her breath as well. He would peek out of the corner of his eye at his neighbor's small, perfectly-shaped nose, her permed reddish hair, and again at those knees flashing provocatively from her open coat, tempting him to touch them. This time they are parted, with a gap of ten centimeters between them. An empty space there between them, like a void.

The train would make a brief stop and then start moving again, and Enden would press his leg even closer against the woman's and fleetingly feel a reciprocal pressure. He would recall how as a young boy he would shove his way into the pitch black cinema hall with the other latecomers, after the topical news digest had finished, so that he could sit in the more expensive back row, although he had bought the cheapest possible ticket. On one occasion some woman sat herself down next to him after the lights had already been put out. He had wanted to sit one or two chairs further away, as the cinema was half empty, but for some reason he didn't. He tried to concentrate on the film, which he had already seen once or twice before. It was an adult film with a naked woman briefly appearing in it. And when that part of the film finally arrived, displayed in black and white on the screen in front of him, he felt the woman's leg against his own, and it started to tremble oddly.

Enden remembered that a little later the woman shifted closer to him, pressing her shoulder against his, and putting her dazzlingly white hand on the armrest separating them. He peeked quickly at her features, still and expressionless like a mask, spectral white in the darkness of the cinema, and wanted to move his trembling leg to one side or shift his body towards the far edge of the chair, but he was paralyzed by a feeling he had never had before. Even when the woman's hand fleetingly touched his thigh he didn't do anything about it. He let the woman's fingers grope him, his whole body trembling, and by then he wanted nothing else but that. The woman's fingers worked their miracles with resolute determination right through to the end of the film, conjuring eruptions of pleasure. Only when the final titles appeared did the fingers depart, and with them the woman herself, shoving her way hurriedly towards the exit.

In a split second that memory would impinge into Enden's consciousness, becoming increasingly more vivid, until he would become aware of an unbearable lust beginning to churn inside him again. He would yearn to push his hardened member into the woman sitting next to him—to rapidly relieve the sudden tension which had overcome him. To free his brain and relax his body, so that he would be able to think of other more important things.

It's ridiculous, Enden would say out loud. Almost out loud, but in fact inaudibly. In his conscious thoughts the phrase would sound like someone yawning in a concert hall, during the deathly silence just before the conductor lifts his baton for the opening downbeat.

It's almost as if we had spoken (he would think, analyzing the situation)*, the leg pressing against me says much more than words alone. And we have made the deal now—uttered our secret* *desires—although both of us have left ourselves time to think it over and we have both prepared an exit plan. But in a moment it could all turn to nothing, it would be enough for one of us to get up and leave the other behind without looking back—it would remain just a chance, fleeting flirtation, or something like that. We could later imagine what might have happened, and it would be as if it had actually happened.*

The woman by his side would sigh quietly, although loudly enough to be heard over the thundering of the train.

Better a bird in the hand than two in the bush—Enden would think with a smile, as his neighbor shifts her shoulder closer against his. Now he would clearly hear her uneven breathing, which would spread quickly to him as well, and turn into what was now a pleasant (no longer unsettling) charge of erotic energy.

The train would change direction, taking a north-eastern course, and the low autumn sun would shine directly into the windows, not the windows next to him, but the ones opposite, and so the rays of sunlight wouldn't reach further than the central aisle, but would come to a halt at the edge of the seat, waiting for the next bend in the track. Continuing the earlier theme, Enden would remember a story he had once heard about how someone on a packed bus had gotten turned on by a woman who had rubbed her bottom up against him completely unambiguously. When the bus stopped by a patch of forest near the sea both of them got off, they did the deed on a patch of heather under the pine trees, and, without exchanging a single word, traveled onwards on the next bus, or the one after it.

As he remembers that story, the vague notion would enter Enden's mind that there is a lakeside pine forest two stops away, close to the railway.

"Tickets please!" a woman's voice, loud and masculine, would suddenly ring out. It would be a demand, an order, forcing the passengers to obey, making their hands reach into their bags and pockets. Enden would shove his fingers into his coat pocket, where something would rustle next to the matchbox and packet of cigarettes. Now he would really be pleased that the train had been late and he had managed to buy a ticket. He wouldn't be daunted by the thought of paying a fine, which was a trifling sum for him, but rather by the thought that the other passengers could get the wrong impression of him. They would take him for a thief—by traveling without a ticket he would be depriving the railway workers of their wages, and it would be impossible keep the railway running like that.

Taking back his ticket from the inspector, Enden would notice that the woman sitting beside him was still rummaging in her bag, and at the same moment he would already realize that she wouldn't find a ticket in her bag. No ticket had ever been bought. There had never even been any intention of buying one.

The ticket inspector would take a step closer. She would squeeze past the knees of the people sitting on the edges of their seats, so as to prevent the suspected fare dodger from getting away. She probably has plenty of experience in such situations, and she would wait patiently with her hand outstretched while the woman fumbled in her bag and turned her pockets inside out. But in the end the ticket inspector's patience would run out, and she would say how much the fine was, opening the imitation leather folder to take out a receipt book.

"I haven't got any money," the woman would say.

It wouldn't have initially occurred to Enden to pay the woman's fine, but when she opened her mouth he would hear her voice: rich, sonorous, cooing coquettishly (which, considering the ticket inspector's gender and stern expression, would be more than a little inappropriate). He would conclude that someone with a voice like that might sing in an amateur choir or act in a theater group. Enden would take a fresh look at his neighbor, and his attention would first be drawn towards the frayed sleeve of her worn-out coat (which would arouse a sentimental feeling of sympathy in him). Then his eye would be caught by her hands, which are not well kempt and show traces of manual work, and on the middle finger of her left hand he would see the ring left from a failed marriage (or maybe following the death of her husband?). Only then would he take a longer look at her face, which would be made up, made prettier, as if she were going out somewhere (to a restaurant, the theater, a concert?!), but it wouldn't be done with expensive products or any skill, just cheaply and provocatively. He would discover that this face was already covered in fine lines and noticeable wrinkles in places, and no attempt would have been made to smooth over them with face cream or powder.

Enden might conclude that the woman comes from the countryside just outside town, and probably lives in one of those rows of new houses built in a village or on a former collective farm—a house without roots that could never be a home to anyone. A place where people come and live for several years before moving on to live somewhere else. He couldn't begin to guess how the people in those houses (including this woman) earn their daily bread. He couldn't know anything about those people's lives. There was no one in his circle of acquaintances who might live in a house like that.

He would suddenly get a feeling that would seem quite odd at the time—he would feel compassion: *times must have been really tough for the poor dear lately, her life has gone awry, fate has been unkind to her, she has been left without the things she deserves in life.*

"Your passport, please," the ticket inspector would say, continuing to perform her duties according to a clear schema that left no place for sympathy, understanding, or any other feelings.

"I don't have my documents with me," the woman would say, at which the ticket inspector would instruct her to come with her.

The woman would be about to get up, her face wouldn't express the slightest emotion, neither fear nor embarrassment—as if she was completely indifferent to what was happening, or was maybe just used to such situations.

"Wait," Enden would say quickly. "I'll pay the fine, how much is it?"

He would have carelessly said that quite loudly: the woman, the ticket inspector, and several other fellow passengers would turn their curious, expectant faces in his direction. The man across from him would pick up his fur hat, push it onto his head, and stand up. The ticket inspector would take a step backwards to let the old man past, then she would squeeze by the passenger's knees and take up position in the vacated seat. She would search for something in her pocket, pull out a handkerchief, and wipe her nose. She would look tired, with a feverish haze in her eyes and dark rings under them.

She's probably ill, she must have caught a cold from a draft, or when her skin was wet with perspiration, Enden would think, taking his wallet from the breast pocket of his jacket.

The ticket inspector would spend a long time writing out the receipt, she would look for the change for a while, count it twice over, and then she would finally hand it to Enden, asking him slowly, as if trying to hold back her rage: "Why did you do that?"

"I don't know," Enden would answer after a brief delay, his voice barely audible, as if he were talking to himself and was taken aback by the unexpected, pointless question. As if he had been forced to question his own actions, because the ticket inspector had hit on something he himself didn't want to admit.

"People should be punished," the ticket inspector would say in an unnecessarily loud voice, almost as if she were announcing her conviction to the whole carriage. And she would get up, rubbing past the passengers knees, displaying the rounded bulge of her bottom under the tight skirt of her work uniform.

"I have no idea how to thank you . . . you know, I was supposed to get some money this morning . . ." the woman would start to say in a hurried whisper, but Enden would bring her to a halt in mid-flow.

"Oh, forget it," Enden would say—for some reason also in a half-whisper—and he would then turn demonstratively to look out of the window, where there would be nothing worth seeing.

People should be punished, he would think, *I said forget it*, he would think.

Enden would now start to feel the almost burning heat of the woman's body against his. The brief nudge, first harder, then softer, of her knee against his own, which was tense with anticipation. Then the nudging would become brazenly provocative, and if he were to accidentally nudge her back, then he would hear (or he would imagine that he heard) a muffled sigh. Now he would have no doubts about where the woman's thoughts were heading. He would have her thoughts mapped out in his head, and he would puzzle over what had made her choose him from amongst the other men. Enden was not so stupid as to believe that he was irresistibly attractive, but he couldn't find any other motivation for the woman's lewd behavior. Maybe I'm just her type, he would conclude, getting excited like a teenage boy, and then it would seem like only unbridled lust could allow him to escape himself and the leaden thoughts weighing on him.

That's how to postpone the unpostponable, he would think. Just ruthlessly grab the time! The train's six-minute delay had made his earlier hurrying pointless. Now six minutes could be turned into sixty, or a hundred and eighty, and in all likelihood the end result would still be the same.

I should start talking to the woman now, he would think as he looked out of the window. When the train starts to brake for the next stop, I'll get up and invite her to come with me. She probably wouldn't get up right away, she'd wait for a moment and then come stand with me and wait for the door to open. When the train stops we would walk silently along the empty platform, then along a narrow track which takes us to the main road, where there would be a patch of forest with twisted pine trees, just a stone's throw away. The whole time I would be walking a little ahead of her, I would feel her at my back, following me, then I would see a suitable stump between the trees, where I could sit down and light a cigarette. I would take a long deep drag of the cigarette and the woman would ask me falteringly what would happen now, at which point I would slide my hand up her cold leg until my fingers reached the warm, clammy spot between them. Meanwhile the woman would have closed her eyes, maybe her body would be ready to offer itself up to me, but her rational side would still be telling her not to: Not here, she would say with a choking voice—let's go to my place, the children are at school . . . and then, after a brief pause, she would ask timidly, maybe stuttering, if she could borrow some money . . .

And it's not that Enden would be unwilling to part with the money, quite the opposite, he would have even offered it himself. He would grin and take a couple of bills from his pocket, and when the woman had hidden them away in her pocket, he would leisurely unbutton his pants and, roughly pushing her head downwards, he would enter her from behind . . .

He would probably only manage a couple of thrusts before he came, but instead of feeling gratified, he would be engulfed in a feeling of total emptiness, overcome by a wave of revulsion with himself and above all the woman, and he would wish that everything from the whole previous hour had never happened . . .

Enden wouldn't want to think about what might happen if this depression were to suddenly turn into rage.

He would have liked to conjure up some arousing mental image, ideally of him entering that woman. It was very likely that the adventure (and it really was an adventure!) would turn out to be quite different, maybe it would even be enjoyable (memorably so). But Enden would be shocked to realize that the cruel images were the most arousing.

Surprisingly, no words would come from his mouth as the train stopped.

But his heart would start beating faster. Enden would briefly look at the woman and would notice a small white scar at one corner of her mouth, roughly a centimeter in length, forking like a tree branch at one end. The woman would force a smile, which would momentarily make her more attractive than she actually was. Enden would smile in response, but he would sense the wretchedness and insincerity of that smile, and the words he had prepared would unexpectedly stick in his throat. He would realize that he hadn't been taking the imaginary adventure at all seriously, and had just been playing with ideas, pretending that he wanted something he actually didn't, and even if the possibility presented itself he would instinctively flee from it at the first opportunity.

In fact, he would feel contempt for the morally degenerate woman, caught between life's spokes, and for a split second he would consider stamping with the full weight of his body onto the tip of her boot, but he would immediately restrain himself. Instead he would carefully place his shoe onto the ground, and navigate his way past his fellow passengers' knees.

Ten seconds or so later, after having stepped onto the windy platform and taken ten paces or so without looking back, Enden would suddenly feel gripped to the core by a sense of regret. Just as if a large fish (a salmon, or a pike weighing more than ten kilos) had slipped off the hook at the very last moment. Or as if he had put a handsome sum of money on a horse that had been in the lead the whole race, but had fallen back just before the finish.

Enden would feel that the sexual tension (like a creeping vine, its shoots slowly growing to entangle him entirely) wasn't ready to leave him alone just yet.

For a moment he would even think about ducking into the filthy station toilet, but he would immediately shudder in disgust—that would be a particularly shameful option, which he would happily exchange for the far more welcome possibility that the woman had actually gotten off the train.

At that very moment the woman would increase her pace, to try and catch up with him and move a little ahead, make herself visible to him. Suddenly that possibility would no longer seem so impossible. Quite the opposite. Enden longs for it and lusts for it, and up to this point in his life he has gotten almost everything he has desired. He would probably also have this woman who has for some inexplicable reason aroused him so much.

Enden would decide to move a couple of steps closer to the end of the platform, as far as the steps that lead down to the tracks. And only then would he look back expectantly.

THOSE ORDINARY THINGS WE CAN'T GET USED TO

I can't understand, and I will never understand, why everything always goes wrong for me, thought Annika, trying hard to hold back her tears.

She felt like a block of wood that someone was doggedly chipping splinters from, so that in the end all that would be left would be a thin sliver, with nothing more to chip away. It's just fate, she thought. Some people have it good all the time, others have to drag themselves through life one way or another. She used the sleeve of her coat to dry her eyes, which were now wet with tears.

The door of the station opened with a loud creak and then shut with a thud, and an attractive woman with two small girls went up to the counter to buy some tickets. As the woman shoved the change back into her purse she cast a fleeting glance towards Annika, and Annika responded with an expression that resembled a smile.

She didn't want anyone to see her crying. That would be like someone peering into an untidy cupboard or a basket of dirty laundry. She had to appear normal to those around her. But she had a splitting headache, and the gulps of wine she had had at Marko's place had only given her short-lived relief.

He's got money to spend on wine, but not for the children, thought Annika, suddenly feeling angry, although there wasn't any point in getting angry. She had already made herself blue with anger, then red, and who knows what else. She didn't have time to get angry anymore, and there wasn't any sense in it anyway. It didn't help her earn any money, it just frayed her nerves.

The door creaked open again and a person in a worn leather jacket entered the station building. His body crashed down onto the bench, his hand reached for the bottle of beer in his pocket, his teeth opened it, he emptied it down his thirsty throat, and then he stared in Annika's direction. What the hell are you looking at, thought Annika, tasting cement in her mouth. She had heard people talk about that, and she thought it might be real cement she could taste now. She recalled that there used to be a water fountain in the station building. Now there was nothing left in the spot next to the heater where it used to be, so all she could do was watch other people slaking their thirst with beer.

Annika had just been slogging away for three days on a potato field. Merle Päraste's partner had taken them to some farm in the middle of Estonia and brought them back again. Autumn had not been particularly rainy, but the cold now threatened to take the potatoes before they had been harvested. This time the work had been pretty decently paid. They had started drinking wine on their way back. She was pretty tipsy by the time she arrived home, and of course Mother had not approved, and had started taking her to task as soon as she walked through the door. By the time Maigi invited her to a party she had been so thoroughly scolded that she didn't need to think for long. She just pulled her coat on over her frock, put her boots on her bare feet, and got into the car. She didn't remember what happened next very well. And what she did remember, she wished she couldn't.

Above all she regretted losing the money. Why, damn it, had she taken money with her at all! Now she was going to be scraping the bottom of the barrel again, she really didn't know how she was going to survive.

You got what you asked for! she chided herself. But what use was that now?

A man came storming into the station building and the door creaked shut with a bang behind him. Outside, the bell was ringing ceaselessly. The man was in his forties, a chubby, slick type with a smooth face, and he was panting audibly. He sat down, landing in the middle of the bench, removed the cap from his shiny, balding head, and started to fan himself with it. The man's light-beige chamois leather jacket, with matching trousers and shoes, created an impression of someone who was always very well-kempt, and he looked out of place, even comical, in the shabby station building. Annika couldn't help grinning. She thought that if she were to see him sitting behind a large desk in some office he would create a completely different impression. He would demand respect, even awe.

But who could have swiped that damned money, she thought the next moment, getting worked up again. When they had gone to buy the wine, no one had asked for money. She remembered that she had bought two packets of candy from the shop for the girls, and she still had them with her. She rummaged in her bag again, dumbly hoping to find something, but of course she couldn't find something that wasn't there. Her fingers just felt some lumps, which were apples.

She realized that taking her purse to a booze-up wasn't the smartest thing to do, but she was worried that her mother would empty it while she was away. And she didn't have time to hide the money. At Kribu's place she had kept her eye on her bag the whole time, but then Marko arrived and, just to taunt him, she started coming on to Villu, who had just been released from prison, and after that everything was just a blur.

That damned Marko, she swore to herself.

The chubby, bald man placed his hat back on his head and went over to buy a ticket. Annika wondered why he was traveling by train. Those types normally have their own cars. Maybe he's lost his license for drunk driving, or he's drunk right now. At that she remembered how it had taken just a couple gulps of wine at Marko's to turn her distress into courage. She had been unable to do anything at all to control the fiery rage which came over her.

"I've lost my driving license," said Marko dejectedly in response to Annika's hectoring. "Now I'm unemployed just like you," he said, pouring the remains of the bottle into the glasses. "You want me to go rob a bank or something . . ."

"Do you realize that your children have nothing to eat," she shouted, to deaf ears.

"Well go and ask for some money from the guy who screwed you last night," Marko said, unusually harshly for him, and he swigged his wine.

Annika took a glass of wine from the table and flung the

contents into Marko's face, then she ran out, slamming the door. Pigs! Pigs! The word rang out in her head.

But compared to that pig Villu, Marko was an angel.

All those things that Villu had whispered in her ear! About how lonely he was, how he hadn't touched a woman in a year and a half, how he was head over heels in love. At first Annika had just played along to tease Marko, but after that the picture started getting blurry, and by the time she came to her senses it was already too late. Villu was thrusting away to the accompaniment of the drunken racket coming from the kitchen.

And then when dawn broke some Russian was having his turn.

When Annika realized what was happening she had immediately tried to push the man off, but he started swearing, and told her that he had paid Villu.

"What do you mean paid?" asked Annika, confused. "I paid three hundred to screw you," the Russian said gruffly.

Annika still didn't understand, and at first she thought it was her basic Russian which was to blame, but when she finally realized what had happened she completely lost control of herself. By that point the Russian thought he had finally managed to explain things to her, and so he doggedly continued his half-finished business.

Things are what they are, thought Annika despairingly, wanting above all to have a shower. Every time she went out her mother would ask her if she had put on clean underwear, as if she were still a little child. Just think how awful it would be if you got run over and they found you wearing dirty underwear, she lectured . . .

When Annika finally escaped the grips of the Russian and got out onto the street, she realized that she knew the part of town where the party had been—it was the same area where Marko lived, or to be more precise, where she and Marko had lived when they were still together. She had wanted to have a shower at Marko's, but when she discovered that her purse had gone missing she got so upset that she immediately got into a stupid, pointless argument with him.

Now Annika was sitting in the railway station, and she didn't know what to do with herself. It suddenly occurred to her that it must have been that damned Villu who had swiped her purse, and she couldn't understand why she had not realized that earlier. Maybe it was just hard for her to comprehend that someone could really be so cruel.

But that bastard was a smooth talker and had Brad Pitt looks, she thought, struggling to hold back her tears.

The body of the beer drinker on the bench opposite was convulsing strangely, and she noticed with alarm that something light in color was sticking out between his fingers, which were clad in leather gloves. Jesus, that idiot is jerking off! There are sick people everywhere, she thought despairingly, and rushed outside, grabbing her bag from the bench.

The door creaked plaintively and then shut behind her with a resounding bang.

It was cool outside, she felt a cutting wind across her bare knees, and the cold reached up between her legs. Annika took an apple out of her bag and sunk her teeth into it. She chewed at the bland fruit, which tasted like sawdust. A fire engine sped along the main road with its lights flashing, and a moment later an ambulance went the same direction, its siren wailing. I should have set fire to that place, she said cursing angrily. That old wooden house would have probably gone up in a flash, and that would have been just what they deserved, she thought, recalling the scene in the trashed room after the drunken party, with Villu sleeping on the floor under the table in some man's arms.

From behind the bare spruce trees a plume of smoke rose skywards, not from where the party had been, but from a different part of town.

She suddenly felt ashamed for having those thoughts of revenge. Maybe right now someone was burning to death, or suffocating in acrid smoke. She had seen fires on television, and she believed that no one should have to suffer something so awful. Not even her enemies . . . But God will punish them, she thought. Such unfairness does not go unpunished.

But then why was God always punishing her?

Why could God not arrange for her to find a fat pile of money right now, or at least enough for her to get home. Her mother wouldn't actually hit her. She would curse her out for a couple of days, but eventually she'd calm down.

When the children came home from school she would give them the candy. A packet of chews for each of them. The girls liked those, and that would cheer them up a bit.

But then what would happen tomorrow, and the day after tomorrow, Annika contemplated, full of fear and anguish. It was an awful feeling. Sometimes it came over her like an affliction, she would feel a pain in her heart and would want to jump out of her own skin. And what made her feel all the more helpless was that this fear had no face: she didn't actually know what it was that she was afraid of.

I can't go home without any money, she thought. If I had behaved myself well, then Marko would have given me some money. He normally gives me something if he can, even if it's only a little. He's a kind-hearted person. But normally he doesn't have any money, because he just can't help pouring it all down his throat. A couple of years ago she had tried finishing off his vodka herself, so that he'd be able to go to work the next day. But how long can you go on like that . . .

Suddenly Annika remembered—how had she not remembered it earlier!—before she had gone to pick potatoes, Malle, one of her mother's former colleagues, had mentioned a temporary job that might suit Annika. She could go and see Malle, find out more about the job, and borrow some money. Malle was sure to be at home. What else could a retiree do in the mornings other than gawp at TV soaps?

When Annika boarded the train that had just arrived, she felt she had found an escape route, that her situation would now start to improve, and that she could put her worries behind her for good.

The carriage was full of passengers. Annika spotted an empty space next to the chubby man she had seen buying a ticket at the station, and she made her way towards it. She pushed her way through to the seat, toying with the thought that if the ticket inspector didn't come by then the whole day would be a lucky one—Malle would be at home, she would get that job, and Malle would lend her some money, which of course she'd be able to pay back from her first paycheck.

The train started with a jerk, and the landscape outside started to slide past, at first slowly, then faster and faster. To the left, the smoke that was rising towards the yellowy-white clouds moved further away until it was completely lost from view. Annika felt the man sitting next to her pressing his thigh tightly against hers; it was uncomfortable, but she had nowhere to run, all the other carriages were probably full just like this one. At least she could sit down in this carriage, and it wasn't cold. Suddenly she felt the man sitting next to her press the tip of his shoe against her boot. She could see his leg shaking.

Another sicko, thought Annika in disgust, and she felt her nose itching. She had barely managed to lift her hand to rub it when the man pressed his forearm up against her breast.

Screw him, thought Annika wearily, and rubbed her nose a bit, stroking the bridge with her finger. As she put her hand back in her lap she pushed her neighbor roughly towards the window with her shoulder. Any normal person would have understand right away that she wanted nothing to do with him, that she was tolerating him sitting next to her only because that was the situation they found themselves in.

Pretty soon Annika felt a trembling leg pushing up against hers again. She would have happily burst out laughing in the man's face, but then she suddenly remembered how once, a long time ago—or was it only twelve years or so?—she and Marko had gone to the cinema, and half way through the film she had felt the tip of Marko's shoe touch hers, timidly at first, as if by accident, and then his leg had started to quiver. Well I never, she had thought, at last he's started to overcome his shyness, and she longed for him to touch her again, but didn't know how to encourage him. So in the end she had placed her hand on Marko's hand, and then she had felt something she had never felt before.

It was love, she thought, getting sentimental. She remembered how Marko had fleetingly pressed his lips against her cheek that evening.

Maybe it had been his shy character and his fear of getting hurt that had driven him to drink, Annika thought, and she sighed.

"Tickets please!" she heard suddenly. The stern, somehow masculine voice was demanding something that she didn't have. She felt a lump rise in her throat as if she were about to start crying: now everything was ruined—Malle won't be at home, the job will have been taken, and I won't be able to borrow any money. Annika tried to imagine what would happen to her next, but she couldn't. They would probably drag her to the police station, she thought in horror. There was nothing she could do, the stern woman who looked just like a prison warden was standing right in front of her, blocking her escape path.

Annika tried to look like an ordinary passenger searching for her ticket. She rummaged in her bag and coat pockets, but the ticket inspector soon got fed up and started to write out a slip for a fine.

"I haven't got any money," said Annika in one quick breath.

"Your passport, please," said the ticket inspector in an emotionless voice, and Annika suddenly felt a rising anger, which was directed at that woman with a man's voice. She was just like the teacher at school had been, an idiot in women's clothes, a lesbian and a bully. It was because of that teacher that Annika had dropped out of school halfway through, and now someone just like that teacher was treating her the same way, in front of a carriage-load of people. No one ever does anything to stand up to those kinds of people, Annika thought.

"I don't have my documents with me," she forced the words out and stood up, as if she were hoping that the ticket inspector would take her somewhere else, where she didn't have to feel the dozens of pairs of eyes devouring her.

"Wait," said the man sitting next to her suddenly. "I'll pay the fine, how much is it?"

Annika sat back down and closed her eyes. A strange hot flush coursed through her body. It started from the nape of her neck and spread to the tips of her toes, and she started to sweat. When she opened her eyes she saw the old man sitting opposite get up and the ticket inspector sit down in the empty space. Then she shut her eyes again, but this time she left her eyelids very slightly open so that the light could shine through, and she saw a hazy image of the ticket inspector's pale knees, which, as decency required, were pressed tightly together.

What's going on here, she thought, suddenly feeling panicked. Clearly this chubby man has taken an interest in me. Maybe I don't look so ugly today after all; it's a good thing I managed to put on a bit of lipstick and comb my hair before I went to Marko's. Then she glanced to her side. At that very moment the man took a black leather wallet with gold embossed corners from his breast pocket and opened it, revealing what looked to be a massive wad of money. He tugged a note from the section of the wallet full of purple kroons—the other section held different bills with light edges. It occurred to Annika that they might be dollars—maybe he was a filthy rich Estonian expat visiting from abroad. She immediately felt so embarrassed about her appearance that she could have cried. Just a shabby coat pulled over her frock, and she didn't even have any stockings on.

How awful, she thought. And then she started to feel uneasy that something about her had caught the man's attention; after all, he was the kind of man who, judging by his clothes and wallet, would have women falling at his feet. And at the first brothel he came to he could have everything his heart—and his dick—yearned for.

"Why did you do that?" the ticket inspector suddenly asked, and Annika flinched at the harsh tone of her voice.

The man didn't answer at first. Annika stared at the floor and saw a twenty-cent coin lying on the muddy reddish linoleum. It was right next to the tip of the ticket inspector's shiny black shoe, and Annika had the feeling that if she were to lean down to pick it up, the woman would tread on her fingers with the full weight of her body.

When the man finally answered, Annika didn't hear what he said, but another voice said loudly and clearly that people should be punished. Why does God always punish me, thought Annika. Why is everyone staring accusingly in my direction.

Maybe I'm punished for not having any money!

I could say something to this man right now, thought Annika when the ticket inspector had gone. Surely he thinks that I'm indebted to him, that he has some sort of claim to me now. To hell with him! No one asked him to come and start flashing his money around . . . But of course I have to thank him now; everyone is staring in my direction and waiting, and I have to show them that I'm not some sort of ungrateful beast. And so, with a hushed voice, almost whispering, she uttered some words of gratitude.

"Oh, forget it," said the man, and stared out of the window with blank indifference.

Annika soon felt the man pressing his leg against her more firmly. She shifted to one side to try and relieve the discomfort, hoping to find a better position to sit in, moving her leg so as to feel less oppressed by her neighbor's proximity.

He's trying to look like he's staring out of the window, but he's probably dreaming up all kinds of sick things, Annika thought. She felt disgust for the man who had just paid her fine, and the feeling grew more and more unbearable.

Like a maggot who has eaten his full, she thought. He thinks he can buy up the whole world with his money. He's pretending as if what happened wasn't part of some plan, but at the same time he's plotting something vile. He'll probably reveal his demands just before the train arrives at the final station. Quietly and politely, so as not to attract attention.

And what should I do? thought Annika. Should I tell him off . . . or not?

When the train started to slow down, the man got up and looked straight at Annika for a moment, and it seemed as if his mouth moved, although she didn't hear any sounds. Annika smiled, without even knowing why. The man pushed past the other passengers' knees and started to move in the direction of the carriage door, without looking back.

Did he say something? Annika thought uneasily. Did he

invite me to come with him? she thought for a moment, but she soon realized how stupid it would be to get up and follow the man now.

But then why not go, she suddenly thought. This stop is probably closer to Malle's place anyway.

The train came to a halt with a slight jolt. Annika leaned forwards, and although she had not yet decided to get off at this stop, she got up, looking like she was weighing something up for a moment, and then started to move hurriedly towards the exit. She had only just managed to step onto the platform when the doors shut and the train started moving away.

The man was walking at a slow but steady pace. When he got to the end of the platform he turned around to look back. It appeared that he was waiting for Annika, and she felt her heart beating faster and faster, in time with the wheels of the train which were starting to turn. She realized that something very ordinary was about to happen with that man, but she also knew that she wouldn't be able to come to terms with it for the rest of her life.

I have to carry on, she thought, almost shouting out loud at herself. I can't go back. I can't turn back a single moment in my miserable life.

But the man took a step backwards and turned around. And then, unexpectedly, he stepped over the edge of the platform. His body was dragged along between the train and the platform as the train gathered speed, and then it was lost from view.

The train continued onwards, looking like it was shrinking, getting smaller and smaller.

The sun came out from behind the clouds for a moment, and the trees, bare apart from a few leaves, were flooded in the cold yellow autumn light. There was a wind blowing, the clouds were moving fast, and the next minute they were already covering the sun again.

Annika walked to the end of the platform, or to be more accurate she started moving slowly in that direction, centimeter by centimeter. Then she picked up her pace and rushed down the steps, where she came to a sudden halt, as if nailed to the ground. Bloody, mutilated limbs were strewn across the tracks. The torso itself was in the corner, by the edge of the platform, a giant bleeding lump. The chamois leather jacket was lying on the ground right in front of Annika's feet, and beside it she could see the black leather wallet with gold embossed corners.

There was no one to be seen nearby. Just as if everyone had died, thought Annika, fighting back the shriek of horror that was welling in her chest.

THE EVENING PAPER, 18 OCTOBER 1996

Mysterious Victim's Identity Now Known

As previously reported, an unidentified male citizen fell under a train at Lilleküla station on Wednesday morning. He had stepped down from the platform and ended up under the wheels of the train as it began to depart. The train driver only found out about the incident when he reached the final station. He defended himself by saying, "Obviously I'm not obliged to stare into the rear view mirror the whole time the train is moving."

The identity of the victim was unclear for several days. The man, who was somewhere in his forties, did not have a single document in his pocket, and not a single kroon was found on him. The accident was reported several minutes after the train had departed, so it is possible to conclude that someone had emptied the victim's pockets.

A number of new facts have come to light. The victim was the businessman Enden Teero. He was known to be an active and practical-minded person. It seems very unlikely that this was a suicide. The fact that he was in Lilleküla that morning prompted questions among several people who were close to him. It is known that he had paid the fine for a woman who was traveling without a ticket. When Teero went up to the carriage door to get off, the woman also stood up. The train driver claims he saw the woman getting out of the carriage at the last moment, but the distance between her and Teero was too great for her to have been able to push him under the train.

Several other interesting facts came to light yesterday. On Wednesday morning, Teero's great aunt, who owned a large property in the suburbs, was admitted to the hospital with serious burn wounds. Although it had been possible to save her from the burning house, she passed away in the hospital. During the periods when she regained consciousness before dying, she had spoken of Enden in accusatory terms. When the neighbors were questioned, it turned out that Enden had been seen that morning going to visit his great aunt. People had been surprised that he was on foot. The fire department concluded that the source of the fire was a faulty electric stove, but they do not rule out that someone could have deliberately placed flammable items next to the stove.

We have established that Enden's great aunt owned several other properties in the Old Town, and that Enden Teero was her only heir.

A STORY WITH A HAPPY ENDING

Master Jogannes Peetson, known in his youth as Joks, then for most of his life as Comrade Peetson, and most recently as Mr. Peetson, turns off the narrow suburban lane on to the main road, stepping out of the silence into the noise. He stops to observe the cars whooshing endlessly past, a slightly startled expression on his face. He has to get across the road somehow, to get to the far bank of the river. At the moment it is clearly impossible. But he doesn't despair, he just waits patiently. The grin that appeared on his face as he compared the road to a river (wide and fast-flowing) is quickly replaced by a decisive look, and the slow and relaxed pace at which he walked down the narrow lane shits to a vigorous forwards motion, as Master Peetson's masterly form is propelled between the speeding vehicles, and happily, as if by some miracle, to the other side of the road. To the other bank, if one continues the comparison of road and river. And now the sun comes out from behind the clouds as well.

The autumn sun comes out from behind the clouds and he sees a broad expanse of water in front of him—a large blue lake, which it takes some time to sail across before a bank of grayish blue clouds presents itself. Illuminated by the powerful beams of sunlight, the leaves on the trees become even more colorful, and the scene becomes more cheerful. Or in fact very cheerful.

A cheerful thought pops unexpectedly into Mr. Peetson's head: I have a good reason to be happy.

And he smiles.

Peetson smiles, takes a hunting cap decorated with small colorful feathers off his head, and wipes the sweat from his face with a square handkerchief. The weather is unusually warm for October. Peetson is overdressed for the weather, and he is not used to walking. He feels rivulets of sweat trickling down his back.

There are two or three people waiting at the bus stop—Peetson doesn't look closely at them. If someone were to ask him later who else had been waiting there, he would answer just two or three, unable to specify if they had been men, women, or children. Peetson's attention is instead captivated by a creature resembling a woman, who is walking along the other side of the road with large plastic bags gathered up in each hand. Walking? No, that's definitely the wrong word. The creature's movements don't really resemble walking, they look more like flowing (or oozing, like mucus?)—just like an amoeba bobbling along, thinks Peetson, with a snort of laughter at the terminology he had managed to conjure up. But a moment later he is no longer in a mood for laughing.

He recognizes (or at least he thinks he recognizes) the woman as his former classmate Lea.

Peetson thinks there is something that resembles his classmate in the way the woman is bobbling along like an amoeba—at least a tiny bit (a grain, a crumb). But that doesn't count for anything in itself. It doesn't arouse any sympathy or any desire to help her. When the woman puts her bags down and leans against the fence, holding on to it like someone who is drowning, Peetson instinctively takes a couple of steps forwards, as if he was going to start running, but he doesn't go anywhere. Instead he imagines with revulsion that the woman on the opposite bank is unable to hold on any longer, and the seething current then carries her to the middle of the river, where the waters close over her head.

But she's not drowning, thinks Peetson, and he tries to imagine what he might do if Lea were to collapse onto the pavement—like a pile of snow melting, like a sandcastle, like a skyscraper that has taken a hit and gone up in flames. Would he rush to help her, would he grab his phone from his pocket and dial 112, would he feel her pulse, and give her mouth-to-mouth resuscitation? Of course he wouldn't. He shakes his head, and an intense feeling of disgust moves up his body and sticks like a lump in his throat, making him feel sick enough to vomit.

Peetson spits (or he makes a sound like spitting, through pursed lips), and in order to try and dispel those sickening thoughts—and particularly so as not to see his former classmate falling over—he drags his eyes away and directs them elsewhere, somewhere further ahead, where his footsteps will follow.

Peetson takes ten slow paces, and then stands still, having noticed something in the shabby, decrepit two-story building across the road (a former bar). In the dark void where the windows had once been, the top halves of young men wearing helmets are visible. Their loud laughter resounds from there down onto the road, where the shiny metal boxes were flowing past endlessly in both directions, some of them giving off foul-smelling fumes from their exhaust pipes.

There are more and more workmen every day, what are they doing there in that dilapidated building, Peetson wonders. Are they starting to renovate those old ruins?

He remembered that there had been several attempts to renovate the building, most recently a few years ago, but they had all given up eventually. Now the building really was dilapidated beyond hope—the lower windows had been boarded up, and in some places a few of the boards had been wrenched off, revealing all sorts of refuse inside, glimmering with reflected light through the darkness—as if the place had been used as a local garbage dump. And to crown it all, the traces of an earlier (recent?) fire were visible through the darkened holes of the upper floor windows—the internal walls and ceilings were charred black.

They're demolishing it, thinks Peetson. How wonderful that they're finally demolishing that horrible structure! Peetson starts walking back in the direction of the bus stop. His (probable) classmate has gathered up her strength, and she hobbles along to the street corner where she disappears behind a tall fence. Then she is lost from view. Just as if she had never existed, Peetson thinks, and then he corrects himself: as if she had never been there.

Then he loses himself in thought. He wonders whether a thought that one thinks in order to continue an earlier train of thought might have some sort of deeper meaning hidden behind it.

A black dog is waiting to cross the road, looking impatient, scurrying backwards and forwards on the spot, whimpering from time to time.

Lea is just like that old bar building, there is no sense in repairing her anymore, Peetson thinks, and then, as if to cover up that last thought, he wonders: Lea was in the same class as me for two years, what was her surname? And he rummages about in his memories, groping his way in the dark. Maybe Lindepuu?—Lea Lindepuu doesn't sound bad at all, but then it would have stuck better in his mind. Then he sees that the dog has given up trying to cross the road—it barks once, as if to indicate its defeat—and then scampers away (actually it limps, dragging one foot behind it) through a hole in the garden fence.

For ten seconds or so nothing happens at all.

Then a green bus arrives at the stop on the other side of the road, some people get off, and an old woman appears, dragging a (visibly) heavy bag from the market. Suddenly an apple core, or to be more precise, half an apple, hits her on the head. The woman cries out, the bag falls from her hand to the ground, and the apples roll out onto the asphalt in all directions, some of them rolling under the wheels of the speeding cars. The woman holds her head in both hands and looks around in alarm. She can't see anything suspicious. In the building with no glass in the windows, up on the attic floor, the young men are laughing, their bodies convulsing in time with the guffawing sound. One of them tries to hit an old man who is hobbling up the road with a walking stick, but he is too far away. The old woman is closer, so they wait as she gathers up the apples which have rolled out of her bag and sets off again.

Peetson feels uncomfortable watching all this. His bus seemed to have definitively decided not to come. He doesn't know what to do, nor does he particularly want to do anything. Some other people have assembled at the bus stop now. They all have indifferent looks on their faces, as if they hadn't noticed anything.

What oafs! Peetson curses the workmen. Then he starts to get carried away: They're assholes, not humans . . . They've got nothing but a heap of runny shit inside their skulls! We used to get up to all sorts of mischief when we were young, but we weren't completely brainless like that . . .

Peetson has traveled back in time to his youth. Suddenly the dilapidated pub building is restored to its former glory and

Peetson is there with his classmates sinking his first glass of beer (or tankard, to use the proper term). In a flash the surroundings change completely—it's no longer a suburb which people come to visit, but a place where people live: where people are born, where they go to school, where they grow up, where they bring up their children to be just like them, and where they will eventually die.

Peetson is startled. He sees the surroundings in a new light. Nothing is as it was just a moment before.

At the age of eighteen he had moved to another town to study and ended up staying there, and after that he would visit his parents' house (where his brother now lives) and spend the night at least twice a year. But bonds had grown weaker with every year, many former connections had disappeared altogether. Even his brother—he concedes with dismay—was like a distant acquaintance, he never confided in him, and his brother's children had never felt any closer than any other children who might happen to come racing up to him on the street or in a park.

"So that's why . . ." Peetson utters out loud, but he can't explain to himself why that affirmative statement came to his lips. He glances briefly at the people waiting at the bus stop, just in case anyone had noticed him mumbling, but everyone is (visibly) busy with their own thoughts. No one eyes him suspiciously. I would in their place, Peetson thinks, and he pictures to himself the people that one sometimes encounters on the streets in town (all the more often recently) who talk to themselves and put you on edge.

As the bus has not yet arrived, Peetson walks past the bus shelter, up the pedestrian path which runs alongside the road, and he soon realizes that he is walking down his old route to school, where he hasn't set foot for nearly a quarter of a century. He simply never needed to. No reason, as they say.

"So that's why," he mumbles again, and he realizes that with the passing years he has become more and more distant from that young man who was called Joks, whom he suddenly finds himself standing face to face with again.

Oh well, so what, he thinks to himself. Many years have passed since all that.

Peetson is not in a hurry. The business he has come to do in the capital will not take more than a couple of hours, and he doesn't necessarily have to do it before lunch. He could wait until even later, and he could even sort the things out the following day. He figures he can allow himself a brief rest. To have a walk in the autumnal suburbs. To take some time out, as they say. He is surprised to realize that he never once went for a walk during one of his previous visits to his parents' house. Always the bus stop and a couple hundred meters to the gates of home, if he hadn't arrived there by car, that is.

The gates of home, he repeats the phrase to himself. When he had kissed his wife Ellen on the cheek yesterday and closed the apartment door behind him, the journey home had started. The return. The arrival back at the place he had once left behind.

The street he is now walking down is pretty close to the house, but to his surprise nothing here is as he remembered it. It occurs to Peetson how ironic it is that people (including him) are so busy with their day-to-day business that they have no time to notice that the world around them has changed. That the trees are taller. That the houses are new or different in some way. The house where Bill once used to live seemed to have been razed from the face of the earth.

Peetson had met Bill a few years ago; he had been discussing some business at a building firm when Bill walked in through the door. It turned out that his childhood friend was one of the firm's owners and Peetson later felt obliged to buy him a drink, since the deal promised to save them a lot of money.

Bill's name was now Ingvar Sild. When, out of force of habit, Peetson called him Bill, he noticed the puzzled look on Bill's and the others' faces.

That evening they had a few drinks in a cozy bar, the alcohol loosened their tongues, and they quickly started recounting old childhood memories. You remember, said Bill. But Peetson didn't remember. You remember, said Peetson, but Bill didn't have any memories to offer that matched with Peetson's.

Suddenly Peetson realized that the man he had thought was his childhood friend was in fact a different Ingvar Sild, whom he had met for the very first time in his life on that day.

Peetson looks over at some newly built houses. They're impressive, but they seem somehow sterile or lifeless. Too prim and proper. And the gardens surrounding them are excessively tidy. A bizarre comparison occurs to him—they're like graveyards, with their freshly planted flowers and the gravel raked around them.

I should go and visit Mother and Father's grave, he thinks, weighed down by a feeling of shame, and he considers the option of setting a course for the graveyard right now. He hadn't been there once since his mother's funeral. She died the previous spring. His father died just two days before independence was declared. He just dropped dead, as they say on those occasions (although this was actually the old man's salvation, Peetson thought, he would have died a slow and painful death during the first years of independence, considering what a good communist he had been).

The thought that walking to the graveyard was not a pointless waste of time brings fresh color to Master Peetson's face. His previously languid, slack appearance is replaced by an energetic sense of purpose. Even his jowls start to move vigorously, although that's only because he had slipped a piece of chewing gum into his mouth.

He thinks ahead to when he is at his brother's place, sitting down having dinner. His sister-in-law asks him what he has been up to that day, to which he replies casually: Oh, nothing in particular, just messed around sorting out some business and visited Mother and Father's grave.

So that's why, his brother and his wife say in one voice—they can't believe that Peetson would have chosen to make such a visit. Suddenly, it's as if he's become a bigger and better person in their eyes.

"Yes, yes," he says out loud, maybe even too loudly, as he is startled his own voice, as well as by the thought that creeps unexpectedly into his mind like a pickpocket's hand.

"Yes, yes," he repeats, quieter this time, and he contemplates that if his brother lived in some other town, then he could have made some money from his parent's house when his mother died. The neighborhood was popular now. Very popular. He could have gotten a million or even one-and-a-half million kroon for all this. Easily one-and-a-half, if not more.

I should consult with an estate agent today, he thinks, starting to make practical plans.

Suddenly a strange feeling comes over Peetson, as if someone had tricked him. Tricked him so cruelly that he starts to see red.

In early spring, when they had buried their mother, no one talked about what would happen with the house. Probably everyone thought it was natural that his brother's family would carry on living there. After all, they had dutifully cared for Mother, who was as helpless as a baby in her final years. They just decided that was how things should be. But was it fair? The younger brother gets to live in a splendid house, sitting on a heap of money, and the older one is left empty-handed? It would have been fairer to sell the house and share the money. His brother would be able to buy a decent apartment and even enjoy a taste of luxury for a while, not just live hand-to-mouth, barely making ends meet, as he does now.

Peetson can't believe that he had never thought about this before. But then he realizes that before he went on that walk he had never thought about how much his parent's house could be worth . . . So what would happen now? His brother might have already registered the property in his own name. But no, he couldn't do that without the other heir's signature. But what if he had stitched up this whole business while their mother was ill? He might have brought a notary to see the senile old woman, who no longer had any comprehension of what was happening in the world, and have her scrawl something with her shaking hand . . .

Beads of sweat appear on Peetson's brow. They're not caused by hot weather, they're icy cold and have been brought on by insult and indignation. There was nothing left to do now but go to court. Take his own brother to court! There was something horribly, risibly banal about it all—he had heard vile stories about how former close friends, and (even worse) seemingly respectable relatives ended up brawling on the court bench over some disputed property. Brothers become strangers to one another . . .

"Damn it!" Peetson sputters loudly.

And it occurs to him that this house, which was in tip-top condition, could be rented out after a little redecoration, and he would pocket at least two hundred thousand kroons a year, as if from nowhere.

Peetson carries on walking, despondency welling up inside him; he turns at the next junction and arrives at the wooded park, where he notices a woman carrying two plastic bags—the same woman who had attracted his attention as he waited for the bus.

What's she doing still puttering about here, thinks Peetson angrily. The track that the woman is hobbling along leads in the direction of the graveyard. He doesn't want to dither about like the old woman, but if he walks past her she might recognize him, she might even start talking to him, begging for money. It could turn into an annoying and unpleasant episode that he would want to erase from his life story immediately and pretend that it had never been happened

Oh well, life is mostly made up of unpleasant episodes, Peetson thinks, as he stops at the thick pine forest and looks around. The only person he can see is the woman with the plastic bags hobbling along in front of him, so he unbuttons his fly. It's especially unpleasant to have to talk about that house business with one's own brother, he thinks as he pisses against the trunk of a pine tree. That will really mess up their plans for the future. It looks as if one of their girls is planning to get married and her groom seems to be living with them already. The other girl is going to finish university soon and mentioned that she was already looking at possible jobs near home. At the moment they've got plenty of room. Too much room. So why not buy some cheap apartments in some high-rise. It's their problem if they really need to live in suburban luxury.

The majority of people live in concrete apartment blocks after all—let them live like everyone else!

Peetson buttons up his fly and decides that it would be best to raise the uncomfortable topic just before leaving. He should finish dinner, put his coat on, and then casually mention that he and his wife have discussed the house business. That he had expected that his brother would deal with it himself. But Ellen had been insistent, arguing that it really would be fairer to divide the inheritance in two. He had genuinely tried to point out to her that she lacked nothing, but Ellen had started nagging him, asking him why he wasn't thinking of his son, and didn't he want to do anything for his future.

The idea of dumping responsibility for everything onto Ellen immediately raises Peetson's spirits. The sun has just come out from behind the clouds again and scattered luminescent patches of light beneath the trees. The hobbling woman (his classmate?) steps into the glowing light and it looks as if she has a halo around her head.

Peetson smiles wryly at the strange optical illusion, steps off the path, walks towards the pine trees, and decides to take the long route to the graveyard. Suddenly a strange image comes to him, in which he seems to be kneeling at his mother's grave and asking her advice about what to do with the house. He hears his mother's voice telling him to do what he believes is fair. Of course! His mother had always loved him the most. When the poor old dear was already quite muddled in the head only the sight of her elder son had brought a smile of recognition to her lips. But she had not been easy to live with. She constantly had bones to pick with his brother's family, and on those rare occasions when Peetson visited he always had to play the mediator role.

Oh well, just my luck that I was living in a different town, Peetson thinks, and then it occurs to him that his mother might have had a horrible fight with his brother's family one day and left her house to him instead. And then when Mother had died, his brother had shamelessly ripped the will to pieces or threw it in the fireplace.

"Damn this unfair world!" Peetson curses, letting his voice ring out this time. There was no one listening, no one to shake their head reproachfully. Here, in the empty pine forest, he felt free. He could rail against the world. He could show that he wasn't some drip who had to play at being magnanimous, whom anyone could have their way with.

There are already some people at the cemetery. Mostly middle-aged or elderly women. They tend to live longer than their husbands, Peetson concludes enviously, but then it occurs to him that there are probably advantages to dying first. He suspects that after one's partner dies, life becomes a sad and troublesome business. Nothing is the same as it was before.

Bizarrely, it seems like his mother and father's gravestone has somehow disappeared from the graveyard. Peetson stops in his tracks and tries to get his bearings. In the spring the trees were bare and the surroundings completely different. It had been the end of summer when his father's funeral had taken place, but that had been a very long time ago. And he had only been to the graveyard on those two occasions. He doesn't even know if the burial mound had already collapsed and been leveled off. After searching in what he thought was the right part of the graveyard several times, he decides to give up and come back some other time with his brother's family.

His legs feel tired so he sits down to rest beside an unfamiliar grave. Liide and August Kask are resting in peace under that patch of land. The ground above them has been raked, there is a bench that has been painted white, and red flowers are blooming in front of the gravestone. Suddenly Peetson doesn't feel so sure about the idea of coming to the graveyard with his brother's family. He can't imagine right now what will happen if he demands the house be sold. The two brothers aren't very close, and they often fought as children. When Peetson left to study in a different city, their relations became lukewarm. Superficial. (Exactly, superficial! Peetson is happy he has found the right word.) Neither of them really cared what happened to the other, and why should it be any other way?

"No reason for it to be . . ." Peetson mumbles reassuringly to himself. It's just that one family gets poorer and the other one gets richer. He should arrange these things in secret from Ellen. She doesn't need to know about all this. I can just play Father

Christmas one day: here you are, my darling, a package holiday to the Canary Islands; son, here's a brand new Audi for you. Just think how happy they would be!

Peetson becomes sentimental, the image of his happy family moving him to tears.

"What a pain . . . !" he says resolutely after a pause, trying to get over his bout of sentimentality. But it doesn't work. I must really love them then, he thinks, getting even more emotional. But then who else would I love if not them. They're the only people in this world who care about me. And they're the only ones I care about.

There is a sandy hillock behind the graveyard wall, where low pine trees are growing. Further off there are towering concrete high-rises marking the edge of the city. Peetson can still remember this area before those buildings were there. They had been at the graveyard for someone's funeral (a relative, or neighbor?). He had gone to wander around the graves, and he had climbed onto the wall and looked down. He could still see the image that was imprinted in his mind back then: a huge expanse of light sand bordered with a dark strip of forest, and behind it the sky-blue (iridescent?) sea.

Now there is only a patch of sand and some low pine trees, surrounded by buildings.

Peetson can't believe the image preserved in his mind. It wasn't possible that the sea had been visible from here. Maybe two memories had become associated with each other in some bizarre way. He can see some garbage, dumped there behind the wall. Bits of junk had been dragged under the pine trees as well. Someone is poking about near the rusty wreckage of a car. It's that old woman who looks like his former classmate.

Was it really his classmate, or was it some complete stranger? Driven by a strange curiosity, Peetson climbs over the wall and steps closer. The woman is pouring water into a small bowl from a plastic canister and washing her hands. She has made a fire between the stones (from pine cones). A thin blue stream of smoke is coiling upwards from under an old teapot, which has seen better days. Plastic sheeting has been fixed over the holes in the car body where the windows had been. That's probably where the woman sleeps.

She sleeps there?! Peetson thinks in alarm.

Then he remembers that he had heard, or read in the news, about how some people (dropouts?) had been thrown out of their hostel onto the street, and now they had to live in the woodland.

Peetson watches the woman's activities from behind a bushy pine tree. Based on her amoeba-like progress up the street he had thought she must be an alcoholic or drug addict, but he doesn't think so anymore. The woman seems to be acting rationally. She knows what she is doing, it's just that her movements are sluggish and lifeless. She is noticeably older than Peetson, so she definitely isn't his former classmate.

When the woman has eaten (something unidentifiable, looking a bit like salad, which she takes out of a plastic bag with a spoon), she pours some brown liquid (coffee?) from the teapot into a tin cup, takes a pair of glasses and a book from the plastic bag, and starts reading. The book is thick and looks heavy (a Bible, Peetson thinks), it must be difficult for her to lug it around. Considering that the woman's health is clearly failing (cancer? tuberculosis?), it looks like a heroic achievement.

I'm ready to wager that it is a Bible, Peetson thinks to himself, and he steps closer to try and make certain. Hearing him or seeing him coming, the woman quickly closes the book, hides it in her plastic bag, and stands up.

Peetson would have preferred to walk past, pretending that he had some business elsewhere, but he feels a surprising urge to approach the woman. He takes his wallet from his pocket and shuffles through it—there are bills of five hundred, one hundred, and two kroons.

It wouldn't be right to give her two kroons, so he steels himself and hands her a one-hundred-kroon bill.

"Take it . . . I hope it is some help . . ." he says hurriedly.

The woman doesn't take the money. She just stares at him. Then she shouts: "Peetson!"

"I'm not Peetson!" says Peetson, and he puts the one hundred kroons down on the ground near the plastic bag and starts walking briskly away, without looking back. He arrives at a spot between some houses not far from the bus stop. His thoughts are in complete disarray. Some of them push their way to the forefront of his mind and flicker vividly for a moment, but then they fade away just as quickly as they came.

Peetson waits at the crosswalk, but a bus unexpectedly stops to let him go. So as not to look ungrateful to the driver, he tries to cross as quickly as possible. A BMW is racing along the road in the other direction, the driver is clearly in a rush—they are always in a rush—and he doesn't have time to react to the bus driver's illogical decision to stop. There's absolutely nothing he can do.

It's evening. The table is set. The family is all together. They are still waiting, putting off starting. Peetson's mobile phone is switched off, so in the end they decide to sit down to eat without him. "Well?" says the father, gazing affectionately at his eldest daughter. She squeezes her potential groom's hand, who clears his throat and says: "Looks like you're going to be grandparents." The father lifts a bottle of champagne onto the table from the floor beside the table leg. He had actually heard the news earlier. His wife sheds a tear. When the happy buzz of excitement has died down a bit, the younger daughter says: "You could have at least waited for Uncle Joks to get here before telling us the news, I would have liked to see the look on his face, I'm sure he would have looked just as bored and indifferent as if he were listening to the time being announced on the radio . . ." No one in this family called him Peetson. Back in his distant childhood he had always been called Joks, and that's what they called him to this day.

THE BEGINNING OF THE END

The Peetson family was sitting around the dinner table. A German dinner service with an alpine motif and some Czech crystal ware were resplendent on the silver satin tablecloth. All of this had been procured for next to nothing some time ago, from the stocks that were specially allocated for Party members. Peetson Senior—may his ashes rest in peace—was a Party big wig, or "Genosse," as people used to say. There probably wasn't a single person who actually knew the meaning of "Genosse," but it was a wonderfully mysterious word, which instilled reverence, or even fear, in the citizenry's subconscious.

Genosse Peetson didn't live to see independence. The final stages of his cancer kept him bedbound. One August morning, when the news came on the radio that the putschists had seized power in Moscow, Peetson shouted out something jubilant but unintelligible, jumped out of bed with the energy of a perfectly healthy man, rushed to the telephone, and collapsed on the spot.

"He died with his ear to the phone," said his son Karl, a photographer with a quirky sense of humor, as he recounted the news of his father's death to his bohemian friends. Karl was named after Marx, but one would have to look to the Bible for the source of his older brother's name, Jogannes (that is, if one turned a blind eye to the unusual spelling of the name on the birth certificate, which was written out by some Russian official). This rather odd name wasn't changed in later years, even when Estonia became independent, and so it remained as a reminder about a particular part of his life story.

The members of Karl Peetson's family were dressed for a special occasion, and they had taken their usual places at the table. His wife Anne-Mai, who had once been a model at a fashion agency and was still a strikingly beautiful woman, his daughters

Monika and Merle, and then a shy young man named Erki, whose expression suggested a constant—unfounded—doubt as to whether he had actually ended up in the right place.

Dinner was supposed to get under way at six, and so everyone had been sure to sort out their things by then. The only person yet to arrive was Jogannes, who was visiting them at the time—he was on a business trip to the capital. Monika tried to call, but uncle Joks's mobile phone was switched off.

"He's probably with his lover," Merle sniggered. Since childhood the girls were in the habit of joking about their (deadly) serious uncle behind his back. They didn't really like him. And their uncle didn't really give them any reason to.

At half past six, they finally sat down at the table. That was the longest they could put it off, otherwise the roast duck would have gotten too dry. There was a pleasant buzz in the air. One of the family members had some news in store to tell everyone. Good news.

Marinated lamprey eels were served for starters. On Sunday they had bought a bucket load of fresh fish from the market—local products, from Narva, the portly woman had said with a heavy accent—and after lunch they had roasted and then marinated the lampreys under Erki's guidance.

"Look at him, earlier he was making eyes, now he's making eels," Karl Peetson joked. He was very happy with his candidate son-in-law. In truth he was always happy with whatever his favorite, elder daughter wanted.

"Well?" said Karl Peetson, looking at Monika affectionately.

Monika squeezed the young man's hand, he cleared his throat and in a slightly over-the-top, ceremonious tone, he said: "Looks like you're going to be grandparents."

Karl Peetson had already heard the news earlier in the day. He lifted up a bottle of champagne from under the table. Merle brought the glasses. A look of happiness and surprise appeared on Anne-Mai's face, but tears came to her eyes.

"You could have at least waited for Uncle Joks to get here before telling us the news, I would have like to see the look on his face, I'm sure he would have looked just as bored and indifferent as if he were listening to the time being announced on the radio . . ." Merle teased.

Then the doorbell rang. "Now you can look at Joks's face until you're sick of it," sniggered Monika.

"Hey dad, some strange old woman is asking for you," said Merle, who had gone to open the door.

Karl got up, wiped his mouth clean with a napkin, and went out to the corridor. The whole family waited around the table in expectant silence. The sparkling wine had been poured into glasses and they were hoping that the soon-to-be grandfather would now say a fitting toast.

Karl took a little time to come back to the dining room. When he did he looked completely distraught. He was holding a blue one-hundred-kroon note between his fingertips, as if he were afraid he might catch some infectious disease from it.

"That old lady was asking for Peetson, but she didn't mean me, she was bringing Joks his money back," said Peetson.

Karl Peetson put the note on top of the television, sat down at the table and stared at the pieces of eel lying on his plate. There were three pieces in a yellowy-brown liquid that was slowly seeping across the surface of the plate. They could hear the tick of the pendulum clock on the wall. It was very quiet in the room.

Finally Karl raised his eyes and said, "That old lady was Joks's former classmate Lea Lindepuu. I remember her from our school days. She wanted to become an actress . . . Now she looks like she's about seventy years old. I don't understand what kind of relationship she and Joks could have had . . . but she talks like some sect member . . . Recently they've spread like . . ." Karl searched for something appropriate to compare them with, but it eluded him.

"They just spout any old drivel that comes into their head, and everyone believes them," he said angrily, after a pause.

The phone in the other room rang. The insistent ringing sounded like a cry for help, getting louder and louder. But no one moved, no one went to answer. Finally Anne-Mai stood up and rushed to the other room, mumbling something to herself.

When Anne-Mai came back to the room, her face was white.

She approached her husband slowly and unsurely, desperately trying to find the right words, and then put her hand on his shoulder.

"My heartfelt condolences, your brother is dead," she said, forcing the words out with difficulty.

No one said anything. No one knew what to say.

Anne-Mai explained: "Some idiot plowed straight into him on the crosswalk. It happened this morning. Ellen only just found out about it. They're leaving the house right away. They'll probably stay with us tonight."

Suddenly they heard a loud and agitated knocking at the window. Everyone turned with a start to look in that direction, mouths agape. An old woman who looked like a bundle of rags was standing the other side of the window. It was clear from her gestures that she wanted to say something important, to pass on some information.

Merle went up to the window, pushed it open and started talking to the old woman as if she were talking to a child: "Please leave us alone, go on home now, go on."

The old lady turned and started to leave, but a few seconds later, when she was a little farther away, they heard her shrill voice crying out again. The words were unintelligible. Merle pulled the window shut, but at the very last moment a few more discernible words slipped through: the beginning of the end.

"She said the beginning of the end . . ." Monika repeated in a frightened half-whisper.

"So what if she did," said Karl abruptly. "People talk too much these days anyway."

"Listen," said Erki all of a sudden. "When those planes flew into the skyscrapers, I was at home sick with a bad cold and a fever. Just out of boredom I turned on the TV, and a Finnish channel happened to be showing a tall building with smoke coming off it. I realized right away that it was New York. The cameras were just focused from long range on the burning skyscraper for a long time, without any commentary. I thought, what kind of stunt are they pulling, it must be some sort of black humor, some trashy film. Then the other plane flew straight into the other building. Suddenly I realized that it was all real and that it was happening right now. I can't describe how I felt inside at that moment . . . Like something wanted to escape from inside me and I couldn't stop it . . . I put on my bathrobe and went out to the stairwell. I just had to talk to someone. An old Russian man from one of the floors above came down the stairs. I tried to explain something to him in garbled Russian. It's only right, he said in response, they deserve it . . . Only then did I remember there was such a thing as a telephone. I went back into my apartment and phoned a friend . . ."

Monika looked at her fiancé reproachfully. "Hey, that's enough, our uncle has just died . . ." she said in a quiet voice.

Everyone at the table was sitting staring at their plates with serious looks on their faces. The champagne was fizzing away in the glasses.

Merle had pulled the window shut, but was still standing there, watching something outside.

SOMEBODY'S CLASSMATE

In fact, Lea had managed to get a few words with Him that evening as well. Not very many. Just a smattering, to use the jocular expression—although this was certainly no joking matter. He had said that things were only going to get worse. That nothing was sacred anymore, and that humankind was digging its own grave. That this was the beginning of the end. There would be maybe a year or two of grace, and after that there would be nothing left.

"But if nothing is left, then no one will cry for anyone," Lea had said. But he had just responded with a gentle smile. That smile could be interpreted in different ways.

"Mother dear, what did he mean by that smile?" Lea asked. Mother didn't know what to say, and so she preferred to stay silent as usual. Sometimes that silence made Lea angry. Just as if she'd lost her voice, she thought, annoyed. And then she was angry with herself for being annoyed. Apart from Mother she had no one else left.

No one left? But had there ever been anyone else? She couldn't remember clearly. All the memories and the images in her head were muddled up like porridge and cabbage. But why did people say "muddled up like porridge and cabbage?" Lea tried to imagine what porridge and cabbage looked like. Porridge and cabbage.

Then it occurred to her that even if she had no one left apart from Mother, there had once been someone who brought flowers for Mother occasionally. Lovely red begonias. At first she mistakenly thought they had popped up from the ground by the gravestone and burst into bloom overnight. But no! Instead, some cunning person had hidden the flowerpot in the sand. Lea decided that it must have been someone who was very deceitful and who was always trying to trick other people.

"Mummy, don't believe them," said Lea, and she stroked her mother's hair.

Suddenly she felt a sharp pang of jealousy. So sharp that it cut into her heart like a knife: she had no one in her life apart from her mother, but someone was constantly bringing Mother flowers. Some secret lover, she thought spitefully. And they're keeping it hidden from me. I'm always the last to find out! That jealous feeling wouldn't leave Lea alone, it stayed with her like an uninvited guest. Eventually Lea got tired of trying to drive the guest away, so she ripped the flowerpot from the sand, and immediately felt relieved.

Now she had to get rid of the flowerpot without anyone noticing, maybe by slipping it stealthily onto someone else's grave. Lea peered around. A little ways away a woman was raking the ground. Another was carrying a watering can. Both were busy with their own tasks, with their noses in their own porridge bowls, so to speak. She found a grave that was overgrown with grass some ten meters away, and that was where she planted the flowers, chuckling to herself as she did so.

But maybe while I was away someone did exactly the same thing, thought Lea as she raked the sand around the grave with her fingers. What a strange idea. She imagined how the begonia migrated backwards and forwards from that neglected grave, finding a new home for itself several times a day. So it's a migratory begonia, Lea thought.

"See what an odd world this is, Mummy," Lea said, looking for a candle end in her pocket. But the candles were all used up. And now was not the best time to go find new ones. There were too many people around for her to start gathering up the extinguished candles from other people's graves. That was best done at dusk, when no one else was in the graveyard.

"No candle, Mummy," said Lea in a sad voice, but then her fingers came across a piece of paper, which rustled strangely as she held it. Lea took the light-blue piece of paper from her pocket and examined the silver strip at one end, which was iridescent with rainbow colors. Like some kind of black magic, a little colored dog appeared and then suddenly disappeared, only to then reappear again. There was no silvery strip on the other side of the piece of paper, but when she held it up to the light a picture of the poet Lydia Koidula suddenly appeared, even though it looked like there was nothing printed on that part of the paper.

"Illusionists," Lea murmured happily to herself.

I might have been named Lydia too, she thought. She had never liked the name Lea. Once, a long time ago, when she had been traveling on the evening train in a carriage illuminated by a dull yellow light, she found herself sitting opposite a man with a broad face and glasses who was reading a book called "Lea." She had recognized the man—he was the famous actor and director Voldemar Panso.

"My name is Lea too," she had said, much to her own surprise. The director had put the book in his briefcase and they started talking. In the course of the conversation Panso confessed that he wanted to stage the play *Lea*, and Lea confessed that she wanted to become an actress.

Lea rolled the piece of paper into a tight tube and shoved it into the sand, then she struck a match and was about to light it like a candle, until she suddenly remembered that this "Koidula" didn't actually belong to her. Peetson had given it to her. Probably just for safekeeping.

But why would Peetson give her his own money for safekeeping?

Lea didn't know. But sometimes people did completely irrational things. Without any ulterior motives. Although Peetson definitely looked like he had some ulterior motive, Lea thought. And then she suddenly felt like she was still the same age she had been when she was on the train with Panso.

And then it occurred to her that Peetson had been her classmate back then.

So that means I must have been Peetson's classmate! Lea realized in surprise. If I was once someone's classmate, then I should still be so now. But then why did my former classmate Peetson say that he wasn't Peetson when I recognized him, and why did he give me his money for safekeeping?

If Peetson said that he isn't Peetson, maybe his life has come to an end. Maybe he has died? Ceased to exist? Lea felt overpowered by such a frightening thought, and she rubbed the piece of magic blue paper between her fingers until it became more and more recognizably a one-hundred-kroon banknote.

If Peetson no longer exists, how can I give him his money back, she pondered, a little annoyed now. Sometimes people just go and do irrational things and don't think about the trouble they cause other people.

Suddenly something occurred to Lea. She couldn't define exactly what the thought was, but she felt very clearly that she had to hurry now. She wanted to run, but her feet wouldn't do what she asked them to.

Why can I never do what I want to do, why do I always feel like someone is holding me back, she thought to herself.

When Lea finally arrived home the door had been torn off its hinges, and the piece of plastic sheeting put up in place of the door had been blown away and was tangled up in the lower branches of a pine tree. Now it looked like a raincoat that the pine tree was wearing. All of Lea's things had been unceremoniously taken from her bags and strewn around, although at first glance it looked like nothing important had been stolen.

Maybe Peetson has been here looking for his money, thought Lea. And then for some reason she suddenly had a vivid memory of how the young Peetson had forced himself on her and carelessly left his child-seed inside her to germinate. She had been trying to forget about that all these years. Sometimes it seemed to her as if it had been lost to oblivion, but then one fine day it all came back to her again.

I wonder if the young Peetson is the same person who gave me this money yesterday, Lea asked herself. But maybe yesterday was in fact today, she thought, feeling a sense of trepidation that grew into real fright. It seemed as if her thoughts were getting inexorably more and more muddled. Just like porridge and cabbage.

But I'm probably not young enough to be anyone's classmate anymore, she concluded.

The book was lying facedown on the ground. It had been ruthlessly ripped from its binding and now was lying with its pages creased and its spine facing upwards among the fronds of heather. They were probably looking for money there, she thought as she straightened the pages. Then she sat down and made herself comfortable in the car seat. She was home now and could read a little. If she got tired she could let herself doze off for a bit. And then she should make lunch. Today she could make some soup. Towards evening, when she felt physically stronger, she would take the money back to Peetson.

Maybe he still lives in that grand house where he lived before, thought Lea. But will he get by until evening without his money?

She had recently found that book next to the garbage cans outside a nearby apartment block, where loads of books had been piled up on the ground, and she planned to start reading it soon. With its attractive reddish-brown leather binding the book had caught her eye right away, and Lea thought it would be a sin to leave such a beautiful, weighty tome lying there. It was of special interest to her because it was written in Finnish. When she had lived in Finland, they hadn't had a single book in the house. Her husband said that books were a stupid waste of money. They had to pay for the television already, and you could get everything you needed from there. Lea was bringing up three children in her husband's house; she just cooked and scrubbed all day long, and didn't have the right to say what she thought about things.

She remembered to this day the envious expressions of her friends when, after endless hassles, she finally boarded the boat with her new husband. You're starting a new life! One that we can only dream of, her friends gasped in admiration.

Ten years later, when she got back to Tallinn and met up with her friends, they asked her about the parts of the world she had visited over the years. Lea replied that she had been to Oulu a couple of times, and that last year they went to Turu, and when she saw the disappointment on their faces, she realized she had been living her life all wrong. As it turned out, some of the girls who had stayed on the other side of the Iron Curtain had traveled through Spain, France, and India, and they twittered on endlessly to Lea about all those jolly trips. She had tried to explain that everything was very expensive in Finland, that ordinary Finns didn't have the time or money to travel for pleasure, but they couldn't understand, or they just stubbornly refused to.

She had asked them what they were whining about, what was so wrong with their lives, and she had felt jealous of them.

Lea opened the book and started reading: *Nyt kelpaa kylpyyn; puhdas amme vettä täynnä, viilea emali, lempeä lauha virta. Tämä on minun ruumiini.*

Hän näki jo kalpean ruumiinsa kylvyssä pitkällään, alasti, lämpimän, kohdussa, tuoksuvalla sulavalla saippualla öljytty, pehmeasti valeltu. Hän näki kuinka vesi lirlirlorisi hänen vartalonsa ja raajojensa yli ja kannatti niita, nosti niitä kevyesti ylospäin, sitruunankeltaisia: hänen napansa, lihan umppu: ja näki kuinka hänen pensaansa mustat kiharaiset karvat virtailivat, virran tukka tuhansien lasten velton isän ympäri virtaileva, kaihoisa virtaileva kukka . . .

That was one of the most beautiful parts of the book. *Vesi lirlirlorisi* . . . Lea looked at her hands, but she couldn't believe that those gnarled, chapped, and grimy hands could possibly be hers. Something had gotten mixed up, hopelessly and irreversibly. Things were not as they should be. *Vesi lirlirlorisi.* She closed her eyes and saw water. She could smell water and feel the caress of water on her skin.

When Lea opened her eyes again, she was sitting on the torn seating of the rusted car chassis and reading a book she didn't understand. The language wasn't the problem—after decades living in Finland she even found herself thinking in Finnish sometimes, but there was something inexplicably amiss with this book. Lea read the words and sentences and she pretty much understood them. In one place, for example, she thought that she was reading about how someone was taking a bath. But at the same time she realized that the text wasn't about someone washing at all. It was as if the words and sentences were constantly in the service of some other purpose, and in the end she didn't understand anything at all.

Eventually Lea realized that this book wasn't intended for reading from beginning to end like other books. The book's pages contained memories from many different peoples' lives, an image here, another one there, and all these different multicolored fragments of memories had been gathered together in one place.

Lea read on. *Kot. Kot. Kotkoo. Kluk Kluk Kluk. Musta Liz on meidan kana. Se munii meille munia. Kun se munii muniaan laulelee se riemuissan. Kotkoo. Kluk Kluk Kluk. Sitten tulee kiltti setä Leo. Hän panee kätensä mustan Lizin alle ja ottaa Lizin tuoreen munan. Kot kot kot kot Kotkooo. Kluk Kluk Kluk.*

—No joka tapauksessa, sano Joe. —Field ja Nannetti lähtevät täna iltana Lontooseen esittämään asjasta kyselyn alahuoneessa.

—Oletko varma, sanoo Bloom, —että neuvosmies lähtee? Minun sattumalta piti tavata hänet . . .

Lea read: *Kuten esimerkiksi?*

Ineksistenssistä eksistenssiin hän tuli monien joukkoon ja yhtenä otettiin vastaan: eksistenssinä eksistenssin kanssa hän oli kenen tahansa kanssa niin kuin ken tahansa kenen tahansa kanssa: kun hän eksistenssistä epäeksistenssiin olisi mennyt, hänet kaikki tajuaisivat ei-miksikään . . .

I really am somebody's classmate, thought Lea.

She shut the book and looked around. At first she couldn't imagine what grim explanation there could possibly be for her finding herself sitting there in a rusty wreck of a car. And then it all became painfully clear. Lea felt a pang in her heart as she rewound her memories back to that day when she was told that her pregnancy had gone too far, and that there was no longer any question of having an abortion.

I must find my daughter, Lea thought, feeling a sudden panic. Then that thought started spinning in her head, colliding with other thoughts, wrenching them apart from each other, turning them this way and that, until in the end everything was mixed up again, just like porridge and cabbage.

Why porridge and cabbage, thought Lea. And then she remembered, she must find her daughter without delay. Finally she found the plastic bag that contained a color magazine, wrapped in plastic. This is the chronicle of life, Lea thought, wistfully. On some of the pages she could look at pictures of

Triin's house. She could see that her little Triin wanted for nothing. She found her prince, thought Lea, just like in a fairy tale.

With a look of total bliss on her face Lea placed the newspaper to one side and they both spent a long time looking at the truth together. Mother and daughter smiled sincerely in unison. They were both happy. They both were satisfied with their lives.

Then He came and told Lea what to do.

LIFE AS MATERIAL FOR A RATHER SAD NOVEL

This summer, or the last part of it, passed by so quickly that I found myself asking: so what was that, then? Whatever the answer, the summer sun was definitely not shining in the sky anymore. We could now look forward to a little less light every day, right on up until Christmas. And there would be plenty of depression and listlessness, eventually turning into a permanent feeling of boredom—if we want to be pessimistic about things.

Over the last twenty years I have always tried to leave my summers free; I turn down any work for almost three whole months. In response to curious people who ask how I have the energy to slog away so hard all the time, I tell them that I always have to have a proper rest during the summer. I believe that summer constitutes the sole purpose and meaning of life for people who live in Nordic countries, and that it would be a sin to let the time run away unused, or to waste it doing something pointless.

But this summer everything went awry right from the very start. The cold spring refused to go anywhere, and I thought I would have to use the horrible weather for painting and only go on holiday once the warmth started to lure me outdoors. I had planned to put on an exhibition of small-format paintings in the Haus gallery, and then the following year there was going to be a big exhibition to celebrate my jubilee in the Art Hall gallery. Like a proper workaholic I wanted to show off an impressive volume of work and watch people clap their hands together and swoon: all of it painted in just one year! Oh the vanity, the vanity.

After Summer Solstice the weather suddenly improved, and our granddaughter came to visit. It seemed a miracle that a six-year-old girl could get on a plane in Toronto, change in Helsinki, and before you knew it, arrive here in Tallinn! I had to sign some travel document in the airport to pick her up, and then our days were filled with entertaining our tiny guest every way we could think of. After ten child-filled days had passed, I realized that I really had to put everything else aside and get on with work without delay, otherwise I would find myself in a bad spot as the deadlines approached.

Although to tell the truth, that was partly an excuse—the only viable one I had—to dump all those unfamiliar ordeals of grandparenthood onto my wife's shoulders.

When the little one departed at the end of August, I realized that I wouldn't be able to have any holiday. As well as the exhibitions, I also planned that year to finish a collection of short stories and celebrate my round-numbered March birthday in style with a book presentation. And that meant I had four months to write most of the collection and prepare the manuscript for publication.

Over the years I had developed a system—or it might be more accurate to say that the years themselves had given rise to the system?—according to which I used the natural light of spring and autumn for painting, and during the darker period of the year I devoted myself to writing. But now both of my professions had their teeth sunk into me like snarling dogs, and I had to get up every morning at six to sit in front of the computer and think up new stories, and then at around eleven I would go to my studio and paint until around five or six. Just like back in my youth.

"Come on, when do you plan to make time for living?" my wife asked. "Art is my life," I answered grandly.

That was how the story went.

It's great to plan for the future and it's wonderful to believe that everything will go exactly according to those plans. But all of a sudden, instead of autumn rains the sun started shining on Estonia, the buttercups started to bloom again, and the Indian summer just went on and on. Sitting at my computer was about as pleasant as being on a torture rack, and it was particularly excruciating to have to be at the canvas painting images of greenery glowing in the sunshine when I couldn't enjoy the real sun, which had been beckoning me invitingly from outside my studio window for several days. It was luring me brazenly into its warm embrace like a lusty woman. Finally I couldn't stand it any longer and I phoned Vladi.

"What are you up to?" I asked casually.

"I'm working" answered Vladi. "I lost two days in a row at funerals. Now I have to make up the time."

He told me that two former classmates, a man and a woman, were buried recently. One was run over and the other slit her wrists, and so, strangely, both of their lives ended on one and the same day.

"Like Romeo and Juliet, kind of," I said, trying to make a joke about the deaths of two strangers.

Vladi was silent for a while. "It would be pretty cynical to describe it like that, but maybe for a fleeting moment they were actually in love with each other. Actually, the woman's story would be pretty good material for one of your novels."

I told him that I was working on a collection of short stories.

"No, it would be wrong to waste that on a short story. It would be like forking out the price of a Mercedes for a second-hand Ford."

I asked him if he had taken a look outside the window lately.

"I have, but I'm working and won't be provoked," he said resolutely.

"I'm working too," I said, although I didn't sound so sure about it.

And so, a couple of hours later we were speeding down the motorway towards Pärnu with a nice big pile of fishing rods on the back seat and a boat on the trailer.

I like going fishing with Vladi because I can talk to him about literature. These days there aren't many people who read books and keep up with literary culture. They are as rare as mushrooms after a rainless summer, and we can't expect there to be many more of them in the future. People don't have time for any other games alongside their professional and personal lives. And it's quite sad to see how even literary people's opinions are derived from out-of-date impressions or information they pick up second hand. All they do is pose and make faces.

Vladi has always been a man of letters to his very core, even if his most recent book was a fishing manual, and fishing is what he is ardently devoted to. Some people are just fortunate enough to make a living from their passion. I, on the other hand, have managed to make a passion from my former living.

I tell Vladi that the story collection I am writing is going to be unusual—it's like a living tree, with shoots coming off the branches. The shoots grow into new branches, which themselves grow shoots, and so on.

"Like a family tree?" Vladi asks.

"Not exactly. The various stories are connected through the characters and situations in them. For example, a supporting character in one story takes on the leading role in another, and a situation the reader is already familiar with is repeated in another story, but this time from a different viewpoint. In the end the reader realizes that all the stories are connected in some way, just like life in Estonia."

"Well he might, if he could be bothered to read the collection from beginning to end. But as far as I know people normally read just one or two random stories, so your carefully calibrated connections will be lost, and the stories will be incomprehensible to the reader."

"No they won't," I argue back. "Each of my stories will be readable entirely on its own, and the overarching meaning of all of them together will be just for the obsessives—like a present to the few readers who treat the collection like a unified work, believing that its compositional principle is the same as a novel."

"It's very refreshing to see such a self-confident writer," said Vladi with a smirk, but I detected a bitter truth hidden in his comment.

"I remember that my computer spell-check used to underline the word '*kirjanik*'* as being incorrectly spelled. When I clicked on the spell-checker, it offered the word '*karjanukk*'** as the correct version. That depressed me for a while," I recount.

"*Karjanukk* . . . I reckon that's the *nukk* that declines as '*nuku*,'*** not '*nuki*'****—that word meant writer back in the

* Estonian for writer.
** A made-up word that could mean "a doll that is part of a herd of dolls."
*** Estonian for doll
**** Estonian for lump.

good old days," Vladi said in response, and that's the last we say on the subject of literature on that particular occasion.

We were very glad that we had been able to force ourselves to leave our work worries behind in town, and considering it was early autumn, the weather was unusually fine. The sun was shining, and the light made the forest look transparent and at the same time multicolored. Each tree stood forth in all its perfection, it was incomparably more interesting than the dense greenery of summer, which tended to subsume all nuances.

It was quite warm, and nearly completely still, as if the wind was indecisively searching for a direction, turning to face each of the cardinal points in turn. Like an uncertain politician who waits until the last moment to press his voting button. We also spent a long time undecided, weighing up our options. Eventually we decided we would fish on the lake that day and put down lots of bait, then on the next day—if the wind didn't pick up—we would fish for perch in the sea, and on the third day we would wake up at the crack of dawn to see if the bait had done its work in the lake. And then back to town. Back to sit in front of the computer screens again.

The moments I relish the most when out fishing are approaching the fishing spot, listening to the lapping of the paddles or the sputtering of the motor, throwing the bait into the water to lure the fish, and getting the tackle ready. At that moment, anything is still possible—a lucky bite, and the fish of your dreams might be thrashing on the end of the hook. But the first minutes usually reveal the truth about fishing: the float sits stubbornly still on the water's surface, and a dark depression starts to come over you. You try to tell yourself that you're not there just to catch fish. That four hours spent on the water is worth just as much as a dull weekend trying to relax by loafing on the sofa in front of the TV. But you don't succeed in deceiving yourself. Your soul needs fresh experiences. The chase and the catch. Your soul craves for a fierce battle with a big fish which is struggling for its very life, followed by the indescribable joy of victory once the fish is thrashing about on the floor of the boat.

But sometimes the fish just don't bite, no matter how hard

you try, no matter what the weather's like. If there's nothing there, then there's just nothing there.

"They'll come for sure," says Vladi. He bombards the water with bait. He changes the hook fitting and places some sort of fancy miracle device onto the hook as bait.

I too believe that the fish will come, not right away, but in about half an hour or so. I've heard the old men in the harbor who have spent their whole lives fishing: "Look at that Vladi, somehow he manages to catch fish in every spot where there are never any to be had."

There is a special art to fishing. Although for a long time I didn't want to admit that. I would fish with just a thick line, a hefty hook, and a fat worm. I thought I didn't need to get into the nuances, I just wanted to land a big fish. But when Vladi was hauling tench and bream onto the boat, I had to be satisfied with the occasional perch. Eventually I got fed up, and decided to get in step with the times. It's strange to admit, but from that day on fishing became much more exciting.

This time, however, there was no excitement to be had at all.

I asked Vladi what had happened to his former classmates.

Vladi doesn't answer, his fingers are moving nimbly, tying the thin line onto the tiny hook—probably the hook housing isn't quite right, not properly calibrated. I smile as I look over the impressive pile of fishing gear on the boat. There's certainly a lot of it, several thousand kroons worth. I think back to when, as a child, I had once managed to pull a one-kilo trout from Vääna River using a rod cut from brushwood and a cork float, and my smile gets broader. I remember how during the Soviet period, when most things were hard to come by, some guys would set off fishing proudly displaying fishing tackle they had procured from abroad or on the black market. That period is already fading from memory, becoming less and less credible by the year, turning into the stuff of anecdotes. Although sometimes it seems to have taken on a more attractive hue as well.

"After those funerals, I couldn't shake the uncomfortable feeling that in our tiny little Estonia nothing can ever stay a secret," Vladi finally started to say, staring down at the antenna on his float, which was barely protruding out of the water.

"One person unravels one end of the thread, the other unravels the other end, and in the end the participants of the story can only hope that their secrets will go with them to the grave. But of course they don't. Everyone knows a little bit, and once you put the bits together, they all know everything. The funeral of that guy who used to be my classmate took place in Tartu, and three other former classmates were also there. But the next day, there were twelve of them at the woman's funeral. A pretty sizeable number. There was a pretty gossipy mood there. After the funeral we sat together for a few hours, and that was when we unraveled the whole intriguing story, or to be precise, we pieced it together from the separate parts. And so now the story is one whole, and some writer can use it and give it a nice literary shape and form," Vladi recounted, trying to stoke up my interest.

The very next moment I wondered why he didn't write the story himself, but then the bitter truth dawned on me that when someone doesn't have much free time, he can't afford to waste it on such an unprofitable activity as writing.

I sighed, knowing that I had no choice but to prick up my ears with interest. Writing was my life, and I had to live that life come what may.

The story's beginning was pretty banal. Joks got his classmate Lea pregnant.

Joks's parents owned an old house that was palatial by the standards of the time. His father was a minister, and that was probably why Joks had a particularly elevated status amongst his classmates, and why everyone thought it natural that the lavish school-leaving party should be held at his place. It was probably at that party that something happened between Lea and Joks, since as far as anyone could tell they didn't seem to be in any kind of relationship. In March Lea stopped coming to school. She just disappeared without trace. She had never been a particularly sociable girl, so no one really missed her. Then one day someone dropped the bombshell that Lea was expecting a child. When they heard that, the boys at school recalled how Joks had bet them he could have his way with Lea at the graduation party, and how they teased him for some time afterwards that he might become a father any day. But then it was all forgotten during the stress of the exams.

The next year Lea carried on where she had left off. Like nothing had happened. She took part in the acting group, and apparently she dreamed of becoming an actress. Her former classmates had finished school and gone their separate ways, and Lea's weekend visits to Paide to see her child stayed her secret back then.

She finished school and tried to get into the drama program. She was a private, withdrawn person. It was like there was an invisible wall separating her from other people, which was probably why Joks had wanted to prove he could bed the girl who played hard-to-get. It seemed odd, not to say silly, that a person who no one really noticed had gotten it into her head that she wanted to become an actress. Of course she didn't get much further than the first round, although people said that Panso himself had spoken at length with her. And then she was lost from sight again for some time.

When she rejoined our social group she was with Joks. This was back in our university days. At first it didn't dawn on us who the glamorous, dolled-up woman could be. In those days there were all kinds of people hanging around Joks. Bearing in mind that his father was a minister, people hoped that their friendship with him would turn out to be useful in the future. No one could quite get their heads around the fact that this was our former classmate Lea. The girl really did look as if she had been completely reborn, from head to toe. Pretty soon rumors started to circulate. People said that she had been seen hanging around with the Finns who were building the hotel, being passed around from one to the other. That she was planning to get married to a Finn. That she was living with a famous actor. That she was married to Joks.

In any case Lea had really blossomed. I remember I was lucky enough to dance with her that evening. She just melted into my arms, and there was no trace of the awkwardness and stiffness that I remembered from the school parties. I asked, rather snidely, whether Joks was a good father. "What do you mean, father?!" she exclaimed in genuine astonishment. I mumbled some vague explanation, but I already suspected that the whole story about her child had just been gossip like everything else. "You know what it's like, people have nothing better to do than blabber and make things up," I blurted awkwardly. Lea started laughing. "I've heard those stories before. But I left school back then because I had to go to the Caucasus to look after my sick grandfather. I didn't have any choice." I remember that Lea said that so sincerely that I immediately felt loathing from the depths of my heart for anyone who concocts false stories about other people.

But of course she was spinning me a yarn. Lea's daughter was growing up in Paide, but Lea kept that information carefully concealed, so when a Finnish builder put a ring on Lea's finger the next spring, he knew nothing about the child. Back in those days getting married to a foreigner was still something out of the ordinary. Like getting out of prison. Like the gates of paradise had suddenly opened up for you. There were always women hanging around the hotel building site, like greedy wasps around an open jam jar. Some of them were chasing the married men who had the hard currency that they could then sell on for a high profit, the others were aiming for the single men, hoping to get themselves hitched. But very few of them actually reached the harbors of matrimony. The Finns treated the women bustling around them just like prostitutes, and who would want to marry a prostitute? Well, Jorma did. His wife had died and he had three little children to look after. He needed a domestic helper whom he could get the bed boards creaking with now and again. It would be double savings—he wouldn't have to pay a babysitter, nor spend money on whores.

And Jorma was indeed an economical man. He would count every mark ten times before he spent it. It's hard to understand what kept Lea with him, why she didn't flee from Finland or start something with some other Finn. She and Jorma didn't have any children together. One can only imagine the lengths he must have gone to in order to avoid getting her pregnant, but he clearly had his own interests at the forefront of his mind.

Lea didn't return to Tallinn for ten years, and when she came it was only for a couple of days. Her mother took care of her daughter, and when Lea visited she probably just passed herself off as some Finnish friend of the family. It was already the 1980s by then, it seemed as if every Estonian had to have their own pet Finn, and traveling abroad was not a big deal for anyone anymore.

The next time Lea came back to her homeland it was already the start of the new millennium, and this time she came back for good. Jorma had died after a long and painful illness. It could have been that Jorma's children sent the stranger in their family packing, or maybe she had started to suffer from homesickness. No one knows for sure what her life in Finland was really like. As is normally the case with moves abroad, you treat it all as temporary at first, you're sure that in a year or two it will be over, but then the new habits get under your skin, and one day you discover you've settled permanently in your new homeland, and you can't imagine your life any other way.

People said that Lea initially rented an apartment in Tallinn with another Finnish woman, and that they partied and made merry there together. You could often see them staggering around town. By then Lea had already started with her crazy talk, but people always put it down to her having had a drop too much to drink. But at some point Lea lost the plot completely. She started living in the rusty wreck of a car behind the graveyard and hunting for food in garbage cans. She quickly started to resemble an ancient crone: just skin and bones, and a disconcertingly scant supply of sanity.

Then last week they found her by Harku Lake. Lea had slashed her wrists, hacking the veins open with a pair of blunt scissors. Prior to that she had been washing herself, and had rubbed a lot of soap into her hair, face, and clothes. And there she lay, all bloodied and soapy, in the shallow waters of the lake. A ruined woman with a Finnish passport in her pocket. Right there on the sand nearby were her plastic bags, in which they found a bundle of unsent letters to her daughter and clippings from newspaper and journal articles featuring the famous socialite and businesswoman Triin Heinmaa.

After the funeral, while I was sitting with my former classmates, the first subject of conversation was Triin Heinmaa. It was evident that the Finns had been there, and had probably organized the funeral, but Heinmaa was not there.

To tell the truth, it was hard to link this important society lady to the story in any way. During her school days Lea's surname had been Lindepuu. In her Finnish passport she was Tamm. Her mother had been married several times and no one knew the name of the child growing up in Paide. Taking into account that Lea hadn't been in her right mind for some time, her collection of Triin Heinmaa pictures could have just been some crazy delusion. She might have believed that this beautiful, successful woman who happened to catch her eye was her daughter. In the final part of her life Lea probably existed in some sort of alternative reality, which no longer had any relationship to the reality that other people inhabited.

Another one of our classmates worked for the police, and the biggest coincidence of the story was that the contents of those plastic bags ended up being investigated by his department. Along with documents belonging to the Finnish citizen Lea Tamm, he found a birth certificate with the name Lea Lindepuu and school reports collected over the years. He was the one who told us about Lea's death.

Joks Peetson was in fact run over a few hundred meters from the spot behind the graveyard where Lea lived her miserable life in that old car. People said that Lea had come to give some money back to Peetson that same evening. One could conclude, therefore, that they had met on the day of Joks's demise.

"And it would be awfully interesting to know what it was they talked about," Vladi says, as if to put a full stop at the end of his story.

But I think to myself that this is a story about three different people, with separate lives and separate fates, who really should have been together as one family, but were not.

Vladi is deep in thought as he watches his float. And I contemplate that if one were to put one's mind to it then this could indeed be material for a novel, which would also nicely accommodate the story of our generation, from beginning to end. But I tell Vladi in an indifferent tone that the book I'm writing is going to be called "Stories with Happy Endings," and I don't see any chance for a happy ending with this sad story.

"Well, death was a pretty happy outcome in Lea's case, if you take a sober look at things," Vladi said thoughtfully.

"But taking your own life is not something that God approves of, so we can't treat this as a happy ending."

"So be it," says Vladi. "But the fact that the evening newspaper didn't carry a headline in bold announcing 'Triin Heinmaa's tramp mother found by the lake with her wrists slashed' could still be seen as a happy ending to a sad story."

"Kind of . . ." I say with a grimace, and I hold my breath as I watch my float gently jerking and then slowly moving to a sideways position, resting on the smooth surface of the water. Maybe a big bream is enjoying my bait, it occurs to me. The float rests on its side, quivering almost imperceptibly from time to time.

"People were also saying that an open book was found on top of the plastic bags by the lake. It was James Joyce's *Ulysses*, translated into Finnish by Saarikosk, open to the last page, which gave the impression, hard as it may be to believe, that Lea had managed to read the book through to the end just before she killed herself," Vladi recounts, as if he hadn't noticed what is happening to my float.

And it happens again. Suddenly the float rises into a vertical position, and then it is lost from sight, sinking to the depths of the lake. I grab hold of the rod and a shudder of joy runs through me as I feel the weight of an enormous fish.

"Kyllä!"* I holler, "Kyllä."

* Finnish: "Yes"

THE CURSE OF LATE LOVE

Mr. Andrus Veiker first met the woman who upset his mental balance in the forest in late summer. It was a still evening, and there was a reddish-yellow sun in the sky. A bird was singing. Gypsy mushrooms, chanterelles, and some fat boletus mushrooms were waiting to be found amongst the shimmering moss and the lingonberry stems. Andrus had walked a good way around the hilly land, which was dotted here and there with pine trees, and when he was almost back at his car he saw that another car had been parked nearby, and a man and woman were clumping about, as if they were looking for something on the ground. Mushrooms, most probably. Andrus didn't have any particular desire to start up a conversation, but when he walked past them the woman smiled sweetly and, pointing at the gypsy mushrooms in her outstretched hand, asked if that type was edible. "Of course," said Andrus in a slightly condescending tone, and he proceeded to give the woman a short lecture on the specific qualities of the gypsy mushroom as an edible type of mushroom. The woman listened, looking at him respectfully, and Andrus glanced at her a couple of times, assessing her pleasant face and appetizing body. "Appetizing" was definitely the right word; for a moment or two Andrus felt a real hunger for a woman—he had lived in celibacy for quite a while, and in fact he had been living, semi-voluntarily, a hermit's life.

The woman might have been somewhere between forty and fifty, a good example of a "MILF," and Andrus imagined her breathing sweet and tender words into his ear in her soft, slightly singsong voice.

But the woman asked a rather more mundane question: "Are you from the area? We're new here. We bought a farmhouse just a month back. In Paatse. Pretty close to the sea. And now we're trying to get settled in. Whenever we have the time we go for walks by the sea, and in the forest."

It seemed they were real city people who had probably grown up in an apartment block, studied to get a profession, slogged away for years, and were now sufficiently well-off to start actually living. A life that would be more pleasant than before. The man was standing a bit to one side, a few steps away, as if he were somehow a witness or observer. He had the sort of blank expression that was impossible to read. The trip to the forest was probably the woman's idea and the same probably applied to buying the farmhouse. Andrus decided that the man was definitely the bystander type, who always obeyed his wife and probably his boss too, just as long as no one bothered him too much or upset his relaxed demeanor. But their car had fancy headlights and was obviously the newest Audi model, so Andrus was inclined to think that the man might himself be a successful businessman or a big boss, and that there was another story to explain why he didn't look very important standing next to his wife.

Andrus put his mushroom basket down, the woman took a few steps towards him and then exclaimed in surprise, "Oh, so you're a real old mushroom hound! What splendid cèpes you've got! Where do those grow, then?"

The word "old" grated with him. The woman probably hadn't intended to stress his age, she just used some standard expression which had gotten lodged in her mind, but when you begin to approach retirement age it's not nice to have people remind you about how old you are. Especially when it's a woman who's so easy on the eyes. Even if it's just implied. "Well, right here on these hillocks," Andrus informed her in a slightly derisive tone. "You just have to keep your eyes wide open."

"Well we must have been looking with our eyes wide shut then," the woman said, and laughed. "Did you hear, Hanno, we have to keep our eyes wide open."

Andrus was surprised, never expecting to hear someone slip a Kubrick film title into a trivial conversation here in the mushroom forest, under the tall pine trees. He suddenly realized that he must have a silly expression on his face, and he was embarrassed because the woman probably noticed it. "OK then, hope you have a good mushroom harvest," he mumbled hurriedly, and started walking in the direction of his car, but after a couple of steps he regretted it. I should have talked to them for longer, he thought. For a moment Andrus hoped that he would hear them call out after him, giving him cause to turn back, but all he heard was a bird twittering away somewhere.

Rather than drive off right away he sat and watched the couple leave the shade of the pine trees with their mushroom baskets and walk up the slope, which was bathed in bright sunlight. Now they'll walk around all those same spots where I've already picked the best mushrooms, he thought sadly. He wanted the woman to feel proud and happy at finding some good mushrooms. I should have quoted some phrase from *A Clockwork Orange* when she made the Kubrick reference, that would have made our brief conversation quite exquisite, he mused, smiling to himself. He started the engine, opened the window, then took a camera from the passenger seat and pointed it in the woman's direction.

Andrus snapped around ten pictures, and then the woman turned around for a moment to look back, so he even managed to zoom in for a close-up of her face. Then he drove back home along the winding forest roads, which were pitted with large waterlogged potholes.

Later, when he was looking at the photos on his computer, he noticed that the woman's face showed no signs of the awkwardness that normally comes over people when they notice they are being photographed. She was simply looking around. Maybe she had wanted to preserve a view of the surroundings to take with her. But when Andrus looked at the photos, they left an odd impression on him. Like nothing he had felt before. Strange. Weird. Inexplicable. It seemed as if the woman was looking straight at him, her eyes full of promise . . . Of course this blonde, wearing figure-hugging light-gray pants and a cream top, and bearing a slight resemblance to Bibi Andersson, was sexually attractive. But he had seen plenty like that before! He was breathing heavily now as he tried to enlarge the pictures to locate the outlines of her underwear under the tight-fitting clothes, so that he could get some idea of what was hidden underneath. But he couldn't see anything. She wasn't wearing any underwear! That discovery—trivial and insignificant in itself—immediately aroused Andrus. "Damn it . . ." he said out loud.

Andrus's wife—Mrs. Veronika Veiker—had been overseas on a work assignment for a long time now, and it had recently become clear that she wouldn't be coming back any time soon. Every time Andrus had to do the domestic chores, which Veronika had usually taken care of, his mood turned black, and rude words came to his lips. He liked to pick mushrooms, and he liked to eat them, but he despised cleaning them. Letting loose a salvo of colorful language, Andrus put his glasses on and, with an air of desperation, started to cut up the mushrooms. On more than one occasion he had spotted a piece of mushroom furrowed with worm tracks amongst the pickled mushrooms or mushroom sauce prepared by some gracious host, and his appetite for mushrooms had quickly left him. For that reason mushrooms were always cleaned meticulously in his house.

A real bore, this life with no wife, sighed Andrus after dinner, having tidied up the kitchen table. Dishwashing and cleaning up also numbered amongst Veronika's domestic duties which were now in abeyance, so Andrus had to resign himself to their inevitability as well. That summer without his wife had been a real ordeal for him, and he had been at his wit's end. He hadn't imagined that the end of his habitual way of life could affect him so much. At the beginning of May he had had the bad luck to end up unemployed because of some intrigue at work. At first he thought it was just a temporary situation, and that if he could get over the feeling of extreme offense, then everything would be fine again. But it wasn't, because suddenly it seemed that no one had any need for him, and the fact that Veronika was overseas made everything doubly worse. Even the fact that he now had more time on his hands and could stay longer at their summer house didn't offer him much enjoyment, because without Veronika all the humdrum hassle spoiled the experience—there was no joy or feeling of freedom in it. This feeling of freedom had been the main thing that had attracted him and his wife to their place in the countryside. The open vistas around the house, the sighing forest and murmuring sea, the endless morning birdsong—these were always the arguments in favor of leaving town, even if the city always held them in its jealous grip and they had to brutally ignore other people's interests just to make a few free days for themselves.

The farmhouse had belonged to Andrus's parents back in the Soviet period, but now that his mother and father were gone the whole responsibility for its upkeep rested on his shoulders. He had grown up there and had come to love the area, and he couldn't understand why their own children cared so little for it. His daughter and her family would come once a summer at most, but his son hadn't been there for several years—and why should he be in a hurry to come and visit his homeland, living in faraway Australia.

That night Andrus had a dream. It was extremely erotic, unlike any dream he had had in years. It was impossible to construct a proper narrative from it, but he knew for sure that he had fallen in love with that woman from the forest. So now he was able to attempt to piece together that narrative again and again in his dreams, and savor the feeling of arousal that spread throughout his body and seemed to have no intention of departing, no intention of separating itself from him, of becoming just a memory.

I'm behaving like a teenager, Andrus thought wryly to himself. But he also experienced a strange contentment, even a vague, happy kind of pride. He pulled the computer onto his stomach and looked at the pictures of the woman in the forest again. She's like the sun, her presence radiates an incredible light, he thought, feeling quite poetic. I wonder what a woman like her does? Is she just the housewife for a well-off husband? But if she manages to fit a reference to a Kubrick film into a couple of sentences of conversation, then she might be pretty smart. Maybe she really is!

The last days of August were warm and the sky was blue. Vacationers' weather, he thought as he got into the car for an after-lunch drive to the beach. The perfect weather for shooting a classic Swedish film. Summer islands and summer adventures, and overflowing emotions. The characters dart from shot to shot, and everyone has a surreal living-in-the moment mood. As if the winter cold and life's problems had never existed. But who cares about Bergman's films these days! He contemplated that if he had alluded to *A Clockwork Orange* there in the forest, the woman probably wouldn't have understood. The age difference between them was probably as big as the time gap between those two Kubrick films. "Kubrick time!" he uttered out loud, as if trying to give the words more weight. Instead of going to the usual beach, he turned off the main road to the right, in the direction of Paatse. And why not—there was a good spot for swimming there, and a large sandy beach.

The woman arrived at the beach when Andrus had already been in and out of the water a couple times and was thinking of leaving. The water was too warm, and the summer heat made him drowsy. He had lost hope of seeing her there on the beach, and was even thinking about going down to Paatse, then dropping by to see a man he knew in the village whom he had once bought fish from, with the hope of finding out in the course of the conversation who had recently moved to the area. The village folk always knew about things like that, and were ready to discuss them in plenty of detail. Usually adding details that went beyond the simple facts of the matter.

The woman appeared from behind the juniper bushes like some apparition, like an angel. Her light-blue summer dress was flapping in the wind, her blond hair was offset with a halo of sunlight. She walked straight up to the water's edge, pulled her dress up over her head, and ran into the sea. Andrus gathered up his things from where they were lying on the sand and trudged up to the spot where he could see the woman's dress shimmering in the sun. When he sat down, all he could feel was the intense throbbing of his heart, accompanied by a kind of gassy gurgling sound, which started to unsettle him. What the hell is that, he thought in alarm.

The woman swam for a long time, and Andrus gradually calmed down. "How was the mushroom harvest then?" he asked in what had become just an innocent inquiring tone. "Oh, hello there! Well, we found an unbelievable spot for chanterelles. We nearly filled a whole basket! Hanno went into town this morning, and it's just so good to be able to talk to someone. No one wants to sit at the other end of the phone when the weather is as good as this, and I was already starting to feel bothered by an odd lonely feeling. We still don't know anyone in these parts. Do you live somewhere nearby?"

Andrus explained that he didn't actually live right there, that his place was a few kilometers away, but that he came to Paatse to go swimming now and then.

"But we still haven't introduced ourselves," the woman exclaimed with a laugh. "My name is Agne."

***

"Last week I got myself mixed up in a pretty strange business," Andrus started to recount. "I once told someone I knew in the film industry about an odd friendship I had struck up years ago. With a homeless guy, one of those bottle collectors, or whatever you want to call them. In the old days they were called tramps. Well, whenever I meet him in town I give him a euro or two, and he accepts the money as if it were my obligation to give it, and from time to time we talk for a bit. Mostly about sports, which he shows a real interest in, although I doubt he was ever a sporty guy himself. I've got this vague feeling that some time ago in the past we were really good friends. In our childhood, or at school . . . I've avoided trying to clarify it, because then that undefined, even mystical bond that unites us would be lost. The mysterious origins of our acquaintance, if you want to put it like that. I want to believe that he was someone from the Komsomol committee at school. That would make a great story: the sorry fate of a Komsomol careerist. Anyway, that person from the film industry I mentioned phoned me one day and asked if my homeless friend is available, because he wants to use him for something. I said that I more or less knew the routes he walked through town, and that sometimes I even tried to avoid the places where I might meet him. The film guy said that he had a plan to dress up some tramp in a decent suit with a white shirt and a tie, but leave him unwashed, and then have him to sort through some trash cans wearing his fancy suit, then take him to some society event with all the snobby elite from the tabloid press, and see what happens. He hoped to get some interesting shots of people looking amazed at seeing a bum in a tie, or of people actually talking to him. After some initial reluctance, which was probably feigned to raise his asking price, Leo—that was the name of the homeless man—was prepared to do whatever was asked of him. My film friend rushed around with him in town all day, and by evening I had the chance to see how Leo carried himself in company. The first thing that caught the eye were his unwashed hands, and his face was bruised and unshaved as if to order, but his shirt was blindingly white. When I stood close I could pick up the stench coming off him. The film guy rubbed his hands together in glee. A little while later Leo was drunk on the free alcohol and it took great effort to drag him out of there before something really bad happened. Out on the street Leo seemed to sober up a bit, but now I just couldn't get rid of him, he was like a stray dog who you stroke a couple of times and then thinks you're his master. So this person, who was actually not part of my life in any way, latched on to me, and I had to be firm and cruel to shake him off."

"And what did that cruel firmness look like?" Agne asked in a soft voice.

"I don't really want to talk about that," Andrus said, suddenly regretting wholeheartedly that he had started telling a story like that. It was remarkable how he had laced his account with greater and lesser untruths, as if to prepare it for performance, although the only person with whom he would have wanted to share an honest account of that ordeal was Veronika, his wife. Andrus had already been bothered for some time by the feeling that he couldn't keep what had happened to himself, that he had to tell someone about it. He couldn't shake off the idea that he had betrayed a friend, since he and the homeless man had actually been good friends back in their institute days, and had run a film club together for several years. The fact that they were once so close was exactly what he didn't now want to admit, even to himself.

"It does seem like a pretty ugly story," Agne said with an emotionless tone of voice. "I can't imagine being in Leo's situation myself, but I'm guessing that the ending to the story isn't particularly happy."

It had started to get light outside. The full moon slid behind the house and the strip of forest was black under the pale sky. I should say something funny or positive now, Andrus thought, but at that moment he remembered what Leo had said: "You dressed me up so nicely, I'm sure it would suit them very well to bury me like this." "Hey, it wasn't me who dressed you up in those clothes!" Andrus had protested loudly, but at the same time he sensed that Leo's words alluded to an uncomfortable truth that had gone unsaid.

"I don't know why I told you that," Andrus said after a long silence. "But those film guys just walk over everyone, they never think about other people. The human race is just material for them to realize their ideas. And what exactly is the ultimate goal? Isn't it all just a form of self-promotion, a way of becoming famous? It's only self-centered people that usually make such a big racket about themselves."

Agne didn't answer, and Andrus could hear that her breathing was deep and relaxed. She had fallen asleep. She was probably half asleep during that story about Leo, and she's hardly likely to attach much importance to it, Andrus thought, getting irritated for some reason, and then he started to feel uncomfortable. Of course, I want to appear better than I actually am to her! Heaven help me, an old man like me shouldn't suffer from thoughts like that anymore!

He ran his fingers gently over Agne's hair, which seemed a bit coarse to the touch, or at least it wasn't particularly soft. And then an odd thought crossed his mind. Maybe he just wanted her hair to be coarse so that something about Agne would be imperfect. He ran the back of his hand across her cheek, which was soft and silky like the rest of her body.

There was already enough light coming from outside for him to observe Agne's face, examine the smallest of details. There was an intense silence all around. Not a sound to be heard. But then suddenly Andrus was struck with panic. He thought he could hear the sound of a car engine, distant but steadily getting louder . . . a moment later he was sure he could see the beams of the headlights passing across the windows of the house.

Andrus's whole body suddenly started to shake, he grabbed his clothes and stormed out through the house. He only began to calm down once he had pressed the ignition button and the car engine started purring. If the engine started, then the key must be in my pocket, he thought, suddenly feeling happy, and he pressed down on the accelerator pedal. Andrus had already driven some way when he realized he was pressing the pedals with bare feet. Yes, his shoes were still in the hallway. They were a very comfortable pair that he had bought just recently.

"Whose shoes are those?" Hanno asked when he saw them.

***

"It's the same old problem," said Andrus, sighing out loud. "The whole town is full of people you know, but no one wants to help. Or they're not able to help. Probably the latter, since times are tight for everyone. Although of course they try to conceal it." It couldn't be helped that the majority of his good friends were approaching retirement like him, and they didn't feel safe in their jobs anymore. It's a cruel world, especially during an economic slump. Someone has to be sacrificed so that you can stay alive. More often than not, that plight falls to a friend.

He and Agne had spoken on more serious subjects as well. They had shared their views, which were often quite similar. Or did it just seem that way to Andrus? "Exactly," Agne would say approvingly in response to something he had just said, and coming from her full lips that single word "exactly" sounded like a long sentence that contained all the arguments for and against. Andrus closed his eyes tight and let the memory of the word ring in his ears: "Exactly . . ."

The sound of the word "exactly" still soothed him to this day, like everything else Agne had said, and he still felt as if the things that she had done for him had caressed his entire being. As if it were a dream, he thought as he remembered everything that had happened, and looking back at it, the whole dreamlike situation really didn't seem to have any basis in truth.

Agne had invited Andrus to come and see their new holiday home, which turned out to be a smart house with a veranda and an attic. "I've lived in apartments all my life. In four different apartments, to be precise, and you can't imagine what a special feeling it is to live in my own house all of a sudden. I'm completely in my own world, where everything is exactly as I want it to be."

As they sat on the veranda drinking wine, with the thin curtains flapping in the gentle summer breeze, Andrus felt like he had wound up in some Nordic film. It wasn't just that the situation resembled a scene from a film: he actually felt like he was in a film himself. Agne was clearly flirting with him. She laughed coquettishly. She looked into his eyes for long periods. She showed off all her female charms.

They had not been together for long, but to Andrus it already seemed like an eternity. It's probably just that we are so suited to each other, he thought as he tried to explain the situation to himself. But what need was there to explain, when everything was just like a sugary love story in which one cliché chases the other until the woman submits to the man she has only just met.

The word "submit," which nowadays just sounds quaintly funny, brought a smile to Andrus's lips. He remembered a funny story from the Soviet Army athletic squad, where he had done his military service. A high-ranking officer named Sitnikov had invited some of the men to his place one morning to boast about how a woman named Musja had "submitted" to him. Sitnikov was actually a pretty despicable sort, like nearly everyone who earned their stripes by groveling to their superiors and brutalizing their subordinates. But the funny thing about the situation was not just the choice of word, but the tragicomic truth that everyone knew—apart from Sitnikov—that Musja gave it up to anyone who went to the trouble of asking. But the memory suddenly brought a bitter tinge to Andrus's smile: did this mean that Agne was one of those loose women, or maybe even a dedicated nymphomaniac, who jumped at every opportunity for sexual pleasure which came her way?

Andrus wasn't some sort of starry-eyed romantic, but rather a highly self-critical and rational person who liked to analyze every single situation and bring clarity and order to his relationships with other people. "In my case that's a flaw that comes with my profession, or maybe it's actually an advantage," he sometimes said, trying to make a joke of that facet of his personality, but he couldn't help being tormented more and more by the question: Why?

What good reason could there ever be for a woman to submit herself to a man who was considerably older than her?

True, Andrus wasn't some creepy old guy with a beer belly, he was actually in good shape—"forest runs and a healthy diet"—and he tried to leave a good impression whenever he spoke. He hadn't told the story about Leo just to idly wag his tongue, but to show off the contacts he had with the film world and the kinds of events he went to.

But that still didn't explain what had happened. He couldn't believe that it was possible that a younger woman would go and fall in love with him just like that, for no clear reason.

What if she just wanted to get revenge on her husband? It was a common situation, and Andrus tried his hardest to identify any evidence that would suggest this. It was likely that Hanno hadn't just gone into town, but had gone to meet his lover, and that Agne had found out somehow and had wanted to take revenge. That's what women were like, apparently . . . although Agne wasn't some kind of shrew, she was gentle-natured and . . . Andrus couldn't find the right words to sum up her character, in fact he was sure that words didn't exist to express everything he was feeling.

***

The beginning of September was rainy, and Andrus waited expectantly for an Indian summer, but it didn't look like warmer weather or sunshine was on the way. The low-pressure areas were crawling across Sweden and Finland, and would then come to a stubborn standstill over Estonia. Despite the bad weather, Andrus felt an urge to go to the countryside, so the following weekend he went for a spin around Paatse, and then dropped by to see the fisherman he knew.

"Oh, them over there . . ." Timmu had drawled when Andrus raised the subject of the new neighbors. He wiped the beer froth from his mouth and gave a friendly smile, then he held the pause like an actor stoking the public's anticipation, but suddenly his wife entered with a crash of thunder and flash of lightning. "You're drinking again, you swine!" the woman howled like a bad-tempered cat, and Andrus, who was guilty of having brought the beer, had to make himself scarce.

Agne's holiday home was rain-sodden and lifeless.

In the evening hours Andrus started searching for fragments of memories, trying to piece together some sort of jigsaw puzzle of indeterminate form. During the hours they had spent together they had chatted almost constantly, but now he had the feeling that he had done more of the talking that evening, and that the conversation hadn't been about anything concrete. Of the things that Agne had said he remembered that some of her friends had caused her grief in some nasty way, whereas some other friends had been just wonderful. It turned out that Agne lived in the city center and that she and her husband often traveled abroad. They had some sort of family business that brought in a good profit, or something like that. As Andrus recalled, they hadn't talked about anything much at length that evening, although it could have been that he hadn't paid attention to the important details. But then a lot of stuff in dreams remains unclear, he thought bitterly, and the whole story did indeed start to acquire a more and more dreamlike quality.

There was nothing he could grab hold of. September came to an end and there was no longer any hope of seeing Agne on the beach or picking mushrooms in the forest. It seemed that those two places offered him the only threads from the story that he could hold on to. He went to Paatse a couple more times to peer at Agne's lifeless house, and once he went by to see Timmu, but all the doors were locked and the village gave the general impression that everyone had suddenly died. That's the end of all that then, he thought sadly once he had prepared his summer house for the winter and realized that there would be no reason to come back before spring. As he drove back to town a bottomless feeling of despair came over Andrus. A complete loss of purpose. Total indecision.

The same thought kept coming back to him again and again: I should forget the whole thing.

But Andrus could have no peace of mind. In his despair he contemplated how strange it was that he had to think about her all the time, although there was actually so little that united them. He started to examine himself more and more often in the mirror, and there he saw an aging, distressed individual who had already turned properly gray at the temples. He tried to smile, smoothing the wrinkles on his forehead and around his eyes, and he weighed up the possibility of having his hair dyed. Dying his hair? That would definitely give his appearance something extra . . . but he couldn't imagine going to the hairdresser and saying: "I'd like to look young again, could you please get rid of all the gray hair."

When he eventually went to the hairdresser, he just had his hair cut quite a lot shorter. A phrase he had once heard from a hairdresser was ringing in his ears: "See, with shorter hair you look ten years younger." When Andrus later assessed himself in the mirror at home he found himself a pretty funny sight, but the feeling passed, and a little while later he was looking at Agne's picture on the computer, and dreaming.

Andrus no longer worried much about the fact that he had been out of work for several months. He had money in the bank, which allowed him to live comfortably for a while. He was sure that at the right moment someone would make him a good offer, and then the days, weeks, and months would start to roll along pleasantly on new tracks. Until then he just had to wait calmly.

But he didn't feel calm at all. He felt sick to the core. He constantly cursed himself for not getting any contact details from Agne, for just sneaking out of the house like a thief that time. Andrus found himself wandering around the old town quite a lot—he had a notion that Agne lived in the Olevimägi part of town, and so he combed the bars and cafés there in the mornings, afternoons, and evenings. They had talked about the plays they had both seen, so he ended up going to the theater quite a lot as well. Of course he couldn't make her just appear out of nowhere. And yet Andrus was constantly haunted by the belief that they would meet again sometime, and so he had to always be ready for that. He was like an actor who had memorized his lines, facial expressions, and movements to ensure that when his moment came his performance would be suitably impressive. Perfect.

But would it really be so perfect? Andrus tried to imagine what it would be like to meet her again in real life. In the mind's eye one can see any situation in a favorable light, make all kinds of plans, and hope that it really will turn out that way. But it never does. Some tiny detail can spoil everything, to say nothing of more serious discords. Something that might have left a wonderful memory is not guaranteed to be as good when you repeat it. He recalled that several years ago he and Veronika had gone to Malmö to visit the Claessons and had spent a few very pleasant days in their company, but then the next time everything was different—not as good, less pleasant, more boring, so they had tried to leave as quickly as possible. It's impossible to bring back moments that have passed, thought Andrus shaking his head, but it was easy to say that, not as easy to really believe it. Just like a little boy, he thought as he scathingly assessed his sorry state for probably the thousandth time. But soon enough he had opened the computer again to look at the pictures of Agne, particularly the one where she had her head turned and was looking him straight in the eye. Why didn't I film her, he cursed himself. Then I would be able to see her in front of me, moving, just like in real life, he thought.

***

Andrus occasionally tried to make a sober and practical assessment of the situation. He had long since realized that the whole thing had been crazy. If only it had just been about sex! He suspected that the sexual part must have grown into something larger. Something deeper. He yearned to be with Agne all the time. He wanted to share everything with her—every germ of a thought, every morsel of food, all his unbridled tenderness. Sometimes he woke up in the middle of the night, twisting and turning restlessly, tormented by the jealous thought that at that very moment Agne would be together with Hanno in bed, and there was absolutely nothing he could do about it.

Thinking about Agne sleeping with her husband caused Andrus to question what kind of impression he had made on her in bed. He couldn't be sure. Maybe he had been in too much of a hurry? Too selfish? He imagined what it would be like to erase everything that had happened and start the story again from the moment when he had cautiously raised his glass and asked how he was going to drive home after drinking. Agne had laughed and answered that he didn't have to, since he was welcome to sleep it off at her place. "Well I certainly wouldn't have anything against that," Andrus had replied, also laughing.

Was it possible that Agne had expected something more from him?

He booked an appointment with the doctor and summoned up the courage to ask for some medicine to boost his potency. When Andrus bought the tablets from the pharmacy he felt as if he had crossed some invisible boundary in his married life, that some unidentified force had taken control of him. He life was twisting, bending, becoming warped, and maybe it was no longer worth living.

It happened at the end of October, when Andrus had to go to Siim Lark's funeral. Andrus couldn't stand funerals, just like many other unpleasant situations in life that people can't stand and try to avoid. But funerals are an important part of life. A funeral is an event that prepares people for something that will sooner or later happen to them. You definitely have to go to the funeral of a close acquaintance. You can feel it inside you that you must. Andrus had worked with Siim during the Soviet period, he had even shared an office with him for a while, and their families had gotten along well—as is often the case with colleagues of similar age and background, and whose children are the right age to play together. When the Soviet system was replaced by the new order, Siim ventured into politics. Then he replaced his wife with someone younger, then that one for someone younger still, and now that young woman was standing by her husband's coffin, her eyes red from crying. Andrus hadn't talked to Siim recently, but he had gotten a pretty good idea of what his old friend was up to from the gossip he had heard and from the entertainment pages of the newspapers. The funeral service took place in a large church in the city center, and there was just enough room on the benches to accommodate everyone who had come to pay their final respects. Andrus took a seat next to a young man, and as he sat there he looked around, searching for familiar faces. "What did he die of?" asked Andrus's neighbor in a whisper. Andrus didn't know and for some reason that embarrassed him. "I don't know, I've just arrived from Brussels," he quickly lied to excuse himself.

And then he saw Agne. Across the aisle, a couple of rows up, not particularly far away nor particularly close, without Hanno, wedged between two portly women. Andrus felt his whole body start to tremble. Then Agne turned her head, just like in that photograph that Andrus had looked at a million times, only that this time their eyes did not meet. For a moment the silly thought crossed Andrus's mind that he should call out her name.

Finally—after what seemed like an eternity—people started to pay their final respects to the departed, and Andrus was already soaking wet like a rag. He had been overcome by successive bouts of sweating and cold shivers, and his spirits were dampened too. The vague notion that had crossed his mind so many times before, that if he was with Agne his life could warp out of shape and break down completely, suddenly became very clear. He already knew for certain that if he were to touch her again, which now seemed like an imminent possibility, his whole life would start to rush headlong towards destruction. None of what would follow had any prospects. It all seemed like a silly story that no one of sound mind would be able to understand. The story would have also been completely incomprehensible to Andrus himself, if he could see it objectively. But he couldn't. He wasn't thinking anymore. He was feeling something he had never felt before, and he knew that it was worth living in the name of that feeling. If only for one fleeting moment.

When they carried out the coffin and people started to disperse, Andrus waited by the door, and from there he noticed that Agne had already started to walk quickly towards the parking lot. He took a couple of hurried steps, then broke into a run. Just before arriving alongside her he slowed down and called out her name: "Agne!" She stopped and turned to look at him, surprised. "Don't you recognize me, it's Andrus . . ." he said.

Agne was looking at him, but her face showed no signs of recognition. "This summer, you remember, picking mushrooms in the forest, and . . ."

"What do you want?" asked Agne coolly, with a tone of voice she might use to get rid of some tedious pest.

"Agne, I thought that we could meet again."

"What for?"

"I think about you all the time . . ."

"Then keep thinking," she said, laughing cruelly. "I really can't imagine why I should think about some self-centered old man who panics at the slightest difficulty and runs out barefoot in the middle of the night. You've got problems, but I can't help you. Go and see a psychiatrist . . ."

Andrus felt someone tug him by the sleeve. "Hey, Mr. Veiker, did you come by car? Maybe you could give me a lift to the graveyard?"

Andrus tore his arm away. The woman who had addressed him was tall, elderly, and dressed head to toe in black. Just like Death, he thought to himself for some reason. But Death is not a woman, he thought numbly as he watched Agne getting further and further away.

A LIFE SHROUDED IN A FOG OF UNREALITY

There were people fighting in the backyard. Hell, how they were fighting—one of them looked like he might have broken the bridge of his nose, the other had bloody knuckles, and the third one had blood literally spurting from above his eyebrow. The women were smoking, the more slovenly one's dress was badly ripped under the armpit, so that whenever she lifted the cigarette to her lips white flesh and dark frizzy hair were visible through the hole, resembling something particularly disgusting. It had rained heavily that night, and the yard was wet with mud. When they finally got the lanky one on the ground and started kicking him, it had turned into a proper mud-wrestling match.

Leo was watching the fight from the second floor window of the wooden house, and he spat, or rather he let the spit dribble out of his mouth and watched it falling towards the ground. Straight into the water bucket which someone had left under the window. "Shit! That old man's snotting into your bucket!" the voice rang out, shrill and piercing. He pulled back, but he didn't manage to close the window, and the very next moment a lump of brick came flying into the room, accompanied by a clod of mud. Nothing else followed, but Leo still pressed himself warily against the stove, and he didn't dare move for a while. By the time he had gathered up courage and slowly crept up to the window, the yard was already empty.

The empty yard was lined with sheds and a fence, which had recently been painted brown. A water pump stood between the house and sheds, looking like some fancy sculpture. It seemed as if he had seen all of this before, but he couldn't be sure. It was more likely that he had seen something that just looked similar, and in reality he had just woken up somewhere unfamiliar. He was in someone's apartment, but he had no idea whose. He had slept on a sofa that had springs bursting out through the worn-out upholstery in two places. It was an old sofa, they didn't make them like that anymore, they normally used synthetic materials to provide softness in place of springs. Usually foam rubber.

Leo was not sure whether the material they used these days was still called foam rubber, it probably had several different names, but then what business was it of his what things were called? The apartment he had woken up in consisted of a kitchen and a room separated off with curtains. Along with the sofa there were three chairs, a table, a wardrobe with a large mirror, and a bed. The bed was a mess, the sheets and blanket were bunched up in a big heap. But there was no toilet in the apartment. It's probably out in the hall, on the ground floor, Leo concluded as he held back the urge to go. One of his friend's houses was laid out just like that, with the hand pump in the middle of the yard as well. In that house the key to the toilet was hanging on a nail by the door. But here there was no nail or key. Evidently things are different in this house, Leo thought, but he was wary of stepping out of the room. There might be someone lying in ambush for him in the hallway or on the landing, ready to give him a punch in the face. For no reason. Or maybe for a reason?

He wasn't so desperate to go to the bathroom that he couldn't wait until later. Better to be patient for a while, until it was safer to go. Life had taught Leo patience. Patience is the mother of wisdom, he would often think to himself, and he would say so to others as well. He sat down at the table and tipped the bottle of vodka towards his lips, but it was completely empty. There wasn't a single drop to dribble out on to his tongue. He was surprised to see that there was only one shot glass on the table. If he had been drinking vodka with some stranger, then surely there should be two glasses. Or maybe he had just gotten so drunk that he collapsed onto the sofa like a rotten tree stump. Apart from the unmade bed there was an uncomfortable feeling of cleanliness pervading the room. There were even three slices of bread placed neatly on a plate. No cigarette butts or greasy plastic tablecloth. And no piles of rags on the chairs or floor.

Leo broke off a piece from one of the slices of bread, but his mouth was so dry that his lips stuck together, and he needed to get some moisture. He stumbled into the kitchen, took a cupful of water from the bucket, slaked his thirst, and then took another cupful back to the table. There was nothing wrong with the bread, it was still quite soft. He figured that if he found himself with a roof over his head and four walls around him he must know the owner of the apartment in some way. No one in their right mind lets complete strangers—especially ones like him—sleep on their sofa. Maybe it was someone he knew from his former life? No, the people from his former life wouldn't live in such modest conditions. They would be enjoying their spacious houses or downtown apartments.

Leo's former life seemed to grow more and more obscured, shrouded in a fog of unreality, yellowing and faded like an old photo, rotting like an ancient building, breaking to bits like . . . like . . . like hell knows what. Thinking about his former life made him angry, so it wasn't worth doing so too often. Things just were what they were.

But he was really quite amazed to see what an orderly state the room was in; it meant that the owner must be a respectable person who didn't drink too much. Maybe he didn't drink at all, which would explain why there was only one shot glass on the table—that would mean that everything was as it was supposed to be, that there was no longer anything unclear about the situation. Leo thought that if he opened the wardrobe door and had a look at what was there, then he would get even more clarity. But it would be wrong to go rummaging about in a stranger's place. It would be quite shameful. He had lived his whole life according to honest principles. He didn't even start to inspect what might be in the kitchen, or hiding in the fridge. He was just grateful for the pieces of bread that had obviously been left for him. Just like the empty vodka bottle, which he could take with him and recoup for some money.

Leo couldn't remember what had happened the previous night, but that didn't particularly worry him. His memory was full of holes, like a sieve that let everything straight through, but that had ceased to bother Leo a long time ago. Things were what they were. But what he could remember was that the previous evening he had been drinking Rein's vodka with him by the pond in the park. The cherry trees were in bloom, the grass was green, and the birds were singing. For some reason Rein had plenty of vodka in his bag, but Leo was not interested in where he had gotten it from and why he was sharing it with him. The spring evening had made him sentimental, and he had cried. Not out loud, he just let the tears roll down his face, but it was reason enough for taking another swig of vodka. Rein had not noticed his sentimental mood, or hadn't wanted to acknowledge his tears. "Have you got some time on Friday?" he asked. A silly question, thought Leo. I wonder what would happen if one day I suddenly didn't have any time . . . ?

But he couldn't conjure up any more images from his memory. That was all. Vodka, the greenery by the pond, and Rein's question. So maybe I'm at Rein's place now? It was a perfectly logical conclusion. But the orderly state of the room wasn't logically compatible with the concept of Rein. The feel of this modest apartment was more feminine. Maybe it was that woman's apartment? But there was a big question mark after that. There didn't appear to be any women's clothes in the room, there were just some newspapers on the table. The *Evening Post*. The *City Paper*. And three tulips were withering in a vase.

The thought that he might be in a woman's house frightened Leo. Things were always a bit dubious with women. You never knew what they might get into their heads. What kinds of desires they were led by and why they might be interested in you. There were ulterior motives in every single move a woman made. Whereas men were just what they were. No messing around.

Shoes . . . Leo pondered. There had been a jacket hanging by the front door, and some shoes on the floor. This time Leo stood up quite decisively, hoping to bring clarity to matters. Should he get out of there right away, or should he sit down calmly at the table? There were some shoes lying beside the doormat, which looked more like men's shoes after all, a pair of well-worn sneakers, and some fairly new walking shoes. They looked like they were his size. He guessed that the man of the house was about the same size as him. Probably just as strong, or just as weak as him. So that if it came to a fight, he might even end up on top. Recently everyone seemed to be fighting, and Leo had ended up in the path of someone's fist several times. Quite by accident, as he hadn't even known the people. One time his face had been literally beaten black and blue, and he had been horrified to see himself in the mirror of the train station bathroom. He couldn't remember anything about the incident. It's possible they knocked him out and then stamped on him. Everything was conceivable. Life was harsh and uncaring. Especially for people like him.

A fridge stood between him and the door—not that it was in his way, just that someone had positioned it against the wall. It wasn't particularly tall or large in capacity, and it was probably pretty old, as it was making a nasty buzzing sound. It's on its last legs, Leo thought despondently as he opened it. The shelves were mostly empty, but two blue cans in the fridge door caught his eye, so he took one out for closer inspection. "Utenos" was the can's name, and another name for it was "Beer." Some foreign stuff. Probably the sort that wasn't fit for drinking?

But it was, and very much so. After a few swigs Leo started to feel like a human being again. It was quite rare for him to feel like a human being, and it usually only lasted for a short period. Soon he would again become who he had been before.

The foreign can had a recycling label on it, which meant that the machine at the bottle bank would accept it, so it was a "liquid asset." "Liquid" was a good word. At least it had meant something good in his former life, so it could probably be put to good use in his present life as well. I should empty the other beer down my throat, then I'll have two liquid assets, Leo deliberated. If the man of the house doesn't drink, then why does he need those cans cluttering up his fridge anyway?

But he could still wait a bit longer before doing that, for the moment he still felt like a human being.

There were newspapers on the table. Leo sometimes liked to read papers, he found them littered around in different parts of town. You just had to know where to look. As he scanned the columns his attention was caught by a bizarre story about a suicide. Someone had hung themselves from the branches of an apple tree in a complete stranger's garden. When the family arrived at their summer house at the end of the week, the unknown man was hanging there behind the house, which had caused a fright. He had even brought a stool with him, climbed onto it, placed the rope around his neck, and then kicked the stool away. The hanged man turned out to be someone well-known, Andrus Veiker, who owned a summer house nearby, and his death aroused a lot of public interest. The reason for the suicide might have been him losing his job. Veiker had been unfairly dismissed from his position that spring, which had probably been a painful blow to him. But why did he have to go and kill himself outside some strangers' windows? When the reporter interviewed the lady of the house, the latter recalled that she had once met the future suicide case picking mushrooms in the forest. And that he had made quite a pleasant impression. He had spoken with some expertise about how gypsy mushrooms were edible.

In any case it was a terrible, horrible story. The family had left town in good spirits to spend the weekend in the countryside, and then they encountered this awful business.

When Leo started reading the obituaries the name Andrus Veiker caught his eye again, since his relatives had filled several columns with condolence messages, and then he noticed that this Andrus had been born in the same year as an Andrus he knew, at which he suddenly realized that he in fact knew Andrus Veiker. That same man who had hung himself from the branches of an apple tree outside a stranger's window. The funeral was supposed to take place today—if today really was today?—in one hour's time—if the clock ticking on top of the cupboard showed the right time!

The idea of going to Andrus Veiker's funeral came to Leo suddenly, just like a flash of lightning appearing from the clouds and striking the ground below. For a moment the past illuminated the present, and like a rumble of thunder the realization came to him that he was going to go and send Andrus, his old friend, on his final journey. Back in their days at the institute they had run a cinema club together that was highly regarded, and they had called it "a black-and-white window on the world." The window was black and white because they showed pirated black-and-white copies of films that had originally been in color. The whole of the Estonian cultural elite clamored to come and watch those films, which for political as well as moralistic reasons were otherwise banned from the cinema screens. It was probably all those previously unseen erotic images that caused the mass public outbreak of sexual passion back then. Andrus and Leo had the power to decide who was allowed to come to the viewings, and this was definitely one of the finest periods of their life.

Leo recalled how the previous year Andrus had introduced him to Hermes, who was working on a documentary film about the old days. The film club and other stuff from the Soviet period. At first Leo tried to get out of it, but then they dressed him up in fancy clothes and had him talk about his life. There was something else linked with this story—figuratively speaking it was dangling off the edge of it—something else . . . some event, or story which had become just a vague fog for Leo. But what did it matter now.

What mattered now was sending his old friend on his final journey.

"Final journey" sounded good. Very poignant. The final journey would of course be nice and comfortable, and it would obviously last forever. The thought that the final journey would last for eternity worked its way deeper into his mind. He opened the wardrobe door and saw a dark suit hanging on the rail. A white dress shirt. A dark-blue tie. Just like the real thing, thought Leo, trying the jacket on. It fit pretty well.

He hadn't felt this kind of strange enthusiasm churning in him for a very long time, and it resulted in him washing, shaving, and picking the dirt from under his nails, so that when he was finally all suited up and he looked in the wardrobe mirror, a perfectly acceptable exterior looked back at him. Looking like that, he could even go to a respectable person's funeral. Which is exactly where he was going. Only after he had let the door with the automatic lock shut after him did he ask "But why?"

The question was like a heavy stone that had rolled around the corner and over his feet. His feet were injured, and now he had to drag them along with him. But he still had to go. If the journey had already commenced, then he couldn't break it off without a compelling reason. He had locked the door behind him and there was no route back. The other blue can of *Utenos Beer* was surely feeling lonely on its own in the fridge. The suit already felt uncomfortable on him. A bit baggy. The pants slipped further downwards at every step.

At the bus stop he rummaged about in his pockets, hoping to find a ticket there, since someone who looked so respectable simply couldn't travel without one. He found a purse with a little money in it. And an ID card with a photo that looked somewhat like him. But the name wasn't his. He suddenly had the unsettling feeling that he was not himself anymore, but someone completely different. But then Leo had thought he was someone else for some time now, and when he slid the purse back into his pocket, he uttered in a half-whisper: "They could bury me in a suit as nice as this."

But then a faintly scornful smile flashed across his chapped lips, because he knew that in real life they couldn't do that to him yet.

TAKE THIS WALTZ

> *You got into this compartment specifically because there was a free space in the corner, on the corridor side, to your left, facing the direction of travel.*
>
> —*Michel Butor, Second Thoughts*

You wish that many things in your life were different, and you recognize your own discontent, but for many years you have tried to resign yourself to how things are—in some ways you have a good life, even a very good one, and it is basically free of worries—so you say nothing as your husband turns off at the first opportunity, onto the road that runs between the low pine trees by the beach. And when the car comes to a halt you close your eyes and let a completely different scene pass across the screen on the back of your eyelids: an expansive seascape where mighty waves break on a sandy beach, and it makes you think, just as Lorca did: *The sea smiles far off. Teeth of foam, lips of sky.*

You sit with your eyes shut, and the murmur of the sea reaches you through the car window. Outside the weather is gray and stormy, but the car keeps you warm and protected, as if you were inside its belly. Whether you like that image or not, you feel comfortable, even cozy there, and at that moment you wouldn't exchange those feelings for anything, so you even feel grateful that this is now your world.

Outside the wind is churning up the seawater. The sea is broken, as a woman from some small island once said as she assessed the rough waters from the harbor quay. That memory comes back to you with a rush of warm feelings, and soon enough an affectionate smile appears on your lips. For a moment you see yourself more than a quarter of a century ago, on a windy summer's day, with shreds of cloud racing across the sky like pieces ripped from a tin roof. You see yourself with your friends from back then, you hear their coarse and sometimes even obscene jokes, you laugh heartily and even feel proud that they are entertaining and sometimes even alarming the people who are assembled on the harbor quay.

You think to yourself that this life was lived to a completely different tune, played in your youth by an orchestra that was inept but well-intentioned, and the piece they played was fragmented, unfinished. That time now seems incredibly distant, and you can no longer see yourself there through your own eyes. It seems as if time has replaced you, turned you into another person. But in the end you just smile at the thought, and then you smile at the fact that you smiled: your usual theatrical, condescending gesture towards yourself.

As if it were better to not take your own thoughts too seriously, and not act on them.

You push the seat back slightly to try and get a bit more comfortable. You take a CD out of the door pocket and cast a fleeting sideways glance at your husband, who is drumming his fingers against the steering wheel and staring tensely out of the window—his head is turned to the left and all you can see of him is the patch of lightly colored skin below his hair line. You wonder what there can possibly be for him to stare at out there, you can feel the irritation starting to rise up through your veins, flowing in place of blood, being pumped by your heart through your body, and you can see the image of him saying "No!" right in front of your eyes.

Your husband uttered that word calmly, without much reflection—in a maddeningly calm tone, as if the wish you had voiced had been frivolous and bothersome. You start to think that he hadn't heard you correctly, or hadn't understood what you said, and like a fool you said the same thing again using slightly different words. He just looked at you briefly, looking genuinely amazed, and reiterated: "Didn't you hear that I said 'no' . . ."

You can feel the irritation flowing in your veins where blood should be, you take the Chopin CD out of its case, and when the CD player swallows it up your anger subsides a little. You imagine the piano player positioning himself on the chair, massaging his fingers almost absentmindedly, fixing his eyes on the row of black and white keys, then closing them for a moment, only to open them again as he ushers forth the first notes, which sound surprisingly like the final chord of the piece. Then another chord sounds, and the pianist's fingers start to race up and down the keyboard, at which point your husband normally coughs a couple of times emphatically.

"Can't you put something else on, you know all that pounding away gets on my nerves," he says.

You pretend that you hadn't heard him.

In despair—or maybe that's just you acting to yourself again—you realize that despite having lived with him for six years you can't bring yourself to see this man as your husband. It's pathetic, you think, feeling even greater despair—and it is probably real despair now, which brings with it a feeling like someone twisting your arms behind your back, or holding your fingers over a candle flame.

You can feel your emotional pain turning into a physical sensation. Real and palpable.

That morning you asked your husband: "Don't you think it's cruel for you to refuse, surely only a heartless person could make such a decision?"

You asked him that in a sharp and hostile tone, which may have sounded like the crack of a whip, a sudden vicious blow to the face, but your husband didn't feel that blow, nor did he hear the crack of the whip, he just shrugged his shoulders, got up from the table, and went into the other room.

Now you wish that the morning conversation had never happened—probably at a more appropriate moment or in a different context your husband would have agreed. You might have been able to convince him. You tell yourself that moments in time are not related like brothers. You tell yourself that even if moments sometimes look identical from a distance, they can actually be as different as black and white, and then you notice that the sound of the piano doesn't seem to be bothering your husband anymore. You could swap the Chopin etude for a nocturne, and you would be engulfed in a wave of romance and tortured longing for something which doesn't exist. You are in defiant conflict with the reality of your life, and of course with the stormy weather raging outside.

You shut your eyes. Not too tightly, which would make the lines around them deeper—you shut your eyes as gently as the CD player pulls the CD in, or like the pianist touching his fingers on the keys, coaxing the music from them. You breathe in the air that has been transformed into music. Your body relaxes and dissolves into the notes, and you realize that you don't care about anything anymore.

You would like to forget about what happened that morning, if only for a moment, but you can't. It's as if the stormy sea were tossing the same unpleasant image in front of you again and again. In that image your husband makes himself invisible, so that your words don't reach his ears and instead collide against an unfeeling, impassive wall and fall lifeless to the floor, to lie there motionless. You feel with terrible clarity that the negative answer has already been polished to a smooth finish, and it will never turn into an affirmative one, or even into a maybe.

You would like to make your life a little more bearable, to find some relief from the growing feeling of helplessness, find something a bit more colorful for your eyes to focus on, but everything is just the same as before, uniform and drab like the sky, where low clouds are scudding over the sea. You feel that if you were to get out of the car and step onto the seafront, those clouds would start to race towards you at immense speed, and would probably knock you right over.

The pianist has now been weaving his musical fabric for some time and you cast a cautious sideways glance towards your husband, because you sense that at any moment he could change position and a look of reproach mixed with tedium would appear on his face: have you still not got the message that I don't like this music . . . Or his expression would suddenly turn angry, and a completely different language would come from his mouth: I know that you want to antagonize me, to pay me back for what happened this morning, but . . .

But your husband doesn't move, and the pianist is allowed to start a new nocturne, one of your favorite pieces, which you long to enjoy undisturbed—those notes have their own special place in your soul, like a scented cushion has its place in the laundry cupboard. It occurs to you that this is the perfect music for this stormy weather, and then you remember that around ten years earlier you heard the same piece playing on a cassette player. At the time it seemed bizarre that someone had dragged a cumbersome cassette player to the seashore to hear the sound of a piano through the roar of the waves. But when that nocturne started and your companion turned the music up to full volume, you had felt you wanted to die, so as to preserve the moment you were in for eternity.

On this occasion you manage to savor the music inside you for a moment or two. Or, on the contrary, you savor yourself within the music, because you feel as if you have somehow become a musical phrase, or one tone among many, or even a pause between some notes. And for the duration of that most eloquent interval of time your husband continues to peer at something outside, situated to your left. And so in the end you also look in the direction his gaze seems to be turned towards, but you can't make out anything unusual.

You already consider yourself lucky that your husband occasionally comes with you to the forest or the seaside. That seems to be your customary thought when you are trying to justify the situation.

You try again and again to justify the past years of your life, to tell yourself that everything is going well, or even very well, that there is nothing to complain about, no reason to shed any tears. Quite the reverse! You have to smile to fend off the intense, jealous gazes of your friends, and sometimes you even flaunt how well-off you are, although afterwards your feel ashamed. But you have less and less shame left in you—it's like an ice cube held in a warm hand, getting smaller and smaller until it just melts away into a pool of water.

Your husband is paying no attention to this music that normally irritates him, and you decide that he probably has something more important to think about—and why not. It's not easy for him to keep up with the young people, he starts wheezing, and when his energy has finally run out he ends up just jogging along behind, with one thought pounding away in his head: will I actually make it to the end? You grin at your running imagery, and you let yourself mock your husband for a moment, as if he were a stranger or distant acquaintance who has gotten himself into an embarrassing situation.

"Hey," your husband says hesitantly, his voice quavering a bit in agitation, "I think I can see a body in the water there. Someone has drowned. Look, there, about ten meters in front of that large rock. No, you can't see him right now, a wave is rolling over, wait . . . watch for when the water ebbs. Look now!"

You look, stretching across your husband and putting your right hand on his stocky thigh, and he presses himself further back into the seat—pulling himself in—so that you can see the beach better between the low pine trees. As you look at the sea you pick up the smell of alcohol, you feel a twinge inside you, but you suppress the feeling, you just keep staring at the beach, where the sea is tossing the waves ashore, one by one in quick succession. They all look the same, but each one is in fact a little different from the other. Then finally you notice a darker object in the churning gray mass, and you also think that it could be someone's head. A drowned person's head.

"It's a rock," you say.

"I've been staring at it for some time, it's a person's head, look, there's hair floating in the water around it. It's a drowned woman I tell you."

"It's a rock," you say calmly, imagining all the hassle it would be if it really were a corpse tossing in the waves over there. You stop and think about the word "tossing." It seems like such a powerful image! Death is tossing the corpse on the water. Just like in Lorca's poem: *Death steps in and out, out and in steps death . . .*

"There has never been any rock over there. That big one for sure, but no smaller ones," your husband says with an inexplicably enthusiastic tone of voice. It seems as if he is longing for there to be a corpse in the sea. Suddenly you see an image of your husband dragging a girlish-looking naked woman onto the beach, and he is clearly experiencing a strange kind of pleasure as he does it.

"Well go and have a look then," you say agitatedly, but you don't think that he will.

You husband doesn't go, instead he reaches across you, pushing you roughly against the seat, and he takes a flat bottle, which is no longer full to the brim, from the glove compartment.

You note in alarm: the bottle is actually nowhere near full.

You don't say anything. You are probably supposed to agree that seeing a drowned person in the shallow waters is a perfectly justifiable reason for taking a swig of something strong. A tangible reason. But you know what will happen soon, and where it will eventually lead. For a moment it occurs to you that you could have gone to investigate—you could have seen the drowned person in the water and pretended that she was just a rock. But you realize straight away what a stupid idea that is. You can't even imagine looking at a drowned person. The scene of a car crash appears before your eyes—a car crash that happened a few years ago, when a woman's body had to be extracted from the metal casing that had crushed her to death. You had only seen it for a moment or two, but it had haunted you ever since. The dead woman appeared before your eyes again and again. You were amazed to see that there wasn't a single injury on her body. A bloodless death, you had thought at the time.

. . . Death steps in and out . . .

Your husband takes another pull from the bottle and offers it to you. Your first reaction is to decline it as you usually do, but then you reflect and decide that it would be better if he doesn't drink the whole thing. He will drink anyway—you know him well enough—but if you help him with it he will drink less, and those twenty kilometers that are left to drive won't be so dangerous, or at least not extremely dangerous.

The strong alcohol courses downwards through your body in a flash, and then it stops, as if it wanted to take a seat and rest its legs. And then a warm feeling spreads through you. Like a little fan heater inside, you think with a sad smile.

"Does that music have to keep pounding away there?" your

husband interrupts your smile, and you watch as he reaches out his hand and presses his finger firmly down onto a button on the stereo console. The sound of the piano is replaced with a monotonous clamor of voices, and one of them—familiar, but you can't remember whose it is—says that we shouldn't treat the truth as a relative value, that despite everything there is still such a thing as the absolute truth, just as there is such a thing as the Christmas Peace, which can never be broken.

"Damn it!" your husband swears. "That's the same stupid talk you could hear at Party meetings in the Soviet period!" He switches off the radio and takes a large pull from the flat bottle.

"It took me around ten years to realize that the period of absolute truth was over for good," he says, still annoyed with what he had heard on the radio. He starts the engine and reverses back onto the road, and then drives a kilometer onwards, to the place where the low pine trees finish and car wheels have made ruts in the ground leading up to the frothing waves. Now he will finally get to the spot where he should have gone to start with. To that place where the beach is wide and the sea is deep. Where the stormy sea has a completeness to it.

You try to imagine what a partial Christmas Peace would look like. Candles are burning, a smell of pine needles is coming from the Christmas tree, Pergolesi's *Stabat Mater* would sound like it was reverberating from the ceiling, walls, and corners of the room. Soft snowflakes are falling gently outside the window but all you can think of is that your husband can't bring himself to give your son a trifling—for him—ten thousand kroons or so. You have no peace of mind because you can't help your child, and although you have no worries about money, you yourself have nothing at all to give. That is what a partial Christmas Peace would look like, and the peaceful part of it really would be very small. On the outside there would be peace, but inside you a storm would be raging.

You can't help remembering how your husband made it very clear to you some time ago that while he might not have anything against living with you, he didn't want to live with your relatives as well. "It's not so hard to remember that," he had said in mocking, sarcastic tone, when you complained one time that your sister urgently needed to borrow some money.

"I'm not a bank," your husband said, "I'm not a bank that just anyone can come and get a personal loan from," he had said, this time without sarcasm.

The beach is windswept and desolate. The dried rushes have been twisted by the wind, the stones are so light in color that they almost look painted, and a bright-red piece of plastic lying amongst them catches your eye. It doesn't suit the landscape, nor the emotional undertones of the scene, and you want to get out of the car to remove the alien entity, bury it under the stones, or bring it back to the car and throw it away later in a garbage can. But it is forbiddingly cold and windy outside—it is December after all—and the mere thought of getting out sends a shudder through your body.

It's vile weather, you think, and you watch how some snowflakes fall onto the car window, only to melt and slide down the glass a moment later.

Your husband has driven away from the corpse-sea—what an image!—and has chosen a spot where he can watch the stormy waters without feeling a constant disgust because of the dead person bobbing in the water nearby. Without being compelled to reach for his phone to inform someone about the person who has died. He had no desire to poke his nose into a stranger's tragedy . . . He isn't obliged to do anything for anyone. That momentary association with something uncomfortable is over and can be put out of his mind for good. Or if he wants to put his mind at rest he can mull over the thought that the corpse can't be brought back to life now anyway, and that someone or other will find it soon enough, and then maybe they will go through the hassle of dealing with it.

But those thoughts don't stop your husband's hand from reaching out for the bottle again and having another decent swig.

You wait until he has screwed the top back on, then you reach out your hand for the bottle. When you try to take it from your husband's hand you feel a rigid resistance, but it lasts such a short time that it almost goes unnoticed. Then when his grip relaxes and you take the bottle you suddenly notice a strange look in his eye, which seems to reflect an odd thought that has just come to his mind.

You can see that he thinks he can read your thoughts. You're mistaken, you think.

When he announced six years ago that he wanted to become your husband, you were astonished. Flattered and astonished. You couldn't imagine what your life could be like with him. You asked yourself despairingly what you would have in common. The only thing you liked about him was that he knew how to dance. Everything else was lousy. You contemplated sadly that you really had absolutely nothing to talk about. But once you had been out with him two or three times, you cautiously conceded that at least he could listen. Or was it just that his lack of conversation made it seem like he was listening?

You had weighed up the situation back then. For your whole life you had lived from paycheck to paycheck, and now you were being offered the chance to have a better standard of living. And there weren't many men left these days who knew how to dance properly. Just thinking about that brought a grin to your face.

You gulp down another mouthful from the flat bottle and the little fan heater inside you starts to warm up your head. You cough to clear your throat and announce: *death steps in and out, out and in death steps, through the tavern door.*

"That was definitely a corpse there in the water," your husband says, as if he were already regretting his decision to drive away from the spot by the pine trees. To run away.

You suddenly remember that you bought a Leonard Cohen CD that morning. You take your bag from the backseat and fish it out. The poet singer or singer poet. Whichever it is, you enjoy listening to him sing, it creates a special atmosphere, it pulls you into the music and plays with your emotions. You had planned to listen to it that evening, when the flames in the fireplace would be greedily devouring the logs, and your husband would be sitting getting drunk on brandy and staring emptily ahead.

You guess that your husband might like Cohen, that listening to Cohen would make his gaze clearer and detach it from the spot where it is normally fixed for long evenings on end. Your husband always looks as if he is cogitating some secret problem, but you can't guess what kind of thoughts he might have, you have nothing to go on, nothing to latch on to, so eventually you lose hope of ever knowing.

You glance at the names of the songs on the CD case, and your attention is grabbed by some familiar sounding titles. "Take This Waltz," you decide, full of joy, and you take Chopin out of the CD player and put Cohen in. At that point some words you once learned come back to you: *En Viena hay diez muchachas, un hombro donde solloza la muerte, y un bosque de palomas disecadas.*

You remember your husband once asked you: "Who is this Lorca again?" Your jaw had dropped in amazement. For a moment you thought it could just be a nasty joke, but in fact you had already realized that the person in front of you had no idea who Federico García Lorca was. Even if the name happened to reach his ears once, it was probably just shaken out again like a bit of unwanted dust. On that occasion, and on many more later, you thought disdainfully that your husband was a real "tipikas"—as people like you called graduates of Tallinn Polytechnic Institute.

Now in Vienna there are ten pretty women, there's a shoulder where death comes to cry . . . the voice starts singing, it's harsh—or maybe it's just rough like the edge of a piece of paper torn from a notebook?—but at the same time it's a very masculine-sounding voice.

You look towards your husband, and he is looking at the stormy sea through the snowflakes melting on the car window. You are sure that this music can't leave him cold, and from the signs on his face it does seem to be moving him. *This waltz, this waltz, this waltz, this waltz, with its very own breath of brandy and death, dragging its tail in the sea . . .*

You have the feeling that Cohen is announcing the end of something. Not judgment day, not the end of all ends, but something simpler—the end of some mood, some state of being, or maybe some feeling. The musical palette is like the stormy weather raging outside, like the foam of the waves, like the early winter landscape waiting for snow. Like the cold dampness that is creeping into every recess of your being

The notes of the waltz are heavy with a yearning for death.

You want to share your inner feelings with someone, to relieve the sweet pain you are enduring, you want something—something very personal—to relieve the nameless feeling which is threatening to break your heart to pieces. For a moment you think about switching off the CD player, but you realize that this won't make anything better. It would just leave an empty feeling, much more destructive than your current condition, which sometimes you even savor.

Oh my love, oh my love, take this waltz, take this waltz, it's yours now, it's all that there is.

You wait until the song finishes before switching off the CD player. You don't want the powerful feeling that has grown inside you to dissipate or turn into something else. You watch as the wind flings the snowflakes against the window more and more violently. You can hear the thunder of the sea even more clearly inside the car now that the music has fallen silent, but it is still muffled. You think about how the raging fury of nature has been softened, so that it is more bearable, no longer dangerous at all.

When the feeling that had possessed you dissipates, dissolves into ordinariness, you say: "Cohen based that song on a text by Lorca, but he has changed it quite a bit . . . he made a real show tune out of it, there's no other name for it."

"Oh really," your husband says, and a moment later he asks you to put the song on again.

You can't recall your husband ever expressing any sort of interest in culture, and you raise your eyebrows in surprise. If you saw yourself in the mirror now you would notice your eyebrows forming arches and a foolish expression of surprise appearing on your face. But you don't object to your husband's request, it even makes you a bit happier. No, not just a bit, it unexpectedly makes you very happy. And so when Cohen's voice rings out over the thundering of the storm again you feel that you have suddenly found something you were waiting an eternity for. You had already declared the search hopeless, but now here was the thing you were searching for, right here by your side.

You look on in disbelief as your husband turns the volume up. As if he believes that increasing the volume makes the sounds bigger, so that he can gobble them up.

Take this waltz, take its broken waist in your hands, you think.

Take this waltz, it's been dying for years, you hear, and you feel a strange anguish as you imagine pushing the car doors open and dancing a waltz, twisting in each other's embrace, on the dead grass of the early winter seashore.

The image seems so unreal.

But then it is joined by another image—this time more alive and more real—of you dancing a waltz at the New Year's Ball. Actually, no one else can bring themselves to carry on dancing, instead they have formed an awestruck circle around you, there are dozens of pairs of incredulous eyes looking at you, and you hope that as the amazement fades the envy in those eyes will be clear to see.

This time you will show them. It wouldn't even be a bad idea to take a lesson or two with some famous dance teacher, who could polish up your footwork and teach you some impressive new move to bring a murmur of awe to the audience's lips.

This grand, colorful image of the waltz you could dance at the ball crystallizes before your eyes, and it doesn't bother you that you have seen similar scenes in several films that were comical and over-the-top. You had always watched those films with a condescending smile on your face, thinking with contempt how senseless all the old people's efforts were, as they strove to leave a trace of themselves in younger people's memories. You couldn't see that you are just the same—written off by most people, tossed aside, labeled redundant. Only now can you see the heroism of the waltzes and tangos the old people dance at parties, surrounded by the younger dancers.

At the same time you can't comprehend why you have been overlooking some important facts.

You still feel good about having unexpectedly done something worthwhile together with your husband, and you cast a glance in his direction—a shy glance—and you see that as he listens to the music his eyes are fixed on the radio panel on the dashboard, as if he is hoping that something visible, something palpable will climb out of there together with the sound of the music. Your heart is beating full of joy like never before as you wait for the final notes of the waltz to fade out. And when the rich tones of the next song—"First We Take Manhattan"—fill the momentary silence, you will turn down the volume and will probably tell your husband about the scene of the old couple dancing youthfully that you just saw in your imagination.

You still don't know the words you should use to lure your husband, but you long for him to be enthused by the dancing idea just like you, so that it can become the focus of the last week before New Year. You already have some idea who to speak to about finding a dance teacher, and you already know who is going to make you a beautiful dress for you to dance the waltz in. You are even thinking about the kind of perfume you will wear. And then of course there are the shoes you saw in a shop window, which you have had your eye on for a couple of weeks now.

"Everything must be perfect," you whisper barely audibly, and your husband sees your lips moving and looks questioningly in your direction. But he gets no answer, so he just twists the top off the bottle again.

"La-la-la-la-la . . . ai, ai-ai-ai . . ." the backing singers sing provocatively, but eventually their voices fade to silence. You think that now is the time to tell your husband about your dancing idea, but instead he takes your limp hand and pulls it onto his lap, then he leaves it to its own devices. And yes—like it or not—you start to stroke around the fly on his pants. And the thought lingers that Cohen's sublime music must have aroused your husband.

You unbutton his fly and your cold fingers start to knead the warm but seemingly lifeless lump of meat. For some reason your husband has switched off the CD player and you have to listen to his breathing against the background of the whistling wind outside. You hold his pitiful shriveled prick between your fingers, and you know that there won't be much more life flowing into it. Occasionally you have contemplated that this must have been the reason why your husband didn't start picking up younger women when his wife died, and instead took someone like you, almost the same age as him.

You can feel a heavy hand bending your neck downwards. You want to push back, but you can't, even though your nose is picking up a smell—an unpleasant smell—and you are thinking that the last time he washed was in the morning, and you're not even sure whether his "thing" got washed then. You cough to try and fight the feeling of nausea, and you straighten your back—this time the hand lets you do that.

Suddenly an image from a film you once saw crystallizes before your eyes, an image of a woman's head being brutally pushed under the water. She is allowed to breathe for a moment, and then she is pushed under the water again and again. You take a deep breath to fill your lungs with air.

You fill your lungs with air, and then let it flow out with a sighing sound, you grab the flat bottle lying by the gear box, and take a greedy mouthful from it, in the knowledge that inexorably you are going to do exactly what is expected of you. But you really don't want to be fired, you think, playing with the silly idea that you are a conscientious worker who is desperately clinging to her job and has to flawlessly perform the boss's every wish. But this thought, which was meant to be funny, doesn't even make you smile this time. With a bitter sigh you spit some saliva onto your fingers, rub it onto your husband's dangling appendage, then you rub that against his shirt front a bit, hoping that it won't stink so badly now. Then you press play on the stereo. It plays the same song you have both listened to twice now.

And so you listen to it again.

A FLOCK OF DELUSIONS

Renald noticed the woman as she got onto the tram. She caught her foot momentarily on the step, but she didn't lose her balance. Then she walked with carefully measured steps to the first empty seat. But for some reason that one didn't suit her, so instead she took another a few rows further back, and there she sat, gazing at her knees, which were a wintery pale white in color. She probably normally wears long pants, Renald contemplated and looked back to the scene outside the window, where there were shiny cars driving past and people dressed in summery clothes bustling on the pavement. A moment later Renald looked over at the woman sitting across the aisle again, and the odd thought suddenly occurred to him that if there had been more passengers in the carriage, then this woman might have taken a seat next to him.

He would have liked to travel side by side with this unknown woman, to peep from time to time at her rounded knees, which were exposed below the hem of her dress.

The woman might have been about ten years younger than Renald, probably around forty. One of those nice mature ones, neither skinny nor fat, he thought as he assessed her. He even found himself having one or two indecent thoughts about her, which really surprised him, given how rarely he had sexual thoughts of any kind recently.

After the sudden death of his wife Maarit, Renald had fallen into a dark depression. It wasn't like he turned into some sort of living corpse, not outwardly at least. He still went to work and he even laughed along with other people's jokes, but at the very first opportunity he would flee human company and lock himself in his apartment, where he did very little apart from sleeping and eating—even the television got on his nerves. True, he sometimes listened to classical music, and he would start to get sentimental as he listened to the beautiful sounds. Sometimes it even seemed that despairing over the cruel tricks of fate brought him a special kind of satisfaction. It was as if his life, which had been flourishing until then, had been smashed to pieces. It was so unfair, and the most upsetting thing about it was that it had happened completely without warning.

Renald had been deeply offended that Maarit had not told him about her serious illness, and had hidden it from him until the very last moment. He realized of course that his wife had only wanted to protect him, but when he finally learned the sad truth it was the unexpectedness that had knocked the ground from under his feet. He was horrified by the inexorable finality of death. It seemed that his wife had wanted to hide her impending death from him, to keep it a secret, and when one day everything inevitably came to light, Maarit was no longer in a state to answer for her actions.

After the funeral Renald was weighed down by a disturbing feeling that it was impossible to trust anyone anymore, even people who were close to him, as if everyone was hiding something from him, lying to him all the time. It seemed that life's true face was ugly, a grimace that promised only nasty surprises, and that to carry on living in a world like that would be wearisome and unpleasant. But the strangest thing about it was that he didn't want to follow his wife, he didn't long for the end of his own earthly life, as is sadly often the case when people close to you die. Quite the opposite, he was afraid of death, and his wife's painful final days haunted him like a nightmare. But at the same time everyday reality oppressed him, and he saw no hope of waking up from it and seeing life around him from a fresh perspective.

The woman's eyes were still fixed on her hands, which were resting in her lap, so Renald managed to look in her direction now and again, and even to observe her at some length without feeling any embarrassment. Occasionally she would scratch the ring finger of one hand, or stroke the back of the other hand. The finger was elegantly formed, well cared for, but the nail was not varnished. It seemed as if the woman was unaware of being on the tram, she was somewhere far away, in the company of other people, engaged in some completely different activity.

When they arrived at the next stop, where Renald was supposed to get off, something inexplicably held him in his seat. Like an invisible hand or fetter, he thought in alarm. But at the same time he realized that he wasn't in a hurry to get anywhere, so he could allow himself a little adventure and wait to get off at the same stop as the woman. He suddenly felt an irresistible urge to see her walking, he wanted to savor the sight of her body moving to the rhythm of her footsteps. He longed to catch sight of some ambivalent gesture she made, or, if possible, to establish her destination.

This strange and unexpected desire made him happy. He felt as if a thin crack had started to appear in the capsule in which he had shut himself for the last few months, that light was starting to seep in, and he even hoped that with the necessary force of will he could tear that crack wide open, and escape to be bathed in light again. Maybe that woman, who is otherwise so unremarkable, is also captive in her capsule just like him, Renald contemplated, and he felt a strange satisfaction at the thought.

At the final stop the other passengers got off, but the woman remained sitting there, and there was nothing in her appearance that suggested she planned to get up or do anything. Renald delayed getting up as long as he could before it became awkward. Maybe the woman isn't going to get off, Renald thought, so finally he got up and started to move towards the door, although he did so with visible reluctance. He really wasn't in any hurry, and given the gentle warm weather he could just as well kill some time in a park, maybe even walk along the trails towards the sea, to the spot where the bronze angel stood holding a cross above her head. There he could sit down on a bench and watch the boats sailing past.

When he looked over his shoulder a little later he noticed that the woman had gotten off the tram after all, and now she was walking at a brisk pace along the same road as him. Renald slowed down even more, and then when the woman passed him he gradually increased his pace again.

Just as he had hoped, he found the movements of the woman's body arousing. The bulges in her tight-fitting dress gave Renald some idea of the pert figure underneath, and he started to undress her with his eyes. He tracked this woman walking in front of him with a greedy gaze, occasionally letting her get a bit further away, only to hurriedly increase his pace and arrive right behind her again.

When she got to the castle the woman walked through the wide-open iron gates. At first Renald thought she would turn and walk through the door into the castle, that maybe she worked in the art museum there or was going to view some exhibition. But instead his quarry carried on walking towards the sea, towards that distant spot at the end of the road where the angel holding the cross was standing.

She is heading for the exact spot where I planned to go, Renald thought joyfully, and suddenly he felt as if there were some strange bond between them, even if it was still very tenuous, almost invisible. An invisible bond, he thought. With a bit of effort I could make it visible, he thought with a smile.

The woman took a seat on the park bench, and the bushes which had just come out in bloom provided some shade from the sun. Renald sat down on the next bench. The waves were lapping quite close by, somewhere behind the lilacs. Renald couldn't see the sea, but he was sure he could feel its presence, as there was an unusual light that made the stones seem noticeably paler in color than they really were.

How nice, Renald mused, as he let his eyes wander across the sky, where he could see occasional clumps of clouds and a flock of small birds circling, then across the fresh radiant greenery of the park until it came to rest on the woman's breasts, which were bulging out from the neckline of her dress. I'm peeping at women like some old pervert, he thought despondently. I'm stalking a stranger, hanging around and watching her lecherously, harboring lustful fantasies.

Right by the bench a buttercup with sparse leaves but a big beautiful flower had forced its way up through the gravel. "What a hero," he mumbled in awe. He cast yet another glance towards where the woman was sitting, and saw that she was staring blankly into the distance. She's probably waiting for someone, he thought. Maybe a blind date—people meet in a chat room or on some dating site, they write to each other, and they agree to meet, Renald mused. That's how these things are done now. At least that's what other people do, not me.

The woman straightened her hair, then raised her hand to her mouth and yawned. It was the yawn immediately following the hair straightening that startled Renald. His very own Maarit had often made a similar gesture. Then he realized that this woman had similar dark hair and almost the same hairstyle as his prematurely departed wife. They were different, yet there was something uncannily similar about them. Renald turned away, so as to stop himself from staring in the woman's direction. He thought about that phrase, "in the woman's direction" . . . All this time he had seen her just as some unspecified woman, some general category, without considering that she had her own life story and a host of personal characteristics that made her who she was.

This woman definitely has her own first and last names, he thought to himself

All of a sudden Renald started to feel an intense regret that very soon he would have to watch some unnamed male arrive and take the unnamed woman with him. The fleeting feeling of closeness, which already seemed to be taking root, would putrefy and disappear, just as the sensual images in his imagination would burn away and leave nothing behind. He liked the metaphor of burning, which conveyed an image of everything being destroyed. Not even ashes would remain to remind him of those sensual images. I'll just have to get over it, he thought, exhorting himself to think more rationally. He sighed.

There isn't any sense in getting close to a woman who reminds me of Maarit, Renald concluded, sighing again at the hopelessness of the situation. It would mean constantly making comparisons, and he could be sure that the winner in such a competition would always be Maarit.

He let his imagination wander to a possible moment in the future when he and the woman would already be close, and she would be looking around his apartment with a contented smile. Her eyes would alight on the photograph of him and Maarit arm in arm, smiling happily. Would that picture be turned around the very next moment, to make the past disappear? Or what would happen when the woman opened the door of the wardrobe to find Maarit's dresses hanging there? Would she gather them up in a bundle and stuff them in the garbage can? Or would she start trying them on one by one, crying out in delight if something fitted her well?

Renald realized for the first time that this woman's figure was of pretty much the same proportions as Maarit's. Just like twin sisters, he mused, feeling a sudden hot flush. If this woman cut her hair a little shorter, then from a distance they would look astonishingly similar.

Renald closed his eyes. The similarity between Maarit and this woman brought him a sweet kind of pain. Those sweet, painful images smelled good, they were arousingly warm and soft, and they seemed so real. Things really could be like that, he thought, and then he opened his eyes to see a group of tourists trooping past him, speaking some foreign language. He saw a gentleman in a light summer suit and a straw hat take a seat about ten meters away. Only a foreigner could look like that, Renald concluded, and then he noticed that the woman was also looking with interest, even curiosity in the man's direction, and he suddenly felt a searing rush of jealousy come over him.

It probably is a blind date, he thought, sighing sadly. They are sizing each other up, then if they are happy with what they see the man will take a rose from his breast pocket, or a newspaper, or whatever object they agreed on, so that the woman will recognize him . . . he had read that this was how things were done, and it was probably true. But it turned out that something completely different was going on here, since the next moment a woman dressed in lightly colored clothes approached the man. He stood up and they walked off towards the sea, laughing loudly.

Renald felt relief, as if a load had been removed from his back, or from his heart. But now he felt vexed by the question of why the woman had looked like she was waking up from a long slumber when she saw the man. Something had breathed fresh life into her, and a moment later when she looked in Renald's direction, he could detect something like a smile on her face. But Renald's shyness made him quickly turn away.

So what if she did try on one of Maarit's dresses, that would be no skin off anyone's back, he thought, as he continued to ponder over that earlier thought.

In his mind's eye Renald could already see himself coming back from work and finding Maarit busy in the kitchen . . . He walks up behind her, slides his hands down her body, pulls her close, and life is just like it had been those twenty happy years when he was with Maarit. In fact he longed to see this woman, who was still a stranger, wearing all of Maarit's clothes, and he hoped that she would smell like Maarit, that she would cook the same exquisite dishes as Maarit, that she would . . . maybe she would even let him call her by his dead wife's name . . .

These fantasies had trapped Renald in their sweet web, and he was feverishly searching for the words he needed to make her acquaintance. Words to break through the shyness and doubts, innocent words that would best serve as a veil for his lecherous desires and unbridled lust. Lecherous desires? No, he couldn't run away from himself anymore. His celibacy had lasted too long. Impossibly long. Renald felt that Maarit would understand him, maybe she would even approve. He was almost sure of that.

But was he completely sure?

The playful thoughts that had forced their way into his head suddenly seemed like a sordid escapade that he'd been dragged into as he slept, against this will. It occurred to him that dreams don't subordinate themselves to a person's will, instead they show shamelessly what the person really wants. Finally he decided that all this was a violation of Maarit's memory, and he started to get really angry with himself.

"Now that's enough!" he muttered decisively, intending to give the woman a final farewell glance that he would season with haughty disdain. But when he looked over at her he saw a smiling face looking back at him. A mawkish smile, as he later recalled. There wasn't a trace of any remoteness or introversion, nor any sign that she was enclosed in her own capsule like him. Her smile was like a handshake that made any distance between them disappear completely. Some inexplicable force he was powerless to resist made Renald get up from the bench. The woman stood up as well, and she started walking straight towards him.

"Want to have some fun for an hour or so?" the woman asked in a slightly husky voice. "There's a fairly cheap motel near here."

"No, no, I've got things to do," blurted Renald as he took a step backwards. For a moment he thought that the woman was about to attack him, that she would twist his arms behind his back and then force him to do something unspeakable.

"Listen, I really need money," the woman said with brazen impatience, and she came right up close to Renald, so that an unpleasant smell of garlic reached him.

"I said I've got things to do," yelled Renald, suddenly losing his self-control, and he turned around and started moving hurriedly away. He didn't quite run, but he walked very quickly, and all the delusions that had engulfed him in a dense cloud dropped one by one onto the pale gravel path, like a flock of birds suddenly falling dead from the sky.

BLOOD-RED WATER, HAZY SKY

The day had started badly right from the beginning. The alarm clock didn't go off, or Ervin didn't hear it; in any case his eyes only opened when he should have already been driving out of his yard. But not all was lost—all the things he normally did in three-quarters of an hour could be sorted out in a few minutes. Instead of carrying out his tasks at a measured pace and reading the interesting headlines of the morning paper by the open window while savoring his coffee, he stormed headlong out of the door. Ervin hated hurrying, especially in the mornings. He believed that the rhythm and feel of the whole day was determined by the very first few minutes. Those first waking movements were like the first sentences of a book that revealed very quickly whether it was worth wasting any time on the rest of the story. But that was far from the end of it. He had only gotten as far as the stoplight by his house when a delivery truck sideswiped his car, bending his rearview mirror backwards. The light had just changed and the truck driver—overweight and agitated—thought nothing of climbing out of his cabin and sputtering some words of apology in Russian, then reaching out a hairy hand to try and wrench the mirror back into place. In his anger Ervin snapped at the man to keep his hands off the car, at which the latter climbed back into his cabin, looking like a dog who has just had a good kicking.

The idea that this man came out of nowhere and drove straight into him hammered away in Ervin's head for the rest of the journey. He had no idea how much it would cost to replace the mirror, and it would have been silly, and in fact impossible, to try and establish the rights and wrongs of that minor accident right there in front of the traffic light. As he parked his car,

Ervin's anger was boiling over. It was probably the helplessness of his situation that made him particularly cross.

"He just zoomed by and smashed it back to front!" he explained in a rage, gesturing with his arms spread wide to Artur, who happened to be getting out of his car.

"I recently read an English novel where something similar happened, and they wanted to kill the careless driver's whole family for it," Artur said as he assessed the car's side mirror, which looked unnatural and quite ugly, like a foot twisted out of joint.

"You read novels?" Ervin exclaimed, and immediately regretted it, but the fact that this young man could engage in any form of intellectual activity surprised him. It just didn't fit with the image of him he had had up until now.

"And why shouldn't I?" Artur laughed good-naturedly, and with one movement he turned the mirror back to its original position.

"Ah, it goes back as easily as that, does it . . . Thanks," Ervin said in embarrassment, and he felt his face flush.

"The Englishman's name was Ian McEwan," Artur said.

"What Englishman?"

"That one who wrote about the mirror stuff. I was amazed to read that the protagonist's Mercedes completely knocked the side mirror off a BMW 5-Series. It didn't just knock it back on itself, but broke it right off. I guess those Beamers must have their mirrors fixed rigidly on to the bodywork."

Ervin inspected his car's wing mirror, which bore absolutely no trace of the recent accident. How odd, he mused, a single fleeting moment can make everything different, turn bad to good, so that all of a sudden it turns out that things aren't as they originally seemed. His eyes followed Artur as he walked across the parking lot at a brisk pace. The young man receded into the distance, but in Ervin's eyes he had grown in stature. "So he really reads novels . . ." he mumbled in respect.

At around half past nine a worried sounding Hannes called and said that Mother was in a bad way again. In a haltering voice his son explained that a friend had phoned him, who had himself been called by a friend's mother whose house wasn't far from their summer house. That person had tried—in dressed up terms—to explain that the situation there was apparently pretty bad.

"Don't beat around the bush—you mean to say that she's drinking again?" Ervin snorted.

"I've got a feeling that we really have to do something this time, but I can't go there myself, I just can't go right away," his son said in tears. "Soon we won't be able to show our faces anywhere, everyone is always pointing fingers at us."

"Come now, it really isn't so terrible." Ervin tried to console his son, but he didn't sound so sure of himself. "I'll try to do something. Thanks for calling."

Ervin Ussisoo, a forty-five-year-old entrepreneur who was doing pretty well in life, put the phone down on the table and glared at his hands, which looked like two freakishly formed animals hunched in front of him. He began to wait for the telephone to ring again, because he knew that the next call would give him some urgent work business to sort out, which would give him a valid reason for postponing the trip to their summer house. Busy at work or something like that. And maybe towards evening he could have a think about how to smooth out the whole business. Although as things currently stood, he had absolutely nowhere to hide.

"Damned hassle," he mumbled.

Helen Ussisoo, Ervin's fifty-two-year-old wife, had recently been taking to the bottle with ever greater frequency. Boozing, in other words. Or to put it plainly—getting drunk. Ervin had long stopped thinking about drunkenness in euphemisms, and he realized that Helen's alcoholism was getting more serious every day. It was like water that had broken through a dam, and now it was mercilessly sweeping away everything that lay in its path. Pretty soon nothing will be left of our nice life, Ervin thought with a sigh as he grappled with an inconsolable feeling of hopelessness. Just when we had managed to get things back on track after all the difficult times.

About a year ago, soon after their younger son Hannes had gotten married and moved out, Helen started to organize frequent drinking binges at their house. "Binge" is a strange word to use, but how else can you describe it when three or four women are chugging wine and chattering on endlessly. Ervin had no idea what they talked about, he just retreated to his room where he mostly read books and listened to music, or for a bit of variety he watched tennis on TV. Ervin wasn't much of a drinker himself; he would obviously have a glass of something when he had to, at a birthday or funeral, but he didn't enjoy it at all. However, he didn't try to forbid his wife's drinking. Let her booze if she wants to. And—to be blunt—the drunken Helen could be kinkier in bed than her refined exterior and manners suggested.

In November Helen had left her job—something had happened there, probably nothing catastrophic, but she didn't want to talk about it, and Ervin didn't grill her. All sorts of things can happen. People sometimes change their jobs, one person comes, another one goes—no one is tied down to one place forever.

And it looked like Helen was in no hurry to find a new job. "I'm taking some time out," she said.

Well that's how it is then, thought Ervin in total indifference, since his wife had gone to work more for her own amusement than economic necessity. Ervin wasn't particularly interested in how his wife spent her days anyway. Ervin lived in his own world—the world of books. He collected them with an undying passion, placing each one lovingly on his bookshelf, and reading most of them from beginning to end. He had slogged away enough in his life to finally entitle him to his "own" world, and he reckoned that his wife would find something to give her satisfaction too. Family life and grandkids . . . he smiled to himself, for he was sure that as soon as children appeared in their sons' families, then Helen would be in the harness full time. So he didn't particularly mind if he occasionally came home to find his wife fairly drunk. He wasn't even very bothered when Helen carried on drinking throughout the evening and—probably out of boredom or liquid courage—started to pick quarrels over trivial things. As soon as the arguments flared up he would lock his study door and then he wouldn't show his face until bedtime. He would often find his wife slumped facedown in the armchair or on the sofa, and he would have to cover her with a blanket.

And so the tally of drinking bouts started to rise: at first gradually, almost unnoticeably, in between or concealed within other bigger events. Then one March Ervin came back from spending the week in Spain to find the apartment looking like a pigsty, with his wife lying like a corpse in their bed, having drunk herself unconscious.

Ervin sat for a long time in the hallway outside their door, still wearing his hat and his coat. It was as if he couldn't bear being in that miserable apartment a moment longer, but he didn't have the strength to leave either.

The time passed by slowly and unproductively, and his thoughts slowly became more and more dismal. Ervin couldn't comprehend what right another person had to mess up his life. In these circumstances, the fact that they had lived together for a quarter of a century and brought up two children now meant nothing. A kick in the backside and out the door to all of that!

Dark thoughts were spinning round Ervin's head, sometimes they became so dark that he even felt ashamed to be thinking them.

In the end he gave in. The rage that filled his heart started to gradually retreat in the face of everyday life. It wasn't possible to turn back time or undo what had happened in his apartment when he had been in Spain. The only thing he could do, and simply had to do in order to try and restore his peace of mind, was to remove the consequences of the catastrophe. So with an outwardly resigned appearance, he started to clean up the mess left behind after several days of debauchery.

Ervin didn't want to know or even to try and imagine what could have happened in the apartment while he was away, but at every step he stumbled across evidence that planted previously nonexistent suspicions, or even repugnant certainties, in his mind. When he finally sat down at the desk in his room—which initially appeared to have been left untouched by the drunken maelstrom—he realized that someone had actually rummaged around in his drawers and even pocketed one or two things. At this, his cup of patience quickly filled to the top, and started to froth and overflow. Without giving much thought to what he was doing, or what purpose there might be in it, he stormed into the bedroom and, in a rage, he started to shake his wife. Her body twisted in his arms like a bundle of rags. And then finally she opened her eyes.

"What the hell happened here! Have you completely lost your mind? Tell me, damn it, tell me!" he yelled, his whole body shaking.

Helen pushed herself into a sitting position, then stretched her legs out over the edge of the bed like a sleepwalker, stood up and tottered to the bathroom.

Ervin watched, numb from shock, as a woman in a ragged, ripped dress waddled from their matrimonial bed, and he saw that one of her feet was bare, while the other sported a single boot.

The sound of vomiting came from the bathroom, accompanied by a repulsive screeching.

That was the final straw. Unable to restrain the dark rage inside him, Ervin grabbed a bronze figure from where it was standing proudly on its pedestal, and moved swiftly in the direction of the bathroom. The door was open and his wife was crouched in a heap next to the toilet bowl with her face down on the floor, like the crumpled remains of a crashed car. The scene excited Ervin's disgust and an insane murderous rage, but then suddenly he was brought to a halt by an image of what could happen the very next moment. And then the next thing he heard was the sound of his own wailing—a ghastly, blood-curdling cry that brought him to his senses with a jolt and forced him to put the heavy figure down. Then he rushed, literally fled, from the house which had long ceased to be any sort of home for him.

Ervin only started to calm down towards the evening, when he had parked his car by the edge of the forest following several hours of driving around wildly, aimlessly. In places there were patches of naked ground starting to appear from under the melting snow.

He thought about what Helen would do if he threw her out of the apartment . . . but then he started to think very rationally about all the unwanted intrigue that could create for his company, especially since Helen had a 40 percent share in it. On top of it all the new apartment was in her name.

He also weighed up the possibility that Helen's alcohol problem might turn out not to be so serious.

Ervin had heard that sometimes even completely hopeless alcoholics were able to go for years without drinking, that there were some special ampules or some kind of hypnotism that would make them physically unable to consume alcohol. There is no such thing as a hopeless situation, there are only people who have lost hope, he thought as he pushed a CD of Sibelius's Fourth Symphony into the car stereo.

Only now did Ervin take note of his surroundings, how the low gray clouds had started to get sparser as they sailed swiftly across the March sky, leaving behind patches that let the bright light come seeping through. The wind was starting to tidy up the sky, he thought to himself.

When the notes of the Allegro started ringing out Ervin shoved a piece of chocolate he had found in the glove compartment into his mouth, and then, as he calmed down, his eyes came to rest on the scenery outside the window. To the right of the road there was an expanse of field, still covered with a muddy carpet of snow, and at the end of it was a striking strip of forest, bathed in light and iridescent with bluish tones. Then suddenly, the incandescent evening sun tore itself away from behind the clouds and appeared right there in front of him. Ervin had the bizarre feeling that the music had made the sun appear. The snow on the field soaked up the evening hues and the previously desolate world suddenly became thrillingly colorful, although the music didn't match this joyous interplay of colors. Sibelius was doing his thing, without providing any particular grounds for hope, asking difficult questions that were left hanging gloomily in the air as the final notes of the symphony gave way to silence.

Ervin's mood had returned to its former state. The fit of rage he had burst into at home now seemed distant and unreal. He couldn't believe that he was the same person who had just experienced that awful crazed feeling that had almost made him strike his wife down. Now Ervin's heart was weighed down with a heavy feeling of guilt, which wasn't so easy to shake off.

"Damn that old bitch!" he shouted, cursing his wife's Finnish friend, who was obviously an alcoholic. Helen had gotten to know her a couple of years ago in Helsinki, when she had to travel there frequently on work business, and the Finnish friend had recently moved to Tallinn. He was sure that if it hadn't been for that Finnish woman, things wouldn't have gotten nearly so bad. Why couldn't Helen see for herself that she was being dragged into the abyss, he thought in exasperation.

The next morning there was an especially radiant sunlight that stuck in Ervin's memory, it was just as if spring had broken out overnight. They spoke forthrightly about the whole business for the first time, both acknowledging the true state of things. Helen was repentant, and very quiet, as if she were ill, as if she had come to the end of the road. But when the conversation turned to doctors, and seeking help to tackle her binging, she put up unexpected resistance, claiming she didn't really have a drinking problem.

"But you do," Ervin said icily. "It's time for you to step back and take a good look at yourself. It won't be long until you're just like that drunk old woman across the road."

"You have to understand, I'm not some kind of alcoholic!" Helen said as she burst into tears. "I promise I won't drink myself drunk anymore, and then you'll see that I'm not."

Ervin had a vague feeling that he might have gone a bit far in his assessment of Helen. It was true that she had nothing in common with the old woman who lived in the wooden house across the road, who could be seen stumbling about with a baby stroller, struggling to fetch herself some "hair of the dog." When they first moved into their new apartment they had been shocked to see an inebriated woman stumbling along with a little baby, but then they realized that the stroller was full of bottles, probably her own empties, and that the stroller was the only thing keeping the woman upright. It was a grim and unsettling sight, repeated week in and week out, until last winter when it suddenly stopped.

That morning it seemed to Ervin that Helen sincerely agreed with everything he was proposing for their future. They decided that Helen should go back to work, that she should avoid at all costs any friends who had a weakness for the bottle, and if she was against going to see a doctor it might be worth asking for help from an alternative healer.

That morning all traces of Helen's drinking binge seemed to be gone for good, the joyous spring sun shone through the windows of their tidy apartment, and it seemed as if nothing really bad or unfixable had happened. Even Helen's bank cards were still all there. That evening Helen didn't reek of beer, wine, or vodka anymore, and she suffered her hangover in silence. But Ervin still couldn't bring himself to sleep next to her. He could still see the recent scene of her stumbling from the bed in ripped clothes as if it were etched in stone in front of him. It was similar to something he had seen once when he was young: a loose Tartu girl who had been used as common property in their dormitory for two whole days. She had also been wearing a high boot on one leg. But that was back then.

Ervin put some bedding on the sofa in his office, and that was the first time since the start of their married life that they slept separately when they were both home.

And so a whole week passed by quietly, and Ervin felt that life had started moving along well-worn furrows again. The day of their twenty-sixth wedding anniversary arrived and when he took his wife to a restaurant for dinner, he didn't even flinch when she ordered champagne. It was an anniversary after all, so it had to be celebrated. That evening he didn't make his bed on the sofa in his office. But to his surprise he still felt a repellent, tense atmosphere hanging over the marital bed, as if he and his wife had become strangers to each other in a short space of time. Then when he finally brought himself to touch his wife, she pulled away. "Don't," she said, in a tone which sounded almost frightened, "I've got an infectious illness . . ."

Ervin felt himself start to shiver, as if he had found himself outside naked in the cold. His wife said nothing more. And Ervin didn't ask for any more details as he was too afraid of hearing something awful in response.

When he got back home from work the next evening Helen was already drunk to the gills. It was impossible to understand anything that came out of her mouth, and she stumbled about from room to room like a giant wind-up toy, colliding with the chairs and walls. At first Ervin just stood there, blankly watching the seemingly pointless activity, until he finally realized that his wife was trying to get dressed to go out. A little later she was dressed up like a scarecrow and was about to leave, but she was incapable of taking a step forwards without stumbling. Now Ervin had work on his hands to try and restrain her. After what seemed like an endless struggle his wife tired herself out, and she fell asleep in the hallway.

In his anger Ervin found himself thinking that he should have let her go. Who cares what happens to her.

The next morning Helen couldn't remember anything. Feeling lower than low, tormented by a bleary guilty feeling, she promised that nothing like that would ever happen again. That that was definitely the last time, that she would pull herself together and . . .

Ervin believed her, or at least he pretended that he believed her, and they spoke no more of it. After ten days or so they went to Ervin's brother's birthday party, where he was panicky and suspicious the whole time, fearing that Helen would end up drunk and he wouldn't be able to show his face from the shame. But nothing ugly happened; on the contrary, Helen behaved with dignity, only touching the glass to her lips when someone made a toast. They arrived home after midnight. Ervin was tired and he slipped off to sleep straight away. But a little later he was woken by a terrible racket to find his wife dead drunk, slumped on the floor with a cut on her head. "Look how valiantly I restrained myself in front of your relatives," Helen babbled. "Surely I'm entitled to a little drinky in reward."

At first Ervin couldn't understand how his wife had gotten hold of alcohol in the middle of the night, since as far as he was aware the house had been emptied of anything drinkable. He had combed every conceivable and inconceivable place like a sleuth, and to tell the truth it was occasionally in the latter places that he discovered the bottles. The possibility remained that Helen had slipped something from the party into her bag. Or stolen something, in other words. Ervin found the idea alarming, and already began to imagine that one of his relatives might have noticed her stuffing the bottle into her bag, and how they would then exaggerate it as they spread the gossip.

So that's how things are, he thought, feeling horror and humiliation.

That incident—really just a trifling matter—was somehow so significant for Ervin that it succeeded in wiping away his last speck of hope. He couldn't turn a blind eye to the situation anymore. All of a sudden two completely different people had started living in Helen's body. One was gentle, caring, and pleasant, someone with whom he could share life's joys, while the other was an unpredictable drunken maniac. Ervin could not help constantly seeing the haunting and foreboding vision of that repulsive old woman who had ruined herself with alcohol and now walked about pushing the stroller full of empty beer bottles.

Ervin realized that he definitely had to do something now, that things just couldn't carry on as they were.

He usually only started looking for a solution or a way out when—figuratively speaking—the water was already knee-high. But when Helen hadn't drunk for several days and the daily bustle of work left no time for thinking, things returned to how they had been before. But only until the next incident, which never kept him waiting long. One evening Helen didn't come home at all. Her phone was at home on the table. Ervin didn't know what to think, or where he should start looking. When Helen still hadn't appeared by the next evening, it suddenly occurred to Ervin that it was maybe for the best . . .

The thought horrified him. "Maybe it's for the best . . ." he repeated to himself. Meaning that if something were to happen to Helen, then the problem would be resolved, one way or another.

Ervin remembered that during one period of his childhood they had lived next door to a man who ended up slumped on the floor in the stairwell nearly every week. His wife didn't let him into the apartment, so he had to sleep his drunkenness off out there. One winter the door to the stairwell had been locked, and the man froze to death in a snowdrift outside. Back then Ervin had realized that his family, and probably the family next door, felt relieved, even happy, that it happened

Ervin's schoolmate Siim had drunk himself to death some years back. And several of Ervin's old acquaintances eked out miserable existences as alcoholics. No one felt any sympathy for them, they were just treated with derision, or people would shake their heads and say that they only had themselves to blame.

Helen appeared a couple of days later like a dog with its tail between its legs, and when she tried to excuse herself with artless lies, Ervin steeled himself and decided to treat her like a common criminal. The weather was already quite warm—it was May after all—and without entertaining any particular hopes or illusions, Ervin drove his wife to their holiday house, where she was supposed to get by without any money, bank cards, or telephone. A week's worth of food in the fridge, and let's see how you manage. It was like being sent into exile, house arrest, or something like that. Helen didn't quibble. She was basically powerless to say or do anything, and she bowed to Ervin's every demand.

But then when Ervin drove to the summer house the following week to deliver some food, he found Helen and her Finnish friend happily boozing together there. He threw the Finn out and promised himself that this time he would be especially strict with his drunkard of a wife. But the next morning Helen was in such bad shape that Ervin gave in and showed a little compassion—he couldn't just let her die—and he brought her a couple of bottles of beer from the shop. Helen promised that it would be the last time she ever had some hair of the dog, and that nothing of the sort would ever happen again. She told Ervin that she had only just realized that alcohol had become a serious problem for her, and that she would do everything in her power to avoid falling back into drinking.

Words, just words, Ervin sighed, although he knew that he had no choice but to go along with her.

A day or so later Hannes phoned: "What's happening? Do you have any idea what kind of state Mother is in?!" Ervin's son had happened to be in the area and he had gone to check if everything was alright at the summer house—that no one had broken in or anything.

Ervin felt suddenly short of breath, and he had the horrible feeling that the chair he was sitting on was swaying under him, as if his office were a ship on a rough sea. He could vividly imagine what his son must have seen at the summer house. He realized that he couldn't hide Helen's drinking any longer, and that he had to face the humiliation and take on the burden of shame. Nevertheless he still had the faint hope that maybe he and his sons could try and do something together to make the situation a little better.

It turned out that Helen had borrowed some money from the neighbor and brought home a whole bagful of liquor. Things had really gotten out of hand. The next day Ervin went out to the summer home, this time together with his sons. And as they drove home that evening he had the impression that his wife's shame and regret were finally genuine.

Helen had to get a grip on things, he thought. Everyone drinks, but only some people end up staring into the bottom of the glass like that.

Some time passed by in relative peace, and then they all went to the summer house for the solstice, where they had a barbecue and drank just soft drinks. Ervin hadn't felt that kind of family unity for a long time; it was if they had all reached out together to pull their mother away from the slippery slope, and that wasn't just some overblown sentimental image—that was really how things were.

The following week there was a terrible downpour, the rain came down for hours on end and torrents of water inundated the city, so that some people even had to use boats to get around. The rains subsided for a bit, but only for a few hours, as if resting and gathering new strength in order to come pouring down again with even greater force.

All bad things eventually pass, thought Ervin when the floodgates finally closed for a bit and the sun came out to shine exultantly. But he felt a heavy foreboding in his heart as he contemplated that good things also pass, and then it's just as if they had never happened at all.

And that was when Hannes called.

***

On the afternoon of that day that had started so badly for him, Ervin got into his car to drive to their summer house and try yet again to rein in his wife, who had drunk herself to oblivion. But he still had no clear plan of action. He realized that life had to go on, but that there was no way it could go on as it was. It was like a car that had gotten stuck in sand—you press on the accelerator but you end up just sinking deeper in. He felt his eyes turn moist. That's just me feeling sorry for myself, he thought, and the self-pity made him feel even more bitter.

What should he do? How could he put things right? He couldn't remember having thought about anything else recently, he would just sit there with a book open in front of him but not reading a single line, just staring pointlessly into the distance, as if he expected the answers to appear out of nowhere.

But was it really possible to find an answer for someone else?

When he was about ten minutes away from the house Ervin turned off the road. The feeling of helplessness had made him tenser with every kilometer and he had to forcibly restrain himself from pounding his head against the dashboard. He sat for some time with his eyes shut tight. There was an unnatural silence all around him, and all he could feel were his fingers trembling on the rough surface of the steering wheel. Eventually he heard a rumbling sound. It was getting towards the end of June and traffic was starting to get busier in the summer-home district. The rumbling brought Ervin to his senses. He suddenly saw very clearly how hopeless the situation had become. He didn't have a single consoling thought. All he could hear was the voice on the radio announcing dispassionately that a thirty-four-year-old alcoholic had killed his mother-in-law and seriously injured his wife during a drinking binge somewhere.

Drunks are an unpredictable bunch, Ervin thought to himself uneasily. He remembered one time when Helen had been drunk and wanted to go out, and he had tried to stop her. Helen had started pounding him in the face with her fists, as if her anger had given her extra strength. She had become a visibly different person recently. Some kind of inexplicable anger was bursting out from deep inside her, although when she was suffering from a hangover she became slavishly submissive.

It suddenly occurred to Ervin that if he found his wife in a bad way, in the grips of a hangover, then the sight of a bottle of beer would be enough to stop her from thinking about what kind of document she was being asked to sign. She would probably just sign it!

The idea that his wife would sign any document that was put in front of her suddenly cheered Ervin up. He even chuckled as if he had heard a funny story, and he decided that the following day he should figure out how to cut Helen out of his life and his business without incurring any major losses, or failing that how he could simply buy her off. If he could get the necessary signatures from her, he could find her a tiny apartment in some little town somewhere and support her with a reasonable monthly allowance. Then it would be her business whether she drank herself to death or finally came to her senses.

He could see it all quite clearly in his mind's eye—but would everything go as smoothly as that in real life?

Ervin knew that Helen was far from stupid, and that despite her drunken state she might realize that Ervin was planning to leave her with nothing. And of course she wouldn't be tied to that little town he had dreamed up! When she had drunk away all her money she would be back, knocking at Ervin's or their sons' doors with pitiful, theatrical promises on her lips. But everyone would realize that they would only hold true until the next time.

Is it really a dead end then, Ervin thought as he started driving again. A road with only death at the end of it?

Ervin couldn't think of a single case where one of his alcoholic friends had actually given up drinking. It's true that people would sometimes say that someone or other hadn't had a drop in however many years, but to him those stories just sounded like the empty propaganda of temperance campaigners, and they were very hard to believe. The scene from that morning suddenly came back to Ervin, when Artur had turned back the bent mirror with a single easy movement, so that everything was like it had been before. And Ervin started to get excited by the thought that quitting drinking would actually mean only a small lifestyle change . . .

But then he surprised even himself as he stopped the car at the roadside shop, and, with a vile malice in his heart, bought three bottles of beer.

The door to their summer home was wide open. He imagined he would find Helen, green in the face, cowering on the sofa, and that she would huddle into the corner when she saw him, hoping to become invisible. And instead of nagging her and raining down words of reproach, he would go and pour her a little hair of the dog, merrily clinking the beer bottles as he went. Unbelievable, Helen would think.

Unbelievable, he would think too, because he was unable to imagine himself in that role.

When Ervin got out of the car, he noticed right away that the blue poppy bush by the front door had been trampled into the ground, and that several faded blue flowers were lying on the earth, each one of them serving as a separate reproach. The luxuriant winter poppies had been the pride of the place back when Ervin's mother was still alive, but now someone had fallen into the bush, or maybe even spent a whole drunken night lying on it.

A moment ago Ervin had been in a relaxed mood, but now the anger flared up in him again. He threw the beer bottles onto the backseat of the car and marched in through the open door. What he saw inside didn't surprise him at all. Broken shards of plates and glasses were on the floor mixed up with food remains, and on the table there were stacks of cups full of cigarette butts. There must have been a larger than usual group here, Ervin thought in agitation. That old Finnish woman probably dragged half the town along with her. He shook his head despondently as he realized how naïve he had been to believe that his tough attitude could put his wife's alcoholic friend in her place.

"You throw that sort out of the door and she climbs right back in through the window," he grumbled angrily.

He walked through the house, but Helen was nowhere to be seen. It looked as if the group of guests had gone their separate ways. Although they might all be curing their hangovers together somewhere. Or stumbling about at the beach, as it was still summer after all. Counting up the number of glasses and cups on the table, he guessed that there was probably a gang of five or six of them. He imagined them bursting in right now, and he realized that there would be nothing he could do about it. They would force him to drink with them, or terrorize him in some other way. If things turned nasty they might do something really brutal or painful to him. And he wouldn't be able to do anything to stop it.

Ervin went outside to inspect the driveway, and he noticed fresh tracks on the wet surface. Maybe they've driven off, he thought hopefully. Helen might be resting somewhere nearby in the shade of the bushes, and he just hadn't noticed her yet. He sat down on the doorstep in the sunshine, trying to calm himself down.

He remembered when his father had begun to build the house. The perestroika-era cooperative businesses had just started to appear. People started to put up little summer homes in the nicest spots they could find. They were all small because there was nowhere to get hold of materials, and it was hard to find capable workmen. You had to do everything yourself, learning how to do the work from handbooks and gaining experience through trial and error. By now a lot of those ramshackle cottages had been turned into proper summer homes. A few years ago he had also done some major repair work, and they had ended up with a decent vacation place for the family.

But look what was happening here now, he thought bitterly. He noticed some movement at the neighbor's place, and he wanted to call out to the woman there and ask about Helen, but he realized just in time that it would be best to keep his mouth shut. Instead he retreated inside, burning up from embarrassment. He could well imagine what the neighbors must have seen. It was a wonder they hadn't called the police. Maybe they had? Maybe the guests had been taken away somewhere to sober up.

He didn't believe that things could have really gone that far, but he still didn't dare to speak with the woman next door. Maybe a bit later. Then he could go and apologize, try to think up some appeasing words and some convincing-sounding promises.

The floor was sticky and there was a box full of empty bottles of Vana Tallinn by the sink. How can they pour that vile stuff down their throats, he thought in disgust. There were some unfamiliar things lying around on the floor. Some bags, a briefcase, a car radio. His first thought was to chuck them all out through the front door, but when he felt the weight of the briefcase he opened it and saw that there was a laptop in it. It looked like an expensive HP and he couldn't bring himself to just throw it away. For a moment he felt tempted steal it. But only for a moment. He didn't want to have anything to do with the people who were taking advantage of his alcoholic wife.

Then his eyes alighted on a video camera lying on the floor next to the car radio. It slowly dawned on Ervin that if it had recently been used then he would be able to watch those shameless, disgusting, sickening scenes that the camera had been witness to in his house. But what use would there be in seeing all that, he asked himself, and he was unable to find an answer. What benefit is there in knowing the truth? Maybe there was more to be gained from shutting his eyes and plugging his ears?

Why do people yearn to see things they know they will regret seeing? Is it just curiosity? Or some inexplicable, subconscious craving?

Ervin quickly took a few steps backwards, as if he were retreating from a force field the camera was emitting, a powerful temptation he had to resist. But he already knew that he would be drawn back in soon enough, that he would reach out his hand and begin watching what there was to watch with a blank expression on his face. That's just human nature, he thought, trying to forgive himself.

But the camera showed him a film of children at the beach. Unfamiliar children running around on the sand and in the shallow water.

Ervin wound the film backwards and forwards and watched the scenes from a family's summer vacation, the kind of thing that would be watched wistfully a decade or several decades later. He guessed that the film had nothing to do with the drinking that had been going on at the house, and that the things that were lying about in the room must be stolen goods.

Someone probably smashed in a car window and took what was there, he thought, numbly at first, as if he were observing a stranger's thought processes. But then the facts of the matter started to sink in, and his hands started to tremble.

"That's all I needed," he mumbled forlornly.

The full realization of all the repulsive things that were going on around him, together with the knowledge that he was indirectly linked to them, dragged in against his will, sapped Ervin of his strength. It felt like time was racing past, and with it the last chance of trying to resolve things, to put them in order, to make them better. But then the startling thought came to him that if his wife was mixed up in some kind of theft, then she might be sent to prison. The idea shocked him at first, but soon became more appealing, and then to his surprise he actually started to like it.

Helen going to prison could solve the problems that had been tormenting him—it would bring her to her senses and force her to stop drinking. Her cossetted existence would be turned upside down and the shock might make her take a long, hard look at her life, weigh up the positives and negatives, and then . . . At this point Ervin's chain of thought broke off. It might seem like a solution for some people, but within his circle of acquaintances it would be difficult to live down the dirty truth that his wife had stolen something. Copious alcohol consumption was another matter . . .

And could the police actually be bothered to deal with petty theft, he mused, as if he were now trying to argue against the idea that had earlier seemed so attractive.

He thought that if things got really bad, he would still do everything possible to bury the story and save his family from the shame. As if to underline this new thought he took the rumpled blanket from the sofa and laid it over the stolen goods. "So as not to catch some chance visitor's eye," he said through gritted teeth.

"It's enough to make me ill," he said despairingly.

Breathing heavily and casting furtive glances in the direction of his neighbor's yard, he walked once around the outside of the house. The trees and bushes that had been planted years ago had grown tall and straight and most of the grounds were concealed from view. All the same, Ervin put on the appearance that he had some business to take care of in the backyard. As if he were looking for something. But I really am looking, he thought. My wife has gone missing.

Helen wasn't in the garden. Maybe the whole group went to the beach together, he thought as he stood under the apple tree grabbing absentmindedly at the piece of rope that was hanging there. The rope was tied to a branch quite high up, and on the grass in front of his feet there was a garden chair that was in pieces. It must have disintegrated in the rain, Ervin thought irritably. Things like that shouldn't be left out. It was a fairly new piece of furniture, but it hadn't survived being left in the rain. He gave the remains of the chair an angry kick.

Since he hadn't seen Helen yet there were still a lot of loose ends, the whole story was unclear, and he didn't know where to start piecing it together. He figured that if he went to the beach to look for his wife he would find her there with the band of drunks and could just take her home. By force if necessary. He imagined the gang of crooks and thieves she was with. Maybe he should give one of them a punch in the face? He got unexpected satisfaction from the triumphant image of him winning a fight with one of them.

At least then I would have actually done something about the situation, he thought.

Ervin took off his suit jacket and pants, placed them carefully inside the car, found his swimsuit in the glove compartment and, hiding behind the car, put them on. After thinking it over for a moment he decided to leave his shirt on, then he locked the car with a clunk, closed the door of the house, and hid his keys under the steps. When Ervin started walking towards the sea, under the shade of the pine trees, he experienced a strange feeling of liberation. All he had with him was his two hands and ten fingers. Nothing more. But suddenly he realized that that wouldn't be enough. He didn't feel free anymore, just defenseless.

***

When he arrived at the beach, Ervin was taken aback by the bizarre color of the sea. The water was blood red, and was completely still under a pale-blue sky and a thin veil of fog. A mass of half-naked people, their bodies seeming to radiate light, formed a restless shifting outline against the sand. Many of them were standing with their feet in the sea or walking knee-deep in the water. Almost none of them were swimming. Ervin got the impression that they were wary of the strange and alarming color of the sea.

A heartrending feeling came over Ervin, as if he were seeing that beach for the first time in his life, as if all the times he had been there since childhood had suddenly been erased. As if through inexplicable circumstances he had ended up in an unfamiliar new place, where he had no idea what to do with himself. He was surprised by a mental image that popped into his head comparing himself to a bug turned into its back. A helpless creature with wriggling legs, striving with its whole being to save itself, without the slightest hope of doing so. The thought grabbed him with such painful force that his hands and feet started moving instinctively. The sand crunched between his toes, and his fingers grasped at the air.

"Strange . . ." he forced the word through gritted teeth, his voice quavering dramatically, but he was unsure whether he was referring to the beach or to himself.

Ervin walked swiftly to the edge of the water. Due to a lull in the wind the surface had become smooth, and it was reflecting the light with a muted glint. The sea really was a reddish color, and at first glance it seemed have become thicker in consistency.

A light mist hung in the cloudless sky. The sun looked like a bright luminescent disc in this hazy setting. The vacationers were moving lazily around casting no shadows, seeming to be hovering above the shimmering sand.

Ervin had spent all his summers at this beach—for shorter or longer periods—so he had basically grown up there, but he had never seen anything as strange as this. It occurred to him that it could be the result of all those endless downpours. Torrents of reddish-brown bog water had flowed down the rivers into the sea and come to a halt there, held near the shore by the current in the bay. Until the wind started to blow.

So there was nothing mysterious about it. Nothing unnatural.

Ervin tried in this way to explain away nature's strange moods, to demonstrate to himself that every unearthly phenomenon had its earthly causes, but this did not calm him down. Quite the reverse—the blood-red sea under the hazy sky filled him with an uneasy feeling. A sense of foreboding was growing inside him, and he couldn't suppress it. It was the painful realization that the world had suddenly changed.

Familiar faces still looked familiar. But he had the vague notion that he only remembered them from the television screen or photographs, that he had nothing to do with them in real life. Only when Ervin started talking to one of them did he remember why he had come to the beach in the first place. My wife has gone missing, he thought.

My drunken wife is hanging around here like a walking mark of shame. I can't pretend that other peoples' opinions don't bother me. Of course they do. He suddenly became very gloomy, and he turned his back abruptly on his interlocutor and walked onwards.

The water was blood red and the sky was hazy.

The sand crunched under his feet, sounding like a sad flock of cranes. Ervin looked across the dunes, seeking something to fix his eyes upon, but Helen was nowhere to be seen. But there was really no reason for her to be there, as she didn't like the crowded part of the beach near the entrance and always preferred to walk further on.

He started to feel as if he had been wandering endlessly up and down the low dunes, but there was still no Helen there amongst the lyme grass, neither on her own nor with her gang of drunks. He responded to greetings from several acquaintances, but he couldn't bring himself to ask about his wife. When he had almost reached the river that was carrying the reddish water to the sea, he felt overwhelmed with tiredness, and he lowered himself down onto the sand. The weather had become oppressive. His shirt, which he hadn't bothered to take off, felt like a wet rag against his skin.

Ervin lay with his eyes shut on the warm sand, and indistinct sounds reached his ears—shouts, a child crying, the murmur of voices coming closer for a moment and then getting further away. He remembered once reading about a similar situation—someone was lying in a closed coffin and listening to people saying things about him which were very different to what he wanted to hear. The protagonist of the story realized that no one was actually mourning his death—quite the reverse, it had even made some people happy. The worst part of it all was hearing people who were close to him talking that way. People whom he had loved, who were supposed to have loved him.

Suddenly Ervin thought he heard a familiar voice. Helen's voice. It still wasn't very clear, he couldn't make out the individual words, but the voice sounded like hers. Ervin felt a pleasant, warm, familiar feeling stirring inside him. He decided not to open his eyes, he would just lie there motionless until he heard Helen call out: "Look, it's my husband, just imagine, I found my husband on the beach!"

Ervin waited for a long time, until he became tired of waiting. Eventually he lost hope, deciding that the familiar voice must have been just a trick of the senses, just a hidden desire which had deceived him into thinking it was true. He didn't open his eyes, he was comfortable just lying there, nothing was bothering him at all. He wanted to make that moment last. In the meantime Helen would probably arrive back at the house and see his car there, then if she still had any sense she would try to get rid of all signs of the drinking binge, clean the dirt from the floor, and at least make things look like they were in order.

Yes indeed, he thought.

When Ervin woke up from his dozing after what could have been either a long or short period of time, the sky had already turned dark. It's about to rain, he thought worriedly, and he sat upright. The sky was covered with dark clouds and streaks of foam glimmered on the darkening water. The beach looked empty, but to the left, behind the mouth of the river, where the beach ended and the high limestone cliff began, there were people jostling about. Ambulance lights were flashing, and it looked like there were police cars. The cars were parked on the cliff, people were gathered by the water's edge, and it looked like something bad had happened down there.

What could have happened, Ervin asked himself, feeling a painful spasm in his heart. He remembered two things at once—an evening a little while back when he had parked the car on the limestone cliff and he and Helen had admired the sunset. Helen had suddenly clung to him with unnatural strength and shouted: "Oh it's awful! The crevice is pulling me in, hold on to me so that I don't jump!" And then he remembered the disintegrated garden chair under the apple tree and the piece of rope hanging down from the branch.

Ervin was gripped by a feeling of panic, but he couldn't move. He kept staring in the direction of the limestone cliff, but he was unable to make out anything clearly. He was completely paralyzed by the thought that Helen had been in a serious accident, that what was happening a few hundred meters away involved her in some way. It was very unlikely, but he still believed it.

But instead of springing to his feet and running to find out what was going on, he threw himself to the ground and buried his face in the sand. He had discovered something that he would have preferred not to know. He had looked inside himself and realized that he was hoping with his whole being that everything would be just as he feared it was.

He had longed for Helen to be dead.

His wife's alcoholism had invaded his life, and stuck to him like mud. He had tried to shake it off but he was covered with it for everyone to see, and it got worse by the day. At that very moment, however, he felt ashamed of himself.

"A person should never think like that, it's inhuman!" he said grinding his teeth. But at the same time he sensed that, deep down inside him, the desire that had briefly surfaced was still there. It wouldn't go anywhere. On the contrary, it was gathering strength and courage, until one day he would no longer be ashamed of it.

Ervin could no longer bear to lie there on the sand, alone with his feelings, so he set off swiftly towards the scene of the accident. There were some people standing on the bridge that spanned the river. "What happened?" Ervin asked. "Oh, someone flung themselves off the cliff again," they said.

His first impulse was to keep going, but he came to a stop in the middle of the bridge. He stood there and watched the raging river waters racing towards the sea. The left bank of the river had collapsed and the river mouth had swollen unusually wide.

Yes indeed, he thought.

AN INORDINATELY, UNIMAGINABLY LARGE BIRD

Will the invisible ever become visible? That question can be answered in the affirmative, assuming that cognition consists only of visible forms.

—René Magritte to Michel Foucault, 23 May 1966

It was a sunny spring morning, the kind when the trees are already in leaf but the cold wind makes you want to grab a warm jacket. Fooled by the sunshine and willfully defying the cold, he decided to go to work on foot. Although it would actually be inaccurate to say "on foot," since these days no one walks twenty kilometers: they take the bus, tram, or taxi—that is, if they can't be bothered to drive themselves.

He noticed a couple of young lovers waiting at the bus stop: they stood there face to face, hand in hand, looking like they were conversing with their eyes; words (which sufficed for everyday matters) suddenly weren't enough. With their eyes they could say the things they couldn't say with words, things that would otherwise go unsaid. The girl's facial expression said the same as her eyes and no onlooker could miss that. He felt envy and regret: for him all this was no more—just yesterday's dream. He couldn't compare himself with that boy anymore—he (and the girl too, why not) had probably only recently lost their innocence. He knew only too well that in his case the sonatas that had been written to those feelings and thoughts were last played a quarter of a century ago (if they were ever played at all).

He noticed how the piercing morning sunlight rendered the girl's dress transparent, and he quickly turned his gaze away—towards the street corner, where more and more people were arriving to wait at the bus stop, some of them groggy from waking, some moody, one of them with a swollen face and puffy eyes. Someone big and flabby stood next to him breathing heavily (wheezing, as if straining from an excessive burden), giving off a stench of garlic, which he must have had generous helpings of the previous night. And then he noticed that the beautiful girl was not in fact beautiful at all; she had a double chin, her face was a bit too flat, and her forehead was covered in pimples. An element of discord suddenly intruded into the girl's consciousness and her expression, previously open and lively, glazed over as if she had put on a mask (like a bank robber just before a heist). Now the beautiful girl in love was no more, and in her place there was just a bird. Yes, she looked just like a bird, with a pointed nose protruding abruptly from her small face, and frightened, staring eyes.

The bus arrived and he was able to observe the boy. That nameless head, which the girl's face had been jealously hiding from view, was now exposed for investigation, and when he saw it he felt angry enough to spit. The person who he had thought was a boy was in fact a middle-aged man, with long hair tied back like a horse's or donkey's tail, which had created a deceptive impression. If earlier he was jealous (of the boy), he now felt pity and sympathy for the middle-aged man, who was ready to sacrifice his peace of mind for a few hours of pleasure and had gotten caught up in some pointless and senseless adventures (with a young girl who herself was head over heels in love!). He knew about these things, he had experienced them himself. When the bus doors opened and he took a step backwards to let the old person in front of him (who was very thin, just skin and bones) get closer to the door, he heard the crows cawing again. All of the surrounding trees were packed full of croaking black birds.

He had forgotten about the birds while he had been watching the lovers (although only the girl was really in love). They had been making his life a misery since the previous evening, he had been thinking about them when he woke up in the middle of the night, and they had made his morning rising especially unpleasant. The noise had suddenly disappeared somewhere for a few minutes, only to return (as an ill-boding reminder) just before he managed to escape. He grinned as he likened the closing of the bus doors and the subsequent journey to a "salvation from the birds." It was a metaphorical expression without substance, a casual figure of speech, since no one would literally need to be saved from some croaking crows.

The crows had arrived yesterday during the day, as Aster, the woman next door, had confirmed. She had been busy in the garden and was able to accurately describe the moment of the birds' arrival. "At first I was shocked to see four of them sitting there just four meters away leering at me with their greedy, bulging eyes, but then when I shouted shoo! they just hopped a little to one side, the cocky, arrogant birds! Then at two o'clock a big flock of them came, the branches of the beech trees were buckling under their weight, they looked like they were squabbling amongst themselves—the vile, ear-splitting croaking sounded like screams—I couldn't stand it for long, I had to escape indoors. I had planned to tidy up the flower bed in front of the veranda, but that got nowhere, I couldn't listen to that screeching a moment longer."

At nine o'clock, exactly when the evening news started, he had received a call from Hunt, who lived in the same suburb. He wanted to know if there were any more details about the rumored plans to remove the mayor and make him stand trial.

"I haven't heard anything about it," he answered, unable to conceal the surprise in his voice (he wasn't just surprised, he was panic-stricken, because he guessed—he knew!—what could lie behind a rumor like that). So to try and hide the stress he was feeling he asked Hunt if there were also countless numbers of crows croaking around his house.

"No croaking here. Not a single crow croaking in our parts, and if one were to so much as open its beak then one of the boys would shoot it down right away."

"It's like a Hitchcock film over here," he said, but he suspected that Hunt probably didn't know much about cinema. "It's a film from the sixties where birds start to attack the inhabitants of a small town, the children can't get home from school because the birds peck them to death. It's a horrible story, but it does have a happy ending," he explained.

"But it's the nineties now," Hunt laughed. "And what's more, the century's almost over."

He couldn't understand why Hunt suddenly mentioned the end of the century, but then he remembered that he had mentioned that the film was made in the sixties. He realized that Hunt was just trying to be witty. But it's one thing to try to be witty, another to actually be witty, he thought angrily. He could even hear the crows' constant cawing through the closed window, and the sound made him shudder in horror.

***

At lunchtime there was something he wanted to do in the town center. An art book had caught his attention in a shop window; it had a picture of a giant rose in a room on its cover. The rose just barely fit into the room, stretching from floor to ceiling and wall to wall. He went into the shop to buy the book.

The shopkeeper (an elderly lady with an elaborate hairdo) was flustered: "Actually, a woman asked me not to sell that."

"I'm sorry?" he asked, becoming flustered himself.

"Actually . . ." repeated the woman with the impressive hair in an almost pleading tone, although she couldn't find the words with which to make the plea. One could imagine her trying to find them, trying to create the most correct and precise sequence of words that would explain and justify what she said . . . but she didn't get to grips with the task.

The situation seemed incongruous, even odd, especially taking into account that this was a shop. He gave up, turning his back on the shopkeeper and exiting onto the street without saying anything more. But when he passed the shop window the book grabbed his attention again. It was a big flower. Very big, the size of a room.

And then he suddenly realized that he was being haunted by an image of a gigantic bird. He couldn't describe the image any more precisely than that. He wouldn't even attempt to compare the bird with the rose blossom. He figured that this must be a question of reality and relativity (in the philosophical sense?!). Or in other words, the problem of comparing two mental images. The rose was in a physical space, a room, so the viewer could determine the size of the rose relative to the room. But the viewer was given no information regarding the size of the room, so it was impossible to know the size of the rose relative to anything else. Similarly, he might have thought of the bird as being inordinately large, but he had to limit himself to it simply being unimaginably large.

Now he knew that he had to buy the book, however much it might cost, because it would allow him to learn something about what this "unimaginable" might mean.

"I'll take that please," he said, addressing the other shopkeeper and pointing at the book in the window with his index finger.

"Oh, you want that one," said the shopkeeper, and her words sounded like a confirmation that she had understood the client's wish. (The book's title was *The Tomb of the Wrestlers* and it was an introduction to the life and works of the Belgian artist René Magritte). The shopkeeper took the book from amongst the other books that were positioned in the window to lure passers-by, then she shifted them back so that the gap wouldn't be noticed, trying to create the impression that the missing book had never been there in the first place.

As he walked past a plaza with some tables and chairs not far from the bookshop he heard his name being called out (in a loud, trained voice, a voice that sounded immediately familiar), and when he looked up from the road he saw an actor whom he half knew sitting drinking beer in the sunshine. He didn't have any particular appetite for chatting, but there was a strange, entreating undertone to the voice, so he sat down next to the famous actor, on a white chair that had been pleasantly warmed in the sunshine.

"Imagine this, I go out on stage and my close friend, or to be precise my lover—that is, the lover of the person I'm playing—has just died, and I—or the character—is completely shattered, every sentence he says—I mean every sentence I say—comes with tears from the very depths of his soul and is supposed to make a theater full of people feel heartfelt sympathy for me—or for the rather camp fellow I'm playing—but all those damned people just start laughing. Just imagine—I say that my life has lost all meaning, and they laugh—I say that my life is over, and they laugh even louder. So I don't say anything more, I just glare angrily at them, and then they start cracking up at that as well. I've been making them laugh for twenty years, I finally manage to persuade the producer to give me a serious role, in the rehearsals everyone says that I'm good, that I'm great, that I was wasting myself with all that clowning around all these years, that I'm really a fine dramatic actor. And then I go out onto the stage to do this serious stuff and they piss their pants laughing."

He tried to console and encourage the actor but soon realized how futile his fine intentions were. The half-drunk man (maybe he was curing his hangover a little too enthusiastically) didn't even need to be helped, he had polished his story down to the last detail, got himself into the role (and only into that role), and he was like a fish in water. But when you realized that his situation was actually more like a fish pulled out onto dry land, then the fact that he was identifying with that situation and taking pleasure in the tragedy of it had a comic effect. But that was inevitable—he was after all a comedian by vocation.

"I'm being stalked by this mental image of a big bird again," he said in a tragic tone that was similar to the one the comedian had used to perform his story.

The actor glared straight at him: "How can a mental image stalk you?" he asked.

***

He told his secretary to tell anyone who asked that he wasn't there. When he had closed the door, positioned the art book in front of himself on the table, and opened it at a random page, the full significance of the sentence he had just said (and had said a hundred times before) suddenly dawned on him: I'm not here.

The picture in front of him depicted boots with toes, standing (?) beside a wall of a house that had been knocked together from unpainted planks. There were some coins lying on the ground in front of the toes. One could conclude that they were a very fine pair of boots: the cobbler had even bothered making toes. But the toes also had toenails, and so one couldn't avoid the conclusion that the boots were actually feet, but the person whose feet were standing there was not actually there himself. The coins were a reference to begging. Sometimes people with no legs have to go begging. But here there were legs which for some reason had ended up without a body, and they were begging.

He had once seen that painting in Stockholm and at the time he had been excited by the fact that this was the first Magritte original he was fortunate enough to see. And he had felt that after seeing the original he somehow had a different relationship with the artist (a more personal one?). As if the artist had somehow become a bit closer to him. But this time he was taken aback by the reference note: Edward James Foundation, Chichester, Sussex. That meant that the picture was actually located in England, not Sweden! So now he started to have doubts about the veracity of his memory, and he decided that he must have seen a different Magritte, and that his memory (that old trickster) had taken a picture from some book that had made an impression on him and placed it in the Moderna Museet in Stockholm.

He snorted indignantly as he read over the text, which explained things: this was one version of the picture (not the artist's original), and another pair of boots with toes was indeed hanging there on the wall in Stockholm. To try to fully clarify the situation, he looked up the details of Magritte's life history: in 1937 the artist had spent three weeks in London, where his host had been the very same Edward James, for whom he dutifully carried out a great deal of work (maybe on his instructions as well?).

A couple of years ago he had happened to see a large Magritte collection in Brussels (thirty paintings, mostly from the later period). He was astonished to see how the literary element (the surrealistic absurd) had pushed the fine art (the emotional impact of colors) to the background. He was left with the impression that the artist had used just three or four colors to paint the picture, deliberately rejecting everything that was held to be important in fine art at that time (what Clement Greenberg would call the "sublime").

He had been particularly disappointed by one of the versions of the "Empire of Light" (he could no longer remember which one), which looked like a badly printed poster. Usually reproductions of paintings left a deeper impression on him, and in the course of inspecting them he could always imagine that the original must have been more impressive. There is an emotional aspect that is integral to looking at reproductions—coming from the knowledge that you're looking at something smaller, worse quality, poorer (etc.) than the real painting. But in reality (!) the reproduction is, thanks to its smaller size, denser in detail and therefore richer in some ways.

"It is only in the case of the Old Masters that one can say that the originals are completely different from even the most technically impressive of reproductions," Vennet explained to the artist when he was complaining about his disappointment with Magritte on return from Brussels. That statement conveyed a lot of things, amongst them the view that Magritte had not been an Old Master.

"Then was he a major artist?" he asked unsurely.

"That's an interesting question," Vennet said. "As far as I am aware a certain Mr. Swift dealt with the problem of scale quite thoroughly back in his day. His object of study was a man named Gulliver, who was first a giant who thought that everyone smaller than him were Lilliputians, and then a Lilliputian who believed that ordinary, normal people were giants."

***

He rejected several proposals that would have lengthened his working day, explaining that he was tired and wanted to sit quietly at home for once. When the day came to an end and he had started on his way home (by foot and by bus), a pigeon suddenly took flight right in front of him, almost scraping his cheek. The shock made him catch his breath as he recoiled from the bird, and he froze still in a defensive posture, but then he noticed the curious look on a passerby's face, and this brought him back to reality. It was only a pigeon, a bird that was slightly larger than average size, bigger than a sparrow or finch, but smaller than an eagle or a pelican. He had no reason to be afraid of a pigeon. A pigeon didn't bear the slightest resemblance (in terms of size) to the bird that was stalking him in his imagination.

But Magritte's rose (in the painting "The Tomb of the Wrestlers") was not necessarily larger than average either. Maybe it was the room that was tiny. Just a room in a doll's house. Everything is small in a doll's house, in correct proportion to a doll's view of the world. In his mind's eye he could see another Magritte work ("Personal Values"), which depicted a room with walls made of cloudy skies. The bed, the wardrobe, and carpets were proportional to the size of the room, but the comb, glass, soap, and shaving brush were gigantic, the same size as the bed and wardrobe. The pinkish-lilac match with the yellow tip seemed to be the largest of all the objects, almost as large as the bed or shaving brush.

He assumed that this picture (from 1952) contained the code needed for reading another picture (from 1960). The rose was inordinately large, it barely fit into an ordinary (normal) room, and that was only if it represented a personal value for someone. But he also couldn't get rid of the image of a room in a doll's house (could it be that normal sized objects had been placed inside a doll's house?), just like he couldn't get rid of the image of the unimaginably large bird that was stalking him.

The writer Toomas Vint (a childhood friend, and some years later a close neighbor) had once told him that if a dream (or maybe some figment of the imagination) started to haunt you, then a surefire way of getting rid of it was to write it into some story.

"It's possible that telling a reader about the dream is just as effective as going to make one's confessions to a psychologist, although I tend to think that it's really just a case of shifting one's own problems onto some invented character's shoulders.

Let him bear my burden and suffer my worries," Vint had said with a laugh.

He weighed up whether he should put the bird image into writing, transforming it into an object of horror for some unidentified other. At the gate of his house he felt quite distinctly how a gust of wind from the wing stroke of a gigantic bird swept his hat off his head (it even ended up lying in the dusty street a couple of meters away from him). But when he looked around there was nothing unusual in the street, even the croaking crows weren't there anymore—that flock of birds seemed to have gone their own way.

He pondered (sadly) why he had just referred to "that" flock of birds, "that" flock which had flown away—just as if dozens of earlier flocks of birds had repeatedly used the trees in his garden as a temporary stopping point, with no plans for making his pleasant neighborhood a permanent nesting place. Birds and people have very different tastes, he thought, and he rang the doorbell because he couldn't be bothered to look for the keys in his pocket. No one came to open the door. As he waited he realized that apart from those crows no other flock of birds had ever stopped in his garden. The crows had been the first.

The sun had been shining in blue skies all day long, but the clouds had started to obscure it and the surroundings had lost their color. The first heavy drops of rain started to patter down. He opened the door and made straight for his room on the second floor. He guessed that he was alone in the large house, but he couldn't be bothered to check whether he was right, and he had no particular need to know.

For a moment the large bird had obscured the sun.

The large bird had obscured the sun, and as it gradually glided downwards on the air currents its diffuse shadow became denser and more distinct, then as it got closer to the ground the area of land under its wings become darker and darker. And then it landed, its legs absorbing the force of its descent like steel springs. The trees under its feet bent like blades of grass, the houses collapsed like matchboxes. People were running, fleeing in panic, crazed from fear and not realizing that they were rushing straight towards the very spot where the bird's foot would step next, bringing with it death and destruction.

***

To begin, I have to clarify roughly how big the bird is, he thought, as he let his eyes wander across the books spines distractedly. The room was full of books, like plenty of other rooms in this small country, which once lived through a strange period of history when books came out in such large print runs that nearly one in ten Estonian speakers could buy a copy of every new work to put on their bookshelf at home (and many saw it as their duty to do so). He suddenly felt that his plan to put that mental image into writing was stupid: it was pointless to invent a person who imagined a large bird, and then to observe him in all those (invented) situations when the bird might appear. The shelves lining his walls were full of thousands of invented situations (or ones which had been copied from real life), and they couldn't really differ that much from each other. The only credible difference was probably the aim—precisely, the aim!—with which a poem, story, or novel had been written. The aim was very important. The aim was in fact the difference.

He remembered Kafka's story about a large beetle. This was a story in which the writer had realized the object of his imagination within the reality of the book (the text), and had then closely observed how reality behaved in response to his imagined object: what happens when something is not as it should be.

It's possible that this had been Kafka's last chance to act before reality started behaving in accordance with his fantasy (that he was a large beetle), at which point his father would have probably put him into a mental hospital. But in that event (if Kafka had been put into a mental hospital), a new (unsolvable) question arises: which reality would have been more realistic, the reality of the Big Beetle, or the reality of the Mental Hospital?

After a brief search (he had a good visual memory and the cucumber green spine of the book flashed up in front of his eyes immediately) the story of Gregor Samsa was there in his hands.

He switched on the computer and started rewriting the Kafka text from his own perspective.

"The Metamorphosis"

One morning I woke up in my bed after uneasy dreams to find myself transformed into a huge bird. I was squatting down, my legs bent uncomfortably under me, my bloated stomach stretching towards the head of the bed and onto the pillow, and my backside hanging over the foot of the bed. When I crooked my head slightly to one side I could see my shimmering rainbow-colored plumage, but when I tried to move my fingers I saw that there were ten feathers at the ends of my wings moving instead.

"What has happened to me?" I thought. It wasn't a dream. As usual, I was in my room, which was a slightly oversized office with the walls covered in familiar bookshelves. There were materials from a municipal government meeting open on the table—I was a senior city official—and there was a picture of me that had recently been painted by a famous portrait painter hanging over the table.

I directed my eyes towards the window, but the wet weather—I could hear the rain drops pattering against the windowpane—made me melancholy. "If I could just keep on sleeping for a bit longer and forget about all this silliness," I thought, but it was impossible. I was used to sleeping on my right side and in my current predicament I couldn't adopt that position. When I strained to try and turn onto my side, I instead fell out of the bed onto the floor. I tried hundreds of times to fit myself into the bed and I closed my eyes so as not to see the wings. But I gave up on these futile attempts when I started to feel a faint dull ache in my wing joints.

"Oh God," I thought, "my job really is a strain! Day in, day out, nothing but responsibilities. And the stress of those responsibilities is much more than a normal official has to deal with—in addition to all that constant dodging and weaving I'm oppressed by the fear that the whispering will come out into the open. Then there are the fleeting sexual relationships with random women, excessive eating, constant swapping of bosses and staff. Damn it all!"

I felt a slight itching in the lower part of my tail: in order to reach it easier with my beak I supported myself sideways against the wall. I found the itchy part, which was bare of feathers and completely covered in red spots, the significance of which I didn't fully comprehend. I wanted to scratch that spot with my beak, but as soon as I touched it I felt a cold shiver run through my body, and I pulled my head back . . .

***

It was already past midnight when he decided that that was enough for now. He would have been happy to live the rest of his life as a fictional bird, but an annoying dull headache forced him to go to bed and rest his head. As he went to the bedroom he thought to himself that from now on he would be living every day of his life just waiting for the evenings, when he could savor the pleasure of writing in the quiet of his office.

His wife wasn't asleep yet, she was sitting there between the pillows, leafing through a color magazine. He wanted to say something to her (something friendly, in a kind voice) but he couldn't find the right words, so he undressed in silence, telling himself: why should I say anything if she doesn't say anything herself. Once he had slipped under his blanket, his wife put the lights out (as if she had been waiting for him all along), and in the silent darkness that descended he could hear the rain beating against the roof. He tried not to think of the scandal that was going to blow up at the city hall tomorrow or the day after, and the consequences for his future career (in all likelihood it would come to an end). He didn't want to think about the future, he just wanted to sleep, but the aspirin hadn't started working yet, and the throbbing pain in his head was growing more and more acute. In order to try and distract himself he began thinking about some of the arousing episodes from his recent trip to Paris. One of these had been with a black prostitute who had gotten him especially turned on. He suddenly became aroused and felt an indiscriminate urge to satisfy himself, come what may. At that point he heard a thundering sound above the house. There was a terrible crash, and then it felt like the bed was shaking or swaying.

"Hey, what about having a little fun," he said to his wife, certain that if she had been asleep then the thundering sound would have woken her up. "Having some fun" was their special phrase, the code they used when one of them was in the mood. His wife didn't answer.

"Come on, how's about we have a bit of fun tonight." This time he worded his wish differently, and uttered it louder and more insistently.

"I'm fed up with your fun," his wife finally said in a tired, irritated voice, and she turned her back to him.

His head was empty for a while, but then feelings of anger and affront started to flood in to fill the space. Throughout the whole course of their married life his wife had never once declined his amorous advances. She always waited patiently for her husband to show his affections, and treated them like some precious gift when he did.

He listened to his wife's snuffling for a bit. Then he pulled the blanket off her and started to push her onto her back. She resisted vigorously, as if it were a matter of life and death. By the time he had finally managed to press himself between her legs, his excitement had subsided, disappeared completely.

"Come on now my strong man, give it to me then, come on give it to me!" his wife taunted him.

He tried to shove his flaccid member into his wife using his fingers, but it didn't work. "So why aren't you having your fun then? Are you too old and feeble for fun now?" his wife hissed, getting out of bed and taking her blanket, with the intention of going to another room to sleep. But he grabbed hold of the blanket and pulled it, together with his wife, towards the bed.

"Where are you off to, wifey?" (He heard his own voice as if it were someone else speaking.) "Into town, I bet? To describe all this in faithful detail to your friends? A person can sometimes be unfit for work, and in those situations one should recall his earlier services and bear in mind that later, once the obstacles have been removed, he will return to work with renewed effort and commitment. I owe a real debt of gratitude to you, you know that yourself. I'm worried about the children too. I'm in a difficult situation now, but I'm striving to work my way through it. Don't make this more difficult for me than it already is . . ."

His wife rushed off leaving him holding the blanket. The rain wasn't pelting down anymore, instead there was just a strange ringing silence, as if a pillow were being pushed down onto his head. He turned himself onto his stomach so he was lying diagonally across the bed and he pressed the pillow onto his throbbing head (to make the quietness even quieter).

This Kafkaesque transformation into a large bird is my escape, he suddenly thought. I'll turn into a large bird and fly out the open window into the endless expanse. Then I will be freer than I've ever been before.

***

He was awoken by a shaking sensation, someone was shaking his shoulder carefully but persistently. He was hot, his body was wet with sweat, and it took him some time to force his eyes open. When he finally did (because the shaking got rougher, more insistent), he saw his whole family (his three daughters, wife, and his wife's mother) in front of the bed, dressed in ghostly-looking white nightgowns. The electric lights weren't on, instead the light came from a single thick candle in his mother-in-law's outstretched hand. "Something terrible has happened," his wife said in a half-whisper. His youngest daughter started sobbing.

"Has the electricity gone off?" he asked, pushing himself upright.

"Come and have a look," his wife said, and they went up to the window. His mother-in-law lifted the candle right up to the windowpane. On the other side of the window there were thick blackish-gray ropes and strings, pressing densely against the glass. It was stiflingly hot in the room.

"The same stuff is covering all the other windows," said his mother-in-law, her voice quavering in fear. "The front door won't open. The telephone doesn't work. There's no electricity."

He took the candle and went down to the lower floor. There was more of that same braiding outside the kitchen window, only it was a lighter gray and made from thinner strings. The women were waiting in silence, watching him hopefully, but he suddenly felt hungry. He remembered that the last time he had eaten had been yesterday morning. No wonder I'm hungry, he thought, opening the fridge and inspecting the contents by candlelight.

"You must do something," his wife said in a timid voice.

"Of course I must," he said as he noticed the roast duck, which for some strange reason made him happy to the depths of his soul. He looked at the kitchen clock, which showed half past six. It should already be light outside by now, he thought as he wiped his greasy fingers on his pajama trousers.

"Have you got a battery-powered radio?" he asked his daughters. They shook their heads. He sighed. He walked around the kitchen shining candlelight into every corner, giving the others the impression that he was looking for something. Finally, a long-handled brush caught his eye. He gave the candle to his wife and tried to smash the window with the brush handle. He succeeded only once he had hurled it with all his might against the windowpane.

Holding the brush handle in front of him like a spear, he approached the window, the lower part of which had shattered. The gray mass was pushing inwards through this gap. He carefully pushed the brush handle into it, and the full length of it went in without meeting any obstacles. Then he took one piece of the string (or whatever it was) between his hands and started to tug it. After a great strain it gave way, then the substance, which resembled palm fronds, started coming into the room. The more that came in, the thinner and lighter in color it became—and then he suddenly realized: the things he was tugging at were down feathers. They were the down feathers of an inordinately large bird that had fallen onto his house. He felt a sudden sense of relief and triumph: the unimaginably large bird was to blame for everything.

***

His hand was already stiff from chopping by the time a glimmer of light appeared through the feathers. He went back to the cellar window and helped his wife and children up (his mother-in-law had felt a pain in her heart and had gone to bed). He wanted the family to experience the joy of freedom all together. As he chopped the last feathers away, he felt as if he had the raw power of a young man. And then they escaped. For the first few minutes they couldn't get used to the light. They blinked and rubbed their eyes with the backs of their hands. When they were finally able to see normally again they didn't recognize their surroundings.

"My God!" his wife called out as she grabbed him by the hand. There were thick green spears growing from the ground, dotted sparsely here and there, chest height and needle sharp towards the top. Not far from where they stood a creature the size of an Alsatian, but resembling a giant ant, scuttled past. They warily started moving forwards, and they found that the green stems were flexible and bent downwards when they stumbled against them. After they had wandered for some time, making a detour around a steaming man-sized hill that gave off a choking stench of excrement, the greenery came to an end and they saw a stone plain stretching out ahead of them. The student from next door was there, tinkering with the car he had bought recently, which had gotten wedged between the stones.

"Listen," his wife said in a whisper so that the children couldn't hear. "I've got the feeling that this bird isn't so big at all, rather it's we that are small . . . we are Lilliputians."

"So what," he said.

"The main thing is that we are free," he said a little later, and he looked at his elder daughter, who was growing more and more animated. He saw that his wife was also looking at her. Despite the troubles they had all lived through, to which the paleness of her cheeks bore testimony, his daughter had grown into a beautiful, buxom young woman.

They remained silent but the look in their eyes said what they both knew instinctively: now was the time to choose a good man for her.

Toomas Vint was born in 1944 in Tallinn, Estonia, where he still lives today with his wife Aili. Since 1971, Vint has earned a living as a freelance writer and painter. Vint's novels and short stories have been nominated for several literary awards; he has won the Friedebert Tuglas Short Story Award twice, as well as the Estonian Prose Award. His novel *An Unending Landscape* is also available from Dalkey Archive Press.

Matthew Hyde is a translator of fiction and non-fiction from Russian and Estonian. Matthew worked for 15 years for the British Government as a translator, research analyst, and diplomat, with postings in London, Moscow, and Tallinn. Following this last posting Matthew chose to remain in Tallinn with his Estonian partner and baby son, where he plays the double bass and translates.

MICHAL AJVAZ, *The Golden Age.*
The Other City.

PIERRE ALBERT-BIROT, *Grabinoulor.*

YUZ ALESHKOVSKY, *Kangaroo.*

FELIPE ALFAU, *Chromos.*
Locos.

SVETISLAV BASARA, *Chinese Letter.*

RENÉ BELLETTO, *Dying.*

ANDREJ BLATNIK, *You Do Understand.*
Law of Desire.

IGNÁCIO DE LOYOLA BRANDÃO, *Anonymous Celebrity.*
Zero.

G. CABRERA INFANTE, *Infante's Inferno.*
Three Trapped Tigers.

JULIETA CAMPOS, *The Fear of Losing Eurydice.*

ORLY CASTEL-BLOOM, *Dolly City.*

LOUIS-FERDINAND CÉLINE, *North.*
Conversations with Professor Y.
London Bridge.

ERIC CHEVILLARD, *Demolishing Nisard.*
The Author and Me.

ARIEL DORFMAN, *Konfidenz.*

ARKADII DRAGOMOSHCHENKO, *Dust.*

FRANÇOIS EMMANUEL, *Invitation to a Voyage.*

PAUL EMOND, *The Dance of a Sham.*

SALVADOR ESPRIU, *Ariadne in the Grotesque Labyrinth.*

JUAN FILLOY, *Op Oloop.*

CARLOS FUENTES, *Christopher Unborn.*
Distant Relations.
Terra Nostra.
Where the Air Is Clear.

GÉRARD GAVARRY, *Hoppla! 1 2 3..*

WITOLD GOMBROWICZ, *A Kind of Testament.*

GEORGI GOSPODINOV, *Natural Novel.*

JUAN GOYTISOLO, *Count Julian.*
Juan the Landless.
Makbara.
Marks of Identity.

MELA HARTWIG, *Am I a Redundant Human Being?*

DRAGO JANČAR, *The Tree with No Name.*

MIKHEIL JAVAKHISHVILI, *Kvachi.*

GERT JONKE, *The Distant Sound.*
Homage to Czerny.
The System of Vienna.

JACQUES JOUET, *Mountain R.*
Savage.
Upstaged.

DANILO KIŠ, *The Attic.*
The Lute and the Scars.
Psalm 44.
A Tomb for Boris Davidovich.

ANNA KORDZAIA-SAMADASHVILI, *Me, Margarita.*

ERIC LAURRENT, *Do Not Touch.*

VIOLETTE LEDUC, *La Bâtarde.*

EDOUARD LEVÉ, *Autoportrait.*
Newspaper.
Suicide.
Works.

MARIO LEVI, *Istanbul Was a Fairy Tale.*

FLORIAN LIPUŠ, *The Errors of Young Tjaž.*

HISAKI MATSUURA, *Triangle.*

ABDELWAHAB MEDDEB, *Talismano.*

GERHARD MEIER, *Isle of the Dead.*

CHRISTINE MONTALBETTI, *The Origin of Man.*
Western.

YVES NAVARRE, *Our Share of Time.*
Sweet Tooth.

WILFRIDO D. NOLLEDO, *But for the Lovers.*

FLANN O'BRIEN, *At Swim-Two-Birds.*
The Best of Myles.
The Dalkey Archive.
The Hard Life.
The Poor Mouth.
The Third Policeman.

CLAUDE OLLIER, *The Mise-en-Scène.*
Wert and the Life Without End.

PATRIK OUŘEDNÍK, *Europeana.*
The Opportune Moment, 1855.

BORIS PAHOR, *Necropolis.*

ROBERT PINGET, *The Inquisitory.*
Mahu or The Material.
Trio.

MANUEL PUIG, *Betrayed by Rita Hayworth.*
The Buenos Aires Affair.
Heartbreak Tango.

RAYMOND QUENEAU, *The Last Days.*
Odile.
Pierrot Mon Ami.
Saint Glinglin.

RAINER MARIA RILKE, *The Notebooks of Malte Laurids Brigge.*

ALAIN ROBBE-GRILLET, *Project for a Revolution in New York.*
A Sentimental Novel.

JEAN ROLIN, *The Explosion of the Radiator Hose.*

OLIVIER ROLIN, *Hotel Crystal.*

ALIX CLEO ROUBAUD, *Alix's Journal.*

RAYMOND ROUSSEL, *Impressions of Africa.*

VEDRANA RUDAN, *Night.*

LUIS RAFAEL SÁNCHEZ, *Macho Camacho's Beat.*

SEVERO SARDUY, *Cobra & Maitreya.*

NATHALIE SARRAUTE, *Do You Hear Them?*
Martereau.
The Planetarium.

STIG SÆTERBAKKEN, *Siamese.*
Self-Control.
Through the Night.

VIKTOR SHKLOVSKY, *Bowstring.*
Literature and Cinematography.
Theory of Prose.
Third Factory.

PIERRE SINIAC, *The Collaborators.*

KJERSTI A. SKOMSVOLD, *The Faster I Walk, the Smaller I Am.*

JOSEF ŠKVORECKÝ, *The Engineer of Human Souls.*

MARKO SOSIČ, *Ballerina, Ballerina.*

ANDRZEJ STASIUK, *Dukla.*
Fado.

GERTRUDE STEIN, *The Making of Americans.*
A Novel of Thank You.

LARS SVENDSEN, *A Philosophy of Evil.*

PIOTR SZEWC, *Annihilation.*

GONÇALO M. TAVARES, *A Man: Klaus Klump.*
Jerusalem.
Learning to Pray in the Age of Technique.

NIKANOR TERATOLOGEN, *Assisted Living.*

DUMITRU TSEPENEAG, *Hotel Europa.*
The Necessary Marriage.
Pigeon Post.
Vain Art of the Fugue.

ESTHER TUSQUETS, *Stranded.*

DUBRAVKA UGRESIC, *Lend Me Your Character.*
Thank You for Not Reading.

TOR ULVEN, *Replacement.*

MATI UNT, *Brecht at Night.*
Diary of a Blood Donor.
Things in the Night.

ELOY URROZ, *Friction.*
The Obstacles.

LUISA VALENZUELA, *Dark Desires and the Others.*
He Who Searches.

BORIS VIAN, *Heartsnatcher.*

TOOMAS VINT, *An Unending Landscape.*

REYOUNG, *Unbabbling.*

VLADO ŽABOT, *The Succubus.*

ZORAN ŽIVKOVIĆ , *Hidden Camera.*

LOUIS ZUKOFSKY, *Collected Fiction.*

VITOMIL ZUPAN, *Minuet for Guitar.*

SCOTT ZWIREN, *God Head.*